D0746057

The Rake and the Redhead

and

Lord Dancy's Delight

∼

Emily Hendrickson

Ⓢ
A SIGNET BOOK

SIGNET
Published by New American Library, a division of
Penguin Group (USA) Inc., 375 Hudson Street,
New York, New York 10014, USA
Penguin Group (Canada), 10 Alcorn Avenue, Toronto,
Ontario M4V 3B2, Canada (a division of Pearson Penguin Canada Inc.)
Penguin Books Ltd., 80 Strand, London WC2R 0RL, England
Penguin Ireland, 25 St. Stephen's Green, Dublin 2,
Ireland (a division of Penguin Books Ltd.)
Penguin Group (Australia), 250 Camberwell Road, Camberwell, Victoria 3124,
Australia (a division of Pearson Australia Group Pty. Ltd.)
Penguin Books India Pvt. Ltd., 11 Community Centre, Panchsheel Park,
New Delhi - 110 017, India
Penguin Group (NZ), cnr Airborne and Rosedale Roads, Albany,
Auckland 1310, New Zealand (a division of Pearson New Zealand Ltd.)
Penguin Books (South Africa) (Pty.) Ltd., 24 Sturdee Avenue,
Rosebank, Johannesburg 2196, South Africa

Penguin Books Ltd., Registered Offices:
80 Strand, London WC2R 0RL, England

Published by Signet, an imprint of New American Library,
a division of Penguin Group (USA) Inc. *The Rake and the Redhead* and
Lord Dancy's Delight were originally published separately by Signet.

First Printing (Double Edition), June 2005
10 9 8 7 6 5 4 3 2 1

PUBLISHER'S NOTE
These are works of fiction. Names, characters, places, and incidents either are
the product of the author's imagination or are used fictitiously, and any resem-
blance to actual persons, living or dead, business establishments, events, or locales
is entirely coincidental. The publisher does not have any control over and does
not assume any responsibility for author or third-party Web sites or their content.

If you purchased this book without a cover you should be aware that this book
is stolen property. It was reported as "unsold and destroyed" to the publisher
and neither the author nor the publisher has received any payment for this
"stripped book."

The scanning, uploading, and distribution of this book via the Internet or via any
other means without the permission of the publisher is illegal and punishable by
law. Please purchase only authorized electronic editions, and do not participate
in or encourage electronic piracy of copyrighted materials. Your support of the
author's rights is appreciated.

The Rake and the Redhead

Dedicated to Jennifer Enderlin
with deep appreciation
for her enthusiastic support
and unfailing understanding.

1

Hyacinthe clutched the letter tightly in her left hand as her right reached out to pull the window curtain of the swaying coach to one side to peer outside. Tom Coachman had slowed the traveling coach, no doubt approaching the inn where they were to spend the night. They were entering a pretty village set in the gently rolling landscape of Oxfordshire not too terribly far from her destination.

The brightly colored sign of the Black Lion Inn hung from above the door to a neat white building. Pink snapdragons bloomed with perky white daisies and orange wallflowers alongside the highly presentable hostelry. The innkeeper could be justly proud of his establishment, she decided when she observed the neat yard and fast-moving ostlers.

She let the curtain drop and turned her attention to her companion and maid, Fosdick. If a more respectable soul existed, Hyacinthe couldn't imagine who it might be. To have Fosdick at her side was the only way dear Aunt Bel had permitted Hyacinthe to dash off to Cousin Jane on an errand of mercy. At the moment the neatly garbed Fosdick looked to have been sucking a lemon from what she termed the havey-cavey scramble across country into the wilds of Oxfordshire.

Which thought brought Hyacinthe's eyes back to the letter again. She had read and reread the missive, horrified to learn her dearest Jane was about to be dispossessed of her precious little cottage, turned out by some heartless man just to improve his *garden!* The village in which Jane lived spoiled his lordship's view, she wrote, so it must go.

"Dreadful man," Hyacinthe declared under her breath. She had no high opinion of gardeners in general and male gentry who toyed with gardening in particular. Her pride still smarted from her previous encounters with his eminence, the rakish and lofty Lord Norwood, while visiting her aunt.

The handsome and dashing gentleman had preferred discussing fertilizer and lawns with Lord Leighton to a pleasant flirtation with Hyacinthe. She could tolerate being ignored for another woman. But fertilizer? Shocking!

It hadn't been their first encounter. She had met his rakish lordship during her brief stay in London, an insult she had kept to herself. Accustomed to flattering attentions from smitten swains, Hyacinthe was mortified to find herself studied through Lord Norwood's quizzing glass and then dismissed. He had as much as declared her to be unworthy of a word, much less a flirtation. It had caused a deep wound, one she could not dismiss no matter how hard she tried.

He must have suspected he had captured her interest, the dratted man. But to depress her attraction in such a heartless manner consigned him to the depths of the most rakish . . . beyond all that was proper. What a pity he was so handsome, such an exquisite dancer, and dressed to the nines upon every occasion. That blond rascal had flirted with every presentable miss and matron in town. All but herself, that was. Oh, the ignominy of it all.

Her only consolation was that the beautiful and accomplished Lady Olivia Everard had chased him quite shamelessly and been given her comeuppance as well.

Heartless, unfeeling man, just like the man who intended to toss Jane from her home. Well, he had Miss Hyacinthe Dancy to reckon with now. She narrowed a pair of fine green eyes and fingered a red curl that had escaped her bonnet while she considered what she would like to do to the gentleman gardener who threatened her cousin.

The traveling coach drew to a halt. Shortly the door opened and the steps were let down by Warton, her groom. Fosdick busied herself collecting the bits and pieces scattered about the interior of the coach.

Hyacinthe gathered the skirts of her dark green traveling dress in one hand and took her reticule with her as she prepared to descend. Her fashionable cottage bonnet caught on the coach door and tumbled down her back, held only by the ribands. Vexed at this disarray to her usually neat person, Hyacinthe paused on the step, intending to push the bonnet into place.

The landlord bustled up, then paused at the sight offered in the door of the coach. Later—when she had peered in a looking glass—Hyacinthe could understand his reaction. At the moment she fumed when the man began to shake his head.

"This be a respectable place, madam. We have no room in this inn for the likes of you." He squared his shoulders with a righteous sniff while motioning her back into her coach.

Seething, more furious than she could recall ever being before—no doubt aggravated by her recollections of Lord Norwood—Hyacinthe stepped down to confront the man. "I am Miss Hyacinthe Dancy, my good man. I require rooms for myself and my abigail plus accommodations for my coachman and groom for the night."

She was insulted at the way his eyes took on a knowing look and roved her slim person. Then the respectable Fosdick materialized at her side and Tom Coachman rounded the coach from where he had been instructing the ostler as to what was required for his employer's equipage.

Just as the innkeeper appeared to be thinking he had made an error, a gentleman Hyacinthe had not noticed before turned to stroll across the inn yard to also confront the innkeeper. And Hyacinthe.

She met his gaze with a fearless tilt of her heart-shaped face, her eyes the frozen green of a northern fjord.

"Well, if it isn't Miss Hyacinthe Dancy," the elegantly dressed and perfectly polished Lord Norwood drawled. "How charming to see you again. I trust you are on your way to Blenheim for the festivities?"

Hyacinthe wasn't sure she could unlock her jaw to give a civil reply. She was not on her way to Blenheim but he couldn't possibly know it. Nor could the innkeeper. Rather than tell an outright lie, Hyacinthe smiled, the brilliant smile for which she and all the Dancy girls were famous.

The innkeeper took a step back, bowed most humbly, then said with a sweep of one arm, "I do beg your pardon, Miss

Dancy. Please to follow me and you shall have the very best rooms I have to offer."

Hyacinthe suspected that Lord Norwood had already claimed the best, but remained silent lest she be labeled a harpy. She bestowed what she hoped was a regal nod on Lord Norwood, then swept past him toward the door of the inn.

She found the infamous lord at her side, placing her gloved hand upon his arm, and behaving as though they were marching in to dinner at Blenheim rather than entering a humble inn.

"I shall lend you consequence, you see," he whispered with a lazy wink from one of his remarkable blue eyes.

Hyacinthe wondered if she could be pardoned for shooting him.

"A male member of the nobility carries a deal of *ton*, you recall. More than a green girl could possibly command. My attentions will insure you a decent supper and a prompt breakfast come morning." He smiled down at her with his well-known and decidedly devilish grin. His astonishing blue eyes held a glimmer of amusement; they crinkled up at the corners, revealing the time he had spent out of doors. Gardening, no doubt, she thought wryly. Or possibly he acquired that attractive tan while at the racetrack, betting on all the winners, for he was known to possess uncanny luck.

She maintained a seething, icy silence until they paused at the bottom of the stairs leading up to the bedrooms. Then she turned to give him a falsely sweet smile and said in a voice dripping with propriety, "You are too kind, Lord Norwood. What a pity we shan't be meeting at Blenheim after all. I understand there usually are a considerable number of gentlemen in attendance at the parties there."

The amusement left his eyes and he gave her a rather thoughtful look. Then with a shake that seemed to say he must have misunderstood what might be concealed in her words, he bowed, relinquishing her hand only after placing a lingering kiss on the delicate glove covering her right hand.

"Until later, dear lady."

"Until later," she echoed. And to herself she added, "Much later; with any luck, never." Once a girl's heart had been wounded, only a fool would seek further injury.

Not until she entered the lovely room on the next floor of the inn and surveyed herself in the looking glass did she gasp with dismay. "Oh!" she exclaimed to Fosdick, who had entered the room directly behind her.

"Oh, indeed, miss," the abigail said in her most reproving tone. "What his lordship must have thought is beyond consideration."

The girl in the looking glass had blushing cheeks and indignant green eyes beneath tumbled red curls. Her green traveling dress clung to her slender frame just a shade too familiarly. What Hyacinthe had considered reasonably proper now seemed a trifle forward in looks, the cut of the dress appearing indiscreet.

Hyacinthe allowed Fosdick to untangle the ribands of her bonnet, then watched as it was placed on the dresser. The pelisse she had worn, only to remove when she became overly warm, was placed on the high four-poster bed. If only she had been wearing that respectable garment with its buttons that marched up to her chin none of this would have occurred. She would have been spared the confrontation with the innkeeper and the interference of Lord Norwood.

Yet she had to admit that she hadn't felt so exhilarated in ages.

It must have been the battle between two of the opposite sex. Hyacinthe—like any true redhead—loved a good clash. Oh, the audacity of the man. His very look had taunted her, bringing back that moment of humiliation when she had been rejected as unworthy of a flirtation by the premier rake in London. Not that she was a flirt. It was the challenge that enticed her. Like any woman worth her mettle, she wondered if she might be the one to turn his head, lure him from his bold ways.

"I trust we shall not see his lordship again," Fosdick said, a question lurking in her voice, a reproach ready to be administered if necessary.

"I hope not, dear Fosdick," Hyacinthe said in a little voice quite unlike her earlier tone of anger and contempt. "I have met the gentleman before, as you may have gathered. We did not precisely agree with one another. In fact, I would be foolish beyond permission to think he intended anything more than his own amusement."

"I see," the maid replied. Indeed, Fosdick probably saw more than her mistress intended, for the maid was wise beyond her years—which put her in the category of Methuselah, most likely.

"His lordship changes his attentions as often as a weathercock alters direction," Hyacinthe mused aloud while she drifted to the window to look down upon the very same inn yard where she had suffered his rescue. "I would have been quite fine had he minded his own business. Once the innkeeper caught sight of you and Tom Coachman, not to mention that dour-faced groom Aunt Bel bestowed upon me, not a soul in the world would judge me improper." She whirled about to give the maid a defiant stare as though to convince both of them of the fact.

"Warton is most amiable for a groom. It would not be seemly for him to be otherwise, miss," Fosdick said, removing the gown intended for the following day from Hyacinthe's traveling portmanteau. "However I have no doubt but that you would have prevailed in the end."

"Indeed." Hyacinthe sighed and returned her attention to the view from the window. While she watched Lord Norwood crossed the yard to chat with Warton and Tom Coachman. With his hat removed, the sun blessed his blond curls with more than radiance. He looked positively angelic. And Hyacinthe knew him to be the opposite. Wretched man.

She leaned forward as though she might catch what was said. Of course she couldn't detect a word of the conversation, but she thought it most strange. Another oddity was that his eminence did not appear the rake she knew from London. But that was silly. The man was the same one she had watched in Town, flirting, dancing, cutting a yard-wide dash through society.

Hyacinthe decided that she quite detested him. He might be heartbreakingly handsome and have manners so polished that young men looked to him as an example to emulate, but he was not a caring person. Beneath that elegant exterior was nothing . . . no heart, no substance. Just when she'd decided that she required those particular qualities in a gentleman she couldn't say, but she did. And Blase Montague, the charming Marquess of Norwood, failed on both counts.

Her heart soothed by this new knowledge, she faced the remainder of her day with more confidence. A rather feline smile crossed her lips. "I wonder if the man who seeks to oust my cousin is like Lord Norwood. I rather believe he must be."

"Then he'd be a gentleman and make no mistake," Fosdick said with a snap. A rap on the door prevented her from continuing in her observations on his lordship.

"Yes?" she said, peering around the door with sharp-eyed suspicion.

A country-fresh maid, her snowy mob cap properly covering brown curls, sidled into the room with a hesitant step, a tray in her hands. Tantalizing aromas drifted from the tray to tease Hyacinthe's nose.

"If you please, miss, his lordship says as how you might like a cup of tea before your dinner. He begs you to join him in the best parlor later." She pressed her lips together in anxious silence after delivering what was undoubtedly a memorized message. It was not every day that a country miss had a chance to make contact with nobility.

"Extend my thanks, but I shall dine in my room." Hyacinthe smiled at the girl, for it wasn't her fault that Lord Norwood offered yet another insult to Hyacinthe.

Once the girl had placed the tray on a table and departed, Hyacinthe turned to give Fosdick a fulminating look.

"It would not be proper for me to join him and he knows it. Why, it could compromise me beyond redemption," Hyacinthe declared indignantly. That that very compromise could place him in the danger of having to offer for her lurked in the recesses of her mind. What a stupid thing for him to do.

"Quite true." The abigail frowned thoughtfully while she poured out fragrant cups of steaming Bohea for them both, for her employer was never one to deny her maid a restoring cup of hot tea. "Since he does know better, one wonders why he did such a thing."

Hyacinthe exchanged a speculative look with her maid. It was indeed a conundrum of the first order.

There was also a plate of fresh-from-the-oven lemon biscuits on the tray. Hyacinthe and Fosdick proceeded to restore their nerves, then Hyacinthe urged her maid to take a rest. The older woman was not quite as stout as she pretended to be and Hyacinthe's tender heart worried about her health.

Besides, Hyacinthe intended to question Tom Coachman about whatever his lofty lordship had wanted with them. Once Fosdick snored genteelly away while stretched out on her comfortable bed, Hyacinthe slipped silently from her room and down the stairs.

She had not made the mistake of leaving without her pelisse buttoned to her chin and her bonnet snugly tied below same. First glancing furtively about, she ventured across the inn yard until she espied Tom and Warton conversing near the doors to the stables. Their talk ceased as she came near.

"Is all well, Tom? Nothing is wrong with the horses, is there?" She clasped her hands before her in genuine concern. Nothing could go wrong here. She felt a need to prove her independence to everyone, particularly Lord Norwood.

"Nay, miss. Just chewing the fat with Warton, here."

Hyacinthe chatted briefly about the day's journey, commented on what might be expected on the morrow; then, as she appeared about to leave, she paused.

"Oh . . . by the bye, I noted that Lord Norwood spoke with you earlier. What did he say?"

"Why, ma'am, he inquired of our cattle and asked if we had far to travel tomorrow. Kindly gentleman, I believe," Tom declared with a genteel smile. It seemed that he had approved of the gallantry displayed when his lordship came to the rescue of Tom's employer.

"You revealed our destination to him?" Hyacinthe asked in a rather quiet voice.

Alarmed, Tom replied, "I hope I didna' do wrong, Miss Dancy."

"No, no," she hastily assured him. "But perhaps you might be less forthcoming should anyone else inquire." Then she turned to slowly make her way back to the inn, deep in thought. So deep, in fact, that she failed to note that Lord Norwood waited for her in the entry hall of the inn.

"Miss Dancy, what a pleasure to see you again."

"Really, my lord?" Hyacinthe answered with a cool look. She had the man's measure. He thought that with no one else suitable available he might indulge in a bit of flirtation with her now. Well, he could take a running leap for all she cared. There would be no flirtation.

He had been leaning against the entry, looking secure with his position in life in general and well-pleased with himself. When Hyacinthe came closer, he stood straighter, bowing elegantly.

"Save your beautiful manners for one who appreciates them, sirrah. And do not bother my servants again, although why you might wish to know my destination is beyond me," she said in a considering way. She continued. "The maid may have informed you that I shall dine with my abigail in my room."

For good measure Hyacinthe drew herself up and flashed a reproving look at him, "Although you must have known that I would not agree to such a shocking suggestion. Your manners are not all they ought to be, are they?" she concluded in a soft voice.

"Blase, confound it, I've been hunting all over the place for you." A good-looking young man with shining dark hair, dark flashing eyes, and a tall, slender form came sauntering up to join the two who confronted each other in the entry. "I might have known you would find the only presentable woman—"

Before he could finish whatever he intended to say, Lord Norwood broke into his speech. "Val, may I suggest you allow me to present you to this lovely lady." He then proceeded to correctly introduce the newcomer.

Hyacinthe inspected the man presented as Valentine, Lord Latham. She had seen the baron about London. He possessed the same reputation as did Lord Norwood. Birds of a feather did indeed travel together.

"Good afternoon, sir," she murmured with just barely the correct amount of propriety.

"Indeed," the good-looking baron replied, bowing over her hand with excessive—to her way of thinking—flair.

Hyacinthe suspected that he might be a shade piqued that she didn't appear bowled over by him or his title. She offered a chilly nod, then marched up the stairs with a well-bred air and measured tread, not to mention a stiffened spine.

"I believe we have been well and truly put in our place, ol' chum," Val said in a reflective voice as he caught sight of a well-turned ankle when Miss Dancy took the last step at the top of the stairs.

"Sorry to interrupt you, but I feared you'd offer her further insult with some comment on her many charms. Miss Dancy is as prickly as a hedgehog." Blase looked up the stairs, catching the same glimpse of that ankle as Val, thinking that Miss Dancy was not quite as he had remembered.

"Much prettier, though. I always did think redheads a challenge. They say they make fiery bed partners. Do you recall that one we met while at Oxford?" He gave his friend a cynical grin, then nudged him along the hall.

The chuckles that followed brought forth a good many shared memories as the two handsome young men adjourned to the common room to enjoy a pint of excellent home brewed.

It was some time later while they applied knives and forks to an excellent roast beef that Val raised the subject of Miss Dancy again.

"Is she someone you knew from Town?"

"I met her once, saw her about frequently. Her brother wasn't in London then, but he's reputed to be one of the finest swordsmen around. And she has a flock of highly protective cousins. I decided it wasn't worth my life to flirt with the girl, even if she is a delectable piece."

"Her brother being . . . ?"

"Sir Peter Dancy. Odd fellow, taken to strange things like mummies and all that Egyptian rot. Began with some treasures brought back from the Egyptian campaign by his father in 1802. But don't be fooled, he's a dashed fine swordsman, as I said. As to Miss Dancy, we may see her again, for she travels on tomorrow."

"Not Worthington?"

"Precisely," came the smug reply. "Miss Dancy does not know what is in store for her." His chuckle bordered on the sinister, but his angelic smile took away any evil from his intent.

* * *

"I hope their lordships have departed by the time we leave in the morning," Hyacinthe said, her manner somewhat distracted from the fine meal their host and the maid had brought to her room.

"You would never deign to speak with them at any rate, would you?" Fosdick nibbled daintily at a roast potato. Her perfect manners would put many of the gentry to shame.

Hyacinthe gave her abigail a cross look. Why was it that Fosdick always had the knack of sounding like a governess, or at the very least a conscience?

"I should never do such a thing, Fosdick. My dear mama taught me better than that before she went aloft." A shimmer of moisture gleamed in her eyes for a moment, then Hyacinthe returned subdued attention to her meal.

All was as she hoped when, after completing a lovely and restoring breakfast in her room, she came downstairs in the morning. It wasn't necessary to make discreet inquiry about his lordship, for all around her she could hear snatches of conversation about the elegant Lord Norwood and his friend, Lord Latham. They had driven from the yard with an amazing flourish that every man around envied, it seemed.

Hyacinthe insisted to herself that she was quite pleased not to have seen them when they left, never admitting that she had peeped from her window—briefly, mind you—when she heard the commotion in the yard below. It was all of a piece—their dashing good looks and that curricle that appeared so rakish and probably bounced unmercifully. A secret smile curved her lips when she considered the uncomfortable drive they must make to wherever they were going.

Perhaps her entourage was not as elegant, nor as dashing, but admiring glances were many when Hyacinthe—garbed today in a neat Nile green pelisse and chip bonnet—stepped into her carriage. Tom Coachman sprung the horses as Hyacinthe had politely requested and they were off.

The miles to Worthington dragged by with seeming tedium. Hyacinthe reviewed all the words she had exchanged with Lord Norwood, debating whether or not she had acquitted herself well.

When at last they entered the pretty village tucked away in a green vale, Hyacinthe drew a breath of pleasure. Granted it was a tiny village, barely qualifying for the name, yet it was exceedingly charming. Some of the old thatched-roof cottages were covered with roses or ivy, tiny yards filled with an abundance of flowers and an occasional cat.

When Hyacinthe viewed her cousin's cottage, it seemed to her that the upper windows peered out from beneath the roof like sparkling eyes from under a shaggy mane. She fell in love with the place all over again.

Tom and Warton busied themselves removing the luggage from the boot and tending the horses, all the while fending off a number of curious children who were drawn by the unexpected sight. Traveling coaches were as rare as a warm day in January around here.

The white-painted door flew open and Jane came rushing down the flagstone path to the neat little gate. A soft gray shawl couldn't hide the thinness of her figure, nor could her smile quite conceal the lines of worry around her eyes. Her pretty auburn hair escaped in wisps from beneath her white cornette.

Hyacinthe absorbed all this in seconds as she hurried to wrap her dearest cousin in an enveloping hug. "It is so good to see you again," Hyacinthe whispered in a voice clogged with happy tears. She was utterly loyal to what family she had, and the thought that some monster would dare to oust her precious cousin from her hearth made her furious all over again.

Once settled in the sitting room located at the front of the ground floor with a pot of tea and cakes, they talked.

Jane Pennington lived as quietly as she pleased, far from the autocratic grandmother she quite feared. The notion that she might have to give up her peaceful existence and wait upon this dragon upset her nerves to the point where she could scarcely discuss the matter.

Rather, she inquired about the journey from Wiltshire and marveled at Hyacinthe's speed of travel, considering the deplorable state of the country roads.

At long last they turned, not without some reluctance on Jane's part, to the matter at hand.

"Where do things stand at the moment, Jane?" Hyacinthe inquired after placing her teacup back on its saucer. "How do the others in the village feel about having to leave the place they have called home for so long?"

"Well . . ." Jane said reflectively, "most are unhappy about being ousted, but a few—those with roofs that need patching and those whose families are too numerous to fit in the space they have—are amenable to the scheme."

"When does his lordship contemplate beginning this dastardly plan? I wish to know how much time we have." Hyacinthe brushed off a few crumbs from her gown, then eased back in her chair.

"I truly do not know. His bailiff came here the day I wrote to you. He informed us that we would be moved, but not when or how or where. As well, the rent is to be raised. Oh, dear," Jane said with a sob, pulling a crumpled handkerchief from where it had been tucked into her sleeve. "What shall become of me?" Then she dried a tear to give Hyacinthe a defiant look. "For I absolutely refuse to go to Grandmama Dancy. The woman would drive me mad in a day."

"Who is this man we must deal with? You never mentioned his name in your letter. At least, I do not think that you did," Hyacinthe reconsidered, recalling the missive that had been crossed with lines in both directions, making it difficult to read.

Jane frowned. "I thought I did. He is Lord Norwood. I hear he is expected to arrive any day now. And then his scheme will be set in motion." She dabbed at her eyes once again, then gave Hyacinthe a startled look when that young woman jumped to her feet and began to pace back and forth across the tiny sitting room, fists clenched, face angry.

"Infamous! Outside of enough! That man . . . just wait until I can fix his hide." She ought to have anticipated this, given his gardening lordship's proximity when last seen.

"You *know* Lord Norwood?" Jane asked in a breathless voice, clutching the arms of her chair in excitement.

"Indeed. And I shall take the greatest of pleasures in seeing that he receives his just desserts!"

2

"What is to be done?" Jane said anxiously, her hand rising to touch her throat in apprehension. "His lordship owns the entire village, the very ground upon which we trod. He is entitled to do anything he pleases with what is his own."

Hyacinthe cast her a frustrated glance, then looked out of the sitting-room bay window at the pretty village green. It was an irregular shape with neat cottages in a line around its edge. In the center of the green a lovely pond was fringed here and there with reeds, enhanced by stately oaks and elms. In ragged order along the far end of the green ranged the Cock and Bull, a century-old inn, then not far away a blacksmith and the usual small village shop that sold practically everything necessary. The ancient stone church, its spire thrusting toward the clouds, occupied a splendid spot on the opposite side, with a tidy little graveyard beyond an old lych-gate.

True, many of the roofs badly needed rethatching and one cottage looked ready to tumble down—witness to bad management on his lordship's part—or his bailiff's. But all in all, it was a charming place. Climbing roses and late-blooming hollyhocks peeking over the hedges that lined the street increased the appeal of the mellowed brick cottages. The village ought not disappear from the face of the earth just to please a whim.

"How does your cleric feel about this? Surely he must protest the destruction of his edifice, one that has sat in that spot for a good many years?" Hyacinthe clasped her hands before her while she contemplated the scene from the bow window of Jane's small cottage.

"Ambrose Clark is such a quiet man, I doubt he would say boo to a goose much less his lordship."

"Oh, dear." Moving closer to the window, Hyacinthe peered out more intently at a figure she noticed. "And who is that man going about as if he intended to buy all the village?"

"That is Mr. Wayland." Jane rose to join Hyacinthe by the window. "While at church last Sunday I heard that he is an architect hired by Lord Norwood to inspect the cottages to see if any are worth moving."

"I doubt he would wish to save anything in that event. It would profit him more to build new. Perhaps he is to design new homes for you all?" Then Hyacinthe considered the rake she knew and shook her head. "I doubt that, for Lord Norwood does not appear the type to be overly concerned with his estate—or, at least, the people living on it." She exchanged a disgusted look with her cousin.

"He has not held the title very long," Jane replied, perhaps in an attempt to justify the young lord's lack of achievement. "He was abroad for some while. Then, after his father died—from a dreadful cold, you know—he returned. He did not spend much time here before he left for London," Jane admitted.

"No doubt he has been cavorting about Town all the while," Hyacinthe replied with a sniff, then added, "when he wasn't out at the racetrack betting on the horses." When she saw Jane's dismayed expression, Hyacinthe felt compelled to note, "He is marvelously lucky, winning large sums with astounding frequency. All that lovely money enables him to cut quite a dash in Society." She turned aside from the depressing view of the angular Mr. Wayland, his legs reminding her of a crane perched at the water's edge.

A look at Jane's hopeful face prompted Hyacinthe to try anew. "Is there no one at all of influence in this area? Someone who might try to reason with Lord Norwood?"

Hyacinthe plumped herself back on a chair, poured a cup of tea, then settled back, waiting.

Jane appeared to consider the matter at length while she reseated herself, then turned an interesting shade of pink when she replied, "Well, there is Sir Charles Ridgeway. He lives on the edge of the village in an old manor house of Tudor vintage. I expect he also must relocate, but I do not know how he feels about it." Jane began pleating the apron she had put on over her dull green gown to protect it while she made tea.

Hyacinthe noted the flush of color and the nervous movement of those spinster fingers. Jane must be all of thirty summers, definitely on the shelf and past her prayers. But Hyacinthe's romantic heart saw no problem, unless Sir Charles was married.

"I fancy his wife and children must be up in arms? It would be difficult to move from a house you like."

"Oh," replied Jane in a flustered manner, "he is not married, although his sister visits from time to time." Since her neatly capped head was now bent, it was impossible to discover what her eyes might reveal.

"I see," Hyacinthe said with a sage nod. Indeed, she thought she saw a great deal. "Well, I had best change out of my traveling clothes and see if Fosdick is able to find a place for our things."

"I hope you will be comfortable in your rooms. I fear Fosdick will have to be content with the small chamber behind yours." Jane rose to walk to the entry hall with her guest, fussing with her shawl as she did.

"She will be," Hyacinthe assured Jane kindly. "And I have instructed Tom Coachman and Warton to settle in at the Cock and Bull. I fancy we might have need of transportation, and I know that you do not keep a coach of any sort."

Appearing cheered at the very thought of having a coach and four at her beck and call, Jane smiled delightedly.

"Mind you, it might be the height of comfort in coaches, but it cannot compare in looks to the dashing elegance of his lordship's curricle. I wonder if we shall see him?" Hyacinthe tipped her head to one side in a considering way while she observed the frightened look that crept over her cousin's face.

"Oh, my. Whatever would we do in that event?" Jane walked with Hyacinthe to the bottom of the stairs where she stood with hands clasped and a worried look in her eyes.

"I shall do something, you may be certain." With those unsettling words, Hyacinthe hurried up the circular staircase to her room at the left of the landing.

Jane decided she had best send for the Widow Smith's girl to help out while her cousin was here. It was easy to see that Hyacinthe would require more than the simple life Jane endured while alone. Although she was *not* unhappy. Reluctant to socialize, the peace of her cottage and the simplicity of village life where everyone knew everyone else appealed to her. She abhorred upheaval. And she very much feared that having Hyacinthe come to stay was like inviting a storm to dinner.

Upstairs Hyacinthe quickly changed into a pretty green sprigged muslin, high-necked and tucked across the bosom, and donned green gloves and her favorite leghorn hat bedecked with an enormous green satin riband. The tips of her green morocco slippers could be seen when she walked.

Before she left she instructed Fosdick to take out the gowns that Hyacinthe had brought along, fearing to find precisely what she did—that her cousin Jane dressed like a country mouse in dull colors and styles. These were new dresses from London, not yet worn. And Hyacinthe's tender heart had decided them a perfect present for her cousin.

"I believe I shall stroll about the village, perhaps check on Tom Coachman and Warton. Would it be unseemly for me to look at the church, since I shan't have my maid with me?" Hyacinthe paused at the bottom of the stairs while her cousin looked on in silent admiration of the fashion plate that had materialized in her humble home.

At last Jane recalled herself. "Of course you may go anywhere. Dressed as you are, there's not a lad around who would dare approach you, nor anyone who might offer insult."

Hyacinthe reflected that she obviously didn't expect Lord Norwood to come around.

She turned to leave the cottage, then paused again. "I forgot to tell you that I bought you a present. Fosdick has placed it on your bed." With a gay wave of her hand, Hyacinthe flitted from the house, drifting across the road to skirt the edge of the village green.

Jane forgot propriety and dashed up the stairs that curved around like those of a church bell tower. Presents rarely came her way, and when she saw the lovely collection of gowns spread out for her eyes to feast on, she burst into tears. Her flurry of emotion didn't last long. Within minutes Fosdick was assisting the slender young woman from her drab green dress into one of pale blue lutestring trimmed in the prettiest lace Jane had ever seen. As she and her cousin were nearly the same size, it required little adjustment to fit nicely.

"If you please, miss, perhaps I might try a different style for your pretty hair." When Jane silently agreed with a nod of her head, the abigail removed the dainty cornette Jane had embroidered in white thread on white muslin. "Ah," said Fosdick in a pleased exclamation, "so soft and silky it is, and the color of a nightingale." Fosdick beguiled Jane into the chair before her seldom-used dressing table and set to work.

Putting thoughts of her cousin aside, Hyacinthe explored the village. It hadn't grown much since she was last here some years before. She thought she recognized a few faces. At the Cock and Bull, Tom Coachman and Warton were pleased to see her, accounting for their time by the high polish on the burgundy coach with delicate gold lines trimming it. Hyacinthe suggested that when not occupied with the coach and horses they might lend a hand at her cousin's house. She was certain there were a few tasks where a man's strength would be an asset.

From the inn, Hyacinthe strolled along the green, crossing to the church. Upon closer inspection she could see that the building could use a new roof. Moss and age had not been kind to it. That was a minus, while surely the antiquity of the building would be a plus in any argument to preserve the edifice.

Within the churchyard she studied the gravestones, noting the dates. Most were from long ago, with a cluster of newer graves to the far side of the building. Inside the church she considered the memorial tablets; shiny brass, softly painted plaster, and two exquisitely carved in marble. How could any man be so heartless as to disturb these relics of the past?

The pews of heavy oak most likely had seen all the people who ever lived in the village. She had a vision of people garbed in the dress of a century past filing into their pews to hear much the same service as served today.

"I say, miss, could I be of assistance?" A high-pitched, beautifully accented voice penetrated her reflections.

Startled and feeling as if she had been hurled through time in seconds, Hyacinthe whirled about to confront a man who had to be the curate, Ambrose Clark. He was a man of moderate height with a thin, intelligent face, bespectacled eyes, and hair that receded to either side of a central portion, resulting in a hairline shaped like the letter *W* upside down.

"I do beg your pardon, for it seems I have surprised you," he said, nervously putting his hands together before him almost in supplication. "That happens quite often, I fear. People come and fall into retrospection."

Hyacinthe informed him of her identity, then looked about her. "It is a very lovely old building," she said, proceeding cautiously.

"Aye," he replied, then sighed. "And that is a problem, for we need a new roof and there is no way we shall receive one. Our only hope is to have the church moved. Lord Norwood has promised to replace all the roof tiles. It would be lovely to work in my office on a rainy day and not have water dripping into buckets all over the room." He tapped his fingers together in a sort of rhythm. "Yes, indeed. However, I suspect there are some among us who do not wish this move."

"Are you not shocked to think my dear cousin, Miss Pennington, might be out on her ear?"

"Oh, indeed, 'tis a great pity," he responded, biting his lip, making Hyacinthe recall a gray rabbit she had once seen. He continued to tap his fingertips together while he seemed to decide on what he ought to say next.

"Can you tell me something of the history of this building?" Hyacinthe had found that most clerics enjoyed expounding on the history of anything, particularly their church building.

"Indeed," he said with more enthusiasm. He then stopped his tapping of fingers to clasp Hyacinthe lightly about her arm and pull her along with him while he gave a lecture on each and every contribution made by the worthies buried here. Then he proudly showed the relatively new organ installed to

enhance the service. It had meant the retirement of the flutist,
violinist, and harpist who had been playing at services for
years.

When he paused in his recital Hyacinthe gratefully inserted,
"I believe I had best return to my cousin's house."

"And I have kept you from her side, nattering on about my
favorite topic. You are a very kind young lady to bear with a
somewhat garrulous old man. I do recall meeting you some
years ago—although you have altered a good deal. You were a
bran-faced little girl with pigtails and ruffled dresses that you
did not appear to like very much." He had a singularly sweet
smile, albeit somewhat timid.

Hyacinthe chuckled at the memory of her freckles—of
which she had but one or two remaining—and those dreadful
white dresses with rows of ruffles and the blue bows that forever came untied. She bade the curate good-bye, reflecting
that he might deem himself old, but she doubted if he was
above forty. Hardly elderly. And about right for Jane, except
he probably didn't have two pounds to bless his name with,
more's the pity.

In the green once again, she caught sight of a nice-looking
man, a bit younger than the curate. Brown hair peeped from
beneath his tall hat. She admired the determined line of his
square jaw. Could this be Sir Charles Ridgeway, whose very
name made dear Cousin Jane turn a pretty shade of pink?

He was headed toward her cousin's cottage with a purpose-
ful stride. Hyacinthe made her way across the green, skirting
the edge of the pond and thinking that the many ducks and a
pair of swans made a very pretty sight, if a bit messy should
one look too closely at the water.

She met him at the gate to the cottage. When she drew
closer to him, she observed that he had a very nice pair of
hazel eyes. Curious eyes.

"I beg your pardon, miss. I had not realized Miss Pennington's company had arrived." He tipped his hat, revealing thick
brown hair covering a well-shaped head.

Hyacinthe nodded in return. "I was so fortunate as to make
very good time. The roads were dry," she explained.

"Ah, yes, that does help." He opened the gate and walked at

her side to the white door, which was opened in a trice by a flustered Jane.

"Oh, my. Hyacinthe, you are come home. And Sir Charles, how lovely to see you." She dithered, clearly ruffled and not quite certain what she ought to do. A pretty blue sprigged dress enhanced her delicate coloring, while the softly draped hair style created by Fosdick made her look years younger and far more comely than the day cap which she had worn.

Hyacinthe smoothly took charge in an unobtrusive way. "I am pleased to meet you, Sir Charles. As my cousin appears to have told you, I am here to help her. My dearest Jane has informed me that you may be required to move as well."

"I have found out today I will be reprieved." He turned to Jane. "I came expressly to tell you that Lord Norwood has arrived and after driving past my home believes it would be a shame to move it. In fact, it may be possible for me to buy it back again." To Hyacinthe he added, "One of my ancestors lost the manor in a card game to one of his lordship's forebears."

"Ah!" Hyacinthe exclaimed, "Then the incredible luck of the present Lord Norwood is a trait handed down?"

"His father must have ignored it, for he plunged heavily into the exchange and lost all he invested." Sir Charles's tone made quite clear what he thought of such an improvident man.

Hyacinthe was puzzled. If Lord Norwood's father had lost so much, how could his present lordship afford the expense of relocating an entire village for the whim of his view? Surely the marquess had not been *that* lucky?

Or had he? If she were more charitable, she might be inclined to believe he gambled to regain the monetary inheritance his father had lost.

Jane nervously gestured to her pleasant parlor. "Please come in. I shall have your favorite beverage in a moment," she added to Sir Charles.

Apparently Sir Charles was accustomed to come here often if Jane knew his favorite drink and kept it on hand. Hyacinthe watched him settle onto a comfortable chair, the largest in the room and located close to the hearth, although it was not a chilly day. The cottage appeared to have a poor foundation, for the floor felt damp to Hyacinthe. Small wonder a fire was kept burning to take the chill from the room.

"Sir Charles, I am very concerned about my cousin," she said softly in hope that her words would not carry into the kitchen. "She does not wish to live with our grandmother. Goodness knows, that dear dragon is a bit intimidating. Not all of us are able to stand up to her, you see." Hyacinthe smiled ruefully.

"Miss Pennington is a trifle shy, but you would think she might manage her grandmother."

"You have never met the lady, I gather," Hyacinthe replied dryly.

"What do you propose to do? I doubt if his lordship will take kindly to anyone interfering with his plans." He shifted about in the armchair as though uncomfortable with the very notion of rebellion. "He means to begin work soon."

"Yes, well," Hyacinthe declared, "I have not formed any plans as yet, precisely. But I will. That dastardly man must not be allowed to destroy this pretty village. Why, it would take years of work to create the charming gardens and pretty scene of the village green. New towns are notoriously barren and ugly," she insisted in conclusion.

"You have a point there. Perhaps if someone were to suggest a different beautification approach to Lord Norwood he might agree to it?" He turned and rose in obvious relief as Jane entered with a tray holding a glass and a bottle of fine dry sherry along with a plate of wafer-thin biscuits, and tea for the ladies.

Hyacinthe watched him as Jane poured sherry into the glass. There were no loverlike glances or hints that he was interested in Jane in a romantic way. Indeed, he appeared to look on her as he must his sister, a comfortable person with whom to chat. Hyacinthe barely suppressed a disgusted and most unladylike snort. The man did not appear even to take notice of Jane's pretty new gown or her attractive new hair arrangement.

"Perhaps we could make out a list of things that we could present to Lord Norwood," Hyacinthe suggested once he had seated himself again. "Might you be willing to discuss the matter with him? For you may as well know that I do not precisely get along very well with him. Besides, I believe it far better for men to consider these matters."

When she glanced out of the window again, she observed Mr. Wayland entering the somewhat obscured house across the way. Tudor in design, it was the oldest cottage in the village and now sat vacant. The image of a stork seeking a nesting site flitted through her mind and she barely repressed a smile.

"I believe that to be an excellent notion," Sir Charles replied, obviously pleased to be considered the one to talk with his lordship. "I agree that Norwood will respond better to another man regarding the matter. But first know that I shan't say anything until the issue of the manor house is settled. I should not like to jeopardize my purchase of it. I managed to buy some of the original land from his lordship's father when he became pressed for funds. I never had the opportunity to approach him about the purchase of my house, as he died before I could speak to him about it."

Hyacinthe decided that while Sir Charles might be a pleasant man, and one who sought to make use of an opportunity, he was not the type to set the Thames on fire. At least he hadn't set his face against her scheme. Or at least as much as he knew of her scheme.

So, with a great many suggestions from all present, a list was drawn up. When finished it contained the basic demands Hyacinthe considered important. But the list was brief—at Sir Charles's insistence. Hyacinthe thought it a very poor thing. She intended to approach the matter from another direction entirely, but decided she wouldn't upset Sir Charles by mentioning it. He appeared to be in much the same state as Jane—a bit reserved, perhaps?

They lingered in the parlor, discussing how the changes might be made. Hyacinthe thought them mad, to be so accepting of what had to be a mere whim on Lord Norwood's part.

"Where shall you live if this house is torn down? And what of your lovely roses and all the pretty flowers you grow in your garden?"

"I do not know in the least," Jane murmured. Tears gathered in her eyes, which she dabbed at with a scrap of cambric.

"And you shall not dip into your inheritance to support me when you may well have need of the money yourself," she added to Hyacinthe.

First tossing an annoyed look at Hyacinthe for distressing Jane, Sir Charles moved to place a comforting pat on Jane's shoulder, which seemed to upset her all the more.

Hyacinthe watched the scene and decided she just might enjoy the role of devil's advocate if it brought Sir Charles around to championing her dear cousin. She considered the list she had written out, then offered it to Sir Charles when Jane had once again composed herself.

"Here, Sir Charles. I wish you well in your efforts."

Hyacinthe doubted he would have any luck, but it appeared to make him and Jane happy. Hyacinthe intended to make her own list.

Across the gently rolling hills from the village and within sight of the church spire and the chimneys of Worthington where it presently stood, two gentlemen studied a list of a considerably different sort.

"Dash it all, Blase, I didn't think to come up here to do an inventory," Val complained good-naturedly. "Why do we not seek out that pretty little redhead we encountered on our way here? Perhaps she has a friend?" he concluded optimistically.

"Neither did I," Blase replied, ignoring the reference to the redhead. "But when I found certain things I believed were here to be missing, I decided that perhaps it was time to do a bit of investigation. And forget the redhead. You don't want any trouble."

Blase circled about the drawing room, making extensive notations as he went. When he compared these with the two other inventories he knew existed, he might discover precisely what had happened while he was abroad.

"Father said he hadn't been forced to sell any of the family jewels or paintings, yet when I checked the earliest inventory I noted that several of the sixteenth-century paintings are missing from the rooms where they were listed and supposed to be hanging," Blase explained. "I want to know if they were moved, stored in the attic, or . . . if they have mysteriously disappeared. I wonder if other heirlooms are gone. I hope to find out."

"Ghosts?" Val asked in mock alarm.

"More likely a thief," Blase replied grimly.

"It wouldn't be surprising considering that only a skeleton staff is here for months at a time," Val said. "At least allow me to help you. Why don't I list all the paintings? I won't be likely to miss any, as none are familiar to me."

Val picked up a sheet of paper and a sharpened pencil to begin listing the paintings in the room. Blase could transfer these items to his master list later on.

The two worked silently for hours, moving from room to room until they ended up in the attic. It was surprisingly clean, with neatly piled goods from past Montagues. A stack of paintings leaned against one of the walls. Val made for this while Blase wandered along the length of the attic poking into various piles.

By dinnertime the lack of light to see and the utter fatigue of it all forced the pair to cease work. They clattered down the stairs to the main floor.

After dinner Val and Blase drifted into the library, where they sought comfort and ease in a pair of leather armchairs and crystal glasses filled with the finest port.

"Val, I am convinced that at some time in the past a bit of skulduggery went on here at Worthington Hall. Either one of my ancestors . . . or a thief . . . absconded with some paintings, all of which would be worth a fortune today."

Val allowed a whistle to escape while he considered all the implications. "Nothing else is missing?"

Blase thought for a few moments, then left the sublime comfort of his chair to cross the room to where a magnificent oil painting of his grandfather hung. He pulled on it and one side swung silently forward on well-oiled hinges. Behind the painting a quite modern safe had been installed some years ago at Blase's insistence. For once his father had agreed. In here the family jewels ought to repose.

He gave Val a concerned look, then swiftly opened the safe. A tiny key always kept on his watch chain opened the final door. He removed several black leather boxes, placing them on the desk.

Val also left the comfort of his seat. "I say, old chap, I've heard you speak of the family gems. Wouldn't miss a chance to see them."

Blase spread out the copy of the earliest inventory, then a second from a much later year, before he opened the first of the boxes. He made a list of each item as he removed it from its place of safekeeping. Emeralds, sapphires, diamonds, and fine rubies winked and sparkled, in spite of being wrapped up and not cleaned for years.

When all had been counted and listed, Blase stared at Val. "There are a few of the gems missing. See here?" He pointed to the oldest list, his finger a trifle unsteady as he marked an emerald necklace, a bracelet of gold set with emeralds, and emerald ear-bobs. "No mention of these appears in this next inventory. I have found no record of their being sold—or given away."

"Perhaps one of your ancestors bestowed them on a lady friend and did not wish his wife to know about it?" Val remarked with a chuckle.

"I doubt such a thing . . . not that many of those gentlemen didn't have lady friends, as you so genteelly phrase it."

"What can you do?" Val queried. He returned to his chair while he watched—not too closely—as Blase restored the jewels to the safe.

Once the painting swung back into place and Blase had joined Val before the fireplace, Blase looked at his friend. "I intend to go to the muniment room and do a bit of sleuthing. My forebears were ever the ones to keep every letter and diary. Mayhap if we check the record boxes for the intervening years between the first and second inventories we might find evidence of a sort. Something to give us a lead in this mystery."

"Us?" said Val in dismay that was only partly mock.

"Most definitely us. I shall need your help. I intend to find out what happened to those jewels and paintings. There must be a clue somewhere. When did they disappear? And who took them?"

3

The next day Hyacinthe studied the countenance of her cousin with a sinking heart. It seemed clear that since Sir Charles Ridgeway appeared to have dropped his opposition to the destruction of the village Jane now wavered in her support for the plan Hyacinthe proposed.

"It looks to me that perhaps I was a trifle hasty in writing you about this, Hyacinthe," Jane said in her soft, hesitant voice the day after Sir Charles paid his call. She played nervously with the ends of her gray shawl.

"Please do not think such a thing," Hyacinthe urged. "Come, look out of this window at the charming village in which you live. It is shocking to think that all this would be torn down merely in order to provide his lordship with a change of view. I suggest that we visit a few of your neighbors, find out how they feel about this matter."

"I believe I could tell you how they think without going to such lengths." Jane said. "Follow me and we shall stroll around the village."

Not quite certain what Jane might say, yet knowing she must do as her cousin requested, Hyacinthe drew on her gloves after first tying a simple chip straw bonnet on her head. They slipped out of the front gate, Jane going first and tugging Hyacinthe along after her.

Jane looked very pretty in her enthusiasm for her mission. Delicate pink cheeks bloomed, a straw bonnet trimmed in deep pink complimented the deep pink print of her new walking dress, one of the gifts from Hyacinthe. The ruffles of her day cap peeped from under the brim of her bonnet, giving an unexpected touch of charm. She appeared a bit different from the drab young woman who had met Hyacinthe at the gate upon her arrival.

"His lordship intends to raise your rent with the new house. Can you or your neighbors afford to pay more?" Hyacinthe thrust at her cousin in the hopes that she might for once be practical about her position.

Jane bestowed a frightened look on Hyacinthe, for the amount of her competence was rather small. The very notion that her rent would be increased was a matter to consider most carefully.

At the house next to Jane's they paused while Jane whispered, "This is Granny Beanbuck's cottage. She is quite crippled, but the most cheerful soul. I buy my bread from her. Although she has difficulty walking, she bakes the most heavenly loaves. I doubt she would wish to move, for a new home might not have such a good oven, nor a boy handy to stoke her fires."

Hyacinthe mentally toted one up for her side. Granny's cottage gave evidence that someone had also planted a pleasant garden in which cabbages mingled with hollyhocks and delphinium.

The next cottaqge had only rows of vegetable behind its ragged hedge. A few sunflowers had invaded one corner of the plot. The muslin curtains hung limply at the windows, unlike Janes's crisp white window coverings. Hyacinthe gave her cousin a questioning look.

"The Hadkiss family resides here," Jane said softly. "Mr. Hadkiss, I am sorry to say, is a man not much given to work. Mrs. Hadkiss, in addition to caring for their seven children—with another about to present its hungry face to the world before long—does laundry and other tasks to keep bread on the table."

"Would they wish to move, do you think?"

"I suspect that Mrs. Hadkiss has given little thought to the matter. She appears to accept what comes her way with no question. Mr. Hadkiss would likely enjoy the move, if only to give him something else to complain about." Jane gave her cousin a stricken look. "I pray you will not think badly of me for my frank comments about my neighbors. I thought it best to be open about them."

"Not at all, for we know that people like the Hadkiss family exist, and not merely in cottages." Hyacinthe looked back at the cottage, now behind them. A tot peeked around the corner of the house, looking wistfully at the fine ladies strolling past. That family was a point for Lord Norwood's side.

"The Widow Smith lives here," Jane gestured to a trim little place, abundant flowers and vegetables intermingling in the little garden behind a low hedge.

Hyacinthe looked at the clipped hedge, comparing it to others much higher, then glanced to Jane for an explanation she felt certain would follow.

"The Widow likes to gossip and so wishes an unobstructed view. She and Mrs. Peachey—who lives across the green from here—take note of all the goings on in the village and debate them endlessly. I expect that even as we pass her house the details of our garments, the fact that I have company, will be carefully observed and discussed over a pot of tea later today."

Amused, Hyacinthe said, "We really ought to pause for a call so she might have the particulars correct."

Jane tossed her an alarmed look, then chuckled. "You are teasing. For a moment I thought you serious."

"I am. That poor woman has nothing more to enliven her life than what occurs outside her home. Pitiful thing."

After giving her cousin a considering look, Jane turned about and retraced her steps to the widow's house.

They were avidly welcomed. The widow, garbed in unrelieved black with only a lace collar to enhance her dress, patted her muslin cap decorated with delicate ruffles. "Oh," she fluttered about, "do come in."

Jane managed to place her request for the widow's daughter to help her out without offending anyone.

When they left fifteen minutes later Hyacinthe wore a somewhat stunned expression on her face. "I have never endured such a grilling. I fancy that is what an accused person must face once in jail."

"You asked for it." Jane smiled at her cousin's countenance.

Her good humor reestablished, Hyacinthe replied with a rueful moue, "But we have made her day, if not her week."

Jane's soft chuckle rewarded Hyacinthe for her efforts.

They strolled along the stone path, Hyacinthe making mental note of the likely positions taken by the Nutkin family, old Mr. Smeed, the village handyman, and the Philpotts, who were quite elderly and apt to resist change.

The little village shop proved very busy today, with ladies entering with empty baskets and exiting bearing them stuffed with parcels. The blacksmith was well occupied, but when he espied Jane, came out to say hello. He brought up the topic of the day.

"Sir Charles says he means to see his lordship about the new cottages. He's collectin' a list from a few of the ladies as to what would be most welcome."

A glance at Jane's face brought dismay to Hyacinthe's heart. She could once again see her cousin wavering. "Well, and that is only proper. What if his lordship ignores these suggestions? What then?" she challenged.

The blacksmith scratched his chin, then allowed, "That's his right, I reckon. This is his land, his village. I might see more work in a new place with people wanting all manner of things made. Perhaps there might be a few extra homes for new people." He gestured to the bench where he had been repairing a clock for the curate. "I gets mostly repairs here, with a bit of shoeing from time to time. I asked for a larger shop, for I could use more space."

"So you support a move? Just to improve his lordship's view? What if the new village site is not so pleasing, with no stream close by, nor a delightful green with a pond and stately trees? What then?" Hyacinthe queried, hoping to plant a doubt or two.

He scratched his head, then replaced the cap he'd removed when first coming to speak with them. "We'll just have to see, won't we?" With that unsatisfactory remark he returned to his workbench beneath the only window in the shop.

The two young women ambled past the graveyard and paused before the church. Hoping to offer a formidable argument, Hyacinthe pointed to the orderly graves, then said,

"These will remain here, I suppose. How can they be disturbed, even if the church is moved? How will the villagers be able to come here if there is some distance involved? Poor Widow Smith could scarcely walk very far to tend her poor husband's grave."

"He was a sailor and was buried at sea, so that is not a relevant point," Jane countered.

"It still seems sacrilegious to me," Hyacinthe mumbled, casting about for another argument. Jane looked confused and bothered, which was about the most Hyacinthe might hope for, she supposed. The curate—whom she had looked to for support—was nowhere in sight.

Not far along the street, just beyond the Peachey house, stood the shabby Tudor-style cottage that had been sitting empty for years, Jane had said. Hyacinthe noted that Mr. Wayland seemed entranced with the place, for he appeared in the doorway as they neared.

"Now, that is an odd sight," Jane murmured. "Whatever can he expect to do with that place?"

"Perhaps he decides if there is anything worth salvaging from a home of such antiquity? Shall we attempt to query him?" Hyacinthe took gentle hold of Jane's elbow to nudge her along the path. Aside from an affronted, almost scandalized glance from her cousin, nothing was said.

Jane managed the introduction with a minimum of words, evidence of her lack of regard for the man.

"Good morning, sir," Hyacinthe offered in a pleasant manner usually guaranteed to bring a smile to any gentleman's face. Mr. Wayland proved the exception. He frowned, and in a most haughty manner.

"I hope you ladies do not intend to poke about this old house. It is in deplorable condition and ought to be torn down." He tilted his head back and took a deep breath as though about to embark on a lecture on the evils of trespassing.

Just for the sake of debate, Hyacinthe slowly shook her head. "What a pity it cannot be salvaged. It has such charm. I should like to see the interior." She moved forward as though she intended to suit actions to words.

"I wouldn't do that, were I you," Mr. Wayland said in a reedy voice that well suited his anatomy. He placed a protective hand on the gate before the house. "I informed Lord Norwood that the house is dangerous and he agreed that it ought to be posted."

Hyacinthe thought the architect a trifle pompous, with his thin chest puffed out with his importance. She noted a book beneath one arm and attempted to see the title if possible.

Seeing her interest, Mr. Wayland thawed slightly. He held out the volume for her to see.

"*Vitruvius Britannicus*? I fail to see how a book detailing the best classical houses in Britain would be applicable here, sir." She was genuinely puzzled. A publication offering designs for cottages seemed more practical to her way of thinking.

That he was most annoyed with her could be seen only by his pinched nostrils and flash of resentment in his eyes that she caught just in time when she glanced up at him. "It is possible to apply the principles of good architecture to the most humble dwelling, Miss Dancy."

Jane declared, "Oh, dear, the hour has flown by. We must return immediately. Good day, sir." She tugged on Hyacinthe, who willingly joined her on a hurried walk to Jane's cottage.

"What an annoying little man," Jane murmured, the worst that she could think to say about him, it seemed.

"Well, in spite of that volume he flaunted, I suspect he is no Henry Holland," Hyacinthe added, referring to the architect who had worked on Carlton House for the Prince Regent.

"Indeed," Jane said faintly, dazzled at the very mention of the London residence. "And have you seen it?"

"Not the inside," Hyacinthe admitted, "Although I have driven past it and think it impressive." Her mind leaped to the task at hand. "So may I offer my plan for your inspection?"

Once they were safely seated in Jane's modest parlor Hyacinthe said, "I think it is abominable that Lord Norwood should oust you and the others from your dear homes. This is what I propose to do in an effort to make him see the light." And she proceeded to present her plan to defeat Lord Norwood with gasps from her cousin now and then.

* * *

Across the gentle hills two gentlemen looked over the contents of a box in the muniment room with dismay. Amid the ancient records and deeds of Lord Norwood's family, letters and diaries were scattered with little regard for dates or order.

"It is a perfect day out. Are you certain you truly wish to begin this task?" Val said in his most coaxing manner.

"Get thee behind me," Blase murmured as he delved further into the box. "Here, you plow through that stack of papers while I see what's in this pile. A task divided, and all that." He began to sort through his heap of material.

Silence reigned until Blase breathed a sigh of satisfaction. "Here it is: the inventory of Worthington Hall, done in the year 1690 in the reign of our gracious sovereigns William and Mary." He replaced the rest of the documents and letters in the box, retaining a fat diary along with the inventory.

Blase took these items and the two men strolled back in the direction of the library, chatting with ease although Blase could scarce conceal his impatience.

"What do you hope to find? The missing paintings listed?" Val asked curiously.

"Precisely."

Just then Barmore, the Montague butler, approached them with an apologetic expression on his face. "If you please, milord. Sir Charles Ridgeway to see you."

"Show him into the library, Barmore." With a resigned glance at Val, Blase quickly entered his favorite room, placing the inventory and diary on the center of his desk.

"And what might your local gentry be about, do you suppose?" Val wondered aloud in his mocking manner. "How do they view your decision to move the village? Are they about to mount a rebellion, or do they meekly fall in with your wishes to remove them from their homes?"

"Oh, I suppose it is all of a muchness—with people on both sides of the matter. These things tend to be the same, no matter what the question."

Sir Charles appeared delighted to be received when he had not written to request a meeting. "Good morning. I am pleased to see you at Worthington Hall, Lord Norwood." His bow was most correct.

"Sir Charles. Won't you be seated?" Blase signaled to Barmore, and within moments a welcoming drink was offered to the guest and to Blase and Val as well.

When they were comfortably seated and had dispensed with the usual sort of chitchat regarding weather, local crop prospects, and the like, the reason for the interview came out.

"I fear there is opposition to the removal of the cottages, sir," Sir Charles revealed after thanking Lord Norwood for leaving his home—which was actually around a knoll and couldn't be seen from the Hall—intact.

"Dash it all, don't they see that it will improve their lives? Their living conditions?" Blase clarified.

"Well . . . as a matter of fact they don't," Sir Charles admitted. "I have put together a list of suggestions from the ladies who live in one of the cottages to be destroyed and replaced. By the by, have you actually notified those who presently occupy the cottages that they will be housed in new ones? When I called upon Miss Pennington yesterday I could not help but feel that she believes she will be without a roof over her head. This, belief, I may add, is nurtured by her cousin, Miss Dancy."

"Ah, the pretty redhead," Val murmured irrepressibly.

Blase exchanged expressive looks with Val before considering the matter.

"I cannot say that *I* have, but my bailiff should have. I have scarcely seen the village in years, except from the terrace of this house. The steeple and the chimneys mar the perfection of the view, you see." Blase leaned back, calling to his mind's eye what he hoped to achieve. "I wish to develop a picturesque aspect, with extensive planting and thinning of the present layout. I may build a cascade along the stream, for Parliament has made it possible to construct a dam, so such a deed is feasible. I have found much inspiration in these books."

He gestured to the shelf behind him upon which rested copies of such books as *Elements of Modern Gardening* by John Trusler and *The English Garden* by William Mason.

Pulling a well-thumbed copy of Humphry Repton's book *Treatise on Country Residences* from this shelf, he held it up and said, "I quite like some of the things this man has to say. I should like to try out many of his propositions, and to that end have invited him to assist me in my scheme."

Sir Charles looked rather dismayed at this evidence that the plans to alter the scenery around Worthington Hall had proceeded so far.

"May I inquire just when this gentleman will arrive?"

"He answered my letter not long ago." Blase rose from his chair to search the top drawer of his desk until he found the item in question. Checking its contents, he looked up at the others. "According to this he accepts the commission and the terms I offered. He has another task to complete which is not too far removed from here. As far as I can figure, he ought to be here in another two weeks."

"And then the fur will fly," Val muttered to himself.

"What about the building of the new cottages? Have you determined a location for them? The villagers would like to have the stream go through the new village, possibly a pond in the green—for they are quite attached to the one they have at present."

"Just how much has Miss Dancy had to do with this list?" Blase inquired in a dulcet tone.

"Oh,"—Sir Charles beamed a smile at the mere mention of the young lady's name—"she was most helpful, indeed. Pointed out to me all the things that could be improved in the various cottages. The Hadkiss family really ought to have a larger place, and Granny Beanbuck must have the best of ovens."

"I suppose she'd have me installing a Rumford stove," Blase murmured to Val in an aside."

Sir Charles heard the remark and, guileless soul that he was, broadened his smile. "I believe that would be excellent. You see, Granny Beanbuck bakes the bread for the village; earns a pittance for other necessities that way."

Blase nurtured a few hostile thoughts about Miss Dancy. The chit would end up costing him a fortune at the rate she was making her suggestions.

"What else, pray tell?" he asked.

Emboldened by the patient look on his lordship's face, Sir Charles continued to enumerate the various points on the list.

"Better foundations?" Blase frowned. "This is an item to discuss with the architect, Wayland."

Sir Charles looked dubious at the mention of this worthy gentleman's name, but said nothing against him.

"What's the problem with the present foundations?" Val inquired, partly out of curiosity and partly to prod his friend into some sort of action.

"Well, the wood beams appear to be directly on the ground with little stone to support them, and the floors are not properly done at all—being of broken stone, so the damp seeps in when it rains and makes it most uncomfortable. And Miss Dancy reminded me that the ceilings are somewhat low, being scarcely seven feet in height."

"And has Miss Dancy anything else to say?" Blase inquired in a deceptively mild voice.

"Oh, yes," Sir Charles replied happily. "She says the bedrooms ought to be better lit with larger windows. and the stairs should be less dangerous—they wind around in a fearsomely steep way at present."

"It seems your Miss Dancy wants a manor house, not a cottage," Val observed with some amusement.

"Perhaps I should consult with her myself," Blase said, again with that misleading calm.

"That would be a splendid idea," Sir Charles agreed. He shifted about in his chair. Something in the atmosphere of the room appeared to make him uncomfortable.

The men talked a bit longer, with Sir Charles inquiring about the purchase of his home. Then he bade them farewell, seeming satisfied with what had been accomplished.

Once the front door had closed behind him, and Barmore's steps could be heard echoing down the hall, Val gave his good friend a curious look.

"So what do you contemplate? Do you actually intend to confront the prickly hedgehog in her lair—or wherever it is they retreat to when threatened?"

"They roll up into little balls to protect themselves, I believe. Had one as a pet when I was a lad." He considered the matter for a time, then a light of unholy glee appeared in his eyes. He rose from his chair and crossed to tug at the bell pull.

When Barmore arrived he didn't blink an eye at the peculiar request from his lordship.

"What are you up to now?" Val inquired, joining Blase by the window that looked out toward the village. "And may I go with you when you leave here?"

"I shan't tell you, and no, I had best go it alone for this," Blase replied with that same expression of wicked delight in his eyes. He gazed at the distant village with a look of boyish satisfaction.

While he waited for his request to be fulfilled, Blase contented himself with a perusal of the inventory. When what he suspected was confirmed, he gave a crow of triumph.

"I gather you found something of interest," Val said from where he still stood by the window, mulling over the possibilities offered by the events of the past hour.

"I was right. There are three paintings, all done by very fine artists of the day. These plus the jewels are listed. Although the latter are referred to in what amounts to a rather oblique way."

"Obviously, your ancestor did not wish their existence to be widely know among his household. Curious."

Before Blase could comment on this, Barmore tapped gently on the door, then entered bearing the small canvas sack.

"Ah, bless you, Barmore. Could ever a man have a better butler than I?" Blase quickly accepted the small sack, then tossed a hasty salute at Val as he headed out of the door.

Giving little thought to what his friend might think, Blase hurried to the stables and mounted the horse that awaited him. In minutes he rode off in the direction of the village, a self-assured smile on his lips.

Since her cousin had gasped and exclaimed so often that afternoon, Hyacinthe gave little thought to another inhaled breath.

"Oh, Hyacinthe, it is he, that is, his lordship, come to seek you out. Why do you suppose he has come?"

Exhibiting patience that would astound her other cousins, Hyacinthe merely shrugged and left the copy of the *Lady's Magazine* to join her cousin at the bay window. Lord Norwood cut a dashing figure as he dismounted, tied his horse to a post on the green, then crossed the narrow road.

"Well, we shall find out soon enough what he wants. He will be here in moments."

"Mercy!" Jane whispered. She answered the door just as he tapped roundly on it.

When he entered the parlor, having to duck his head through the low doorway, Hyacinthe repressed a smile. He stared up at the ceiling with a definite frown. Apparently Sir Charles had made his call on Lord Norwood.

"I wonder if I might consult with Miss Dancy alone, Miss Pennington. I promise to be most circumspect, but I would never upset you and I fear we may exchange words."

Jane jumped to her feet, declaring she simply had to fetch a loaf of bread from her neighbor, Granny Beanbuck. She whisked around the corner, remembering just in time to grab her shawl.

"What is it that is of such a private nature, sir?" Hyacinthe said, eyeing the wiggling sack in his hands with some misgiving. "I trust you realize that we must be most careful, for Mrs. Peachey will have taken note of your arrival. Jane had the good sense to slip out of the back door. Yet—"

"It is like living in a glass bowl," he muttered, casting an annoyed look at the bay window.

Then he turned to face Hyacinthe and her heart fluttered with alarm at the wicked gleam she thought she saw in his eyes. "I repeat, what is it?"

"Since your arrival you have been doing your best—from what I have been told—to turn my villagers against me and my project. Can you not see it will be to their ultimate benefit?"

"No, actually," she replied simply.

"I offended you while at the inn. If I apologize most abjectly, you will cease this interference?"

Hyacinthe tilted her head, looking at the premier rake of London trying to assume a humble aspect. It was very difficult not to laugh. In fact, it was impossible. Her silvery laughter pealed out in the room, resulting in a look of tight-lipped outrage crossing his lordship's face.

"Miss Dancy, you live up to your reputation."

She sobered quickly at that comment. "What do you mean, sir?"

"You are as prickly as a hedgehog, 'tis said." Blase didn't add that he was the one who had coined that remark. "To that end I offer a token." He held out the wiggling sack, which Miss Dancy accepted with obvious reluctance.

She eased the contents of the sack onto her lap. "A hedgehog!"

The bewildered animal, some ten inches in length and bearing hundreds of spines as a defense, looked about it with alert brown eyes. Its nose quivered as though hunting for a familiar scent.

"*Touché*, Miss Dancy. Or ought I say, *en garde*?" His look of devilish amusement was restored, Hyacinthe noted.

"You declare war on me?" she inquired in an innocent manner. "I believe you ought to prepare for a counterattack. I am not one of your milk-and-water misses, you know. Consider yourself warned."

4

"It is a dear little thing," Hyacinthe said as she watched the hedgehog scuttle off to bury its nose in a pile of leaves and debris in one corner of the area behind the cottage. "I shall call it Harry—for rather obvious reasons."

"It is spiny, not hairy," Jane objected, eyeing the flurry of flying leaves with skepticism.

"Looked to me as though they were hairs that were stiff on the ends, but what do I know. I have heard tell that a hedgehog is a gardener's friend, eating all those nasty slugs, snails, and beetles." By now the little animal had totally disappeared beneath the leaves—for the rest of the day, most likely. From somewhere in the back of her mind, Hyacinthe recalled that hedgehogs were most active at night. In fact, they were quite busy little creatures.

"Well, I do not know what prompted his lordship to bring you such a peculiar gift. Really, to order me from my own home!" Jane declared in a miff. "I had a time of it to sneak from here to Granny Beanbuck's house without Mrs. Peachey seeing me, I can tell you."

"He issued me a challenge of sorts."

"*That* is the outside of enough," Jane said with rising indignation. Then, her forehead pleated with both worry and curiosity, she asked Hyacinthe, "What manner of challenge?"

" 'Tis odd, for I am not certain. He declared me to be as prickly as Harry the hedgehog, and said I was to be *en garde*, as though this were some sort of fencing contest."

Jane sank down on a wicker chair that Mr. Smeed had mended for her. "Contest?" she echoed faintly. "Oh, I beg of you, do not do anything you might regret."

Hyacinthe had the grace to look a bit uncomfortable at this sign of her cousin's concern. "Well . . . I did say he ought to take care of a counterattack."

"Is that a fencing term as well?" Jane asked in a faint voice.

"Yes." She could see her cousin was still puzzled, so she continued. "My brother, Peter, is a dab hand at fencing. I have learned quite a bit merely by watching him. I have vowed to have him teach me someday, for it looks to be jolly good fun."

"Oh, my," was all Jane could reply, and that in a fading voice.

"Well," Hyacinthe said, rising from where she had knelt and dusting off her hands after tossing the sack into a pile of refuse that was due to be burned, "I intend to do a bit of calling today."

"No," Jane said a bit more stoutly.

"Indeed. I have seen not one assurance from his lordship that your lot will be any better following the removal. Have you any proof that he actually intends to build new housing—other than that frippery Mr. Wayland who wanders about with book in hand?"

"Well, not exactly." Jane rose from her chair to follow Hyacinthe to the kitchen, where she proceeded to scrub her hands in a basin of water.

"What does that mean?" Hyacinthe asked.

"Sir Charles assured me that I must have it all wrong. And you know what a peagoose I am about such things. I am not like you. I cannot speak up to people. I like my peace and quiet; living in this little village is my notion of heaven on earth. The mere thought of London frightens me speechless." Jane clasped her hands together before her as if in supplication.

"I know that, silly. And because I care a great deal about you, I insist upon seeing that you continue to enjoy your quiet backwater life. Not all butterflies are gaudy and ostentatious. There are dainty little things that flutter around in rural gardens quite happily. And you are the dearest of people." Hyacinthe gave her cousin a hasty hug, then bestowed a fierce glance toward the doorway through which Lord Norwood had left not long before. "But I shan't have you hurt, nor put out of your dear little cottage."

"Sir Charles said that I shall have a lovely place to live. Really, he did," Jane told Hyacinthe.

Deciding she had best say nothing that she might regret later, Hyacinthe murmured something about changing from her morning dress and left the kitchen.

Once dressed in a suitable gown for calling, Fosdick having arranged her hair in pretty curls, one of which draped over her shoulder in a fetching manner, Hyacinthe set out on her own. Jane had declared she could not face the prospect of joining her cousin, which suited Hyacinthe to a tee.

After a casual stroll around the village green and offering a handful of crumbs to the ducks, Hyacinthe made her way toward the Peachey home. Like the Widow Smith, Mrs. Peachey preferred to keep her hedge low. Although she also embraced the widowed state, she chose to retain her married status rather than be called widow. In an unguarded moment she had explained to Jane that it made her feel younger, somehow.

Mrs. Peachey was not quite so obvious as Widow Smith. She showed Hyacinthe into her parlor, concealing her curiosity with tea preparations and a flutter of chitchat about one thing and another. Mostly she talked about the coming upheaval and what it might do to her cats.

"They are all I have," she revealed to Hyacinthe while stroking the fluffy white cat that had crawled up into her lap. Then seeming to realize her words might be construed as a bid for pity, she changed the subject.

"Lord Norwood called at Miss Pennington's cottage this morning. Odd time for a gentleman to come calling, I'd say?" her hand, threaded through the cat's thick fur, paused while her bright dark eyes watched Hyacinthe with sharp intensity.

"He brought me a gift." Hyacinthe smiled, then added, "He heard me mention that Jane had a problem with snails and slugs and had one of his men locate a hedgehog for us. I'll confess that while it is a most unusual present, Jane seemed pleased to have the animal in the garden." Hyacinthe was amazed that the heavens didn't open up to strike her for all the lies she had uttered as of late. However, she found she could not bear to spread about malicious stories regarding Lord Norwood.

"That was surprisingly thoughtful of the gentleman," Mrs. Peachey said. She resumed stroking her pet.

"I gather you are the repository of the history of this village. Have you ever considered writing it down? It ought to be done so the children of future generations would know what life was like in the little spot before it was destroyed."

"Destroyed?" Mrs. Peachey exclaimed. "I'd not thought of it like that, but you are correct. The village and its past shall be gone. So much has been lost already."

Glancing out of the window, which was bowed like Jane's, Hyacinthe observed Mr. Wayland making his way to the moldering Tudor house next door.

"My, that gentleman has a passion for old places," Mrs. Peachey commented. "Why, the other day he came to call and asked a hundred questions about the village and particularly that house. One would have thought it really did have treasure hidden in it."

"Treasure?" Hyacinthe echoed. "How fascinating. My cousin said nothing about a tale like this."

"Possibly she don't know. Mind you, there may be nothing to it, most likely 'tis all a hum, but . . ."

"Yes?" Hyacinthe said eagerly.

"Well, the old story goes that around two hundred years ago—or thereabouts—there was a redheaded woman living there who was kept by the then Lord Norwood. Mind you, I've nothing against red hair, yours is a glory, but it seems that she was declared a witch, having a rare ability with animals. His lordship-that-was-then defended her, and soon she was spending a goodly amount of time with him, if you catch my meaning."

Then Mrs. Peachey appeared to remember just who sat in her parlor and she flushed slightly. "Of course, being a single lady, you may not, for such tales really are not the sort for young ladies."

"Not at all, I find them most interesting. And yes, I believe I do know what you mean. My Aunt Bel spoke of a woman like that once. Do go on."

Reassured that it was permissible to soil the ears of a maiden lady with her tale and relishing a new audience, Mrs. Peachey continued. "The story goes that he gave her jewels and other fine things. Then hard times came, his lordship went away, and not long afterward she died."

"And so?" Hyacinthe prompted, well aware that Mrs. Peachey was trying to draw out her dramatic offering as much as she could.

"When they went in to take her off for burial not a thing could be found. She was gone, with only white curtains waving in the breeze."

"There was no body?"

"Aye. No body and no jewels or anything else that anyone could find. And believe me, they have searched the house time and again over the years with no success."

Hyacinthe took a sip of her tea, reflecting on the bizarre tale she had just heard. Did this account for Mr. Wayland's fascination with the Tudor house? Did he believe the tale and search for treasure?

"No one has lived there in ever so long. Certainly not as long as we have been here. The house just sits neglected, sinking further into decay each year. 'Tis haunted, some say," Mrs. Peachey concluded with relish.

"Haunted!" Hyacinthe whispered, captured by the image of the beautiful redheaded woman who had mysteriously disappeared so long ago. Jewels and treasure were enough to make anyone dare the risk of ghosts to search the house, but not a trace left behind? "No body ever appeared?"

"Well, some say she weren't really dead at all. That she slipped off to London to be with his lordship. That she paid her servants to tell the tale. They left soon enough, so the story goes."

"I think you ought to record every word of this story, Mrs. Peachey. And you ought to put down the history of every house in the village. I feel certain that between you and Widow Smith the entire record of this village could be collected. It would be a memorial to the village once it disappears and a great accomplishment for you!"

Mrs. Peachey was struck dumb by the words she'd just

heard. She clasped her hands to her bosom and could scarcely wait for Hyacinthe to depart so she could consult the Widow Smith on the project.

Once again strolling along the green, Hyacinthe stopped to study the Tudor house. What had truly happened to that woman so long ago? Had that particular Lord Norwood been as devilishly handsome as the present holder of the title? She simply had to find out. But, she realized, her shoulders sagging a trifle with the admission, how could she? Ladies did not call upon gentlemen. It wasn't done.

However, he had issued a challenge, one she had no intention of ignoring. What to do? A gleam entered her eyes and she hurried home.

"Do you know of any stray kittens?" she inquired of Jane after entering the cottage.

"Granny Beanbuck always has a collection of cats . . . to keep the mice and rats from her flour and breads. Why?"

"I believe I ought to repay the gift Lord Norwood bestowed upon me. He deserves a token of appreciation." A crafty expression crept into Hyacinthe's eyes.

Jane sank down upon a chair, favoring her cousin with a dismayed look. "Why is it that I suspect you of ulterior motives?"

"Because you should. Why did you never tell me the romantic tale of the Tudor house?" Hyacinthe sketched the story for her cousin.

"That lot of silly nonsense? I feel certain Mrs. Peachey made it up."

"I doubt it, for it has the ring of truth. And you needn't look at me as though I don't know what *that* is. I want to know more, and to do that I must see Worthington Hall, or at least the picture gallery. Help me, Jane."

"Mercy!" came the faint reply.

"I shall summon my coach, then call upon Granny Beanbuck," Hyacinthe decided promptly. "I do wish to compliment her on those heavenly cinnamon buns that she makes. Perhaps I ought to bring a sample along for his eminence, so he could see how important her oven is!" Hyacinthe's eyes danced with delight at her plan and she took her light cloak from the tiny stand in the hall before opening the door again.

"Hyacinthe," Jane protested weakly. She watched as her cousin skipped off along the village path in the direction of the Cock and Bull, then retired to restore herself with a cup of tea. She had been doing that quite often lately.

Within several hours all was in readiness. Tom Coachman and Warton presented themselves before Jane's cottage promptly when bade. Various curtains twitched when Jane and Hyacinthe, dressed to the nines for calling upon his lordship, left the cottage to enter the carriage, followed by the stiffly proper Fosdick.

Hyacinthe surveyed with satisfaction the sack she had made from pretty striped muslin and tied with a cherry-red riband. "My mama always taught me to give better than I receive."

"I doubt if she had anything like this in mind, dearest," Jane said.

However, she seemed to have reconciled herself to whatever scheme her cousin had in mind, for when Hyacinthe returned after obtaining a surplus cat from Granny Beanbuck, she found Jane in a receptive mood.

As though sensing something of what was in Hyacinthe's mind, Jane said as they set off in the coach, "I am fortunate to have someone who cares for me. Just think of Mr. Smeed and all the others who have no one at all." She reached over to bestow a pat on her cousin's gloved hand.

Hyacinthe turned to the window, partly to overcome her emotions and in part to survey the scenery that spread out on either side of the burgundy coach while they smartly bowled along the road that led to the Hall.

" 'Tis pretty here. Rolling hills, lovely trees, small well-cared-for farms in the distance. I cannot think what Lord Norwood means when he says his view needs improving. How can one possibly improve on this?"

"He said he wished to enhance his view," Jane said mildly.

"Enhance? And needs to destroy homes to accomplish it? Bah," Hyacinthe declared inelegantly.

The coach drew up before the house with a flourish, and Warton let down the steps for the ladies. Hyacinthe stood by the coach, examining all she saw while waiting for her cousin to gather up herself and her reticule.

"Now remember, I wish to see the portrait gallery. You must help me think of a way," Hyacinthe whispered.

Warton rapped at the door, then announced the ladies to the butler. Hyacinthe went ahead, but Jane tagged close behind, as though afraid to be two steps away from her stronger and more determined cousin. Fosdick trailed behind, set on lending countenance to her ladies.

"We are here with a small gift for Lord Norwood," Hyacinthe explained. "He was so kind as to bring us one yesterday. Oh, this is Miss Pennington, and I am Miss Dancy."

Not by a flicker of an eyelash did the butler reveal what he thought of this invasion of a gentleman's establishment by two young women and a maid.

They were ushered into a very charming sitting room and left there. Jane gave Hyacinthe a stricken look, then turned to the door as though to flee while she could. "This is insanity!" she said in a whisper.

"Nonsense. This is war," Hyacinthe whispered back.

They heard the clatter of footsteps on the stairs—at least two people. Perhaps that other man, the one with the shining dark hair and considering dark eyes, was here as well. He was far too unpredictable to consider for Jane. Sir Charles would do nicely once brought around to realize it.

"Miss Dancy? What a surprise. And Miss Pennington. To what do I owe this honor?" That he had doubts about whatever it might be lurked in his expressive eyes.

The man from the inn, Valentine, Lord Latham, sauntered in behind Lord Norwood.

"Miss Pennington, allow me to present a good friend of mine, Lord Latham."

Lord Latham bowed over Jane's hand, turning her into a flustered muddle with his polished compliments.

Hyacinthe decided she had best get to the heart of the matter immediately. The sack was becoming a trifle much for her to manage, she acknowledged when a set of claws came through the muslin.

"Since you were so kind as to bring me a gift, the very least

I could do was reciprocate," she said with a proper little curtsy.

"Why do I have the feeling that I ought to beware of the bringer of gifts?" she heard Lord Norwood murmur to his friend. He stepped forward, a hand outstretched in seeming resignation.

Smiling, Hyacinthe placed the sack into the hand, whereupon he yelped. The claws had found a target.

Obviously stifling a string of words he longed to fling at her, he opened the bag, dumping out the orange-striped kitten with little ceremony.

"A cat?"

"A tiger cat, my lord," Hyacinthe replied demurely.

The animal huffily switched a very fluffy tail, then began to investigate its surroundings.

"How novel," Val commented. "A cat from a cat."

Jane gasped at this bit of wicked language.

Hyacinthe thought it improper, cynical, but rather amusing. Naturally she did not reveal her reaction.

Lord Norwood suggested that they all be seated, and then gently queried Hyacinthe about her day while keeping a wary eye on the kitten.

She gave him full marks for perceiving that she had not made the call merely to present him with the tiger cat, which had been cleverly named Tiger by Val.

The butler appeared bearing a tray with tea and biscuits, and a bottle of ratafia should they care to indulge a bit. Hyacinthe bit back a smile when Val took note that he was expected to take tea with the ladies.

"Thank you, Barmore," Lord Norwood said, adding "please remove this animal to the kitchen." The man picked up the cat by the scruff of the neck and gingerly took it from the room accompanied by affronted yowling.

Jane fidgeted at her end of the love seat where the young women had decided to sit. Hyacinthe knew she had to act quickly or all would be lost and the daring call would have been in vain. If she could lure his lordship into a hunt, he might forget about the destruction of the village.

"You have a lovely home, Lord Norwood. While calling

upon the villagers I have heard fascinating stories of your ancestors. Indeed, I quite long to see what they looked like." After this blatant hint, she wondered if he would deny her the pleasure. He didn't disappoint her. He did look a trifle startled at her request, however.

"Why, I should be pleased to show you the gallery when you have finished your tea. I wouldn't wish to deprive you of anything."

"Except Jane her home," Hyacinthe flashed back sweetly.

"Aha!" Val said softly. "I begin to see the light."

"You only think you do," Hyacinthe murmured back in the same tone. She drained the cup of excellent Bohea, finished the last of her biscuit, then rose, dusting off her fingers with a napkin as she did. "I expect we ought not delay. I fear we are a bit improper as it is, but I just knew you'd appreciate the kitten."

"Indeed," the somewhat stunned Lord Norwood replied. He gave his friend a significant look, then the four walked in the direction of the picture gallery at the rear of the house.

When they went up the stairs to the first floor, Hyacinthe observed how polished and immaculate everything looked. Good housekeeping was not always to be found in a bachelor establishment, or so she'd been told. Her brother had a terrible time finding someone who would put up with his place, but then he had all those mummies!

"Here we are," Blase announced at the door to the gallery. What the devil these two females were doing here, ostensibly looking at his ancestors, he couldn't imagine. After the wicked gift of that nasty little beast, he'd decided he had best humor them.

They strolled along the length of the hall with Val making suitably naughty comments along the way.

"Are you never serious, Lord Latham?" Jane asked at long last when he had shredded the character of a particularly bored-looking lady.

"Not if I can help it, my charming Miss Pennington. Might I counter with a question of my own? Are you never silly?"

She surprised him with her reply. "At times." Her glance at her cousin seemed to imply a connection between the two.

At last they paused before a gentleman of the late sixteen hundreds. Blase admitted he resembled the chap, but stopped at that. From what he had read in this fellow's diary during the past four days, he had a reputation that put Blase in the nursery brigade.

"Who was this?" Hyacinthe inquired after checking the date at the bottom of the frame.

"He was also named Blase Montague. It's a name that pops up in the family from time to time." He waited for her to comment, for he was certain there was a reason somewhere in her desire to see these pictures.

"Most appropriate, I'd say." She tilted her head·to give the painting a considering inspection. "Do you know that there is a fascinating story about him? Mrs. Peachey told it to me this morning. After hearing it, well, I just had to see what he looked like."

Something rang in the back of Blase's mind. "A story? One the villagers repeat?" He gave Val a meaningful look, then concentrated on the miss at his side.

"Well, and it was not so terrible, sir. Nothing scandalous, at least I doubt if it is. Unless he murdered her and hid her body someplace. I'd not thought of that before."

"Miss Dancy, *if* you will be so kind?" Blase wished he could shake the pert young woman who stood close enough·so he could detect the spicy carnation scent she wore. It suited her, for she was a spicy morsel of a woman. He swung between wanting to kiss her and wishing he could shake her, for she was as naughty as could be.

With a final glance at the painting, Miss Dancy turned away to retrace her steps to the doorway. "We really ought to be going."

Blase lost his temper, something he rarely ever did. He strode up to Miss Dancy, took her firmly by the arm, then marched her along down the stairs into the library, where he pushed her onto a chair.

"I repeat, Miss Dancy. If you will be so kind? I should like to know this story you heard. I have a particular reason for wishing to hear it."

Hyacinthe glared at the man she frequently referred to as

"his eminence" because he was so intimidating. After silently debating a moment, she nodded.

"Mrs. Peachey said that when he was alive there was talk that he was involved with a redhead who lived in the Tudor house. Come to think on it, there was no mention of a family. I wonder if he established her there." When Lord Norwood gave her a dark look, Hyacinthe continued, "It was said that he bestowed 'jewels and treasures' on her. Yet, when it was known that she had died, the people who entered the house found the curtains open—no body and no treasure of any kind. Is that not a mystery?"

"Jewels? Nothing about what kind they might be?"

Hyacinthe rose from the chair where she had been so unceremoniously pushed and edged toward the door. "Nothing. But one can only wonder if they remain hidden in the house."

He strolled after her, stopping her in her tracks when he said, "And why did you wish to see his portrait?"

"Well . . . I wanted to see if he resembled you, I suppose." She knew she had upset him the moment the words left her mouth. Oh, if she could only learn to guard her tongue. Slipping away down the hall—seeming not to run but covering the marble with rapid steps—she waited for Jane by the front door. Lord Norwood had followed at her heels.

"It has been, er, interesting, sir. Thank you for the tea and the viewing," Hyacinthe said politely, then ducked out of the door before his lordship could commit murder or whatever promised by the look in his eyes.

Jane had joined them at the door. With a muddled murmur of words, she dashed after her cousin, both of them popping into the coach before the gentlemen could prevent them. Although what they might do, she didn't know. And didn't want to find out. Fosdick left the house, following her young ladies at a more seemly pace.

"What did you accomplish by that foolishness?" Jane demanded to know once they were safely away from Worthington Hall.

"His ancestor most likely did her in, for he looks to have a temper equally as bad as the present lord. Certainly they resemble one another," Hyacinthe said after examining her sleeve to see if any sign from that firm grip showed. "We can but hope my ruse works and he decides to investigate."

They discussed the matter all the way to the cottage, deciding they would prowl around the Tudor house sometime when Mr. Wayland was occupied elsewhere.

At Worthington Hall Blase walked at Val's side back to the library, a frown marring his handsome brow.

"I would wager there is something in that tale of hers," he said.

"Then you believe it?" Val asked incredulously.

"You forget, I have been reading his diary. He describes his love as having hair like flame, with a temper to match. It is my theory that he gave her the jewels and the paintings. But why did they never turn up anywhere?"

"Interesting. When do we commence a search of the Tudor house?"

Unsurprised at the conclusion his friend had reached, Blase replied, "Tomorrow morning, early. I shall assign that snooping Wayland to surveying the land I have set aside for the new cottages, and perhaps he can stake out the foundations with the help of the masons he hired. That ought to keep him out of our hair."

"But what of Miss Dancy?" Val inquired with a devilish grin.

"She is another matter entirely. We can but hope that she turns her attention to something else."

"You amuse me, Blase. If I know anything about women at all, you will have to rise early to beat her to it."

"I cannot believe she brought me a cat."

"I noticed he scratched you. Were I in your shoes, I should be a little wary of the redhead. I suspect she also has claws and would not hesitate to use them." Val smiled narrowly as though recalling something from the past.

"Perhaps a ride would be in order. I confess that this alteration I planned is assuming proportions I'd not considered when I began."

"Bit off more than you can chew?" Val taunted gently.

"Not in the least," Blase replied, stiffening slightly at the implication that he might fail in his plans. "I shall find the jewels and paintings, mark my words. And the prospect from my terrace will be developed as I envision, with the help of Humphrey Repton."

Val merely chuckled while they went up the stairs to their rooms to don riding apparel.

Across the gentle hills Hyacinthe dismissed her coachman and groom, then guided Jane inside the cottage. Fosdick took their bonnets and pellisses, disappearing without questions or remarks.

"I doubt that man has changed his intent one whit. But"—Hyacinthe spread her hands wide and excitement colored her voice—"he believes those jewels and other treasure *do* exist. Well, we shall see who finds them. Perhaps I can uncover the missing items, then use them as persuasion. And if his rakish lordship thinks he will succeed with his plans to destroy history, he can think again. I am more determined than ever that he shan't prevail!"

5

"I believe we might steal over there now. It is far too early for either Mrs. Peachey or the Widow Smith to be up and about." Hyacinthe leaned from her dormer window beneath the overhanging thatch roof to peer out into the half light of early morning. Quite a few ducks and the two swans dotted the green with their feathered presence. They were relatively quiet, with only soft quacks to be heard. Not a soul was abroad at this hour.

"This is utterly mad," Jane protested—quietly, lest she wake Fosdick. It seemed that the formidably proper abigail intimidated Jane far more than Hyacinthe, for Jane appeared quite hesitant to do anything that might shock the woman.

"Well, we do not wish the entire village to know what we are about. Come." Hyacinthe closed and latched her window, then motioned Jane to follow her from the pleasant bedroom.

They tiptoed down the stairs until they reached the tidy slate-floored entrance hall.

Hyacinthe eased the bolt on the door, then slipped outside without the slightest sound.

"What a good thing you put a spot of oil on those hinges yesterday," Jane observed in a mere whisper while they continued their almost-silent progress across the green.

A pair of ducks followed their movements, quite obviously hoping for a few crumbs, and one of the stately swans gave them a rude stare for disturbing its inspection of the morning tidbits to be found.

On the far side of the green the old house rose amid a tangle of climbing rose brambles and weeds, with an occasional clump of pinks and wallflowers gone wild peeping from the confusion of greenery. The footpath had been cleared so they were able to avoid snagging their serviceable gowns, worn expressly to tolerate the inevitable dust that haunted old places.

They found the front door well and truly locked, as were the windows to either side. Not to be deterred in what she declared to be an intriguing investigation, and recalling the daring exploits of her more adventuresome cousins, Hyacinthe persevered.

Around to the rear of the house she discovered that the entry to the scullery had been left ajar.

"Lovely!" she whispered. Not knowing how soundly Mrs. Peachey slept, the girls agreed to whisper until safely within the old house.

They slipped silently into the house, then placed the door precisely where it had stood—nearly closed.

Jane peered through the gloom. "I can scarcely make out a thing," she complained.

The floor above them squeaked and Jane reached out to cling to her cousin's arm.

Glad for the comfort of her touch, Hyacinthe said, " 'Tis nothing more than an old house. Come." She drew Jane along with her until they reached the front parlor. "We shall begin here," she decided.

Once their eyes became accustomed to the poor light, the girls looked about them with raised brows.

"It would seem that someone has begun an investigation before us," Jane observed with a noticeable tremor in her voice. "Things have been shifted about in an obvious search. There are footprints in the dust."

"How curious that Mr. Wayland did not mention that a trespasser had invaded this house when he cautioned us against coming here," Hyacinthe commented. "One cannot help but wonder if the gentleman has notions of his own."

"You mean he intends to hunt for the treasure for himself? But that would be dishonest," Jane declared roundly. The floor creaked again and she again drew closer to her cousin.

"We are hunting as well," Hyacinthe reminded her. "However, should we find something, we would assuredly hand it over to Lord Norwood, although he does not deserve it. I should be happy with the fun of finding something hidden for so long. And if it serves to persuade his lordship to forget about the ruination of the village, more to the good."

Jane shook her head. "Well, I do not see how you expect to find anything when 'tis obvious that someone else has explored this house before us."

"I suspect that Mr. Wayland has not found anything, for if he had, would he not take himself off with his loot?"

"I suppose so," Jane said doubtfully.

"Here," Hyacinthe directed, "you begin in this corner and I shall start at the opposite. There are still pictures on the walls, so search behind them for hiding places. The carpet—motheaten as it is—has been rolled up, so I suppose that the last hunter has already inspected the floor."

The cousins worked quietly for some time before they met at the far side of the room. Both were somewhat dusty, with cobwebs draped decoratively across the day cap Jane had donned over Hyacinthe's objections.

Hyacinthe cast a disgusted look about the room. "I doubt there is anything hidden here. Shall we go upstairs?"

"Why not the kitchen?" Jane wondered, while she followed her cousin up the worn steps. The wood had a depression in the center of each stair tread, and the girls held up their skirts to avoid gathering up the layer of dust that covered them.

"I doubt if she was well acquainted with that room were she the mistress of a wealthy man," Hyacinthe explained. "I am encouraged there's no evidence of someone else having been up here, for the dust has not been disturbed."

The floor creaked and groaned as they gingerly made their way along the upstairs hall. There were four bedrooms—all paneled, with mullioned windows—and a small storeroom. They peered into each of these, noting the absence of furniture in all but one room.

"I wonder where the ghost is said to lurk," Hyacinthe murmured while she poked and prodded everything in sight in the unfurnished rooms. She entered the room that had the remaining furniture with Jane close behind her.

"Cousin, you are anything but reassuring," Jane said as she bent to look under the bed, its tattered hangings covering elegant although dingy lines. "There is no carpet here, either," she observed while checking the inside of a beautifully decorated commode now stained with age.

"The place smells of decaying wood and mildewed fabric." Hyacinthe made her way to one of the many-paned windows, opening it just enough to allow a breath of air to wash through the room and send feathers of dust flying.

Jane sneezed, then looked apprehensively about her. "I thought I heard sounds from below," she whispered.

They paused, standing utterly still. What appeared to be footsteps reached their ears, followed by a scraping noise as though something were being dragged across the floor.

Jane turned pale and reached out to clutch Hyacinthe's arm.

"I believe there is something or someone belowstairs," Hyacinthe murmured.

"Or the ghost of that woman," Jane whispered, holding a handkerchief firmly to her nose lest she sneeze again.

"I wonder what she was like?" Hyacinthe whispered back. What sort of woman would appeal to the dashing, rakish gentleman who leaned so casually against a stone wall in that painting? While he seemed so correct in dress and manner, his eyes had held secrets. They held laughter and a knowledge of the world that Hyacinthe could only guess at.

Had he murdered her as Mrs. Peachey hinted? Or had she taken her treasures and stolen away to London? About to investigate a closet beneath the eaves at the far end of the room, Hyacinthe froze as she heard footsteps on the stairs.

"Quickly, no one must find us here!" Pulling Jane along with her, Hyacinthe scurried to the closet, then closed the door when they were safely inside. They were in what had been a paneled room, from what could be seen in the gloom. A mere slit of a window revealed little. Evidently clothing and other necessities had been kept in here, with the space used as a dressing room.

Jane tugged at her cousin's sleeve, motioning to the door, beyond which could be heard voices.

"Well, Val, this must have been her room." The steps crossed to the window that Hyacinthe had opened.

"Appears as though someone has been here recently," Val commented.

"Wayland said he had been examining the house to see if anything was worth salvaging," replied Blase.

"Well, I hardly expected it to be her ghost," Val said. He chuckled at his friend's expression. "Did you?"

"I'll confess I did not know quite what to expect. I'd not be surprised to find our little hedgehog over here poking her face into what does not concern her."

"Ah, the prickly redhead. She's a charmer, I'll wager, were you to persuade her into your arms or bed."

"She's a gently bred female, Val. Best confine those sort of observations to others, if you know what I mean." He chuckled in a somewhat suggestive manner. "Not but what I'd not relish the opportunity to do a bit of an—shall we say, investigation?—should the opportunity arise."

"Do any of the paintings we have seen so far match the description in your inventory?" Val queried while strolling about the room. He grimaced at the filthy painting above the bed. Once at the far side of the room, he tried the handle of the door to the closet, opened it to peer inside, then closed it without going into it.

"What was in there?" Blase inquired lazily while he checked under the bed to see if any of the floorboards might be of a different type or have been pried up lately.

"Dressing room. Nothing of importance there."

"Well, I expect we had better inspect it before we leave here. Who knows, she might have had a hiding place in there with her clothing and whatever furbelows a lady kept then."

"Very well," Val said, propping himself against the wall to watch while Blase continued his search. He tapped walls, pried at the broad oak planks that served as flooring, scrutinized the ceiling to see if a panel might conceal a hiding place.

"Confounded Tudor style offers far too many places for concealment. The carvings on these wooden panels could have a spring catch in any one of them."

"Or a secret door to stairs where we'll find the skeleton of the poor dear, locked in by her unscrupulous maid, foiled in her intent to flee to her lover."

"Val, remind me never to permit you access to one of those gothic novels again." Blase gave his friend a patient look, then added, "You might help, you know."

"I suspect we already have sufficient help," Val said, nodding his head toward the closet while holding one finger to his lips to silence Blase.

Blase frowned, then sighed. "Hedgehog?" he mouthed.

Val nodded.

Giving the room a final inspection, Blase shook his head in disgust. "If there is anything here, I cannot fathom where it might be."

"Think Wayland may have found it?" Val said softly.

"Stashing it away for later disposal? Anything is possible, I suppose. I believe my architect will bear close watching."

Taking exceedingly quiet steps, he edged over to the closet, turned the knob, and with a swift motion threw the door open and stalked inside.

"Good heavens," Hyacinthe complained, "you could give a person an attack of the spasms crashing in like that."

"Aha!" Blase said in a nasty tone, "I thought we had found our ghost! And how is our little hedgehog this morning?"

"Quite well, thank you. *He* is noisily settling into a cozy spot at the bottom of the garden, busily munching snails and slugs and whatever else hedgehogs eat. Harry is quite a treasure. May I ask our tom cat how he is getting along?" Lord Norwood appeared most annoyed with her comparison of him to a tom cat. She barely suppressed the grin that longed to break forth. "Mr. Wayland cautioned us so strongly against coming into this house that we simply had to find out what might be here," Hyacinthe said in a disarming way, offering Blase a conciliatory smile.

"He has been here often?"

"Every day," Jane said, while brushing away a cobweb that chanced to float before her. She smoothed out her skirts, then covered her nose again to prevent another sneeze.

Val shook his head in apparent amusement, his grin widening as he realized the disreputable sight the two young ladies made.

"What do you say we adjourn to the outside and a bit of

fresh air?" He offered Jane his arm, which she accepted with obvious reluctance. It seemed she still recalled his comment that there was nothing of importance in the dressing closet. That would rankle any lady, even one convinced that she would never wed.

"I am able to manage perfectly well on my own, thank you very much," Hyacinthe said politely to Lord Norwood when he offered her his arm. "I would like to inspect this room more than we were able. You came and we felt it best to hide, for we truly did not know who might be coming up those stairs. Why, it could have been anyone."

"Indeed. I think we shall join the others, however. I will return here later to do a bit of hunting on my own."

"You are a spoilsport, sir," Hyacinthe said with vexation. "This would be the most likely place for a woman to conceal something of value. Perhaps there is a secret compartment behind that little painting over there, the one in the shadows."

Blase strode over to examine the painting, which he proceeded to remove from the wall in order to see it better. The dim light offered by the window proved insufficient, so he left the dressing room and marched down the stairs to the rear of the house with Hyacinthe trailing directly behind him. Here he managed to wipe the dust from the picture, then studied it more fully.

"Is it one of them?" Val said softly, for Jane had made it clear to them all that Mrs. Peachey might appear in her backyard at any time.

"I believe it is. In which case the others ought to be around here somewhere. I wonder if I ought to tell Wayland to forget this house for the moment."

"Or keep him so busy elsewhere that he has no time for anything involved with this house," Val suggested.

"Excellent notion," Lord Norwood replied, a grin lighting his handsome face.

About then the sun chanced to light up the yard, reminding them of the advancing hours. Hyacinthe took Jane's hand to edge around the house. It would be best for the two of them to disappear while the gentlemen were otherwise occupied. She had a distinct feeling that Lord Norwood was not best pleased with her at the moment. Yet she had helped find his painting.

She saw the men glance up just as she and Jane began to hurry away from the house and across the green. The ducks protested, fussing in a noisy way, when the young women skirted the rim of the pond.

"We probably have awakened Mrs. Peachey—not to mention every other soul in the village—with all this racket," Jane commented when Hyacinthe tugged her past the gate and into the cottage.

"All but Granny Beanbuck, who must have been up for some time. I smell her cinnamon buns. Do you think that after we clean up we might manage to purchase a few for our breakfast?"

"Indeed," Jane warmly agreed.

They hurried up the stairs and into their respective bedrooms. In short order they were appropriately garbed for a possible meeting with two irate gentlemen. Jane's hair had been restored to shining neatness, while Hyacinthe's red tresses curled provocatively about her heart-shaped face.

Hyacinthe set about heating tea water, although she was not accustomed to such labors. One did what one must, she had long ago decided.

When Jane returned bearing a heaping plate of warm and very-fragrant buns, the aroma filled the little kitchen.

With such an incentive, Hyacinthe quickly poured the boiling water into the teapot, taking care not to spill any on herself. Rather than eat at the kitchen table, she loaded a pretty painted tray with cups and saucers, napkins, and a large plate heaped with a prodigious number of cinnamon buns inside a white linen napkin to keep them warm. There was easily enough for four.

Jane eyed the repast in the parlor with audible misgivings. "I think you are being presumptuous."

"They will be reluctant to intrude upon Granny Beanbuck," Hyacinthe declared with feminine certainty. "But I believe that the aroma of fresh-baked cinnamon buns will be nigh onto impossible for any male to resist. How thankful I am that you bought such a splendid amount."

"Yes, well, I thought that Sir Charles might stop by later this morning, and he is very fond of them." Jane blushed a painful shade of pink.

Hyacinthe had consumed the first bite of one of the delectable buns followed by a dainty sip of tea when a loud and very impatient knock could be heard on the door.

"I will handle this," she whispered to Jane. Moving from the parlor to the little entrance hall, she cautiously opened the front door just a little. Upon seeing Lord Norwood and Lord Latham waiting, she opened the door a trifle wider, looking at them with wide-eyed innocence. "Yes?"

"Why won't more girls use that word," Val muttered in a plaintive voice.

Ignoring his friend, Lord Norwood bowed slightly, then sniffed the aroma of cinnamon buns that floated from the parlor. "I believe we have something to discuss."

"Perhaps you will join us in a morning cup of tea? And fresh-baked cinnamon buns, of course." When both men surged forward, Hyacinthe stifled a grin at their boyish enthusiasm. "I feel certain that we have sufficient."

"Why do I feel that you mentally added 'even for you' after that remark?" Val said in a jesting manner.

"Well, and I did, I suppose," she confessed.

Within short order they were all seated in Jane's parlor sipping cups of strong Bohea and nibbling utterly delectable, fairy-light cinnamon buns.

Lord Norwood was exceedingly hungry after that tramp through the house, then finding someplace where he and Val might clean off some of their dirt before presenting themselves at the Pennington house. When he had consumed two cups of tea liberally laced with milk and three of the buns, he spoke.

"I believe we must have some sort of understanding. Mr. Wayland is correct about one thing. You ought not go into that deserted house. You might be hurt, or something worse."

"What do you mean, worse?" Jane inquired.

"I think he implies we might be murdered, or something equally dire," Hyacinthe explained dryly.

"But if he proceeds with his plan to tear down the village, we shan't have the opportunity to explore that once-lovely old place. It must have been very charming in its day," Jane reflected.

At this reminder of his intentions Hyacinthe grew very quiet, giving Lord Norwood considering looks over her teacup. He appeared to be unaware of her change of mood, for he blundered on.

"Precisely. I believe I shall instruct Wayland to commence laying out foundations for new cottages at once," he said, bestowing a sad look at the last bit of bun that remained on his plate.

"Even with autumn approaching? I fail to see how you can accomplish much before spring," Hyacinthe observed carefully.

"Oh, the workers are willing to proceed through most of the bad weather, except for snow," he assured her.

"Then we ought to pray for a cold winter," Hyacinthe muttered under her breath.

"Still not resigned to the move, Miss Dancy?" Lord Latham asked, his bright eyes dancing at the prospect of a good argument.

"I think it is the most stupid, insensitive, and utterly selfish thing I have ever heard of," Hyacinthe declared stoutly, glaring at his lordship in a quite defiant manner. "The very idea of destroying a person's home merely to improve a view is sheer nonsense."

She could see that Lord Norwood was barely hanging onto his composure. A dull red suffused his cheeks and he compressed his lips, no doubt to prevent him from blistering her ears with his reply to her forthright denunciation. She had to give him full marks for reasonably good manners.

"Hyacinthe!" Jane cried in a totally mortified voice.

"I cannot apologize for my excess of passion regarding this. Tell me, sir, will the rents go up on these new and splendid—and no doubt costly to build—cottages? It would be folly to construct them and not gain a respectable return for your money. That would be a poor investment."

"And what do you know about landlords and investments?" Lord Norwood said in a strained voice while failing to answer her question.

"When my dear papa was alive he taught me a great deal, perhaps knowing he had not long on earth. Since I have the practical head, whereas Peter is the dreamer of the family, Papa decided I had best know as much as possible. I understand far more about this matter than you suspect. I doubt you can toss a great sum of money away on tenant housing without a sufficient return . . . unless you have been far luckier at the racetrack than I had heard."

He frowned at her words, taking a few moments to digest them. At last he placed his teacup on the table close at hand and rose as though to depart. "I gather there is little more to say on this matter."

Hyacinthe also rose, facing him with her hands in a composed clasp before her, her little chin tilted defiantly up at him. "I daresay you have the right of it, sirrah. Unless you change your mind. I should be most grateful in that event," she said graciously, with a nod.

"I wonder what that might involve," Lord Latham murmured in his mischievous way.

"I do believe that your nurse ought to have spanked you more often, Lord Latham," Jane said repressively.

"I fear she had other things in mind, dear lady," he said, with a very distant and somewhat forbidding look on his face.

Hyacinthe thought it best to change the subject immediately before Jane could press for an explanation. While she had no notion as to what his unfortunate experience might have been, it obviously was one that still bothered him.

"Is that Sir Charles I see coming up the walk?" she said.

Jane promptly forgot the note of suppressed anger that she too had heard in Lord Latham's voice and immediately went to answer the door.

"Sir Charles," she could be heard saying in a happy voice. Jane's feelings were highly transparent to Hyacinthe. She wondered if Sir Charles might possibly be aware of them. And if he were, what did he think?

The proper gentleman entered the parlor with a look of great surprise at discovering guests in Miss Pennington's parlor at this hour of the morning. He bowed correctly, then at

Jane's urging took her chair and accepted a cup of still-hot tea with a plate bearing a large cinnamon bun.

Jane perched on the arm of Hyacinthe's chair until she rose to cross to accompany Lord Norwood and Lord Latham to the entry. "Do entertain Sir Charles, please, Jane," Hyacinthe told her. "I will tend to our departing guests."

"Pray do not leave on my account," Sir Charles protested. "In fact, I wished to ask Lord Latham about that fishing gear he mentioned to me the other day."

With a smiling look of resignation at Lord Norwood, Lord Latham again seated himself, obviously prepared to share his knowledge with Sir Charles.

Jane looked torn between chagrin that Sir Charles wished only to converse with Latham and hope that she had a possible beau in her parlor.

"I believe I will walk with you to the green, if you do not mind," Hyacinthe said to Lord Norwood as he prepared to leave. "Not having the slightest interest in fishing, I would rather feed the ducks."

"Please give Miss Pennington my thanks for the buns and tea. They were most welcome. Although"—he gave Hyacinthe a searching look—"if she is as hard-pressed for funds as you implied in your impassioned statement regarding rents, I suspect it is you who purchased the buns this morning."

"Jane's competence is very slight, barely sufficient for her to reside here. Most would deem it shocking that she lives alone, particularly when she might live with her Grandmama. But Jane is the tenderest of creatures. I fear she would wilt into nothing under our grandmama's domination. I intend that she be able to keep her home," Hyacinthe stated, giving her tormentor a frosty glare.

"Yet do I not detect an interest upon the part of Sir Charles?" Lord Norwood asked in a rather mocking tone while guiding her across the road.

Hyacinthe withdrew from him slightly. "It is not my place to speculate upon her *or* his interest, sirrah."

"You mean you have not figured out a way to bring them together?" He was on the verge of laughter, she noted ruefully.

He was a wretch—far too handsome and too certain of himself by half.

"I have not considered the matter," she answered in lofty tones, her air somewhat marred when a duck waddled over to nip at her skirts.

Blase supposed he could have reassured her that he had no intention of raising her cousin's rent. Yet he rather enjoyed these sparring matches with the delicious Hyacinthe Dancy. "I shall do what I must, dear lady," he said at last, deciding that his words could be taken several ways.

The lovely face that belonged to the most spirited and sparkling woman he had met in some time became most angry. Apparently she was not taking his words in a positive way, to say the very least.

She tossed the handful of crumbs she had carried from the cottage to the ducks that had drawn close in hope of a treat, then advanced upon him in a manner he could only think of as menacing. In fact, she reminded him of the swan that bore down upon them from the other side of the pond.

Absently he observed Sir Charles and Val exiting from the Pennington cottage, Mrs. Peachey pausing to chat with the Widow Smith, and Ambrose Clark wending his way along the path. It seemed half the village was out early this morning. Then he focused on his fiery, temperamental redhead.

"You are a beast, Blase Montague!" she hissed at him, reminding him again of the approaching swan. "An utterly wretched, selfish, inconsiderate, thoughtless beast."

With those words Hyacinthe stepped forward to give Blase a vehement push. Caught off guard by the suddenness of her movement, he had no defense. Waving his arms in the air in the hope of regaining his balance—and a futile hope to stay on dry land—he plunged into the pond.

The filthy water was chilly and, worst of all, contained duck feathers and a lot of other things he preferred not to consider. He surfaced and shook his head, then tried to climb from the pond, Fortunately the pond was shallow, so he could stand on the bottom with his head above water. However, he found himself unable to make any progress.

The rocks were covered with green slime and a goodly bit

of muck. He slipped and slid, trying to find purchase on rocks that defied him. With a determined grip on a couple of slimy rocks he made another attempt. At last he managed to exit the pond, dripping green mess and dirty water all over, feeling as though he badly needed a bath. *And* feeling most angry.

Miss Dancy, hands covering her face in presumed horror over what she had done, backed away from him—as well she might.

"Words fail me, Miss Dancy. But I daresay I shall think of some presently." He bowed, then squished his way toward where the blacksmith had his carriage and horse tied up.

If there was a soul in the village of Worthington who did not view his lordship, all wet and mucky, striding toward his carriage that momentous morning, he or she would regret it always.

Val ran to catch up with his friend, and from somewhere behind him Blase could hear the sound of laughter . . . unrestrained, bubbling, very feminine laughter of the sort that eventually hurts the ribs.

6

"I cannot believe that you did such a terrible thing," Jane scolded. "Do you think it will make Lord Norwood more kindly disposed to the plight of the villagers? Or to me?"

"He implied that he would raise your rent. I fear I just exploded. To think of all the money he has won at the racetrack . . . and then to treat you so! It is the outside of enough," Hyacinthe said indignantly. "The man has no heart, no sensitivity, no soul. He is little better than a monster!"

"I wonder why he wagers at the racetrack so constantly," Jane mused. "Surely he does not need the money? Does he?"

"Every gentleman of the *ton* is a gambling fool," Hyacinthe told her with a shrug, "with the exception of my brother." But the query set her to thinking. What if Lord Norwood truly did need the money—to run his estate, for example. What if his father had squandered the money on an ill-advised scheme, losing the lot?

It would be a good thing were Lord Norwood to take his winnings to improve the estate, the farms and homes of his tenants. But not, she reminded herself, to fritter away his blunt on such a foolish project as a picturesque view for his garden. Or turn his tenants from their homes. Who knew what nonsense Mr. Wayland would design? Likely uninhabitable places that looked pretty but were impractical to live in.

Yet to be fair, she had to admit that she had acted badly. Her Aunt Bel would have been scandalized, and well she might. A young lady simply didn't do such things. Even if it was hilarious.

Vexed with herself, she rose from her chair in the parlor to pace about the small room. Then she paused, an impish look covering her piquant face with its small pointed chin. She gazed at her cousin defiantly.

"But it *was* amusing. I tried not to laugh, really I did. To see that lofty man reduced to a green slime-covered mess was truly diverting. I have endured too many insults from him not to appreciate *his* receiving a setdown."

"I did not know he had insulted you," Jane exclaimed, her manner inviting Hyacinthe to confide but not demanding such.

Hyacinthe looked toward the window, recalling her feeling of humiliation when he had stared at her through his quizzing glass then proceeded to ignore her, as much as telling her and the world that she was far beneath his consideration. To presume to flirt with her while at that country inn was entirely too much to tolerate, an indignity for which he ought to be heartily ashamed.

" 'Tis a long story. It involves a flirtation gone awry, I suppose." She drifted from the room and out to the garden. It might be soothing to watch the hedgehog, if the little fellow would come out. So far she had only seen him at an early-morning hour, so perhaps he napped during the day?

The flowers were pretty, simple cottage-garden varieties. The lovely colors and fragrance proved an excellent substitute for the animal's antics. She wandered about the orderly garden, admiring Jane's efforts. Lord Norwood would do better to emulate Jane, with colorful flowers, restful trees, and cleverly trimmed shrubs.

What did he actually want, anyway? What, precisely, was a picturesque view? She dimly recalled reading some nonsense in the newspaper, a debate on the merits of landscaping an estate to emulate a painting, or something ludicrous like that. It seemed vastly foolish to her. Expensive, as well, if one went about demolishing an entire village to accomplish that whim.

The sound of voices from the cottage brought her about. She retraced her steps, entering the kitchen only to pause.

"So you see, Miss Pennington, it would seem to me that you have more to gain than to lose by supporting his lordship in his landscaping scheme," urged Sir Charles, his voice coming from the parlor.

"My cousin said he planned to raise my rent. I cannot afford that."

"Dear lady, is there no one to whom you can appeal? No home in which you may take refuge?" Sir Charles queried gently.

Hyacinthe pictured him leaning forward, his concern visible on his pleasant square face.

"Only Grandmama Dancy, and she terrifies me," Jane replied with a note of alarm in her voice.

Hyacinthe stayed where she was, reluctant to intrude, but deciding she had best know the direction of this conversation—just in case Jane needed her help.

Figuring that they might welcome some tea, Hyacinthe tiptoed about, placing the kettle on to boil, cutting some bread into wafer-thin slices, then adding biscuits and arranging a tray to take into the parlor.

"We shall have to see what can be done," Sir Charles said in his kindly manner. "I have often wondered that such a gently reared lady would choose to live by herself. I believe I understand now. Young women have a difficult time of it, it seems."

"Particularly if they wish to be independent. 'Tis not done, I have been told repeatedly," Jane confessed in an incensed voice. "It seems 'twere far better if we move in with some relative to become an unpaid servant."

To Hyacinthe, standing in the middle of the kitchen, these were remarkable words. She had nearly dropped the tray when that somewhat bitter voice denounced the custom that nudged spinsters to take their place where relatives might find them useful. To be sure, most unmarried ladies seemed to feel they must earn their keep. Yet all those she had met lived in fear of being sent away if they somehow displeased. It must be a dreadful existence, living in the shadows as it were.

Was she fated to end up with that as her own destiny? Would she become a patient attendant to her aunt or, horror of horrors, her grandmama? If Sir Charles failed to marry Jane, perhaps Hyacinthe would end up living here, spending her days pottering about in the garden. With her tidy income, they could manage quite nicely. It was a point to consider, she thought bleakly. Maybe they could travel.

"Oh, Hyacinthe," Jane cried from the doorway, disconcerted at finding her cousin in the kitchen, "I thought you were in the garden. Sir Charles is here and I intended to serve tea."

Hyacinthe smiled at her cousin's pink-cheeked dithering when Jane glanced at the teapot, gazed absently at the bread and bun container . . . then did nothing.

"Tea is ready." Hyacinthe carried the tray past Jane and into the parlor, placed it on a low table, then curtsied to Sir Charles in what she hoped might be considered a conciliatory manner.

He rose, bowing slightly while he studied her face. "I trust you have recovered your composure from earlier this morning?" There was the faintest hint of censure in his voice, but his eyes danced with the memory of his lordship dripping pond water while squishing along the village path.

"Indeed, sir. Mr. Clark read me a lecture on the evils of a bad temper." Hyacinthe exchanged a rueful smile with Sir Charles that spoke volumes.

"I would wager that you would do the same thing again, however," he said with a lift of his brows.

"Lord Norwood implied that he would raise the rent for my dearest Jane once she moved into his precious new cottage. If she would allow me to pay the difference it might be allowed, but she is a wretchedly stubborn and independent girl," Hyacinthe declared. "Few people know the real Jane. You ought to see her beautiful darning, sir. Why, it looks put there on purpose. I have an exquisite butterfly on my sheet to cover a hole that dared to appear. It is a wonder what she can accomplish."

"Hyacinthe!" Jane managed in a strangled voice.

"Forgive me," Hyacinthe said demurely, "I know what a modest creature you are, but once in a while it is necessary to tell the world what a splendid and talented woman you are. Is that not so, Sir Charles?"

"Hm?" he asked, his attention fastened completely on Jane.

Hyacinthe merely smiled and sipped her tea. Perhaps Jane would not find it necessary to pay the higher rent after all.

"That wretched female laughed at me! There I was, dripping wet from her having pushed me into that detestable pond, and she had the audacity to laugh!" Blase complained while tossing his ruined pantaloons in the same pile that contained a favorite coat—also ruined—hose, and a shirt that had green spots and dirty muck that he doubted the laundress could get out.

Val turned from the window to study his good friend's indignant expression. A smile lifted one corner of his mouth. "I had no idea that I would be so entertained when you invited me to visit."

"This was not my idea, and you know it," Blase fumed, stomping around to the tub. His ire subsided when Smithson assisted him into a soothing bath.

Ordering a bath in the late morning had caused some surprise in the kitchen, but the hot water quickly appeared when the staff heard that his lordship was in a towering rage.

"Ah, how good to become clean," Blase said with a sigh from behind the screen that sheltered him from a draft and close to the small fire to prevent his being chilled.

"You didn't smell particularly charming. That pond ought to have a better flow of water so it wouldn't become so stagnant . . . not to mention smell devilishly bad."

"I must remember that when arranging for the new pond," Blase said, a wry note in his voice.

"Have you thought of trying to win her over to your side?" Val asked, returning his gaze to the distant scene. "Why not invite her and her cousin, and perhaps Sir Charles as well, for tea—or something? Then you could take her out to the terrace to explain what the vista could be, how your changes will create a grand, picturesque view? I can just imagine you on the terrace, with one arm around her—to direct her gaze—pointing out your sad want of a proper prospect."

The sloshing ceased while this proposal was duly considered.

"She'd never come."

"She came with the cat, along with Miss Pennington and that sour maid," Val reminded him.

"The *tom* cat. That was an insult."

"Have you forgotten you presented her with a hedgehog? What has happened to your sense of the absurd?"

More sloshing could be heard behind the screen when Blase rose to step from the bathing tub. Before long he appeared garbed in a fresh shirt, well-made cream pantaloons, and white hose. He leaned against the door to his dressing room while footmen appeared to clear away the remains of his bath.

His hair was still damp from its washing, clinging in blond curls about his head. Blase's shirt clung to a powerful physique not gained from lolling about. His pantaloons graced well-formed legs that more than one lady had sighed over. And he looked down his aristocratic nose with the air of one well-born.

Val commented, "Pity she could not see you now. She'd forget her opposition to your scheme and chase after you. She ignored you in London, you said?" he needled.

"I ignored her," Blase snapped back, then paused. "Although I must admit, if she was interested in me, she never revealed it by the flutter of an eyelash."

"A bit of wounded masculine pride there?" Val jibed. "I don't know why you should want her attention, even if she is a delectable morsel and promises a fine time of it in . . . " His words trailed off suggestively. "There are other women. Miss Pennington would make some gentleman a fine, quiet, undemanding wife."

"Sounds dashed dull, my friend," Blase growled, pulling on first one boot, then the second.

"True," Val happily agreed. "So will you?"

"Invite them to the Hall?" Blase thought of seeing Miss Dancy again in his home, showing her the view he intended to improve. Hyacinthe? A more unlikely name he couldn't imagine. She should have offered soothing calm, like a lavender lily in a garden instead of red fire and white lightning. And then he recalled that fire and lightning were far more stimulating than a tranquil lily. Although as he recalled she was a delightfully fragrant armful, not that she had remained in his arms for more than seconds.

"All right. I shall send off the invitation. Better invite the curate as well."

"Might as well make it the entire village while you are at it. Just pray for good weather." Val stared out at the gathering clouds and wondered what the volatile Hyacinthe Dancy did now. He thought her name appropriate, for she bloomed like an exotic flower in the midst of that little village.

Hyacinthe finished her cup of tea, then excused herself, murmuring something about Fosdick coming down to keep them company.

Leaving Jane dithering behind her, Hyacinthe hurried up the spiral staircase, thinking this was another place where there could be improvement in cottage design. This staircase was murder. What might happen if they needed to go down in the dark, even with a candle, chilled her spine.

In her room, she explained Miss Pennington's need of her to the awesomely correct abigail. Once the pleased maid left to hurry down to the parlor and thus chaperone Jane, Hyacinthe got busy.

She knew that Mrs. Peachey usually visited the Widow Smith at this time of day. It was an ideal time for snooping about the Tudor house.

Had anyone questioned her enthusiasm for a house owned by her tormentor, the very man who had ignored her and now threatened to tear down Jane's home about her very ears, she would have been hard-pressed to explain. It was the legend.

Donning a serviceable gown and emulating Jane with a head covering, Hyacinthe slipped down the stairs and out the back door. Clouds gathered off to the west; it would undoubtedly rain before long. Ideal weather for snooping.

She first made her way to the pond, offering the ducks and swans a handful of crumbs as a purpose for her stroll.

Then, after a careful inspection of the village, she ambled in the direction of the church, only at the last moment turning aside into the Tudor house greenery. No one could see her now. Her dull green gown blended into the shadows cast by an old oak tree.

Her heart beat rapidly when she slipped past the scullery door and into the kitchen. Going on the same premise as before, she ignored that room as well as the next, slipping up the stairs as silently as she might.

Although there was not the least need for quiet, she felt it suited her purpose, not to mention the mood of the house. Were there spirits here? Did the ghost of that long-ago red-head—Hyacinthe had not forgotten that bit of information—linger in the shadows of these rooms?

After another perusal of the empty bedrooms, checking paneling and floorboards much as Lord Norwood had done, Hyacinthe paused on the threshold of the large bedroom.

If she had lived here, mistress of that madly handsome rake, what would she have done? If you figured that the girl had been murdered—what a dreadful word that was—it meant her treasures were most likely still hidden in the house. Unless someone over the years had found and stolen the lot.

Yet Lord Norwood had just found a painting that apparently had been part of this treasure, and found it right here, or at least in the dressing room. After one more survey, Hyacinthe crossed to enter the little room. She began to examine every panel, every irregularity in the walls.

"Oh, pooh, this window needs cleaning. I can scarce make out the design on the wall." A tattered cloth tossed to one corner served as a means to•scrub the window a bit cleaner, enabling Hyacinthe to see much better.

She was just about to pry at a peculiar knob in a carved design when she heard sounds from below. Frantic lest she be found here, not knowing who the intruder might be, she hunted for a place to hide. Those steps were now on the stairs and the intruder would undoubtedly be in here before many minutes passed.

In the far side of the room she spotted a screen folded and leaning against the wall. Quickly and silently she set it up so that it would conceal her in the deep shadows and close to the wall, so unlikely to arouse interest.

Behind this screen so many years ago, the cherished mistress of that dashing gentleman had changed her elegant clothes. They must have been elegant, although Hyacinthe had no way of knowing. Yet in her experience she had noticed that those lovely women of questionable reputation seemed to dress better than the respectable but often plain, wives.

Her fears were realized moments later when the door opened wide to admit a man. She peered through the crack between two panels of the screen to inspect this person. It didn't take her long to realize who it was. She barely stopped herself from exclaiming his name aloud. Mr. Dudley Wayland!

Fortunately he ignored the screen and thus missed her presence. He went to the same panel that Hyacinthe had suspected to begin digging about with a penknife, evidence he'd been here before. In moments the catch snapped and a portion of the design opened to reveal a secret chest.

Hyacinthe scarcely suppressed a gasp of dismay. She ought to confront the man, but she was hardly of a size to do this and she had no weapon, nor could she call Norwood.

Wayland produced a soft sack from his coat pocket, velvet by the looks of it, then poured in the contents of the chest. Before leaving the little room, he replaced the chest, closed the secret panel, then glanced about the room.

Hyacinthe held her breath, praying she'd not be detected. Any man who would steal could do other nasty things as well.

She waited until she heard his steps retreat down the stairs and cross the rooms below. When he had left the house, she dared to slip from behind the screen. Dashing quietly to the window in the bedroom, she glimpsed Mr. Wayland in the tangled greenery behind the house. He tucked the velvet sack into his coat pocket, then mounted his horse. In moments he had disappeared from her view.

"Drat and double drat!" she fumed, kicking at a tattered bit of drapery. "If I had been a man, I could have stopped him, captured the treasure." Even if she contacted Lord Norwood, Mr. Wayland would have hidden the items.

Returning to the little dressing room, she touched the same place Wayland had touched on the carved panel, then inhaled with satisfaction when it sprang open to reveal the same little chest. It was empty. She removed it, then inspected the space where it had sat for so long. Back in the dim recesses she noticed a black box.

Excitement building, she daringly reached in, ignoring hazards like spiders or bugs, and pulled the box out.

It was long and slim, covered with fine leather. Taking an anxious breath, she opened it to discover a delicately wrought bracelet of gold set with emeralds. At least, she would wager they were emeralds.

A second examination by the light of the bedroom window increased her conviction. She clutched the lovely piece of jewelry to her breast, wondering what she ought to do with it. She had to give it to Lord Norwood. It belonged to him.

She took another look at the exquisite piece, admiring the rich flash of color from the deep green stones. How beautiful. With a resigned sigh, and wondering if she would ever wear anything half so fine, she closed the lid of the handsome box, then returned to the dressing room to replace the panel just as Wayland had done. The jewel chest she retained. This also belonged to his lordship and might be lost if the house was to be torn down.

A light drizzle fell on her while she ran across the village green to Jane's cottage. Skirting the pond, she recalled her father's motto: *Qui dabit recipiet*. He who shall give will receive. Perhaps in giving this to Lord Norwood she would receive a respite for her cousin?

Hurrying through the gate and up to the door, she was taken aback to find it whisked open and the man who had been occupying her thoughts standing before her. She halted.

"Come in, come in. I shan't bite you," Lord Norwood said with good humor.

"I must speak with you," she said breathlessly. "Come into the parlor, I have something to show you, that is, for you." She knew she puzzled him, but she could scarcely blurt out all that had happened in the last half hour.

When they stood in the center of the cozy parlor, Hyacinthe thrust the two items at him.

"These are yours. There would have been more, but someone else took them before I could reach them."

"What the . . . ?" He accepted the chest and the slim box. Placing the chest on a nearby table, he opened the box first. Inside he found the bracelet of emeralds in their intricate gold setting.

Jane gasped when the green jewels flashed in the dim light.

Holding up the bracelet by one end, Lord Norwood studied

Hyacinthe's face. She knew she must be flushed, for she had dashed madly through the mist to reach Jane's cottage.

"Wherever did you find this?"

"Well, I located the little hiding place where she had stashed her jewels. The rest were in that chest, or casket, I suspect they may have called it. Had I just a bit more time, I might have been handing you the entire contents of that as well."

He turned to place the bracelet back in the box, then inspected the little chest. "Who took them?"

"Dudley Wayland," she said quietly. "Did you chance to see him ride off just before I returned? Had I a weapon, I would have shot him. Or something equally dreadful. I could not tell precisely how many items there were or what they were. He dropped them into a velvet sack, then made off with them while I remained helplessly behind."

At his look of inquiry, she added, "I may be silly, but I am not so foolish as to court disaster."

"There are a few who might argue with you there," he murmured.

Val stepped forward from where he had remained half hidden in the shadows. He picked up the bracelet, nodding.

"You agree with me that this matches the description I have?" Lord Norwood demanded.

"Indeed. How do we proceed from here?" Val inquired.

"He must not be allowed to leave the estate," Hyacinthe stated in no uncertain terms. Then she said, "Perhaps he believes himself safe from discovery."

"This is a nasty turn of events, for I quite like his designs and it will delay things considerably for me to find another architect, then continue *if* I can persuade him to follow the same plans. And *if* that chap will be able to work with the men that Wayland has already hired."

Something suddenly occurred to Hyacinthe and she gave his lordship a narrow look. "What are you doing here, sir? I confess that I'd not thought to see you in the village again so soon."

"After our little *contretemps*, you mean?"

"Well," she confessed, "I cannot think of a more inopportune and embarrassing occurrence."

He raised his brows but did not flash that charming grin at her, and her heart sank.

"I came to invite you all up to the Hall for tea the day after tomorrow."

Hyacinthe exchanged a look with Jane, who in turn glanced to where Sir Charles quietly stood off to one side of the room.

"I believe we should be pleased to accept your gracious invitation, sir," Jane said politely. She bestowed a hesitant smile his way, then edged back to stand beside Sir Charles.

"The drizzle has let up. Could you show me the panel in question?" Lord Norwood asked, taking hold of Hyacinthe's elbow and steering her from the room even as he spoke.

"Of course," Hyacinthe said. She could not fail to observe how breathless she remained, especially since he had drawn so close to her side. Her heart did odd little flips and flops that quite puzzled her even as they left her somewhat shaken. Never had she been so intensely aware of a man as she was of Lord Norwood.

Had she actually presumed to call him Blase Montague as Jane claimed? Everyone knew his name and family, but one did not use it unless rather intimate. *That* word caused her cheeks to bloom like one of the roses in the Tudor garden. Where had her wits gone? What a crackbrained girl she was becoming!

"If you will have the goodness to go ahead, I would see the secret compartment."

Hyacinthe pulled herself together and attempted a composure that she certainly didn't feel. Once in the house she carefully made her way up the stairs. Opening the door to the dressing room, she made directly for the cleverly carved panel. By using her thumbnail she did the trick, and the hidden door popped ajar.

"Well, I'll be!" he exclaimed. He thrust his hand deep into the recesses, groping about the back of it lest anything had been missed.

"I should explain," he began, turning to look directly into her eyes.

Hyacinthe felt her knees suddenly weaken; her heart began that alarming pattering again. Those amazing blue eyes had a powerful effect on her.

"These jewels are part of a collection bestowed upon his mistress by my esteemed ancestor. That he had no right to give away something that belonged to the family did not appear to bother him. Perhaps he intended to take them back at a later date. Somehow he never did." Norwood gave her a wry smile that cut to her core. "I had heard about the missing gems, as had others in the family. None of us had done anything about it, for it was presumed to be hearsay. A fanciful story, if you like."

"What made you search?" she whispered.

"I wanted to do an inventory of the estate. When I discovered listed jewels missing, I feared a thief." He reached out to pick a cobweb out of the curls that peeped from beneath the little cap she wore.

"What will you do about Mr. Wayland? You must not let him profit from his thievery." She sounded as though she had just completed a mad dash—breathless, with a pounding heart beating a mad rhythm.

"It is a dilemma," Lord Norwood said, taking a step closer to Hyacinthe. He pulled her cap off, placing it in her hands, then ran his fingers through her tumbled curls.

She found it impossible to retreat; her feet refused to move. She stared up at him feeling trapped, assailed by a tumult of emotions she'd never known before. Why did his light touch affect her so?

She cleared her throat, knowing that if she had any sense at all she would march away from this rake. Yet she could not move.

"I must thank you for all you have done," he whispered, hovering over her, his lazy grin teasing her.

The words to the effect that it was quite all right were never spoken, for he leaned down to place a warm kiss on her lips.

She'd not been kissed like this before. Indeed, had scarcely been kissed at all. This bone-melting sensation was totally different from past experiences. When she opened her eyes, she gave him a confused look.

"You are welcome," she whispered back, bemused, then forced her feet to move and fled the room and the house as though a demon chased her. Perhaps it did.

7

Blase stood in the small dressing room feeling as though he had been struck on the head with a falling rock. He raised his right hand to touch his mouth. Was he mad? Had the pond water affected his brain? He felt like ten kinds of fool. Thrusting his hand through his hair, he considered his dilemma.

He had just kissed the little termagant who was making his life *most* complicated at the moment, whose brother was undoubtedly the finest swordsman in England, who had very protective relatives, and . . . who was eminently kissable. What a passionate delight she had proven to be. Utterly delicious.

Amazingly—all things considered—the casket holding the emerald bracelet remained in his left hand. He'd quite forgotten it in the heat of the moment.

Leaving the dressing room, he wandered down through the house and out to the tangled garden. Here he found Val leaning against one of the old oak trees, his expression of cynical amusement about what Blase expected to see. Today it rubbed him the wrong way.

"I daresay you find this all vastly diverting." Blase gave his good friend a look of exasperation.

"You have a spot of dust on your cheek. Miss Dancy did as well. Might I inquire what happened when that fiery young woman revealed the hiding place? It seemed a rather innocent occasion, although you might have been well advised to have the abigail along. She's a proper dragon," Val pointed out while strolling over to join Blase.

"You may inquire all you please. It does not follow that I shall tell you, however." Blase turned away, avoiding those sharp eyes that always saw too much. He began to walk toward the blacksmith's where they had left their horses.

Absently he noted the twitching of curtains in various cottages as they strolled along through the village. The locals were undoubtedly having a fine time with all the goings on as of late.

"Noble fellow," Val replied sagely. "Never could abide men who kissed, then told."

"I wonder if you would enjoy a splash in the pond," Blase mused, glancing toward that murky water inhabited by all the ducks and the pair of swans. "Perhaps you might think that vastly amusing as well. I wonder how you would look attempting to climb from that dreadful water while trying to find purchase on stones covered with slimy green muck."

"Enough," Val said, hastening around to the far side of Blase, maintaining a comfortable distance from the pond.

"One would think you didn't trust me," Blase complained, assuming a wounded look.

"Nor do I. If memory serves me right, you tossed me into the sea once. Ruined a perfectly good coat and vest, not to mention shrinking my favorite fawn pantaloons. Can't recall why."

"That was a relatively mild matter. Certainly not as annoying as this. However, it did serve to cool off that head of yours." Blase tossed his friend a grin that revealed his good nature had been somewhat restored.

"Well, I shall take care to avoid a repetition. Water ought to be taken in small doses, preferably heated, and with sandalwood soap."

Blase halted in his steps. "Blast," he muttered. "I had best go and reassure myself that Miss Dancy will still come to the Hall."

"Think you might have given her a disgust of you?" Val chided in innocuous banter.

Blase didn't reply to his friend's needling, but turned to stride back to Miss Pennington's cottage. Curtains twitched again, and he felt almost virtuous in providing entertainment for the village. He bowed in the direction of the Widow

Smith's cottage, to be rewarded with another flutter of muslin at her window.

"You are disconcerting them, my good fellow. They like to think they are unobserved," Val told him.

"Hah!" Blase snapped. "They are about as inconspicuous as that pond over there."

At which reminder Val strolled to the far side of Blase once again.

At Miss Pennington's cottage they were ushered inside by Jane, a pleasant smile curving her lips at the sight of the two gentlemen.

Blase decided that—given their amiable greeting—Miss Dancy must not have revealed all that had happened at the old house. When he looked at her, she fixed her gaze on her hands, but other than a slightly higher color, gave no indication of her inner feelings.

Racking his brain to think of a reason for their return, he said, "I merely wished to thank Miss Dancy once again for her help." He held the little chest up while keeping a careful watch on her.

She rose from her chair to move to her cousin's side, her hands clutching each other before her. She said nothing. Her cousin stepped forward as though to compensate for Miss Dancy's lack of response.

"Do you believe you may think of a way to relieve Mr. Wayland of the treasure while keeping him here to complete his work?" Jane asked quietly.

"Perhaps you will be forced to abandon your scheme," Miss Dancy said with a flash of those incredible green eyes.

"I feel certain I will think of something. When you see the view from the terrace, perhaps you will understand why I feel this is all necessary."

He was rewarded with a rather belligerent stare from Miss Dancy. Then she sweetly said, "Somehow I doubt it, Lord Norwood."

Feeling somewhat defeated—although he realized he ought to have expected such a reaction—Blase bowed to the ladies, then reminded them before taking his leave that they were expected at the Hall for tea.

"I should say that you have a fence or two to mend as yet, my lad," Val observed while keeping a wary eye on the pond and his best friend.

"You may say that, or anything else you please. What a tangled mess this is becoming," Blase muttered. He strode past the cottages, not paying attention to the fluttering curtains this time. At the blacksmith's he impatiently exchanged a few pleasantries with the man, then mounted his bay and rode off in the direction of the Hall, followed by Val.

From the parlor window Hyacinthe watched the men ride past the pond, then turn toward Worthington Hall.

She ought to have denounced that wicked man. Rake! He had earned his reputation in London, if this was a sample of his behavior. In the back of her mind—and heart—she almost wished that he had sincerely meant that remarkable kiss.

"Come, dear." Jane drew her to the sofa, just the right size for the small parlor. "Something has overset you," Jane probed in her gentle way.

"Nothing at all," Hyacinthe denied stoutly. She had begun to realize that if she explained what had upset her it would complicate her life. She had done her best to calm her nerves while returning to the cottage. A glimpse of Mrs. Peachey had helped enormously. It served to remind Hyacinthe that she would be as affected as that rake were she to reveal his ill behavior. Gossip would ruin all Hyacinthe's plans for her future.

"All this racketing about in musty old places may not overset your nerves, but it does not a *thing* for your hair," Fosdick declared. "Allow me to make repairs, miss."

Since Fosdick rarely insisted on such a thing, Hyacinthe suspected she must indeed look a fright. Nodding her acceptance, she preceded the abigail up the narrow stairs. It was just as well that she escape, she decided. Had she remained in the parlor, Jane might well have wormed from her the dreadful secret.

Two days later Hyacinthe, with Jane and Fosdick at her side, drove along the lanes until they reached the main avenue to Worthington Hall.

"It is an impressive place as it stands. I fail to see why he must improve his view by destroying the village," Hyacinthe murmured yet once again when their coach drew up before the entrance.

"Did you not say that Carr included the house plans in his book *Vitruvius Britannicus*?" Jane whispered as they slowly mounted the steps to the imposing front door. To either side of them tall Corinthian pillars soared in splendor. Jane gave a speculative glance at the upper windows just barely visible.

Hyacinthe nodded in agreement, then said, "I suspect that is the reason that Mr. Wayland totes that volume about with him, the odious toad. It is far too heavy a book to carry in the ordinary way."

Before they could decide who would have the pleasure of pulling the bell, the lovely carved door opened quite magically to reveal Barmore. The butler might be said to have almost beamed a welcome at them. He bowed, then led them along with him.

After settling Fosdick on a comfortable side chair in the Great Hall (Barmore tended to speak in capitals when it came to the house, it seemed), he continued on through to the next room.

"The Yellow Damask Room, my ladies," Barmore announced proudly. He ushered them along to a group of attractive chairs placed about a polished console table that held an arrangement of autumn flowers. "Their lordships will be along directly. May I say they intended to be here to greet you, but a small crisis arose."

Hyacinthe murmured something gracious in reply. Rather than settle on a chair she chose to wander about the room. She could see the elegant crystal chandelier reflected in the looking glass that hung above the marble fireplace surround.

"Could you tell me anything about the room?" Jane said. "Since you appear to have done a bit of boning up, that is."

"This is an Adam's fireplace, and I think he designed the consoles along the wall," Hyacinthe said thoughtfully, racking her brain to remember what she'd read. "The paintings are mostly Italian except for that one over there by the man called the Greek, El Greco, that is." She strolled about the room, offering details when asked. Jane remained most prudently seated on a yellow-and-white-striped chair, yet watched her cousin with great interest.

The unusual mantel clock had struck two when a stir at the door, not to mention the heightened awareness Hyacinthe felt, revealed that the gentlemen had joined them.

"I do apologize, Miss Pennington and Miss Dancy," Lord Norwood said smoothly. He strode across the carpet to reach Hyacinthe, subtly guiding her to join the others, who were dutifully seated by the console table.

"I hope it was nothing truly serious," Hyacinthe said while her eyes dared him to say it was a mere nothing that had kept him from his guests.

"Actually I was finalizing plans to have Wayland watched. His every step will be monitored."

"Oh, good," Jane exclaimed.

"I hope you know what you are about," Hyacinthe murmured in a voice only Lord Norwood could hear.

Another stir at the door brought the curate to join the group, Ambrose Clark seemed quite at ease with the party, joining Jane to converse on the problems of the church roof, particularly over his study, which leaked more badly than ever.

Before Lord Norwood could reply to Hyacinthe's provocative remark, Barmore returned, followed by two footmen and a maid. They carried trays with enough tea and splendid pastries for a party twice their size.

"Oh, I say, I fear I am a bit tardy," Sir Charles said as he breezed into the drawing room. "Had a spot of bother just before I planned to leave."

Barmore saw to his tea, thus relieving the ladies from the task of deciding who might serve as a hostess. Neither was likely to desire the position, Jane being too shy and Hyacinthe reluctant to put herself forward.

Conversation remained general, in spite of the curate's obvious desire to return to the subject of his leaky roof.

Hyacinthe set her empty cup on its saucer, then placed them on the table, glancing about the room to note the tall windowed doors which apparently led to the terrace beyond.

When she chanced to look at Lord Norwood, she met his thoughtful look briefly, then dropped her gaze to her lap.

Every time she looked at the dratted man, that kiss came to her mind, like a particularly disturbing dream.

"Would you join me for a walk on the terrace? I should wish you to see the view as it is and what I intend." His deep voice broke through her introspection.

Startled, she rose from her chair with alacrity. She did not want him to assist her or touch her in any way. Perhaps she feared her reaction?

Walking just slightly ahead of him, she stood aside so he might open the door, then swished past him. On the terrace she came to an abrupt halt, delighted with the old-fashioned geranium and ivy filled urns and fanciful stone railing. "Lovely."

Appearing to ignore her pleased reaction, Lord Norwood drew her along with him by the mere force of his presence. At last he came to a halt. Hyacinthe dutifully looked in the direction he pointed.

"See the spire and that dreadful cluster of roof lines? What I intend to create is a smooth sweep with a mass of trees planted in a diagonal line." He pulled a drawing from his coat pocket to show her.

Wishing to be fair, Hyacinthe studied the drawing, then gazed out across the verdant lawns and hills dotted with stately trees. It was utterly beautiful and she'd not wish one thing altered if it were hers.

"Well, you will do as you please, no doubt. But I think that spire rising in the distance is most charming. It adds a solid English touch to what otherwise would be a rather bland landscape." Her demure glance at him was just as bland; only those green eyes were afire with mischief.

Blase studied the saucy face turned up to gaze at him with a feeling of total frustration. He was torn between wanting to throttle her and to wrap her in his arms, smothering that adorable face with hungry kisses. He would begin with the freckles, then proceed to even more interesting places.

Moments lengthened as the silence stretched on and on. They stared at one another, measuring, sizing up the opposition as it were. He could feel a sizzling tension in the air, vibrating between them. Still she remained silent.

"Hyacinthe—" he began, speaking the name he used when thinking of her.

"La, sir, you must deem me a forward baggage, to use my given name without permission," she interrupted, a storm cloud drifting into her eyes. Hands clasped tightly before her at her waist, she glared at him with the air of one vastly insulted. He wondered if she held her hands thus to keep from slapping him and was thankful of her restraint.

Blase could think of no London miss who would have objected to any familiarity he might have used, including use of a first name. Indeed, he had found most women eager to become intimate in any way possible. Miss Dancy made her feelings regarding him painfully obvious.

"Forgive me, since we are joined in a sort of battle, I daresay I thought it easier," he said smoothly.

"Convenient," she said with a cool nod. "However, I fear it would look a trifle forward on your part, for I cannot consider calling you Blase."

She said his name in a husky whisper, the very sound of which did the strangest things to his nerves.

"Whatever you wish, Miss Dancy," he replied after clearing his throat of an obstruction.

The door along the terrace opened. Miss Pennington, Ambrose Clark, and Sir Charles, with Val at his side, emerged from the house to amble along, admiring the view, commenting on the abundant geranium blooms.

"It is a perfectly splendid view, Lord Norwood," Miss Pennington observed enthusiastically while studying the distant church spire and cluster of thatched roofs.

"You cannot detect the leaks in the church roof from here," Mr. Clark added darkly.

"Lord Norwood wishes to eliminate all the buildings from that pretty vale, replacing them with a strip of forest," Hyacinthe explained, mostly to Jane.

"Of course," Jane replied quietly. She turned quite pale, obviously recalling his intent for her cottage.

"Was this sketch drawn by Mr. Repton?" Miss Dancy inquired, holding out the paper Blase had handed her earlier.

"No, I fear it is my own poor work."

"Perhaps Mr. Repton will have other suggestions to offer? He may even *like* the church spire and the thatched roofs," she suggested in what Blase could only feel was a decidedly snide manner.

"Come, we may as well return to the house. Perhaps you would like to see a few of the rooms?" he said in an attempt to draw them all from the distressing topic of his intended alterations to the landscape.

The more Miss Dancy opposed his plans, the more determined he was to implement them. He hadn't examined his motives to see if he was prompted by pique at a woman who quite obviously detested him or by a more commendable goal.

She made appropriate comments when they again viewed the long gallery, a repository for family portraits and immense pieces of furniture that could be housed nowhere else.

"Isn't that your infamous great-great-grandmother, Blase?" Val asked with a cynical lift of his brows.

"Infamous?" Miss Dancy quickly repeated.

"Well," Blase replied with a dark glance at his friend, " 'tis said that she ran off with a friend of her husband's when she discovered the redheaded mistress ensconced in the little village cottage."

"Oh," Hyacinthe cooed, "she did not care to be supplanted. I believe she must have loved her husband very much to be so angered by his turning away from her. She appears to have been exceedingly lovely." Actually, she made a fitting wife for the gentleman with the roguish eyes.

"Rumor has it that she had a wretched temper," Lord Norwood snapped back.

Hyacinthe smiled, satisfied that she had made her little point, yet noting it seemed the Montagues did not care for women with a temper. Fine. She smiled again, then observed that Lord Norwood looked uncomfortable.

"I should like you all to call tomorrow, if possible," Sir Charles requested while they strolled back to the main entry hall. "I believe it is my turn to entertain." He appeared to address them all, yet looked at Jane when he spoke.

Hyacinthe and Jane departed shortly after agreeing that it sounded like a delightful outing.

Although Hyacinthe had her reservations about viewing the prize pigs Sir Charles touted with such great pride. She said as much to Jane later while awaiting their coach to arrive at the front door of the Hall. "I shan't wish to come overly close to their pen, for they are known to have a dreadful smell," she concluded, wrinkling her nose. "Perhaps we might remain in the house?"

Jane gave her a look bordering on indignation, then nudged her forward as Tom Coachman drew to a halt with a great flourish. Fosdick quietly followed them.

"Have you ever seen the inside of Sir Charles's home?" Hyacinthe asked as she settled back on her seat.

"No, indeed, for how could I? It would not be seemly for a single woman to call upon a gentleman," Jane reminded her with gentle reproof.

"Yet he is free to call . . . or not call . . . upon you," Hyacinthe quietly observed.

Jane's pink-cheeked silence revealed more than she knew.

The following morning glistened brightly. A shower had passed through during the night, leaving little puddles for the ducks to enjoy. The air was rain-washed fresh, and various country scents teased their noses when the two cousins drove along to the lovely old home belonging to Sir Charles.

"We might have walked, you know," Jane protested at what she termed an extravagance.

"Nonsense. I have those two men eating their heads off, not to mention the horses. We might as well use the coach and arrive like ladies rather than dusty country misses," Hyacinthe said in a spirited way.

She could see how enchanting Jane found the Tudor-style house. Upon their arrival, Jane stepped from the coach and merely stood, absorbing the gentle lines, the soft greenery that cloaked the exterior.

"Too much ivy," Hyacinthe decided. "I predict it will cause the brick to crack, and then you'll have seepage and all sorts of other problems."

Jane bristled with annoyance. "I think it is utterly charming.

And just when did you become such an expert on houses, anyway?"

With a demure flutter of eyelashes to hide her pleasure at Jane's animated defense of the house, Hyacinthe replied, "My father was ever curious about houses. He bought his copy of *Vitruvius Britannicus* when it was published in 1771. I confess to looking up the Hall when I knew that you lived close to it. And as to knowing about houses, well, that is simple common sense."

Jane's disbelieving look was quickly banished when Sir Charles himself opened the door to greet them.

"Ladies, this is indeed a pleasure. I cannot think why you have not come to call before." He beamed down at Jane, then ushered them in. Hyacinthe was quite happy to be neglected, trailing behind them with a smug little smile.

She decided that Sir Charles must be a bit neglectful of his memory, for to her knowledge they, particularly Cousin Jane, had not been *invited* heretofore. But, since Sir Charles was such an amiable man, and appearing increasingly interested in Jane, she'd not tease him about it. Her smile faded when she caught sight of the others in the room.

Lords Norwood and Latham stood by the fireplace. They bowed in the direction of the ladies, but did not move forward. Latham wore a sardonic expression as he watched Sir Charles play the attentive host to Jane.

Ambrose Clark hovered not far from the table, where an assortment of delicacies had been placed. A magnificent silver teapot sat close by a silver teakettle steaming over a flame. Mr. Clark wore a hungry look that suggested he could do justice to the entire display. Did the man never have enough to eat? Hyacinthe wondered.

Then she observed Mrs. Peachey and the Widow Smith seated by a many-paned window, looking much gratified to be included in the group.

The little party proved quite jolly, thanks to an unexpected talent for story telling on the part of Mrs. Peachey, possibly prompted by the glass of sherry she had sipped before the others arrived.

At last it came time to view the prize pigs. Much to everyone's surprise, Mrs. Peachey and the Widow Smith joined the others.

"This is like a parade," Mrs. Peachey observed with a girlish giggle.

"Did you have anything to do with the additions to the group?" Lord Norwood inquired of Hyacinthe.

Since he had spoken to her in an undertone, she replied quietly, "Not at all. Sir Charles must have taken pity on the ladies. I quite enjoy them."

"Even when they quiz you on your matrimonial prospects?" Lord Latham asked, his voice tinged with tartness.

"They mean well. And you notice that I did not respond. Indeed, I have determined to hop on the shelf, for I believe I shall journey to distant lands rather than marry. I shan't have to contend with another Season in Town, nor wonder if a man courts me for my fortune or my face."

"Likely neither," Lord Latham shot back, a grin on his handsome face. "They are more apt to seek you out for that wit you reveal when you least realize it."

"Well, it would be a comfort to think it was that," she countered amiably. Why was it, she wondered, that when Lord Latham teased and almost flirted with her, it affected her not in the least. While on the other hand, the mere presence of Lord Norwood had the power to send her nerves sizzling, her blood tingling, and her head spinning in a whirl.

"Is something wrong, Miss Dancy," Lord Norwood asked in concern. "You shake your head."

"No. Where are these prize progeny anyway? I don't detect their proximity." She sniffed the air, curious as to how far they must walk. It was disconcerting to stroll along at Lord Norwood's side. She tilted her parasol slightly so she might not see him at all.

"Allow me," the dratted man said smoothly. He removed her parasol from a suddenly limp hand, then held it over her head better to shield her from the sun. It placed him in far better view, however, and much closer.

Then a sharp turn in the path revealed a splendid pig sty, far superior to the average one. Inside, an enormous sow balefully inspected the viewers with one malevolent eye while keeping a watch on her offspring with the other.

"What a quantity of bacon and ham that would be," Ambrose Clark declared reverently.

"I daresay it would," Lord Latham agreed. The two gentlemen wandered ahead, discussing various meals of bacon and ham they had enjoyed in the past.

On the far side of the sty Sir Charles explained the pedigree of the animals to Jane. The two widows gazed, looking rather doubtful, for a few moments, then walked back in the direction of the house.

Hyacinthe glanced at Lord Norwood, wondering if he felt this most peculiar beguilement when close to her. Odd. She detested the man. Yet when he drew near, her resolve seemed to melt. No, she scolded herself, she must be strong, be firm.

"Hardly dainty, are they?" she observed in what she hoped was a serene manner.

"Indeed," he agreed.

He was laughing at her; she sensed it even though he merely smiled. Another of those little insults. Not as serious as that kiss, but it served to remind her that they were piling up. One by one those indignities increased.

Affronted by his attitude and recalling all he intended, Hyacinthe undid the ribands of her bonnet. The wind did the rest of the deed. The wickedly expensive head gear from a fine London milliner went sailing over the fence into the sty to land precariously atop a wooden box. Here it perched, ready to topple into the muck at any moment. The pig eyed the bonnet as though wondering if it was some new sort of food.

"Oh," cried Jane, "your beautiful new bonnet!"

"I fear it is lost!" Hyacinthe cried in return, clasping her hands before her in an attitude of dismay. She turned her emerald eyes upon Lord Norwood, beseeching him without a word.

He closed his eyes for a moment, then met hers, frowning with apparent resignation.

"Never fear, Miss Dancy. I shall rescue it for you."

He handed her his hat, then removed his coat and draped it over the fence. In seconds he climbed to the top of it. Unfortunately, he lost his balance on the topmost board. With a truly spectacular waving of arms and legs, he dived into the mud and mire of the sty.

His muttering might have blistered their ears but for the mud that persisted in clinging to his face.

"Good heavens!" Sir Charles cried, opening the gate to rush to his guest's assistance.

One of the piglets dashed out the gate to freedom, followed by three others before Jane had the presence of mind to close it. The piglets squealed and grunted while running around the yard. Garbled language burst forth from Lord Norwood, while Sir Charles and Jane attempted to soothe him.

In short order the two men slipped back out through the gate. A young farm lad who had lingered in the background captured the piglets, returning them to their pen.

Only Hyacinthe watched the scene as though frozen in her slippers. Had she actually intended that disaster to happen? Had she realized how utterly wretched it would be for his rakish lordship?

She had. Only sheer willpower kept a guilty grin from her face.

8

Once the piglets were returned to the sty, Lord Norwood removed from same, and the chaos somewhat reduced, his lordship turned to where Hyacinthe stood transfixed in a mixture of naughty delight and conscience-stricken remorse.

"I fear your lovely bonnet will never be the same, Miss Dancy. Pity," he observed with what she perceived to be a note of satisfaction, holding out the battered bonnet now dripping with mud. It had tumbled the same moment he made his extraordinary dive.

"It was a favorite, but one cannot predict what nature will do, can one?" she said with all due humility.

"Perhaps," he muttered, turning to Sir Charles, who was urging him to the house where a cleaning up and change of garments might be effected. The two men hurried off, Lord Norwood shaking clumps of mire as they went and Sir Charles murmuring words of sympathy and carrying the undamaged coat that had providentially been removed before the accident.

Lord Latham strolled over to join Hyacinthe, looking at her through his quizzing glass as though she were a heretofore-unknown species of butterfly.

"I particularly detest the affectation of London dandies with those odious quizzing glasses," she said quietly. "Perhaps I ought to acquire one of my own. Do you like being inspected, Lord Latham?" Hyacinthe concluded in quiet indignation, while holding up an imaginary magnifying glass and glaring at him.

"Actually, I usually use this to depress the encroachment of those green lads from the country who think they are all the crack merely because they have learned to tie a respectable cravat." He lowered the glass, then dangled it about on its little gold chain while eyeing her. "You know, I believe Blase would be well advised to bring a change of clothing with him whenever he is about you. You seem to draw disaster like a magnet. Are you magnetized, Miss Dancy?"

"Hardly," she snapped back, her eyes flashing. This man saw entirely too much to suit her.

Fortunately for all concerned Jane bustled up at that moment quite atwitter.

"Dear me, that poor man. First the village pond and now a pig sty. What next?" she mused with a thoughtful look at Hyacinthe.

Turning away from the sight of the pen with the dreadful mire that had formed from the recent rain, Hyacinthe tamped down a sense of pity for her opponent. The man was a monster, willing to oust widows and old men from their homes. She took several steps toward the house.

"How's the hedgehog?" Lord Latham asked idly.

Hyacinthe shot him a suspicious look, then said blandly, "Quite well, thank you. And how was Tom Tiger this morning? I mean the cat, of course," she added sweetly.

Lord Latham chuckled, then glanced at Hyacinthe before taking her arm, as well as Jane's, to guide them toward Sir Charles's tasteful but plain home. They sauntered along at a leisurely pace.

"The confounded animal refused to be banished to the barn," Lord Latham confided. "It has taken up residence in the house, specifically in Blase's bedroom. It seems it prefers to snuggle in the rich softness of his bed rather than the plain straw in the barn."

Darting a look at her tormentor, for she was certain there was a hidden taunt in that tale, Hyacinthe merely smiled, then turned to include Jane in the conversation. "Cats are so odd. There is no accounting for their preferences."

Jane looked rather puzzled at the exchanges between the two, which seemed to have nothing to do with Lord Norwood's spectacular dive into the pig sty. "To be sure," she murmured vaguely. When they approached the house she looked at it as though not quite certain whether they ought to enter or not.

Just as Hyacinthe was about to urge them inside, Lord Latham paused, staring off in the general direction where the new village was to be located.

"Did you know that an army of masons and carpenters have begun work on the new cottages? Several stone shells are completed and the carpenters are busy on the interiors. It will not be long before the first can be occupied. Do you know whose it will be?"

Jane spoke up. "I fancy Mr. Smeed will be first. He is hard of hearing and accustomed to being alone, so he will not mind being the first."

"Needs an ear trumpet?" Lord Latham asked. "I believe I saw one in the attics not long ago while we were hunting for . . . some things," he concluded lamely.

"The jewels, I'll wager," Hyacinthe said softly, looking at Lord Latham with a knowing gaze.

"As to that, I had better remain silent. Best for you to inquire directly of Blase." He opened the door, thus ending all speculation.

He ushered the women into the drawing room, where Hyacinthe was unaccountably glad to see the Widow Smith and Mrs. Peachey settled in for a comfortable tea before the pleasant fire. The house might be plain, but it possessed all necessary comforts.

Hyacinthe watched her cousin when Sir Charles entered the room.

"Ah, you have returned. Norwood is abovestairs. We found some clean clothes that will do him until he reaches home. It would be a shame were he to catch an inflammation of the lungs or worse." His eyes sought and held Jane's gaze as he imparted this bit of information. She nodded in wordless reply, moving toward him to converse in softly spoken words.

Hyacinthe walked over to stand by the two older ladies, who were enjoying the lavish tea set out by the capable housekeeper employed by Sir Charles.

"Poor Lord Norwood," Mrs. Peachey said after a sip of tea. "One would think the man jinxed."

"Indeed," the Widow Smith added. "Or at least when around a particular redhead." She smiled amiably at Hyacinthe. "Although this young lady does not seem the sort to inspire mischief."

"My red hair does not give me regrets in the least," Hyacinthe answered, knowing full well all the tales ascribed to people with red hair. She was certain she had heard them all. "It might be unfashionable, but I like it."

The curate, who had been quietly standing by the tea table munching on a piece of particularly delectable nut torte, now entered the conversation. "It is good to be content with what the Lord has given one," he declared piously. He quite ignored his leaking roof in that respect.

The gentle hum of conversation, not to menton the consumption of tea and biscuits, came to a pause when the object of their mutual pity entered the room. Only the crackling of the fire could be heard other than the click of boots crossing the polished wood floor.

With a bow in Hyacinthe's direction, he strolled across the room to accept a glass of restoring port from Sir Charles.

Lord Norwood went to stand by the mullioned window, the glass of ruby port in his hand. He looked remarkably fresh, his blond curls tumbling over his forehead in an engaging manner. A wry smile tugged at his lips when he observed how the others watched him.

"Well, old chap," Lord Latham said in a pleased voice, breaking the silence that engulfed the room, "Sir Charles did well by you. I vow those pantaloons could be your own, and go well with your coat."

The fawn stockinette pantaloons might have been made for the slightly shorter and stockier Sir Charles, but adapted themselves well to Lord Norwood's taller, leaner frame. The crisp white linen shirt and elegant waistcoat looked quite splendid.

But then, Hyacinthe admitted to herself, if one were to toss a hemp sack over his head, Lord Norwood would contrive to make it look dashing.

"I shall order a waistcoat much like this from my tailor in London. My mishap is not in vain, for I found something much to my liking." He raised his glass to Sir Charles in a toast. Norwood's gaze, when it settled upon Hyacinthe, made her very uneasy. He could not possibly guess that she had intentionally allowed her favorite bonnet to sail away with the wind. No woman would do such a silly thing.

"What a pity the wind took Miss Dancy's bonnet like that," Mrs. Peachey said with a nod of her own bonneted head, unconsciously echoing Hyacinthe's thoughts.

"Especially since it appeared to be securely tied," Lord Norwood murmured clearly enough so that Hyacinthe heard him. He had crossed the room, ostensibly to avail himself of the lemon biscuits that were heaped on a plate. Tart yet sweet, they were truly excellent. He took a bite, then darted her a look. "Delicious."

"No doubt," she replied with equal care.

"Things often surprise a chap. Like this biscuit." He held it up for her to see. "Expect it to be sweet, and here it has a sharp tang to it. Don't expect sweet things to bite a fellow."

"Really, sir?" Hyacinthe said innocently. "I thought nothing could surprise a London . . . beau like you."

"I consider myself duly warned."

"I understand the first of the new cottages is about finished," she said, striving for a neutral voice.

"Indeed," he said, his face turning serious. After a thoughtful glance at Lord Latham, Lord Norwood switched his attention back to Hyacinthe.

"Jane thought Mr. Smeed would be the first to move," Hyacinthe continued.

"Not all the people are resistant to improving their lives," he said with a hint of a taunt in his voice.

"I fancy the houses are made with the same damp floors, twisting stairways, and unhandy kitchens as the present?" Her smile might have been neutral, but her eyes warned him that she was prepared to do battle.

He leaned against the fireplace wall, then studied her hostile face. "Why don't you ride over soon to see for yourself? I cannot guarantee that *you* will have no ill befall you, but I trust you are a daring girl. It goes with the hair, I believe."

"*I* believe I have mentioned before that I quite like my hair color. Unfashionable it may be; it runs in my family. I would

not consider a wig or dye, as some have urged," she concluded
sharply.

She found the look of genuine horror that flashed across his
face most rewarding. Not examining her reasons, she smiled at
him. "There are some people who feel it necessary to be a
fashionable blond in order to be happy. Or to marry well.
Since I am not in the least interested in the latter and quite
content with my red hair, my life is pleasing to me."

"That others could be as well," he answered with a pensive
look, then glanced at her again. "Yet you would deny me happiness. You would stand in the way of progress," he countered, taking a sip of his port.

The room grew silent at his words. Mrs. Peachey exchanged
looks with the Widow Smith. Jane drew closer to Sir Charles
as though seeking support from him.

Hyacinthe chose her reply with care. "That depends on what
you consider progress, I suppose. And achieving happiness at
the expense of others must not be satisfying. Or so I should
think," she ended meekly.

The others waited breathlessly for Lord Norwood's reply to
this provocative remark. Then the plump housekeeper entered
the room, whispering a message to Sir Charles.

"Mrs. Grigson tells me that a messenger has come from
Worthington Hall. Mr. Repton has arrived."

The two widows put their heads together to softly discuss
the latest development.

Hyacinthe turned to face her adversary. "You had best consult with him at once. I shall look forward to his reaction to
your scheme. Do be sure to tell him of the antiquity of the
church. Perhaps with that leaking roof he may consider it worthy to be a picturesque ruin."

"Now, Hyacinthe," Jane cautioned.

Lord Norwood inserted a comment into whatever she intended to say. "I shall ask his opinion. But, as I foot the bill for
everything, he will inevitably have to bow to my wishes."

"Well, happy sawing, tearing down, planting, or whatever
you intend to do next, then," Hyacinthe said.

"Ah, dear lady, your look wounds me," he replied. He
placed his empty glass on the table, then took one of her hands

in his. The farewell kiss he placed on it was light, his lips scarcely touching her skin. Yet she felt it acutely and trembled. And what was worse, she suspected he felt her tremble.

She flashed him a look that dared him to comment on her weakness.

He merely smiled, that lopsided smile that had melted hearts from one end of London to the other. Those intense blue eyes crinkled at the corners, and they held knowledge. He knew. Oh, he definitely knew she was not completely immune to his charm.

Hyacinthe gritted her teeth, then bared them in a parody of a smile in return. "Good-bye."

"Parting is such sweet sorrow," he murmured provocatively while slowly releasing her hand. He turned and walked across the room with jaunty steps. Hyacinthe and Jane walked behind him.

In the hall, he accepted his rumpled shirt, neatly brushed waistcoat, and cleaned pantaloons with a sigh. "Mrs. Grigson has done an admirable job, but I fear these are beyond redemption. Thank heavens my boots were easily cleaned. Hoby would never forgive me were I to confess that this pair had been ruined in a pig sty."

Hyacinthe met the challenge in his eyes with a cool look from hers. "How fortunate your tailor has your measurements. You need not interrupt your scheming here to return for fittings."

"You thought that I might?" he said with an arrested look on his face.

Vexed with her unguarded tongue, Hyacinthe said, "I merely thought it would be the thing to do. My mantuamaker always insists upon my presence for final fittings."

"How fortunate your wardrobe has not been decimated in that case." He bowed again, then left the house with Lord Latham cheerfully trailing along behind him, whistling a merry tune.

Alone with Jane in the hall, Hyacinthe also prepared to depart. Jane touched her arm and said in a low voice, "If I thought you had a thing to do with that disgraceful episode at the pig sty I would send you packing, cousin or no cousin."

"I had no control over the wind. And besides," Hyacinthe concluded triumphantly, "that was quite my favorite bonnet."

"I know you mean to help me, and I recall that list of things you might do to Lord Norwood. This was not one of them. Yet the notion that you might try such a trick with the idea it would help me lingers in my mind."

Incensed that her cousin would not immediately crow with delight at the discomfort wrought to their adversary, Hyacinthe drew her shawl over her bright hair and turned to leave. She made polite remarks to Sir Charles, who had just returned from seeing their lordships off, then walked to where Tom Coachman and her carriage awaited them.

The ride to Jane's cottage was silent for the most part. When they reached the house, Jane paused before the front door to study Hyacinthe.

"Do you plan to ride over to inspect the new cottages as he suggested?" There was no need for her to identify who "he" was. They both knew.

"I shall arrange for a horse in the morning. I believe I will find the expedition most illuminating." She turned back to inform her groom of her wishes.

Warton promised to have a suitable mount waiting for her.

The following morning after the girls had feasted on Granny Beanbuck's cinnamon buns and cups of hot tea, Hyacinthe donned her favorite riding habit of jade green with jet buttons down the front. On her head she wore a shako made of jade felt trimmed with a black plume. Her image in the looking glass appeared more confident than she felt.

"Do be careful, dearest," Jane cautioned. "There are ever so many dangerous objects around a building site."

Hyacinthe promised, then mounted the horse her groom had obtained. She waved to the curate as she jauntily set off in the direction of the new village.

It would be horrid, she knew. There would be no stately trees, just a row of plain houses, all the same with no character, no pretty gardens. She had seen one of these model villages elsewhere and detested its newness, its sameness, and its almost depressing quality of cheerfulness.

She met no one on her ride. Lord Norwood would most likely be occupied telling the celebrated Humphrey Repton just how to design his landscape. If Lord Norwood had such set ideas, he ought to have done the wretched business himself.

She rounded a bend in the road and came to a halt. Before her a sort of organized chaos met her eyes. Piles of lumber were stacked haphazardly to one side of the proposed main road through the new village. Houses were in various stages of construction. Lord Latham had not exaggerated in the least when he said that an army of masons and carpenters had descended upon the place.

Then she observed Mr. Wayland.

She dismounted with the help of a convenient block of wood, looped the reins over a branch, and set off along the road.

"Good day, sir." She approached him with curiosity. Had he hidden his cache of jewels in a safe place? She would dearly love to find them, just to taunt Lord Norwood with his own inability in that direction if for no other reason. "I see you carry out your employer's directions with enthusiasm. Such speed is truly amazing. It must keep you on the go from sunup to sundown."

He preened himself a little, and gave her a lofty look. "I do what I am paid to do."

"Have you worked with Mr. Repton before?"

"He arrived yesterday," Mr. Wayland said by way of an answer. "I look forward to adding his name to my list of collaborators," he added with a trace of pomposity.

"I should like to view the cottage that is nearly completed," Hyacinthe informed him, taking a step toward the first cottage of what appeared to be a depressing row.

He bowed, then frowningly accompanied her in her inspection tour.

She said nothing when she viewed the flagged floor, but noted that the foundation looked dry and sufficiently deep to prevent problems with damp. The kitchen had a pump, which meant the owner would not be required to venture out in bad weather to fetch water. The stairs were somewhat better than in the old village, with broader steps and less sharpness to the angle of turn, but she was not impressed with the house. Not in the least.

"I fancy all the houses will have the same design?" she inquired in a bland voice.

"Naturally," Mr. Wayland answered with pride. "It saves costs, you know. Lord Norwood does not wish to waste his money."

"He could have saved a great deal of it if he had just left well enough alone in the first place," she murmured to herself while strolling across the room to peer out of the window at the construction across the road.

Mr. Wayland gave her a sharp, curious look, but did not question what she had said.

"If you do not mind, I shall wander about, trying to envision what the village will be like—eventually—in a long time," she added softly.

Intent on completing this job as fast as he could, Dudley Wayland eagerly agreed, and bustled off to oversee the carpenters he had hired.

Hyacinthe glanced about the little parlor, then went outside. The house appeared far too close to the road to permit a charming garden such as the present Worthington cottages boasted. Why, if there would be space enough to allow a few flowers to either side of the door, that would be all. Dreary. The only variation she could note was that some of the cottages had bay windows alongside the entry door.

She trudged around to the back of the cottage, noticing the absence of windows on the sides. A thatcher had arrived, and with the help of his men commenced to work on the roof.

"Well, Miss Dancy," came a familiar voice, "what do you think?"

"Lord Norwood!" she exclaimed. "I thought you would be in conference with Mr. Repton this morning."

"And so I am. He wanted to view this site before we ride over to the area I wish to improve."

She glanced past Lord Norwood to see an older man. The gentleman did not appear well and she sent Lord Norwood a questioning look.

"He still suffers from a carriage accident he had some years back. He accepted this commission as a favor, for he knew my father. The younger man at his side is his son, John. He travels about with him now, and I suppose is in training to take his father's place eventually."

Hyacinthe felt pity for the older man. She hadn't expected this development. The poor man most likely needed this commission, unable to perform as in the past. She hastily turned away and felt her ankle twist on a scrap of lumber. With a cry of pain she ended on her posterior in a mixture of sawdust, mud, and mortar.

"Why, Miss Dancy, I believe you have met with an accident! Allow me." Lord Norwood assisted her to her feet. He brushed her off with care, then frowned in dismay when he saw how she compressed her lips in pain upon attempting to walk.

"Please, help me to my horse at the end of the road. I believe I had best return to Jane's cottage. I have injured . . ." She didn't finish her sentence, for a lady did not mention an ankle, or her leg for that matter. Hyacinthe might be a bit daring, but she was not lost to all propriety.

Suddenly she found herself scooped into his arms and carried away from the building site. He paused where Mr. Repton was studying the plans for the village with Mr. Wayland at his side.

"Miss Dancy has injured her ankle. I am taking her up to the house. Perhaps Mr. Wayland will be so good as to show you the area I most wish to improve."

She could hear the vexation in his voice and suspected he wished he had not invited her to inspect his new village. Were it not for the pain she felt, she might be pleased at this spoke thrust into his wheel.

Blase placed the young woman, who was becoming increasingly heavy, on his horse, then mounted behind her after tossing a few instructions to one of the men regarding her animal.

"You ought to have exercised more care. Anyone with a bit of sense should know there are hazards about a building site," he scolded. She was so still, so pale. Her face had turned so white that the three tiny freckles on her nose stood out in bold color. He drew her closer and urged his bay to greater speed.

"I was curious to see the new village."

Now he became truly alarmed, for her voice had grown faint, and there was none of that fiery spirit he admired.

Reining up before the front of his home, he called for Barmore while sliding down, then carefully eased Miss Dancy into his arms. She appeared even weaker, although trying valiantly to allow no sign of her pain.

"Oh, I say, sir," said the butler with anxiety. He held open the door, then barked out a succession of orders while Blase rushed down the hall with Hyacinthe in his arms, Barmore right behind him. At the end room, Blase paused. Barmore hastily opened this door, then assisted with placing the injured girl on a chaise longue near the window.

"Mrs. Earnshaw and Smithson will be here directly, my lord," he said quietly, referring to the Worthington Hall housekeeper and Blase's valet.

"I ought to have been taken to my cousin's house," Miss Dancy protested faintly.

"Miss Pennington is a lovely young lady, but not likely skilled in the treatment of injuries. Mrs. Earnshaw oversaw all my childhood afflictions, and Smithson is adept with sprains and breaks."

At this bit of information Miss Dancy looked about to truly faint. She said, "I doubt if I have a break, sir. Perhaps a sprain," she allowed, then gingerly leaned back against the pile of pillows. She glanced about her room seeming to note the feminine touches here and there.

Blase repressed a smile. "My sister stays here when she visits. It was originally my mother's room."

"I see," came the soft reply. Her lashes drifted down over pale cheeks and a look of intense pain suffused her face.

Smithson entered the room with the housekeeper right behind him. He carried a black bag that must have looked ominous to the wary Miss Dancy. She peeped at it with obvious misgivings.

Mrs. Earnshaw shooed Blase from the room and he couldn't repress a grin at Miss Dancy's patent relief at his departure.

"What's all the commotion?" Val said, strolling up with marked curiosity.

"Do you recall that I urged Miss Dancy to inspect the new village? Well, she did. And she fell—I suspect spraining her ankle in the process." Blase walked over to stare out the window.

"Pity, that," Val replied with genuine regret. "Now what happens? Your little redheaded nemesis will be unable to cause you any trouble, so you ought to have clear sailing." He joined Blase, but studied his friend instead of the view.

"I didn't wish her hurt."

"Ha!" Val laughed. "After all she has done to you? I do believe you have gone soft in the head."

"The wind took her bonnet," Blase replied to the jibe, knowing he didn't sound very convinced.

"If you believe that, I have an old racehorse to sell you," Val scoffed.

"For all her temper, she's a taking little thing," Blase said in his own defense—and possibly in hers. "She passionately defends her cousin and her home. I have to admire loyalty like that. I wonder how many cousins truly care for their family as she does." Blase transferred his gaze from the landscape to his friend.

"I hope you have ordered a new supply of coats and pantaloons in sturdy fabrics that will take a few tumbles, dousings, and shrug off mud. If she stays here you will need them." Val gave a disgusted snort, then walked through the room to the door at the far end that led to the entry hall. Here he paused and turned to face Blase.

"By the by, as we agreed, I searched Wayland's rooms after he left this morning. I found nothing, and I think I must have taken apart everything there. No jewels, no sign of that velvet sack that Miss Dancy mentioned. Are you certain that she did not take that pouch for herself? Giving you just the bracelet as a sop?"

With that explosive conclusion, he left the room.

Blase again faced the window, only this time he saw nothing. Was it possible? Could Miss Dancy in her misguided loyalty to her cousin do such a dastardly deed? He didn't wish to believe it of her. Turning away from his view that was soon to be improved, he walked back to the room where she was being tended.

Just as he was about to open the door, Mrs. Earnshaw bustled from the room, her face set in a resolute expression.

"Miss Dancy?" Blase inquired.

"You did right bringing her here so Smithson might tend her. Better than any doctor, he is. Poor mite, her ankle is badly sprained and must be paining her something fierce. I'm off to the stillroom to find her something soothing." She paused, then stared at him with a look he remembered from his childhood. "She is not to be upset, mind you."

"I must speak with her, however. It is important."

Smithson approached just then, so Mrs. Earnshaw went on her way.

"She sprained her ankle?" Blase repeated, although he knew the answer.

"And is in pain, as no doubt Mrs. Earnshaw told you. I'd advise that she remain here until the pain subsides. Perhaps her cousin could join her, lend her countenance as it were?" the valet said, knowing full well how gossip could travel.

"Ah, yes, propriety. What would we do without it." Blase murmured. Then he dismissed Smithson after a few more words of instruction.

At the door he paused to view the beautiful Hyacinthe Dancy. Could she really be capable of such treachery as Val suggested?

9

"You really ought to have taken me to my cousin's cottage," Hyacinthe Dancy insisted, albeit quietly. She still reclined on the chaise longue where Blase had placed her, the injured foot now propped on a pillow. She looked wan and fragile, those tiny freckles still standing out in bold relief. Tendrils of deep red hair clung to her forehead and cheeks.

Without thinking, Blase crossed the room to brush the strands of hair away from her face. It was a curiously intimate gesture that was lost on him, but drew a puzzled look from Miss Dancy.

"I fear that would have been a bad decision for you. Mrs. Earnshaw will take care of you far better." He supposed he sounded rather gruff, but his concern for Miss Dancy had affected him more than he had thought possible.

"I would wish that Fosdick and Jane could tend me." She gave a vexed swipe at her riding skirt. "How stupid of me to be so careless. I ought to have known there might be hazards present. 'Tis all my fault. I pray you will not blame any of the workers for my irresponsible actions." She gave him a concerned look that seemed to come from her heart.

"I shan't," Blase replied abruptly. However, he wasn't about to make it easy on his antagonist. She had countered him at every chance. She had cost him two coats with her silly schemes. Yet there was something in Hyacinthe Dancy that made him want to change her mind, make her see what he saw.

"I cannot remain here," she insisted. "You must see that. Why, the speculation, the gossip . . . It is amazing how word can wing its way about the country with such speed, particu-

larly if the gossip is malicious." She pressed her lips together
then studied her hands now folded in her lap.

"I decided to send for the doctor," Blase said, hoping to
mollify her. "He ought to lend a touch of respectability to the
situation. I'll grant you this—if he says you may be moved
we will take you to Miss Pennington's. Although how you
might go up those stairs is beyond me."

"Aha! You do see what I mean about those stairways! They
are dangerously narrow and steep. I trust you mean to alter
that in the new cottages?"

Blase was startled at the change in Miss Dancy. More animated, she leaned forward to make her point with a flash of
those green eyes. Then she winced and fell back against the
pillows with a sigh of frustration. When tears brimmed in her
eyes, Blase sank down on the chaise at her side, taking one of
her hands in his.

"If I agree to see that the stairs are indeed improved, will
you agree to consider my garden plans?"

"Do your London friends know that you are become a *garden* rake?" Her color yet pale and the usual twinkle in her fine
eyes dimmed, she managed a strained grin at him.

He cringed at the pun, shaking his head at her while quite
forgetting to release her hand.

"The doctor is here, milord," Mrs. Earnshaw said from the
doorway. She had most likely noticed his position. Fortunately
she was not the sort to spread rumors. Blase dropped Miss
Dancy's soft hand and left the doctor in charge.

Mrs. Earnshaw whispered that they had been fortunate to
find the doctor attending an injury on the estate, so he had
been close by. Then she shut the door so she might assist the
doctor. After all, an ankle ought not be exposed to a gentleman
who was not a husband!

Blase paced back and forth across the library while the doctor examined Miss Dancy's injury. On, she was most likely as
tough as old boots with a core of pure steel. On the other
hand—and here he paused to stare off across his garden—she
was a delicious armful from her feathery red curls to her
dainty feet, and she wore a spicy scent that reminded him of

the red and white carnations in his garden. Spicy. Somehow the word, as well as the scent, suited Miss Dancy to a tee.

"I understand the doctor is here. Any verdict as yet?" Val popped his head around the corner, then strolled across the library to join Blase.

"No. I'd not thought to send for him, but Mrs. Earnshaw suggested it might be a seemly thing to do," Blase confessed.

"And what if he declares that Miss Dancy should not be moved?" Val gave Blase a sly grin.

Blase shrugged. "Then I suppose I will have to send for her abigail and Miss Pennington to lend countenance."

"It would be interesting—having your adversary under your roof." Val toyed with a paperweight on the desk while watching Blase.

"Oh, she is not all that bad," Blase felt compelled to say in defense of the young girl who had seemed so soft and womanly and now lay in the next room close to tears and in pain.

"Look at it this way . . . if she were a horse, would you bet on her?" Val said, a look of mischief dancing in his eyes.

Blase gave him a surprised look, then chuckled. "As spirited a filly as she? Why, there's no doubt she'd win any race by several lengths."

"And what about the emeralds? Have you considered that if she stays here, I could investigate the Pennington cottage— under the guise of obtaining something she particularly desires." Val's expression revealed his rather cynical notions of Miss Dancy.

"I cannot like the insinuation that she has stolen the gems," Blase protested.

"Then where are they?" Val tossed the paperweight in the air, watching the flash of color as it twirled about.

Blase gave him a bleak look. "I confess I do not know."

Before they could continue along this line the doctor opened the door, joining them with quiet steps.

"She ought not be moved for a time; that is one of the nastiest sprains I have seen. I suspect she will receive far better care while here. Although she seemed very concerned about propriety—as is only right," commented the man, who usually saw to farm injuries and not those of a gently reared young lady.

Blase exchanged glances with Val, then said, "I will send for her cousin and abigail. Miss Pennington is all that is proper."

"And," Val inserted with a twist of his mouth, "Fosdick, her abigail, is an undisputable guardian of virtue."

Giving the two peers a curious look, the doctor issued a few suggestions, then went off to have words with Miss Earnshaw.

"Do you really mean to go snooping about?" Blase queried softly lest his voice carry to the next room.

"Indeed. Who knows, I may join the Robin Redbreasts." Val hooked his thumbs inside his waistcoat, then tilted back his head to give Blase a narrow, suspicious look.

"You? A Bow Street Runner?" Blase laughed, adding, "It would take more than curiosity to turn you into a detective."

There was a sound from the next room that ended their conversation. Blase, followed closely by Val, hurried to the door. They were greeted by the sight of Miss Dancy attempting to leave the chaise longue.

"Here now, what do you think you are doing?" Blase demanded, rushing across the room to her side.

"I cannot believe I must remain here. Surely I could go?" she pleaded, then sank back against the pillows as the pain grew more intense.

Tears of frustration brimmed her eyes, eyes that reminded Blase of deep green pools. He was lost in them a moment before he came to his senses. "No, but you must be uncomfortable as you are. May I be of help until Mrs. Earnshaw returns?"

She shook her head, then apparently changed her mind. "My jacket. Help me take it off, please."

She fumbled with the little jet buttons that curved up under her bosom, succeeded with that task, then shifted slightly. Blase tugged at one cuff, easing that sleeve from her arm, then reached around to help with the other.

He discovered that in so doing he was very close to her and was momentarily dazed. She smelled deliciously spicy. She leaned against him briefly, as light as thistledown and far nicer. Then he recalled those missing emeralds. Could she truly have taken them?

The sight of her delicate cambric shirt, tucked and curving so faithfully to her figure, brought him to his senses as nothing else might. He tossed the jacket aside, then looked to where Val stood, arms folded across his chest, his eyes revealing his amusement.

"There is nothing more we can do here." A sound at the door brought Blase around. "Mrs. Earnshaw," he said with great relief. "I believe there is much you can do to make our guest more comfortable."

"Mr. Repton is desiring to speak with you, milord," she replied, bustling across the room to stand by Miss Dancy. Presumably the folds of sheer cambric draped over the housekeeper's arm constituted a nightdress. The image of Hyacinthe Dancy attired in the sheer cambric drove him from the room with more than necessary haste.

"Well," Hyacinthe observed, "you would think I was contagious."

"He is that anxious to have his plans for the garden and view implemented, miss," the housekeeper replied evenly.

She ably helped Hyacinthe from her riding costume and into the delicate, lavender-scented nightdress trimmed with white ribbons. "This was his mother's gown but she always took care of her things. You are of a size, I believe, or near enough. Now, let us put you under the covers of the bed. I believe you could use a bit of sleep after taking the powder the doctor left for you."

With that, she carefully helped Hyacinthe into the bed and tucked the covers about her with an attention that Hyacinthe found especially kind.

"Thank you for all you have done. It is an extra burden, I'm certain." Hyacinthe's eyelids drooped. She swallowed the mixture that Mrs. Earnshaw handed her to drink, then fell back against the pillows.

The housekeeper paused by the side of the bed, studying the young woman who had affected her master so strongly. She had not missed that tender look of concern, nor the gentle way he held her hand. Did he know how he felt? she wondered. Oh, these coming days were not to be missed for anything.

When Fosdick and Jane learned about the accident, they flew into action. Fosdick packed what she deemed necessary. Jane slipped over to Granny Beanbuck's cottage to obtain a few cinnamon buns, which she was certain would make Hyacinthe feel better.

It was not long before they were prepared to depart.

Jane opened the door to discover Sir Charles on her doorstep. "Oh!" she exclaimed. "You startled me. We were just about to summon the coach to take us to the Hall. Poor Hyacinthe has suffered a terrible accident."

"No!" Sir Charles cried in alarm. "May I offer my carriage, dear lady? I feel certain you must wish to drive there as soon as may be."

"What a thoughtful man you are," Jane told him. She gathered her bits and pieces, motioned Fosdick to leave the cottage, then joined Sir Charles.

When they reached Worthington Hall they found the patient asleep.

"I would like to see her—just for a moment," Jane said softly to Lord Norwood. She held in her hands a small sack from which emerged the aroma of fresh cinnamon buns.

"She sleeps," he cautioned.

Not allowing such words to deter her, Miss Pennington set forth behind the housekeeper in the direction of the bedroom.

Fosdick didn't bother to ask permission but also followed along to the bedroom where her charge slept.

Jane exclaimed softly when she saw her dearest cousin stretched out on the bed, looking so white and still. She placed the cinnamon buns on a nearby table, then edged toward the door. "There is nothing I may do for her at the moment," she admitted. She left the room, looking close to erupting into tears.

The abigail peered about the dimly lit room, then studied the strained face of the girl. The injured ankle, still elevated on a pillow, made a high mound near the foot of the bed.

"I fixed a sort of a cage to keep the covers off that poor

foot. Dear girl," Mrs. Earnshaw said, "she made not one whimper, although anyone could see she was in pain."

"She's a game one, she is," Fosdick agreed. She consulted with the housekeeper a bit longer. When the other woman left, she emptied the portmanteau of the things she believed necessary for the next few days. Fosdick was the sort of person who firmly believed in being prepared for any event, so the bag held a great deal.

In the entry, Barmore guided Miss Pennington to the drawing room, where the gentlemen awaited her. She chatted with Lord Latham and Lord Norwood while seated next to Sir Charles.

"Did the doctor say it would be very long before my cousin may return home?" Jane queried gently with a dubious look at Lord Norwood.

"As soon as the pain permits her to be moved. Between the swelling and the nasty ache from the sprain, she does not feel quite the thing at the moment," Blase said.

"Poor girl," Sir Charles murmured, looking as though he harbored a few other thoughts about Miss Dancy but was far too polite to utter them.

"Did you reach any conclusions with Repton, Norwood?" Val said, sounding quite bored with the topic of Miss Dancy's injury.

"Indeed." Blase rose to look out of the window in the direction of the soon-to-disappear village. "We will begin planting the woods to sweep up that first hill immediately. Miss Dancy will no doubt be pleased to learn that Repton believes we ought to keep the church—the tower will make a splendid ruin." At Jane's dismayed gasp, he turned to bow in her direction. "We will also build a new church in the center of the new village, of course. Mr. Clark shall have his roof that does not leak."

"Oh," Jane said with an uncertain note in her voice, "that will be splendid, I'm sure."

"How does the rest of your plan progress?" Sir Charles inquired with a thoughtful look at Miss Pennington, who wore a worried frown on her pretty face.

"Two more houses are almost ready for occupancy. I be-

lieve the Nutkins and the Philpotts are to move next," Blase
concluded with satisfaction. As an afterthought, he said, "And
of course their old cottages will promptly be demolished."

At Jane's second gasp of dismay, Sir Charles patted her
hand in a gesture of comfort.

"And what does he say about your terraces?" Val asked
slyly. "Miss Dancy seemed to admire them greatly, as I recall."

"They shall remain as they are," Blase replied, not admitting he had argued with the famous landscape designer regarding that matter. As Miss Dancy had pointed out, their beauty
added to the consequence of the house. He was not so set in
his ways that he could fail to see reason when presented with
convincing arguments.

Just then Barmore entered the room to offer tea to Miss
Pennington while Blase saw to the liquid refreshment for the
men.

When she had finished her tea, Miss Pennington set off to
check on her cousin, then seek out her room. It was located
next to where Hyacinthe slept, and within minutes Fosdick entered to consult with her.

"Miss Hyacinthe ought to be able to come home shortly,"
the abigail reported with satisfaction.

"I fear there will be fireworks to rival a Guy Fawkes Day
celebration when she hears that more cottages are being torn
down," Jane said with a wry look at Fosdick.

"Oh, dear me," Fosdick muttered.

"At least the old church will remain . . . to become a Gothic
ruin," Jane concluded, sighing. "What Hyacinthe will say to
that doesn't bear thinking."

It was quite as Jane has feared. When apprised of the latest
developments, Hyacinthe erupted. Fortunately Lord Norwood
was off with Mr. Repton and his son, so he was spared her fire
and fury.

"That heartless monster," Hyacinthe fumed from her bed.

"Dear," Jane reminded her, "he is transporting the families
into their new abodes in fine style. Mrs. Nutkin is that pleased
with two extra bedrooms and her husband is kept busy all day,

quite exhausted come evening what with the work to be had at the new village." She exchanged a significant look with her cousin, both knowing that an exhausted man was less likely to be interested in what Mrs. Nutkin would as soon have him avoid.

Instead, Hyacinthe attacked the abandonment of the old church. "While it might need a new roof, surely it should not be allowed to molder into a ruin!"

"I cannot answer that, my dear," Jane admitted.

A gentle rap on the door brought the information that the curate desired to offer a word of comfort to the injured young lady.

Exchanging a resigned look with Jane, Hyacinthe nodded to Fosdick. The gentleman entered hesitantly, then approached the bed as though she might bite him.

"Good day, Miss Dancy. So sorry to learn of your tragic accident. But things will happen, you know. The Lord's will be done," he concluded with a look at the ceiling.

"That's very comforting to know," Hyacinthe said wryly.

"I suppose you have heard that I, that is the village, will have a new church," he said, animation lighting his face for the first time. "Not merely an ordinary roof, but slate of the finest quality. There will be no leaks in this roof, I can assure you," he concluded with great pride. "Sir Charles expressed an interest in donating a lovely baptismal font. Oh, this is a great thing for the village. Did you know that more cottages are to be built than existed previously? We shall grow. There will be progress."

"And progress is far more important than history or the security of one's loved home," Hyacinthe said softly.

He appeared disconcerted for a moment, then smiled. "To be sure," he said, apparently taking Hyacinthe's words at face value.

When Blase entered Miss Dancy's room just before dinner, he did so with caution. He had been warned that she had heard of the changes and not been pleased at all.

"It promises to be a fine day tomorrow. If your injury permits, perhaps you will be allowed to be carried to the terrace."

"So I may enjoy the view?" she shot back swiftly. "I daresay there will be fewer rooftops to mar it by then."

"I gather the curate or someone has been to call."

"He was here," she acknowledged.

"I thought you might admire the sight of the new trees being planted. There will be hundreds added to the parkland," he said with enthusiasm. "And the little stream has been dammed up to create a rather charming waterfall. When your ankle is better, I will take you to see it. Mr. Repton believes that it will be a soothing sight on a hot summer day."

"I fancy he is correct," she said, her fingers pleating the bedcover. "My injury seems to be improving. I believe it will be no time at all before I will be able to return to Jane's cottage, although I doubt if I will be up to viewing a waterfall for some time. I should like to see the village before it disappears," she concluded, her fine eyes mocking him with a flash of green.

Blase avoided meeting her eyes. He feared he might reveal something he would rather keep to himself. Val had gone to the village late in the afternoon, ostensibly to fetch something for Miss Dancy.

"Do you suppose that we might become a bit less formal? Since you reside here—even temporarily," he asked, not liking to use her surname when "Hyacinthe" was so much more charming to say.

"I scarcely believe that would be proper," she answered quickly. "I am well aware that such a change would be reported to others just too eager to gossip."

"And you have no desire to be linked with me," he finished. Odd, how it truly piqued him to know that she quite detested him. Well—perhaps that was too strong a word. Maybe disliked would be more like it. But he had always known the admiration of every lady he saw, and this cut him to the quick.

"Even if you have become the *garden* rake?" she gently chided. "Indeed, I regret to admit you are not my ideal. For it is not polite to tell your host that he fails in any aspect, is it?"

Blase decided that he had asked for that setdown and paused by the door on his way from the room. "I trust that Mrs. Earnshaw has seen to your comfort?"

A faint pink stained Miss Dancy's cheeks. "She has been quite wonderful to me. You are most fortunate in your servants, sir. And from what I have seen, you have a lovely home."

Somewhat mollified, Blase marched to the library, where he found Val hunting through the shelves.

"Looking for something to read?" Blase said in mock horror. "I am really failing in that case. Shall we plan an outing tomorrow?"

"I had enough today. Blast it all, I believed I would find the emeralds concealed in Miss Pennington's cottage."

Blase permitted himself a smile, albeit a small one. "And?"

"Not a blasted thing," Val admitted in disgust. "It is a small place and there are few spots in which to hide things." He leaned against the wall of books, giving Blase an assessing look. "Your Miss Pennington is a remarkable person, in that she doesn't collect vast quantities of absurd things. My sisters do, the silly twits."

"But no emeralds."

"No. So . . . where do we go next?"

"I wonder if Mr. Wayland has placed them in an entirely different hiding spot. See if you can nose about, learn more of his movements. Perhaps your valet, or my head groom, could chat up the locals at the nearby tavern."

"It's a thought," Val replied, rubbing his chin with a considering look. "I'll confess that I had hoped Miss Dancy had taken them."

"It would have been very convenient," Blase said, trying not to appear as pleased as he was. He didn't choose to inspect his reasons for wishing her innocent. Perhaps it was easier to view Mr. Wayland as a culprit?

Since she insisted that she was much improved, Hyacinthe was carried out to join the others in the drawing room after dinner. Blase lifted her in his arms, thinking she felt like an armful of flowers or something equally light. He took great care to prevent her foot from further injury when he placed her on a sofa.

The evening went well. When Blase rose to take Hyacinthe back to her room, she gave them all a firm look.

"I fully intend to return to Jane's cottage on the morrow. Not that I do not appreciate Lord Norwood's gracious hospitality, but I feel much more the thing. And it is better that I go." Her words were decisive.

Blase knew there was no arguing with her. Perhaps he might be able to persuade her to return to study his view later on. He still felt this imperative to convert her to his position. Yet she still looked very pale and fragile.

"Whatever you wish," he said.

"You do not really mean that, you know," she murmured provocatively in his ear while being carried back to her bed.

The next few days passed surprisingly quickly considering Hyacinthe's inability to get about. She remained in bed at first, then managed her way down the stairs to recline on the sofa in the parlor. She became adept at hopping about.

Everyone she had met in the village called to offer sympathy and inquire about life in the great house. Of course it was most subtly done, but between the Widow Smith and Mrs. Peachey there was precious little that wasn't learned about the way things were done up there.

Sir Charles called as well, but Hyacinthe soon decided that he was far more interested in how Jane fared with her invalid than in the invalid herself.

One fine day Hyacinthe could tolerate being inside the house no longer. With the help of Fosdick and a cane Sir Charles had brought for her use—bringing forth Jane's great admiration—she set out to sit on the green. Here she could watch the antics of the silly ducks and admire the beauty of the haughty swans.

While she sat relaxing in the shade of a fine old tree, one of the Nutkin children approached her. It was one of the older of the girls and she wore the saddest expression Hyacinthe could imagine.

"Sukey, dear girl, what troubles you?" Hyacinthe asked when the girl hesitantly approached her.

"Me brothers, miss." Once the barrier of actually speaking

to the pretty and sympathetic lady was broken, the girl poured forth her tale. "They tease me somethin' fierce, 'cuz I can't fly a kite for nothin'."

"That will never do," Hyacinthe declared briskly. "Allow me to help you, if I may. First, I must inspect your kite." Seeing the dubious expression on the girl's face, Hyacinthe assured her, "My brother taught me years ago, and I do not believe you ever quite forget how to do something like this."

The kite proved airworthy in her estimation. The ragged tail needed a bit of improvement, but after adding her handkerchief to the end, Hyacinthe decided it would do.

"Now you must run so, holding the kite like this before you release it." Hyacinthe demonstrated the proper way to hold the kite, then urged the girl to run across the green.

"Look, miss, 'tis flying!" Sukey cried with delight.

The success went to her head. Sukey Nutkin ran and ran until she was red in the face from her exertion and about to drop from sheer joy at besting her brothers.

Then disaster struck. The kite slipped from her tired fingers to sail up into the branches of the spreading oak.

Mrs. Peachey, who had been looking on, declared, "What a shame, Sukey was enjoying herself so much." All knew how rare an occurrence this was for the overworked Nutkin daughter.

The Widow Smith, also a spectator, suggested a gentle tug on the string, while old Mr. Smeed—who had returned here for the afternoon because he was lonely all by himself—offered the opinion that the only way to get the kite down was for some young lad to climb up to fetch it.

"Me brothers ain't about to bring it down," Sukey said, fighting the tears that threatened to fall.

Since all the other young men were over at the new village working on the new cottages, there seemed no hope. The kite was undoubtedly doomed to hang limply from the tree limb to forever decorate the tree. Hyacinthe wondered if it would mar the view for Lord Norwood.

Somehow it failed to surprise her when the object of her thoughts appeared in sight. He had a way of doing that lately. He strode to her side, a frown on his brow.

"Ought you be sitting here? 'Tis very public," he said, casting a look about at the throng of people who all seemed to be peering up into the tree for some odd reason.

"I grew bored with the parlor," she admitted. "Poor Sukey needed someone to show her how to fly a kite. And now that she's learned how, the dratted thing landed in the branches."

Every face turned to him. Blase's heart sank, for he realized what they expected. Oh, perhaps they didn't actually *expect* him to climb after the blasted kite, but he knew he would diminish in their eyes were he to walk away from Miss Dancy's appealing look. Not to mention the disappointment he knew would spring into Sukey's pale blue eyes.

"I shall climb up to fetch it for her," he said with far more enthusiasm than he felt. Remembering his previous experiences with Miss Dancy, Blase removed his coat, tossing it on her lap.

The climb was a simple affair, for the oak tree was superbly arrayed with stout limbs spaced nicely apart. He managed to reach the kite with just a little effort. Complications arose when he tried to return to the ground. The kite in one hand—for he didn't wish it to sail away—and the other hand assisting with his descent, he found the going tricky.

"Look out!" Miss Dancy cried.

Her warning proved too late. A branch broke under his weight and he felt himself slipping. He let the blasted flag go, vowing to buy another if necessary, and grabbed at passing boughs.

The ground he fell upon was cushioned by long grass, but he was well aware that his pantaloons had suffered greatly.

"Oh, sir, you've ripped your—" Sukey immediately turned as red as a beetroot and grabbed her restored kite, mumbling a "thank you" before dashing off.

She had done it again. Somehow Miss Dancy had managed to bring him to grief once more. And what was worse, she looked as though she was ready to burst into laughter at any moment.

"I am so sorry, my lord," she said in a choked voice. "What a dreadful thing to have happen." She handed him his coat to cover his exposed posterior.

The rest of the villagers drifted off to discuss the disaster, their chuckles floating back to taunt him.

"Miss Dancy," Blase said with great forbearance, "you really are a dangerous woman."

"What a lovely thing to say,'" she replied, this time breaking into peals of laughter. Blase found himself somewhat reluctantly joining her.

10

"She doesn't have the sense God gave a flea," Val chided while they rode along the track from the Hall to the new village.

"I would never go so far as to say that," Blase said sharply. "However, this last bit of teasing has gone too far."

He supposed he was overreacting to the situation. It was unreasonable to blame Hyacinthe Dancy for his fall from the oak tree, thus splitting his pantaloons and making himself a laughing stock for the villagers. That the premier rake of London should be placed in such a position was appalling, however. And she was the one who had silently urged him to fetch the blasted kite.

She had called him a *garden* rake. While he had laughed with her, it had served to remind him that Miss Dancy possessed a lamentable sense of humor.

And that cat she had saddled him with! The dratted animal had taken over his bedroom not to mention his bed, and acted as though Blase ought to cater to it. When Smithson had served the cat kippers, they had been on a china plate, if you please. No ordinary crockery for that animal.

True, the little fellow did have a winning way about him and had proven to be a good mouser. But still, a man didn't have a cat for a pet; he had a sturdy, sensible dog, for pity's sake.

"What do you intend to do about her?" Val queried.

Blase knew full well that his friend expected him to perform some devilishly nasty bit of retribution. Blase couldn't think of a thing he wished to do to Hyacinthe Dancy that was along such lines. Not after holding her in his arms. And then there was that memorable kiss. She had never mentioned it, but he found it impossible to forget. But he would. He must. It would be absurd to become more deeply involved with that red-headed tease.

"What I intend to do is forge ahead with my plans. I told Wayland to hire more stone masons to work on the church. We also need a few more carpenters to speed up completion of the houses. The sooner the new village is completed, the sooner Miss Dancy will give up and go away."

"And you wish her to be out of your life?" Val gave Blase a look that clearly told how he doubted this. Fortunately he said nothing more, so Blase didn't have to defend himself one way or the other.

"I want to find those emeralds first. I cannot believe she has taken them. Why would she give me the bracelet in that case?" he demanded.

"To put you off her trail," Val said, obviously trying to sound like a detective. "You see, if she can make you believe that by handing you the bracelet she's innocent, she can keep the rest of them. You must admit, she would look rather luscious arrayed in those emeralds on that delicate white skin with her striking eyes." Val's grin reminded Blase of Tom Tiger after it had produced a mouse for his appreciation.

"But," Blase reminded his friend, "you found nothing in her belongings."

"True," Val admitted with a frown, then brightened. "Perhaps they were in the portmanteau that the abigail brought to the Hall after Miss Dancy was injured. People often stow important possessions in peculiar places, like a portmanteau. Especially if they are away from home. And it appears she has no home, for she seems to drift from relative to relative."

"Pity you didn't find occasion to examine all her belongings while she was up at the Hall," Blase wryly concluded. The thought that the beautiful Miss Dancy was without a close family bothered him. Her brother ought to provide a proper establishment for her or take her into his own home. She needed watching over. "What about Wayland?"

"You know I have had my groom keeping a sharp eye on him whenever yours was busy. Nothing out of line has been observed. He is either innocent or dashed clever. In spite of my inclination toward the beautiful and dangerous Miss Dancy, he does bear more surveillance."

They entered the road that led through the center of the new village. It was not cobbled as yet, and the puddles of water here and there prompted caution. The entire area looked raw and unsettled. No flowers such as Miss Dancy seemed to desire graced the front of the cottages; no trees grew in the village save a few paltry beeches and willows scattered around the edges of what would be the village green. The new pond had yet to form from the stream that now flowed along the lowest part of the proposed green, but at least they were spared the abundance of ducks and the two swans.

"I must speak to Wayland about the street. There should be sufficient ground for gardens in front of the cottages."

"Yes," Val agreed. "I've noticed Miss Dancy appears quite fond of gardens. Wonder how her hedgehog is faring?"

"Last I heard it was consuming every slug and beetle in Miss Pennington's garden. I suspect Miss Dancy has been feeding it bowls of bread and milk as well, for she said something about being worried the little thing might have a difficult winter."

"Animal lover, then?" Val said with a grimace.

"Well," Blase said, "it's nice to think she cares for something. She seems to have a total indifference to men."

"Men? Or you in particular? I must say, it's dashed amusing to see that little bit of a damsel turning her nose up at you when you're the quarry of nearly every woman in London." Val grinned with decided cheer at the thought.

Blase ignored this provocative remark. Instead he stiffened, studying his architect as he spoke with a man.

"What is it?" Val murmured, reining in to see what had caught Blase's attention.

"I believe I just saw my esteemed architect accept a bribe. I'd swear the delivery chap from the quarry slipped him something." Blase narrowed his gaze.

"Wouldn't be anything new, I suppose," Val said quietly.

The two men dismounted, tied their horses to a convenient post, then slowly approached the architect from behind him.

Wayland and the man standing beside the load of stone were in deep discussion. Try as he could, Blase did not actually see Wayland pocket any money. It had been the appearance of accepting it that had struck him so forcefully. He could prove nothing.

They apparently caught the delivery man's eye, for he spoke rapidly to Wayland, then turned away to the dray.

Wayland spun around with a smile of greeting on his angular face. "Lord Norwood! I have good news for you, sir."

Momentarily diverted, Blase said cautiously, "And what is this good news?"

"We have begun tearing down the cottages in the old village and this chap will carry useable stone from there to this site, cutting down on what we need from the quarry. It will save time and money." The architect looked enormously pleased with himself. And there was not one sign of guilt in his face.

"Both would be welcome," Blase murmured. His suspicions regarding the emeralds must be coloring his entire attitude to Wayland. He had only Miss Dancy's word on the jewelry. Not that he wished to believe in her guilt.

Old Mr. Smeed had ambled from his new cottage to approach Blase. He appeared to have something on his mind.

"Good day, Mr. Smeed," Blase said courteously. He caught Val's eye, motioning with a nod of his head that Val should investigate the area for him while he kept the architect by his side.

Val nodded back ever so slightly to show he understood, then sauntered off down the road, carefully avoiding puddles. He made a show of checking each cottage as he went along.

The older man nattered on about the dust and noise from the building and the great progress that had been made, then came to the point. "Granny Beanbuck's worried that you'll not have a proper oven for her. Depends on her baking, she does. Claims she'll not move so much as a chair until she kin try it out first."

Blase exchanged a look with Wayland, then sought to allay these fears. It took much of the morning to arrange transport for the elderly Mrs. Beanbuck, then properly test the new oven. She brought the last of the morning's dough with her and set about forming her loaves with her customary skill.

Blase found he did not like her narrow-eyed scowl overmuch.

"Canny old lady, isn't she?" Val commented as the bread went into the new oven. He had silently sidled up to the group under cover of the bustle of checking the fire in the oven and cajoling the old woman to make her attempt.

"Come on, let her be while you tell me what you have found—if anything. I trust you inspected the office Wayland set up in that unfinished house across the road?" He exchanged a look with Val, who had strolled along at his side out to the center of the road.

"Indeed. Dash it all, I found not one thing that you might not expect to find in a temporary office. Of course, it was a bit difficult to hunt about, what with the carpenter popping in and out ever so often. I have become disgustingly creative with my excuses, I'll have you know." Val kicked at a small stone in his scorn of his success, or lack thereof.

"I appreciate your efforts," Blase said softly. He glanced to where his architect conferred with a stone mason. "Wayland showed no nervousness at your absence, either. Apparently the gems are not here."

"So what do we do next? Kidnap Miss Dancy so as to examine the remainder of her belongings?" Val muttered with a sly glance at his friend.

"I may try to persuade her to go on a picnic one of these days if the weather is decent." Blase glanced at a puddle, then off to the horizon where some gray clouds had formed, promising another shower before long. "Too much rain and we'll have a devil of a time finishing these cottages in time for the winter."

"Here comes Mr. Clark. I do believe the good curate is ready to do stonework himself in order to speed things up." Val chuckled at the eager expression on the gentleman's face.

Blase chuckled too. "His nimble footwork dancing around the puddles might serve him well at something, but I'm not certain it would be of any use in laying stone."

"He'd do most anything to get a roof that didn't leak."

"Good day to you, my lords." Ambrose Clark rubbed his hands together in a gesture of satisfaction while glancing back to where the church was slowly taking form.

"It seems good," Blase agreed.

"He hasn't run into Miss Dancy yet," Val said under his breath. Blase heard what he said and gave him a dark look.

"Ah, yes, the young lady does seem to have a most unfortunate propensity for accidents." Mr. Clark assumed a pious mien, then added, "One must not judge another too harshly, for you know not what lies in the heart."

"You might say that," Blase murmured. Then, with another stern look at Val that cautioned him to guard his words, he guided the curate toward where the church would one day stand in simple glory.

The curate began to inquire about certain aspects of the church plans, gesturing nervously with his long fingers. Blase decided he would beg leave of the curate to ask Miss Dancy if she and her cousin would join them on a picnic. He'd ask Sir Charles as well so he could entertain Miss Pennington. While they were away, Val—who detested anything as provincial as picnics—could sneak into the Pennington cottage to perform the rest of his investigation. Not that Blase truly expected Val would find anything incriminating, but it would silence him and remove a taint of suspicion from the lovely Miss Dancy.

Of course were Val to discover the jewelry, it would be another matter entirely.

It was sometime later before Blase was able to leave the new village. Granny Beanbuck somewhat reluctantly allowed as how the oven appeared promising. Since Blase had gone to the expense of a new Rumford stove for her, he accepted her words of probability with wry resignation.

The curate finally ran out of questions, his last act to wave a letter from the bishop offering a few words of advice for Lord Norwood. Blase accepted the letter with a slight bow, then marched away.

"I vow, I shall be more careful when I next come here," he commented to Val. "One would think *I* am the master builder instead of the one I hired."

"But you are ultimately responsible and they all know that," Val pointed out.

Which brought Blase to the matter of Miss Dancy and Miss Pennington. He was heartily sorry that he had left Miss Dancy with the idea that the rents would be raised substantially. His bailiff has suggested such a raise, but what with the effects of the war and all, there were few who could manage it. Blase figured he would have to attend a few more races in the hope of winning enough blunt to make up the difference.

The two men rode along the route to the old village, pausing when they came to where Sir Charles lived. That gentleman was out in his stable area and waved to them.

It was the opportunity Blase sought, so he motioned Val to follow.

After the usual chitchat, Blase extended his invitation. "It will be a simple thing, but I thought Miss Dancy might enjoy an outing after being confined with her injury."

"Indeed," Sir Charles fairly beamed at them. "I shall enjoy escorting Miss Pennington. You know, it is a shocking thing for her to be alone, which she will be once Miss Dancy leaves here."

"Quite," Blase said with a glance at Val. "I was unaware that Miss Dancy was planning to depart soon."

"Well, as to that I cannot say," Sir Charles replied sagely. "I confess I have been most concerned with Jane, that is, Miss Pennington." His face reddened slightly, then he added, "I've been thinking that since my situation has improved—what with my father passing on and my inheriting—I might afford a wife." He studied the faces of both men as though to know their reaction. "You did say that I might buy back the manor house my ancestor lost to yours."

"I did and you may. As to Miss Pennington, I feel certain that the lady would welcome such a proposal, for she shows a marked partiality in your direction." Blase gave Sir Charles a smile of genuine encouragement. This solution would end two problems. Sir Charles would get a wife and Miss Pennington a husband and a home without rent.

"Perhaps the day of the picnic?" Sir Charles said softly with a pleased nod.

Blase and Val left shortly after that.

Val burst into laughter once they were around the bend. "Turned matchmaker, Blase?"

"Why not?" Blase grinned at him. "Now to dispose of Miss Dancy."

When they reached the Pennington cottage a few minutes later, they found Miss Pennington about to depart to fetch the mail from the village shop where it was brought every day. She turned about to invite the gentlemen inside.

"For I must tell you that Hyacinthe has been quite blue-deviled. Why, if her ankle does not heal more quickly I fear she will sink into a green melancholy!" Jane said with some concern.

"It is slow to mend, I gather. She seemed to enjoy her time by the pond," he recalled.

"I fear she overdid. Anyway, the rain showers put an end to that. It is difficult for her to reach the garden by herself. Although she does enjoy sitting there at dusk to watch for her hedgehog."

Jane opened the door and they entered into the parlor to find Miss Dancy seated on the sofa, her foot propped up on a stool, looking for all the world like an old lady with gout. Her greeting revealed mixed emotions—joy at a change of company and dismay that the callers should be Lord Norwood and Lord Latham.

"Good day, sirs. From the touch of sawdust I gather you have been over to the new village. And how do things progress?" she asked politely.

Blase detected a flash of fire in those green eyes that warned him to tread cautiously.

"Well, I do believe," he replied blandly.

"And when do you tear down the lovely old Tudor cottage across the green? I am surprised that Mr. Repton did not consider that in the vein of a rustic refinement for your distant prospect. It reminds one of an old painting." Her face wore a pensive expression, one almost of sadness.

"As a matter of fact we did discuss it,'" Blase admitted. He was totally unprepared for the sparkle of hope that lit her beautiful eyes. Indeed, her entire face came alive and she leaned toward him with eagerness.

"And what did you decide," she asked, quite as though his reply was the most important decision to be made.

Blase found himself in a quandary. Mr. Repton had definitely felt that the house offered a touch of the picturesque, but Blase had thought to tear the cottage down. Instead, he now found himself gazing into Miss Dancy's remarkable eyes and saying what he'd not intended to say.

"It shall be allowed to stand. At least until it may become dangerous."

"How utterly delightful!" she exclaimed as though Blase had done something wonderful. "Did you hear that, Jane? That lovely old place shall remain as a memory of the village that once was. I am so glad," she said with genuine warmth.

Blase smiled, then wondered if she perhaps recalled that kiss they had shared in the closet of the Tudor cottage. Could she possibly have a sentimental attachment for that reason? He did not flatter himself it might be so, merely reflecting that the cottage was an appealing sight. He decided to proceed with his picnic plan.

"We hoped to invite you both to a picnic on the next fine day," he said with a half-smile. "Miss Dancy could do with some fresh air and Sir Charles declared he would enjoy escorting Miss Pennington. I can promise some fine views," he coaxed with a cautious eye on Miss Dancy.

Jane Pennington blushed, while Hyacinthe Dancy resumed her pensive look. It was Jane who answered.

"We should be pleased to accept, my lord. I will bring some of Granny Beanbuck's famous cinnamon buns as a treat. Fosdick intended to go shopping one day soon. That would be ideal."

The gentlemen professed themselves delighted and left shortly after.

"Do you think?" Jane cried. "Could he actually? Oh, I suppose it is nothing more than Lord Norwood inviting him along and his being polite," she concluded, her face losing its animation.

"It is difficult to know what gentlemen think. When I see

Lord Norwood I cannot help but recall the little song about the sad maiden. You know, the maiden who begs the man not to deceive her, and how can he use a poor maiden so? The last verse is particularly apt." She sang it in her high, clear soprano, a rather shrewd gleam in her eyes:

> "Soon you will meet with another pretty maiden,
> Some pretty maiden, you'll court her for a while;
> Thus ever ranging, turning and changing,
> Always seeking for a girl that is new."

"Well, while I think that a nice little song, I do not believe it applies to Sir Charles. He has not been in the way of chasing young maidens. Only lately has he come into some money, and he attends to his estate rather than socializing."

"It quite relates to Lord Norwood, however," Hyacinthe said. "I wonder how long before . . ." Then at the sight of Jane's frightened face, she stopped. "Well, we can only believe we do the ladies of England a favor by keeping him occupied so that he cannot inflict his charm elsewhere."

"Perhaps the mail has arrived," Jane said hurriedly, moving toward the door. "It is usually here by now."

"Would you be so kind as to buy us some peppermints when you go?" Hyacinthe begged, hoping to cheer her cousin with a treat. "And take my reticule in case there is a letter for me. I vow the postage seems to increase every month. Fancy, I must pay at least twenty shillings for a letter from my aunt!"

"Of course I shall," Jane said, taking the reticule from the sofa and leaving at once.

Hyacinthe had not meant to upset her cousin and regretted her thoughtless words. However, she could not help but worry. Unless Sir Charles came to the rescue there was nothing left but to persuade Jane to permit Hyacinthe to assist her. For some time she contemplated ways in which she might accomplish this.

Hyacinthe heard the front door shut and turned to greet her cousin. Sitting quietly on the parlor sofa had taken its toll and she welcomed a diversion.

"The mail has come and there is a letter for you. It's two

sheets, so must have a great amount of news. It was franked by Lord Crompton. Do you know a Lord Crompton, my dear?" Jane said, sounding much impressed. She handed the letter to Hyacinthe, who promptly broke the seal and unfolded it.

She read the letter with a growing sense of dismay. While lovely news, it was not the sort she had hoped to receive.

"What is it, Hyacinthe? You look as though someone has died." Jane sank down upon the sofa, her face full of concern.

Hyacinthe refolded the letter, trying to think just how she would tell Jane the bad news.

"The letter is from Aunt Bel," she began.

"With whom you stayed before you came here," Jane prompted.

"Indeed. She is to marry the Earl of Crompton shortly."

"But that is wonderful. I am so happy for her. Why the long face?" Jane gave Hyacinthe a puzzled look.

"Because," Hyacinthe said with deep regret, "I had hoped we might go to stay with her until we could find another place for you to reside, some little cottage you would like. Cousin Chloe will go to live with Grandmama Dancy while Aunt Bel and her new husband go off on an extended wedding trip. We can scarcely invite ourselves to stay in a house where everyone is gone. Indeed, Aunt Bel will have had her things removed to her new home and Montmorcy Hall will sit empty until Cousin John returns from wherever he is traveling."

"That means you have nowhere to go, does it not?" Jane gently queried, her eyes soft with sympathy.

"Well . . ." Hyacinthe desperately sought an answer to their dilemma. "We might try staying with my brother. Only . . . as you know, Peter is fascinated with those horrid Egyptian mummies and that dreadful collection of peculiar objects our father brought back from Egypt. I truly do not think I can bear to live with a nasty old mummy."

Jane gave Hyacinthe a horrified yet fascinated look. "Do you mean he actually has them in the house? How frightful!"

"Then you agree with me on that? We must find another place to live. Surely there are other cottages to rent. I shall help you."

"I like it here," Jane said stubbornly. "It is quiet, charming, and I have friends." She no doubt thought of Sir Charles, as her face looked wistful and her eyes grew dreamy.

"If we were to put our money together, might we not afford something rather nice? With a lovely bit of garden for you. And my hedgehog," Hyacinthe added as an afterthought.

"I know of no such situation," Jane said, shaking her head thoughtfully. "I spoke with Lord Norwood's bailiff the other day. I did not wish to trouble you with what I learned, but it is not good. He told me the rents are to be higher, much higher, on the new cottages. It is more than I can manage. And I know of no other place to which I would care to go. Now that Cousin Chloe has moved in with Grandmama Dancy, that rather eliminates her as well. Not that I particularly wished to live with her," she added.

"Then what are we to do if you will not permit me to pay more of the rent, stubborn girl?" Hyacinthe said quietly. She clasped her hands in her lap, suddenly speculating on a life amid the decay of the Tudor house. "It is all his fault, you know. What a pity he wasn't stuck in that pig sty," she said grimly. "He'd have succumbed to something dire by now and we could remain here." She shared a look with Jane and sat wishing Blase Montague to the ends of the earth.

"I do so want to retain my independence. Oh, Hyacinthe, I am truly afraid," Jane said in a whisper.

"I am as well," Hyacinthe agreed, then handed her clean handkerchief to a quietly weeping Jane. Another line from the little song returned to her. "Oh, my innocent heart you've betrayed."

11

The following days brought significant activity and change to the old village of Worthington. Granny Beanbuck's cottage began to tumble as the workmen tore it down stone by stone. What wood could not be used again was trundled away for fuel. Windows and doors were carefully removed for future use elsewhere. Nothing would be wasted.

Jane stood in the garden, watching as the chimney toppled to the ground, a cloud of dust rising in its place.

"How I shall miss the aroma of cinnamon buns in the mornings," she murmured to Hyacinthe, who stood at her side also watching the destruction of the cottage.

"I fail to see why his elegant lordship could not have been satisfied with his view as it was," Hyacinthe complained to Jane and the hedgehog, who had been startled from its sleep by all the racket and now poked a drowsy head from under a leaf.

"What did I hear you call him yesterday?" Jane said, beginning to stroll to the house.

"The garden rake," Hyacinthe snapped. "All of London society will be vastly amused to see how rustic he has become. The premier rake of the Town, reduced to tree plantings and fertilizer. I vow they will think he has gone to seed!" She chuckled when Jane groaned at her joke.

"But you do not go to town, so how will they know?" Jane said, holding the door open for her cousin to enter the cottage.

In the house all was neat and smelled faintly of lavender and carnations, a distinct contrast to the uproar and musty dust next door. Hyacinthe gave a look about her, then turned to Jane.

"We could forget about those nasty mummies and fling ourselves upon my brother in the city. Perhaps he will store them elsewhere if I beg him prettily. Otherwise, we will have to find another cottage at a rent you can afford . . . unless you will swallow that silly pride of yours and allow me to help you. Can you not see that *if* you will let me pay most of the rent, you could have one of those dratted new cottages? I am certain Sir Charles would wish you to be close by," Hyacinthe concluded, hoping this might be a persuasive finish to her argument.

Jane gave her cousin a distressed look, "I cannot diminish your inheritance in such a manner. You may have need of it." Then she confided, "I fear that Sir Charles is not as interested in me as you seem to think. He has never sought my company for any purpose other than casual conversation. I doubt the man knows how to flirt."

"Think what a blessing that will be, then," Hyacinthe crowed. "How many women would love to have a husband who did not persist in flirting with another?"

"Who said anything about a husband!" Jane cried, looking most alarmed.

"Well, any woman of sense being single and in need of a home must necessarily look about her to see if there is an unattached and eligible gentleman in the neighborhood. And Sir Charles is all of those, you must admit."

"True," Jane agreed. She paced about the room, wringing her hands as she went. "But I could never be forward or try to trap him, as I know some women do to catch a husband. That is why I failed in my Season . . . I could not flirt with that in mind."

"I know what you mean," Hyacinthe replied quietly. "I fled London for several reasons, one of which was that I could not see myself wed to any of those beaux who clustered about me."

"And the one who attracted you?" Jane said with a gleam in her gray eyes.

Hyacinthe turned away from her cousin to study something out of the window. Rather than answer this probing question, she looked at the Tudor house. Mr. Wayland could be seen wending his way—empty-handed—in the direction of the new village.

"Did you not say that Mrs. Peachey wished to consult with you about a particular design for a cap? Why do you not bring it over to her now?" Hyacinthe said softly.

"Of course," Jane said, her bewilderment at this complete change of topic quite clear in her voice.

"And I will do a bit of looking about the village, since my ankle is so improved," Hyacinthe said in the mildest of tones.

Jane gave her a sharp look, but said nothing regarding her cousin's overly innocent expression.

They left together. Hyacinthe tucked her cousin's arm in hers and chattered about the ducks and whether or not they would peaceably make the move to the new village. Jane concluded that it would take a bit of coaxing to bring them all, including the swans, to a new home.

Just when they drew even with the Tudor cottage, Hyacinthe paused. "Think about my offer—*do*. Unless you can bring Sir Charles up to scratch, you must decide upon some path for your future."

"I promise, although I meant what I said about your inheritance. But what a horrid expression, 'up to scratch.' You make him sound like a chicken." Jane made a face that quite expressed her feelings.

"Well?" Hyacinthe chuckled at Jane's grimace, then sobered. "I intend to do a bit of hunting about. Should Mrs. Peachey wonder, tell her I am investigating the old garden. She will never question that, I believe."

"Since when have you become enamored of old gardens—just in case she should ask?"

"Ever since I saw Mr. Wayland leave this house not long ago. He carried nothing in his hands, which I think rather curious. And just what was he doing here when Lord Norwood said that this house is not to be torn down?"

"Oh, do be careful," Jane whispered. She searched the area about them with a casual turn of her head, then set off toward Mrs. Peachey's cottage with a light step.

Hyacinthe clutched her shawl about her more tightly, then entered the tangled web of a garden with hesitant footsteps.

Someone had made an effort to clear away the worst of the weeds. The grass, such as it was after many years of neglect, had been scythed.

She wore a small, neat bonnet tied securely under her chin. Fortunately her gown was of plain stuff, not likely to suffer from dust and cobwebs. Although she devoutly hoped the spiders had not been busy since she was last here.

The rear door again stood slightly ajar. Hyacinthe slipped inside with practiced ease, then began her inspection of the interior.

Nothing in the kitchen area appeared to have been disturbed. The dust covered all surfaces in an even layer and no trace of footprints could be seen other than on the path that had been made by herself and Lord Norwood and Lord Latham when they searched. She must not forget that Mr. Wayland had also roamed the premises. Which were the prints he had left today? she wondered.

In the paneled parlor, she saw nothing untoward. Sadly shredded draperies hung at the windows but it mattered little as the panes of glass were so dingy that it was difficult to see anything anyway.

Hyacinthe grew thoughtful while slowly plodding up the stairs. If Wayland had left no trace of his visit on the lower floor, whatever he had been doing here must be found upstairs. She hurried on to the first of the rooms.

Considerably later and covered with a film of dust and cobwebs—the spiders seemed to have been busier than ever before—she entered the largest bedroom. The tattered bed hangings swayed in a draft of air.

Checking about her, she noted that one window was cracked open a trifle. She walked over to investigate the area, but found nothing. Then she turned to face the dressing room as she called it. She had not returned to it since that day of the momentous kiss.

Taking a deep breath, she walked across the room, then opened the door. Nothing appeared to have changed. She began a more minute inspection, going over panels, studying the floor. She thought Mr. Wayland had been in here, but it was difficult to tell. The little hiding place didn't have anything in it that had not been here before.

That did not mean that he could not have concealed his loot elsewhere, however. Hyacinthe felt a strong urge to find those jewels. She wondered if Lord Norwood suspected her of keeping them, giving him only the one piece. Naturally she would never do such a thing, but he didn't know that. He might have seen her around London, but that hardly constituted a knowledge of her character. She did not give him high marks for his powers of observation.

Except, she noted, he must pay attention to race horses to have won such enormous sums in betting on the races.

She listened a moment to the creaking of the house. A gentle wind tore at the trees that hovered over it, causing branches to brush against the roof and walls. No other sounds reached her ears. Had she perhaps hoped that someone would come? Certainly not Lord Norwood, she scolded herself.

Feeling frustrated at her inability to discover where Mr. Wayland had concealed his stolen goods, she walked to the window, wiping a small place on the pane with her sleeve. From here she glimpsed the village store. What on earth was going on over there? Then she realized that the shop owner must be in the process of removing to the new village. The new shop was barely ready to accept the goods transferred, yet away they went. Even as she watched, another load of goods was carried from the shop to be placed on the dray, which was ready to depart. The lad in charge of the transfer set off toward the new village, plodding along the track with care.

Jane would feel more isolated than ever. One of these weeks Mrs. Peachey and Widow Smith would go, and then Jane and Hyacinthe would be the last people left. At least Lord Norwood had promised to leave Jane's cottage until last. Although that wasn't of great help.

Drat it all, why could she not have persuaded Lord Norwood to abandon his stupid scheme? Giving up on her hunt—only for the day, mind you—she marched down the stairs and across the green until she was again inside Jane's modest home.

Fosdick was clearly horrified at her appearance. She tut-tutted and fussed over her charge like a mother hen. Hyacinthe submitted to a change of clothes after a rather thorough washing. Mostly her hands and face were in need of repair; the gown merely needed scrubbing in soapy water.

Once restored and garbed in a charming moss-green mull trimmed with clusters of ivory ribands and pale pink satin roses, she hurried from the house, Fosdick trailing her. At the Cock and Bull she found her coachman and groom. They chatted quietly while working on the coach leathers.

"How soon can we be ready to depart? I wish to go on an errand." She gave Tom Coachman an expectant look.

The men allowed as they could have the coach ready in a trice, which Hyacinthe interpreted as about thirty minutes at best.

Strolling away, she watched more of the contents of the shop being hauled to a dray.

"She ought to have offered a few things at a special price so she would not have had so much to move," Hyacinthe observed to her maid.

"Well," Fosdick said sagely, "as to that, she will need the same items at the new shop."

As soon as the coach was ready, Hyacinthe climbed inside with Fosdick following, and they set off along the road that led to the Hall.

"I do not approve of this gamboling about, young lady," the proper abigail said with a sniff.

"You do not have to approve, dear Fosdick. Just manage to attend me." Hyacinthe folded her hands meekly in her lap while she considered precisely what she would say to his lordship when she confronted him. It was far too late to stop the destruction of the village. What could she best hope to accomplish with this visit?

She firmly rejected the notion that she might wish to see the dratted man. While he was as handsome as could be, he was totally ineligible. What woman wanted a husband who preferred fertilizer and planting to her! That he might not always be absorbed with altering this view didn't occur to her.

Barmore hurried down the front steps to greet her, escorting her into the house with flattering promptness. Fosdick quietly trailed behind, once inside seeking a chair in the vast entry hall.

"I failed to send word that I wish to see Lord Norwood. Dare I hope that he is in this afternoon?" Hyacinthe asked with a demure smile.

"As a matter of fact, I believe he just finished his nuncheon. Allow me to inform him of your arrival, Miss Dancy." He paused, then added, "May I also hope that your injury is entirely healed?"

"Indeed, Barmore," Hyacinthe said, flashing the famous Dancy smile at the butler, "I feel quite the thing, I assure you. How kind of you to ask."

Looking gratified at this fulsome reply, the butler disappeared from the drawing room, leaving Hyacinthe to amuse herself until Lord Norwood should deign to appear.

She did not have long to wait. That peculiar sensation that had assailed her heart before startled her again when she turned from the window to see him enter the room.

"Miss Dancy," he said while crossing to join her. "To what do I owe this pleasure?"

"I fear my wits have gone begging, sir," she admitted, suddenly thinking she was a silly peagoose to come here. "It is far too late to halt the destruction of the village, much as I wish I could. Jane is terribly upset and that distresses me. I cannot persuade her to allow me to help her with the rent. Perhaps you would allow me to pay part of her rent? She has such impossible pride."

"Yet you admire her, for I can hear it in your voice." He thought for a minute, then offered his arm. "Come with me. I would have you look at my view again, for it is constantly changing."

Hyacinthe reluctantly permitted him to take her arm and usher her out to the terrace. The geraniums still bloomed in spite of the chill that now hung over the countryside at night. Their spice scented the air when she broke off a leaf to crush in her hand.

"Well, sir?" she said, not encouraging him in the least.

"The trees must grow some, but surely you can use a bit of

imagination to see how it will be in the future," he said with enthusiasm, pointing off toward the village.

Young saplings marched up the hillsides; a great deal of earth had been moved since she was last here, creating a different contour. And she was forced to admit that it truly looked lovely. What vision to be able to see that the change would be so charming.

"I believe I can envision some of what it will be," she allowed. "I shall miss the old village."

"The church steeple and the roof of that Tudor cottage you admire so greatly still stand," he reminded her.

"And lovely they are, too." Recalling what she had seen that morning, she turned to face Lord Norwood. "Have you discovered anything more regarding the missing jewels? The reason I ask is that I saw Mr. Wayland coming from the Tudor house shortly after Granny Beanbuck's old cottage was razed. He walked rapidly toward the new village, not stopping to check on the dismantling. He carried nothing in his hands, and since the house is not to be torn down, why was he there? I thought it most curious."

"I'll wager you went over to investigate."

Hyacinthe dropped her lashes in confusion at the gleam she observed creep into his eyes. Did he recall what had happened when they had been at the old cottage? Surely a rake such as he would likely forget a bit of dalliance. It was only a brief kiss, after all. But, her heart reminded her, it had affected her most strongly.

"I did," she managed to reply. "I found no evidence he had hidden something there. However, it would be logical if you think about it. He may believe we have thoroughly investigated the place, so feels safe to return his loot there."

"Interesting theory. I had best bring Val along and do some more investigation." He turned back to his new gardens. "But come with me for the moment. I wish to show you my new planting of roses. Come next June, they will perfume the air with their fragrance. I also discovered a new variety that blooms in July, so to extend their season."

"Perhaps one day we shall have roses that bloom until frost," she said, willingly going across the terrace and down

the steps into an area neatly planted with a clever layout of
rose bushes. There were a great many plants. The ground
around them was covered with a mixture of straw and manure,
judging from the smell. She wrinkled her nose in distaste, but
said nothing. After all, this sort of smell one encountered
every day while on the road or in town.

"And over here," he continued, while tugging her along
with him, "I intend to have an Elizabethan knot garden. Val
and I found some old plans in the muniment room with a list
of plants and their arrangements. I think you might admire it
very much."

Puzzled why he might care what she thought of his new gardens, Hyacinthe admitted that this particular one appealed to
her. She said as much. "Perhaps it is the charm of the old cottage, but I like the idea of an old-fashioned garden. What a
pity you could not restore the garden around the Tudor cottage. Did your ancestor also include plans for that, or did his
plans extend only to the occupant?" Her smile was mischievous, but she was still relieved when he grinned back at her.

"Do you recall she is recorded as a pretty redhead?" His
grin widened when he saw her discomfiture.

"Perhaps I ought to restore the place, then," she said. "I
could take up residence with your permission and pity."

"I cannot see that you would need my pity, Miss Dancy," he
teased. "I might be able to offer something else, however."

She turned away from him, feeling that the conversation
had taken a perilous turn.

"The weather has improved and Val insists that tomorrow
will be better. No rain, he declares. Could we plan our picnic?"
He guided her along various paths which now held an occasional yellow chrysanthemum or purple China aster. A few
other fall-blooming flowers were clustered in a bed near the
steps.

She paused at the bottom of the steps to look about her.
"That would be lovely, although I will confess that I doubt
you could find views that might rival these gardens. *You* may
have the distant perspective. *I* prefer the detail and scent
around me."

"We shall see," he promised, then returned her to the entry
hall where Fosdick awaited.

The abigail wore a disapproving frown and gave Lord Norwood a frosty glare.

On the way back to Jane's cottage, Hyacinthe considered her call to Lord Norwood. It had availed her nothing, but it had planted an idea in her head.

"Fosdick, do you think that the Tudor cottage is beyond hope?"

"Not in the least, miss. My mother lives in a house of an age with it and goes along right well." The maid gave her mistress a shrewd look, then added, "I fancy were it to receive a good cleaning it would improve considerably."

"Have you been there?"

"No, but I saw the gown you wore—nothing but dust and cobwebs on it. There must be several girls in the village who would like a bit of pocket money what with moving to a new house and all."

"Are you actually encouraging me to clean a house that does not belong to me?" Hyacinthe gave Fosdick a disbelieving look.

"Aye. What better way to draw rats from a hole?" the maid replied with an innocent air.

"Hm, I shall think about it," Hyacinthe murmured in return. She resolved to seek out all the willing hands she could find. The Widow Smith's girl would be the first to approach.

Across the gentle hills Val chided his host. "You mean you had the chit here and you did not let me know? I wondered why you disappeared so hastily after our meal, not to return for ages."

"You are ever the gallant with ladies. I was only protecting Miss Dancy from your charms." Blase gave his friend a teasing glance, then strolled along the hall in the direction of the muniment room.

"What? Are we to bury ourselves on such a perfect day?" Val cried in dismay.

"I wish to look over that box once again to see if perchance there could be a paper or two I missed the first time. I would like to know more of the history behind that Tudor cottage. By the by, Miss Dancy informed me that Wayland had been snooping around there this morning. She didn't see the chap arrive, but he left there conspicuously empty-handed."

"You think he may have returned to the scene of the crime, so to speak, to replace the jewels in what he considers a safe hiding place?" Val said, excitement coloring his voice, supplanting his usual air of ennui.

"It could be. Miss Dancy said something about cleaning up the garden, and I believe I'll see that it is done. Shame to have the place go to ruin."

"When it will remain empty? Why bother?"

Blase felt like a fool to reveal that he did so because Miss Dancy wished it done. Rather, he gruffly replied, "Sound management practice. I believe it would be possible to find someone who prefers the country to the village."

Val didn't refute his remark, but he gave his friend a very curious look. Blase ignored it.

They spent an hour or so in the muniment room, then took the papers Blase unearthed to the library. Here he relaxed in his favorite chair while studying them.

"Do they help?" Val inquired. He had established himself in a comfortable chair by the window where he could see the distant hills and still view the cozy fire burning in the grate.

"I found the floor plans of the cottage. It seems my esteemed ancestor had a clever passage built so he might slip down the hidden stairway in the event that someone was coming up the main steps."

"You mean in case his wife sent someone looking for him? I say, that seems unlikely."

"Why else would he put in such a thing?" Blase studied the plans, which included a scheme for a garden. The writing was faded and difficult to read. "Come over here to see if you can decipher this print. Time has not improved it."

They huddled over the old set of plans until between them they felt they had figured out the original.

Blase gave his friend a satisfied look. "I believe I should like to duplicate the original garden. It would be a curiosity."

"By all means. I think it would add to your picturesque view." Val said this with no change of expression to indicate he was other than his usual cynical self.

Equipped with dustcloth and broom in hand, Hyacinthe daringly marched over to the Tudor cottage. Behind her several of the village women straggled along similarly equipped. All were dressed for the purpose of attacking the dusty house.

Hyacinthe acted the general and deployed her troops most efficiently. In short order, the tattered draperies went out to the rubbish heap and the windows began to sparkle, pane by pane. Following the generous application of lemon-scented beeswax on the paneled walls and other surfaces, the spice of sweet-smelling rushes and herbs strewn across the freshly scoured floors, and fresh air sailing through the rooms, the house soon took on the appearance of a habitable cottage.

Hours later Hyacinthe looked about her with great pleasure. Jane had joined her at midpoint and added her efforts.

"I am a dab hand with polishing, if I do say so," she said with modest pride.

"Everyone has been marvelous," Hyacinthe said. She sought out her reticule and promptly paid each woman a generous amount for her work. Not only had they come when asked, they must have left their own work undone. Hyacinthe doubly appreciated that.

Once alone, she and Jane sank down on the bottom steps of the staircase, looking about with satisfaction.

"Did you realize it would be so lovely? Just look at that floor. The parquet pattern must be as beautiful as the day it was put down."

Hyacinthe glanced at Jane, then took a deep breath before imparting her information. "I mentioned the house to Lord Norwood and said it was a pity that it go to ruin. I also said we might move in here, since he does not plan to tear it down. It is larger than your cottage and certainly more attractive, what with the patterned windows and all the other little touches given it. It must have been built with love," she said softly.

"You do recall the story about it, that his lordship's ancestor housed his doxy here."

"Are there any ghosts?" Hyacinthe inquired idly.

"None I know about, but one never knows," Jane answered gloomily. "I shouldn't feel comfortable thinking that first redhead was lingering about here."

"We had best clean up, then have our supper. I, for one, am famished," Hyacinthe declared as she rose and walked to the rear door. There she paused, looking about the spotless kitchen with a tired smile. "What a shame that girl of long ago couldn't see this place now."

"It wants only furniture, I believe," Jane agreed. Then she gasped and blushed. "I forgot to tell you in all the general commotion. Sir Charles met me after I left Mrs. Peachey. He invited me for a little drive to the new village, then insisted he take us up to the picnic tomorrow. He believes the weather will be fine, but suggested I bring an umbrella anyway. Oh, Hyacinthe, he was so *caring*." Jane gave her cousin a pleased smile, then slipped past her and hurried toward her cottage.

Hyacinthe looked about her again, thinking of the fine wood, utterly worm-free, used for the bed upstairs. Well, she thought with a philosophical shrug of her shoulders, she could always move over here. If Jane married Sir Charles, she would be able to spare a few things. And Hyacinthe could purchase the rest in Woodstock. All she had to do was convince her garden rake that it would be a good idea.

Firmly closing the door behind her, she also considered the other reason she'd had the house cleaned. No sign of the jewels had turned up. Yet she felt they had to be here. Her instincts told her they were. Her instincts were never wrong. In which case, she reflected as she entered Jane's cottage, she had best prepare for a wedding between Sir Charles and Jane and hope that Lord Norwood would not object to a tenant in the Tudor cottage. He hadn't said no.

It was some hours later when she awoke for no reason at all. She remained perfectly still, listening. Nothing.

She slid from beneath her covers, grabbed her soft velvet robe, donning it while crossing to the window.

Across the way she could see small rays of light coming from the Tudor cottage! They wavered, most likely because of branches that were in the way. But there was no doubt in her mind; someone was in that house. *Her* house to be. The one she had cleaned up so she might move there.

She stuffed her feet into her morocco slippers and skimmed down the stairs as quietly as she could.

Without considering the impropriety of her actions, she slid back the bolt on the front door, than began to cross the green. A glance at the upstairs windows revealed the lights up there. Was it Wayland? She picked up a stout limb, just the right size for knocking a man over the head, and continued on her way.

12

"What do you make of all this?" Val said while looking about the spotless bedroom. A light aroma of beeswax and lavender scented the air. No dust motes or tattered draperies remained. The carved oak bed frame—what remained of the mattress had been consigned to the rubbish heap—glowed with the patina of age and diligent rubbing.

"A band of pixies has descended upon this place since we were last here," Blase replied with amusement. He scratched his head in bewilderment. "I wonder why? I vow the fussiest housekeeper could not find fault with the house. Who could possibly wish to turn this old place into a habitable cottage? What happened to the tales of ghosts or whatever prevented others from renting it over the years?"

"Do you suppose whoever cleaned this house also searched for the jewels?" Val strode to the dressing closet to fling open the door and peer inside. "Why did we think it necessary to come here at night?" he complained. He motioned for Blase to bring both lanterns into the room.

Blase followed, standing bemused when he surveyed the efforts of his particular pixie. Not only did the room shine with polish, the windows sparkle, and the floor gleam sufficiently for it to serve as a looking glass, but the folding screen had been joined by a pretty little pine chair and a small table—both equally well-polished.

Blase set one of the lanterns on the table, then began examining the paneled walls. "I have the feeling that whoever did this intends to move in here," he said over his shoulder. "Perhaps after the others have moved to the new village he will settle in here to set up housekeeping with no one the wiser."

He quite forgot he had tacitly given Hyacinthe Dancy permission to live here.

"You would see the fires in his chimney, however," Val reminded him.

"Perhaps. It could be that he is counting on my going off to a Christmas party elsewhere, then haring off to London following that." Blase turned to face his friend, a speculative look on his face. "You also think Wayland has something to do with this?"

"He would appear the logical one," Val agreed.

"Well, we will have to upset his plans. Let's comb every inch of this room, for we both sense the gems must be here. How fortunate I have the original plans and my pixie removed the dust. Now to find the concealed catch that leads to the secret stairs."

He showed the plan to Val again, and they set to work. The house was chilly, the work frustrating, but both men were most determined to succeed.

Hyacinthe stared at the cottage, watching the light move from room to room. With only starlight and a half moon to guide her, she had stumbled all the way across the green. The stout limb had helped her keep from falling. She hoped it would serve her as well when she hit the prowler over the head with it.

Taking a firm hold of the tree limb and her courage, she advanced upon the house, sneaking around to the rear and the door that opened to her touch. Although after today she would be able to enter through the front, for she had found the key and oiled the lock and hinges.

She glided across the kitchen floor, thankful she need not worry about bumping into furniture. With the floor plan well imprinted on her memory, she went mostly by touch and recollection. Once she found the stairs, she began a cautious assent, one step at a time.

Blase paused in his examination of the spot he felt most likely to have the secret catch. Raising his head, he listened, then shushed Val.

"I think I hear something."

"A pixie?" Val teased.

Blase tossed him an annoyed look, then tiptoed from the dressing closet out to the bedroom. With only the light that escaped from the closet, this room was dimly lit. He could see well enough, certainly sufficiently to see the intruder. Looking around, he could discover nothing to hand to use as a weapon. He crept up to the door, standing to one side, waiting.

Hyacinthe rounded the top of the stairs, hoping that the intruder had not heard that squeaky step. Why hadn't she oiled *that* dratted thing? With painstaking care she edged her way along the hall until she reached the main bedroom. Here she paused, listening. She heard nothing, but she could perceive a faint light coming from the small dressing closet. Her nerves tightened and her heart pounded faster. In moments she would face this man.

Raising her trusty stout limb over her head, she nudged the door open wider with one foot, then slowly entered the room. From the corner of her eye she sensed a figure to her side.

Spinning about, she crashed the limb down upon the hapless intruder's head with all her might—which admittedly wasn't great. The man staggered, then fell back against the wall, sliding down to rest on the floor with a satisfactory thump.

Then Hyacinthe realized who it was!

She sank to the floor in horror at what she had done. While it might be forward to be so bold, her concern outweighed any propriety. She drew his head upon her lap and bent over him. Stretching out a hesitant hand, she gently probed Lord Norwood's head, seeking a wound. "Oh, I am dreadfully sorry, my lord," she said softly, wondering if he would be all right.

"Blase! What the . . . ?" Val dashed around the corner with a lantern in hand, then abruptly halted before succumbing to laughter.

Blase gazed up at his nemesis with a resigned look, then winced as her hand touched the injury to his head. The only tolerable part of this all was being cuddled in her lap.

"I believe your pixie has returned to the scene," Val said, trying to control his chuckles.

"Miss Dancy, may I ask what brings you here in the middle of the night?" Blase said with what he thought was praiseworthy restraint. He nudged the tree limb away with his foot, waiting for her reply and reluctant to move.

"I saw lights. Since this house is unoccupied, I grew worried. It would never do for some vagrant to set fire to a perfectly habitable cottage when I had just finished having it cleaned." She drew herself up, a righteous tilt to her chin and an indignant fire gleaming in her eyes. Had she not presented an amusing picture in her lace-edged nightcap and green velvet robe, she would have passed for a dragon.

Blase unwillingly rose to his feet, opened one of the windows to toss out the branch, then turned to face her again. "Why did you clean the house? Not that it doesn't look splendid, but it *is* unoccupied, as you just pointed out."

She clasped her hands together and stared down at the floor. "I thought it a shame that this house should be neglected. Jane suggested that the local women would welcome a bit of money—what with moving into new houses and all—so I hired as many as I could to help. And besides . . . you said I might live here." She gave him an accusing glare.

"I see." Blase glanced at Val, then winced, for his head hurt like the very devil when he moved.

"So you had a sort of protective interest in the house?" he said mildly. "And when you saw a light over here you felt it necessary to investigate—even if it was the middle of the night?"

"Indeed," she replied eagerly. "The very thing. How clever of you to guess." Then she appeared to recall her improper dress and began to back toward the open door.

"You are to leave us now? Just when we are about to open the secret panel?" He had no idea what possessed him to reveal their intent. Why would he want this exasperating and dangerous female around?

She stopped her retreat. "Secret panel? There is a concealed passage in this house? How exciting!" She took several steps toward him. "May I see? Then I promise I shall vanish from sight."

"I told you she was a pixie," Val muttered.

Blase gave him a look that quite silenced him. Motioning them to follow, Blase returned to the other room, dutifully trailed by Val and Miss Dancy.

She quickly espied the plans and eagerly scanned the layout before joining him where he had been puzzling over the secret entry.

Running a delicate hand over the wood, she paused at a knot—or what appeared to be a knot. "How odd," she murmured. With a twist of her hand, she pressed her thumb against the knot and the panel slowly creaked open.

A rush of stale, dust-laden air greeted them. Cobwebs draped the walls and ceiling of the staircase, festooning it with ghostly shadows when the lantern was brought to play on it.

"I say," Val murmured.

"Quite," Blase replied.

"Well," Miss Dancy said in a bracing voice, "do you intend to stand there all night? I would like to know where this goes." With that observation she took one of the lanterns and began to march—most carefully, mind you—down the steps.

Blase grabbed the other lantern and with Val directly behind him hurriedly followed the intrepid Miss Dancy.

The steps made a sharp turn, then continued until they reached the bottom and a door. Miss Dancy depressed a dull brass lever and the door swung open, squeaking its protest at being disturbed after all these years.

Miss Dancy stepped forward and looked around her. Blase followed. Val paused on the threshold, assessing what they all saw.

"The rubbish heap!" Miss Dancy exclaimed.

"I see where the old mattress went," Blase observed.

"And the mice that had made it their home. This house needs a cat," she snapped.

"I'll be happy to volunteer Tom," he offered in what he considered a magnanimous gesture.

"That will not be necessary," she whispered back as though suddenly mindful that voices could carry in this little village in the silence of the night. "Granny Beanbuck has a spare cat she will be pleased to offer. A sister to Tom if I make no mistake."

Blase stepped forward, although he didn't know quite what

he could say to her. He was furious, intrigued, ached like the devil, and wondered what she was *really* up to. To top it off, he felt a nearly uncontrollable urge to gather the delicious Miss Dancy into his arms and kiss her until she was as senseless as she had intended him to be after that knock on the head.

"Good night," she said softly. "I am truly sorry about your head. Is the picnic still to be?"

"What? Of course," he muttered, trying to gather his wits about him.

Feeling oddly dejected, Hyacinthe hurried off into the darkness, stumbling here and there. She had not taken a lantern and now wished she had. But someone might have seen her and that would never do, gossip being what it was.

She hurriedly slipped back into Jane's cottage, drew the bolt into place, then walked up the stairs as quietly as a mouse.

From her window she glimpsed the light from the lanterns as it flickered about the yard. Then it disappeared into the house and she guessed that the two men had returned to the upper floor. In minutes the light glimmered from the bedroom and she knew she'd been right.

She waited, watching. After a bit the light disappeared. Figuring that they must have gone back to the Hall, Hyacinthe made her way to her bed, curling up under the covers with a great deal on her mind.

She drifted off to sleep while trying to figure out how to persuade Lord Norwood that she would be the ideal tenant for the Tudor house even after bashing him in the head with a stout limb.

In the morning Blase met his guest at the breakfast table with a yawn and a wince.

"Head still hurt?" Val inquired, placing his coffee cup down on its saucer with a clink.

Blase gingerly rubbed the offending part of his head. "You might say that. For such a slip of a girl, Miss Dancy is most capable."

"I wonder if that is part of the curriculum at Miss Twickenden's School for Young Ladies of the Gentry, or wherever Miss Dancy went," Val mused. "It could be that we have touched upon a secret training—that of preparing girls to defend themselves against all comers."

"I rather believe it's instinctive—at least with her." Blase filled a plate with food, then joined his friend at the table.

"She is a walking disaster, isn't she?" Val commented while selecting another slice of cold, dry toast. "I do not know why your cook cannot bake rolls like Granny Beanbuck's. Would Cook's feelings be irreparably damaged if we sent off for some? They were very good," he concluded wistfully.

"Send for some if you like. Doubtless the groom would be more than willing to fetch them—especially if he could sample one or two."

"I shall remember that for the morrow," Val said. "So . . . weather permitting, you are to picnic today while I search her cottage. Are you prepared? With Miss Dancy along you had best wear something old and ready for the rubbish heap. And certainly ascertain that you have a supply of liniment and bandages about the house before we leave."

"I do not know why I tolerate that young woman," Blase grumbled between bites of egg.

"Usually one does that sort of thing when one is more than fond of said young woman," Val said obliquely.

Blase gave Val a sharp look but offered nothing in rebuttal. Indeed, words failed him. How *did* he view the delicious Miss Dancy? What a fetching little thing she had been last night in that lace-trimmed muslin cap and soft velvet robe. Those lovely eyes had flashed green fire at him, and she had snuggled him against her in a delightful manner.

"I wonder what she's up to," he murmured.

"Wants something, you may be certain," Val said dryly. "They all do. There isn't a female alive who does not wish for more than she has."

"Ah," Blase countered, well acquainted with Val's jaundiced view of the female portion of the population, "but what does she wish?"

"I'll wager she will let you know soon enough." Val finished his coffee, then pushed his chair away from the table.

"You don't suppose . . ." Blase said slowly. "No, it could never be that. It would be highly improper."

"What? Do tell," Val urged. He propped himself against the wall by the window, tilting his head while awaiting Blase's reply.

"With Miss Pennington smelling April and May around Sir Charles, do you suppose Miss Dancy actually intends to live there? I could not credit what she said last night. She had mentioned something about not liking to live with her brother or her grandmother. She previously lived with her aunt. I read that *she* recently married and is off traveling with her new husband, the Earl of Crompton. It would seem that Miss Dancy has no home to call her own." He exchanged looks with Val.

"And she would rather live in a haunted old Tudor cottage than rent one of your new houses," Val concluded with a nod.

Blase also rose from the table, crossing to the window to join his friend. "I shall take great interest in her request. For I believe you are correct—she has something up her sleeve besides her arm."

Hyacinthe splashed some of her precious carnation scent on her bosom and neck, then dabbed a bit on her wrists. It would never do for a lady to reek of scent, but she did adore the perfume.

"Are you nearly ready, love?" Jane asked from the doorway. She looked charming in a soft golden-yellow wool gown trimmed with gray rosettes. Her brown hair peeped from beneath her chip bonnet decorated with tiny yellow roses and knots of gray riband.

Accepting her coquelicot Poland mantle from Fosdick, Hyacinthe wrapped it over a matching gown, a particular favorite of hers. Fastening the mantle at her shoulder with an antique brooch, she turned to face her cousin. "Well? Will I do?" She touched the brim of her most cherished bonnet, one trimmed with bunches of red cherries.

"Fetching," Jane declared with admiration. "That shade of poppy red is most becoming on you, in spite of your red hair. Hurry, Sir Charles is to come at any moment."

"And you do not wish to keep him waiting?" Hyacinthe

chuckled, then followed Jane downstairs after thanking Fosdick for her excellent efforts and wishing her a lovely day in town.

Sir Charles drew up before the cottage promptly, his smile of greeting flattering Jane.

Hyacinthe took a good look at the pair and decided she would not have to worry about Jane. Rather, she had best find a place for herself.

It was not time for her to depart as yet, however. Jane would need bolstering until the wedding, for wedding there would be even if those two were not aware of it yet.

The picnic was to be held not far from the home farm of Lord Norwood's estate, in a pleasant glade through which flowed the same stream that made up the village pond.

When they arrived at the scene Hyacinthe found herself hard put not to smile at her cousin and Sir Charles. They had said little but exchanged discreet smiles and looks all the way.

With a sigh, Hyacinthe turned to greet Lord Norwood, then looked about for his friend.

"Val detests things like picnics. He decided to remain at the Hall. I suspect he may go riding later. Something to do with Granny Beanbuck's cinnamon buns, I believe."

"Jane brought some with us, for she had noticed he seemed very fond of them. What a pity."

"I doubt they will remain uneaten." Leading her along the stream, he softly inquired, "You slept well last night after all the excitement?"

"Once I saw the light had gone, I popped into bed and slept like a top until morning. And you? Your poor head. It must ache something fierce this morning. May I repeat how sorry I am?"

"Oddly enough, I believe you."

That exchange appeared to permit both of them to relax. Hyacinthe enjoyed his company for once. He seemed to take pleasure in hers as well.

The repast that the cook at the Hall had prepared was likely enough to feed a small army, but Hyacinthe and Lord Norwood attempted to do justice to it.

Jane and Sir Charles appeared lost to most everything. At

last he murmured some nonsense about showing her the late-blooming flowers he had observed along the stream, and the two strolled off in that direction.

"Smelling April and May," Lord Norwood said quietly.

"Do you think he will offer for her?" Hyacinthe dared to ask.

"Shouldn't surprise me in the least. The man needs a wife to help him on his estate. Fortunate he inherited instead of his elder brother. That character was a fool of the worst sort. He was killed while traveling, which enabled a good man to receive what he ought."

"With those acres restored and the manor house once again in his possession he will have a proper farm?" Hyacinthe inquired, figuring someone ought to ask on behalf of Jane.

"Indeed." Lord Norwood looked amused. "Sir Charles came over this past week to settle the matter. The house has returned to his family, where it should have been these many years."

"Gaming can bring terrible losses. Yet you do well at the racetrack, or so I have heard. Has no one ever wondered at your amazing luck?" she had the temerity to ask.

"If they have, it has not reached my ears. I may be a rake, Miss Dancy, but I have the reputation for being an honest rake." He gave her a look that made her wish to disappear.

Hyacinthe could feel her cheeks turn pink. Embarrassed, she sought for something to say in reply and couldn't think of a thing except to apologize. "I did not mean to cast aspersions, sir."

"I expect you did not. People are naturally curious. And I confess I have an uncanny bit of luck at the racetrack. I avoid cards, however, for my luck does not extend to them."

"How interesting," she said politely, knowing she ought not inquire further. "Do you suppose we might also take a stroll? That chicken was delicious, but I think I ate more than my share."

"Ah, yes. With Miss Pennington and Sir Charles scarcely touching their food, someone had to eat," he said approvingly. He rose to his feet, then extended a hand to assist her.

The scenery proved exceedingly lovely. Golds and yellows splashed the trees with autumn color. An occasional patch of russet peeped through the remaining greens and browns on the hillsides. The stream flowed quietly over pebbles and past the rushes, in no particular hurry to reach its goal. Hyacinthe felt the same.

She was glad they had chosen to walk in the opposite direction from the others. She'd not wish to interrupt something promising.

"You look well in that color, most surprisingly," he suddenly offered.

"I know, it is curious given my red hair. I believe I explained before how I feel regarding the color. What is that up ahead? A garden in the country?"

"Wildflowers, I expect. They seem to do remarkably well along here."

"But they look like a garden! Oh, do say I may have a little bouquet. Not all of them, for I'd leave seed, but a few, please?" She clasped her hands together, thinking the array of autumn flowers quite lovely. They were on the other side of a fence, but it did not look to be a formidable obstacle.

"When asked so prettily, how could I possibly refuse?" he said as gallantly as anyone might wish.

"Mind the fence," she felt obliged to caution.

"Hang the fence, it's the bull on the far side of the pasture that I'd best steer clear of," he replied with a laugh.

She could see no sign of the animal and said so. "Perhaps your man has moved it to another pasture for the day?"

"We can but hope so. Val would say I am tempting fate," Lord Norwood muttered as he vaulted over the fence to advance upon the mass of wildflowers.

He bent to gather an armful of wild angelica, woodbine, wild asters, white campion, harebells, and clustered bellflowers with a bit of greenery for contrast.

Hyacinthe was absorbed in finding a piece of moss so she might keep the flowers damp until she reached the cottage. When she looked up after locating a particularly nice clump, she froze in horror.

"Blase," she whispered, so forgetting herself as to use his first name, "that bull you mentioned before? The one you wished to avoid? I fear he is advancing on you. *Now*. What can I do?"

Lord Norwood slowly straightened, then turned to see a nasty-looking bull approaching him from over the hill. It seemed evident that the fellow did not like having his territory invaded. Not in the least.

"I've heard tell that the chaps in the Spanish bullrings wave red capes at them," he murmured.

Hyacinthe had already dropped the moss. Now she swiftly undid the brooch at her shoulder, dropped it into her reticule, and slid the Poland mantle down until it hung limply to the ground.

"He is coming nearer," she cautioned, edging closer to the fence. She placed a foot on the first rung of the fence, thankful that it was neither a stone barrier nor a hedge. "Can you take my mantle?"

He turned again to cross to her side. It proved a mistake. The bull charged at him, covering the ground at a frightening speed. Poor Lord Norwood didn't have a chance, really. He was picked up and tossed aside like a limp rag. He fell to the ground with a ghastly thump. With a sideways glance she could see his body . . . exceedingly still.

She swung herself over the fence, forgetting any care for propriety or her clothing. Taking the bright coquelicot mantle in the hope that the color would deflect the bull from its target, she waved it about, slashing the air with red.

"Can you edge away from that nasty animal?" she cried. No reply was forthcoming.

The bull paused in his attack on the intruder, then inspected the bright cloth being waved at it with curious eyes. Hyacinthe daringly advanced, attempting to come between Lord Norwood and the animal. She continued to wave the mantle about, her fears for her dear Blase's safety foremost in her mind. It didn't occur to her that she was placing her own life in great danger.

Behind her she could hear what sounded like someone slowly making his way through the long grasses and flowers. A few soft groans reached her ears, making her more determined than ever to keep the bull at bay until Blase could reach the other side of the fence.

"Hyacinthe!" Jane cried in dismay.

"Be quiet, woman," Blase said, sounding clearly in pain. "Unless you wish to see your cousin trampled to death."

There was a pause, then Hyacinthe heard him say, "Keep waving the mantle, but begin backing up. There is nothing in your way," he instructed in a gruff, pained voice.

She could hear how difficult it was for him to speak. Following his directions, she sidled across the pasture until she reached the fence. Before she could think of how she was to negotiate that, what with the bull still advancing on her and not being able to turn her back on it, she was snatched from behind. Over the fence she sailed, landing on her feet with a thump.

At first she thought Sir Charles had pulled her to safety. When she saw him standing by Jane, she turned to look at Blase, and was utterly horrified by what she saw. He leaned against the fence, his blue coat sadly torn, grass stains on his fine gray pantaloons, and his face covered with stains and dirt. When he moved toward her, he limped slightly.

Without consideration as to how her words or actions might appear to the others, she said, "Thank God, you are all right. I would never forgive myself if anything serious had happened to you." She gently brushed off his face with her mantle. "You poor man. Was ever a person so beleaguered as you?" she murmured. "Another coat, and those poor pantaloons are quite ruined, I fear. First your head, and now your leg. You will wish me to Jericho."

"Hyacinthe!" Jane blurted out, "you did not do this on purpose, did you?"

Hyacinthe stopped what she was doing. She could see the doubt creep into Blase's eyes. "Of course not," she stoutly denied. But the doubt had been planted. Blast Jane, anyway. Why did she have to say something so utterly dreadful?

How could Hyacinthe convince Blase that she couldn't hurt him, not intentionally, not anymore? Not since she had realized that she loved the dratted man. Her garden rake.

"It was an accident," Lord Norwood said evenly.

"He went in there to pick me some wildflowers. The bull was nowhere in sight at the time," Hyacinthe cried. She darted looks at Jane and Lord Norwood. "I truly did not wish him harm. Truly!" Tears of frustration and reaction stung her eyes and she turned aside to fumble in her reticule for a handkerchief.

A somewhat crumpled and partially soiled scrap of linen was thrust into her hands by the man at her side.

She mopped her eyes, then gave Jane a defiant stare. "I may have harbored a few unkind thoughts about Lord Norwood in the past. But, dear cousin of mine, I'd do nothing to willfully hurt him. Not *ever*." She turned away to take Lord Norwood's arm with the intention of assisting him to where the carriage had last been seen.

"Val will never let me hear the end of this, you know," Lord Norwood said with a wince when he stumbled on a rock.

"I shall try to explain. You must have a doctor examine you carefully," she insisted, guiding him away from a rut.

They reached his carriage and with a stricken face she watched his painful climb into it. He leaned forward slightly to stare at her a moment.

"Tell me, Miss Dancy, what is it that you would wish above all . . . in regard to the Tudor cottage, that is?"

"Why," she said, looking at him with wide eyes. "I should like to live there. You said I might," she reminded him.

"I was afraid of that," he muttered. "I'm not certain I'd survive it, my dear."

Hyacinthe stood very still in the center of the road when his carriage drove off toward the Hall. He detested her. He must. She wondered how she could endure without him.

13

The reaction of his staff at the Hall was about what he might have expected, given the sad state of his appearance.

Val merely took one look at his torn coat, grass-stained pantaloons, and battered person . . . and laughed. "At least you did not wear your best remaining coat," he said after his amusement had abated.

"You might at least express a bit of sympathy, old chap," Blase complained to his friend while they walked up the stairs to the master bedroom after Blase had ordered hot water to be brought up.

"I told you she was a dangerous woman," Val countered. "You are dotted with scrapes and bruises from head down as far as I can see." They walked down the hall until reaching Blase's room, then entered. Val strolled to the windows, where he found a seat with a view of the hills.

Smithson must have anticipated a calamitous end to the outing, for he had a tub awaiting the hot water, towels set out, and clean clothes spread on the bed. In short order the water arrived, even before Blase had stripped off his shirt and the ruined pantaloons.

Blase gingerly eased himself from the remaining pieces of clothing, then sank into the tub of hot water behind the screen and in front of a glowing fire. "You don't know the whole of it," he replied in response to the charge against Hyacinthe. "Do you know that when that bull tossed me toward the sky Miss Dancy whipped off her mantle, clambered over the fence, and deflected the perverse animal from a second stab at my carcass? Just before he charged I had muttered something about the bullfighters in Spain using red capes. She may never have seen such a display, but she certainly saved my hide by waving her mantle about beneath his nose. I was able to crawl to the fence, slither under it, and reach safety. She was remarkably brave."

"Champion," Val murmured, quite subdued by this revelation. "She endangered her life to protect you? Amazing. Sounds like a regular Boadicea."

"And she did not ask for anything while on the picnic, either." Blase sighed with pleasure while he soaked in the hot water, then began to soap his face and arms to remove the mud that smeared them.

However, he refrained from mentioning the doubts that Jane Pennington had raised with her accusation. Could Hyacinthe Dancy hate him so much that she might wish him dead? Preposterous. Why would she have dashed to his rescue if that were the case? Still, she might think he would be sufficiently discouraged to abandon his plans.

That was a piece of nonsense if ever he heard any. Even were he so inclined, things had progressed too far to be altered at this late date. No, he did not want to accept the idea that she harbored malicious intent toward him. Regardless, he would do well to be on his guard when near her.

The memory of her close to him, his arms about her when he pulled her to safety, returned. Combined with that promising kiss in the cottage and her gentle, remorseful caress (true, that was after hitting him over the head), it created a tantalizing recollection—one that was hard to dismiss. He wanted Miss Dancy, but dare he pursue her? It could be a hazardous course! She certainly did not encourage a fellow, what with her concerted efforts to half kill him.

"You have not asked what I found," Val said quietly some minutes later.

"Well, *did* you find something of interest?"

"Nothing," Val admitted. "I approached from the rear, and since there are a number of workmen tearing down another cottage in the area, I doubt if I was noticed. They don't bother to lock the back door, foolish women. Wonder there was a thing in the house."

"But?" Blase urged, relieved to hear Miss Dancy proven innocent.

"The remarkably neat Miss Dancy has an impressive lot of jewels, a nice collection of gowns and whatnot, and everything else you expect to find in a woman's room, but no emeralds of any kind, antique or otherwise, stashed in the bottom on her portmanteau and other luggage. Odd, that. You would think that some man would have given her stones to match her eyes ages ago." Val tilted his chair back to rest against the window surround while he apparently considered Miss Dancy's eyes and lack of emeralds.

"She isn't that old, my good fellow, not too long out of the schoolroom," Blase said, oddly pleased that Miss Dancy did not possess signs of gifts from gentlemen—not that any proper miss could or would accept such things. But Miss Dancy was not the ordinary run-of-the-mill woman. She appeared to have her own set of rules to live by.

"So what do we do next?" Val said with a sigh. "Oh, I just remembered, your curate chanced by just as I was leaving the old village, full of messages for you. Had I known of your injury, I'd not have suggested he present them to you in person."

"I will be a little sore, nothing more than that. No broken bones, thanks to Miss Dancy." He allowed Smithson to spread soothing ointment on his scrapes after reluctantly leaving his bath, then pulled on his clothes hurriedly.

"Correct me if I'm wrong, but wasn't she the reason you landed in this pickle in the first place? She has been behind every disaster that has occurred so far."

Blase refused to discuss it further. Picking a bunch of wild-flowers seemed innocent to him, but Val could read catastrophe into anything a woman did. The two men went down to the drawing room where the good curate awaited them, having decided to promptly do as suggested.

"Oh, I say, Lord Norwood, you look to have had a bit of an accident," Ambrose Clark declared in dismay.

"Nothing, nothing," Blase muttered with a look directed at Val daring him to say otherwise. "What is it you wish to discuss?"

"Well, it is this, my lord: I do believe we ought to bring as much as possible from the old church—associations, you know. The cross, the font, pulpit, the screen as well, all ought to fit in the new building. I should think the bells might be rehung as well. Certainly the new organ should be moved," he finished, looking at Blase with hope in his eyes.

With a glance at Val, Blase sought to reassure the curate that the organ would be transported as soon as possible along with the other items, and that he would also try to see that the good man received an elevation, since the vicar assigned to this church hadn't been seen in these parts in an age.

Across the hills from the favorable meeting between lord and curate, Hyacinthe stormed about the little parlor in hurt frustration.

"I cannot think how you could say such a thing," she accused her cousin for the third time. "Surely you know me better than that, to even *think* for a moment that I might wish him dead—for he could have been killed had that bull not been lured away from him."

Dismayed by the outburst, Jane tried to soothe her cousin as best she might. "I confess I was a trifle upset, as it appeared Sir Charles was about to propose to me, and your cries stopped that. Perhaps I am merely dreaming, to believe he has an interest in me," she concluded with a sad face. She accepted her cousin's regrets, then left the room to prepare a tray of tea and biscuits.

Hyacinthe sank down upon the chair close to the window, staring out with unseeing eyes. Now that she considered what she had done, she felt all trembly. Nerves, she decided. After all, she didn't challenge a bull every day.

There was, however, another matter to consider—her discovery. She had most unfortunately fallen in love with the very man she opposed. Why, she detested him. He would force all these villagers from their old homes, then raise the rents on the new ones—just to improve his view. That was reprehensible. Dreadful.

She wished it might be otherwise. But, she reminded herself, he had ignored her all the while in London, flirting with every other woman in sight. He was exceedingly good at charming the ladies. He certainly charmed her without half trying.

"Miss," Fosdick said from the doorway, "I believe someone has been in the house while we were gone."

Hyacinthe snapped from her considerations to stare at her abigail. "You cannot be serious."

"Your belongings have been shifted about; nothing is in quite the same place as it was," the maid asserted.

From the doorway Jane gasped at this revelation. "Nothing like this ever happened before all this tearing down began," she said. "It must be one of the strangers."

"Have you seen evidence that anyone forced entry?" Hyacinthe asked, ever practical.

"Why would they need to? The back door was left unlocked," Fosdick said with a disapproving look at Jane.

"I never did need to lock up before," Jane said in her own defense.

"Was anything taken?" Hyacinthe asked while she hurried across the room out to the bottom of the stairs.

"Not a thing, which is most curious, if you get my meaning," the maid replied in a voice laden with import.

Hyacinthe paused, slowly turning about to face Fosdick. "That is *most* curious, indeed. Why bother to enter a house, go through belongings, then take nothing? Not even my jewelry?" she added in disbelief.

"Nothing," the abigail confirmed.

"Why?" Hyacinthe sank down on the bottom step, contemplating the matter.

"Well, if you were to ask me," Fosdick continued, "a person might search for a particular item, and if he did not find it, leave without taking anything else."

With a gasp, Hyacinthe jumped to her feet, then dashed up the stairs, taking care not to bump her head on the low part at the top. Her room seemed as always, neat and orderly. Fosdick had followed and now watched.

"Everything has been shifted about," her maid said, pointing out a few.

"Mr. Wayland would have an excuse to be in this area. He comes over here quite often to see how the men do. Maybe

Lord Norwood found the jewels, has taken them away, and Mr. Wayland believes *I* have them."

"Excuse me," Fosdick inserted, "but Lord Latham did not join you on the picnic today. Remember, I was nowhere near here; Tom Coachman took me in for a bit of shopping."

"Surely you do not think Lord Norwood would send him to spy on me?" Hyacinthe cried, hurt at the very notion that the man she loved would further distress her. "That would be utterly horrid!"

The abigail failed to respond. Hyacinthe returned to the parlor to relate what she had seen and discussed.

Jane ventured a strained smile and suggested they consider the problem over a cup of tea.

Later, while strolling about the village—ostensibly to relax her nerves and enjoy a bit of air—Hyacinthe mulled over the mystery. Someone had entered her room—for nothing else in the house had been disturbed—but had taken not a thing. It bothered her to think that either Mr. Wayland or Lord Latham would go through her possessions. Obviously someone believed she had the antique jewels.

But that puzzle aside, she must face her real dilemma. Lord Norwood. She had seen the look of doubt in his eyes when Jane accused her of deliberately luring him to the field. While she had admittedly pushed him into the pond, and assuredly permitted her hat to sail into the pig sty, she hadn't intended him to fall when he rescued the kite. And she certainly had never intended his life to be imperiled while venturing to gather a few wildflowers.

Yet would he believe that? Would he suspect her of wanting him dead? No! her heart cried. Not the man she had come to care for—even if it was against her will. But there were good reasons for him not to have complete faith in her.

She knelt down to examine a duck that nestled along the bank of the pond. "You do not think I could be so heartless, do you?"

The duck rose, shook itself, then waded into the pond and swam off.

"So much for evidence of innocence."

"Miss Dancy, are you all right?"

Hyacinthe jumped to her feet, startled by the high, thin voice of the angular architect. "Mr. Wayland, you quite surprised me. Have you been in the village long?"

"No, I had to supervise some work on the church," he replied in an important manner.

"I see." Which meant that Lord Norwood's friend had come around to snoop in her things if Wayland could prove he was elsewhere. The knowledge pained her, for it doubtless meant that Lord Norwood had planned the picnic with that very thing in mind. It hadn't turned out the way he planned. Nothing had been found in her room, and he had ended up somewhat battered and bruised.

Mr. Wayland glanced at the Tudor house, then sidled up to her. "Have you observed people around that house?" He gestured in that direction with a nod of his head.

"Why, I hired the village women to clean and polish it. I intend to move into that house, for it is most charming and I do not mind being in the country. I daresay I can persuade a distant cousin of mine to join me here to maintain propriety if Jane requires an extra person." She dare not hint that Jane would wed Sir Charles, for the poor man had not mustered up his courage to propose.

Dudley Wayland paled at her words. Hyacinthe considered it an odd reaction to her innocuous proposition.

"Why, surely you would not wish to live so far from others," he said, his manner most agitated.

"I like a serene life," she said, quite forgetting that her life had been anything *but* that since coming here.

He muttered a few more sentiments along the same lines, then marched off in the direction of the new village with a few backward glances that seemed rather ominous.

"He most definitely does not wish me to move into the Tudor cottage. I believe I shall consult with Lord Norwood's bailiff regarding the rental of it. Surely he cannot resist the notion of an income from property that would just decay otherwise." With a somewhat calculating look in her eyes, she retraced her steps to Jane's cottage. "I can tell him that Lord Norwood agreed."

Once in her room, she again paused to look out of her window across the hills in the direction of the Hall. With all that had happened he must surely detest her. Never mind that she had detested him for ages. All had changed. The shoe was on the other foot, so to speak.

"Fosdick, I intend to rent the Tudor cottage. There is something quite havey-cavey going on over there. What better way to find out than to be on the premises?" She pulled on a gray pelisse over her coquelicot gown. Best to be inconspicuous in what she did.

The maid assisted her efforts, then stood by the door before Hyacinthe made her way down the stairs. "You are no doubt walking into danger, renting that place. However, I won't leave you, rest assured of that."

Hyacinthe gave her a grateful smile, then hurried from the house in search of the bailiff.

She found him not far away in the old village. He was looking over the remains of several cottages that had been torn down.

Hyacinthe might love Blase Montague, but she thought him mad to attempt so silly and expensive a scheme. Nevertheless she wished to make atonement for all she had done to the poor man, even if she had undoubtedly ruined any chance she might have had in charming him. And she must rent the Tudor cottage to do so. She felt it in her bones.

"Sir? I have something to discuss with you." Since the man rarely chatted with the guests in the village, he was clearly startled at her request.

Sometime later, and much pleased with her success, Hyacinthe returned to Jane's cottage waving a written agreement in the air when she entered the parlor.

"We may move into the cottage across the way anytime we please," she declared to an astounded Jane. Behind her, Fosdick nodded as though she had quite expected this.

"I shall hire some of the workers to carry your belongings over there if you will agree to the scheme, and Tom Coachman and my groom will help as well. We shall be settled in a trice! In fact, perhaps I ought to buy your furniture, for I feel certain that Sir Charles will come up to scratch one of these days."

Jane looked unconvinced, but a hit of pink crept into her cheeks as she considered her cousin's words. "I suspect you pay more than your share," she scolded gently. "We will settle that matter later."

"I shall begin to pack," Fosdick declared, then disappeared up the stairs.

"I wonder if Sir Charles will think me comfortably settled if we transfer my things over there," Jane said with a worried frown sometime later. "Do remember that his concern was for my homeless state."

Hyacinthe shook her head. "I truly doubt that is the case now. I believe he is quite smitten. You might mention that I intend to invite a distant cousin of mine to move in here with us. Then he will have no qualms about asking you to marry him. Nor will he fear that I shall come along with you." Hyacinthe knew full well that often a single lady would be invited to live with relatives. It placed a strain on all, particularly in the early days of a marriage. She did not intend to create more problems.

With the abundance of workers available in the village, it did not take long for her coachman, groom, and several strapping men to remove the belongings from Jane's cottage over to the Tudor place.

Mrs. Peachey and the Widow Smith bustled across the green to find out what was happening.

"I declare, such goings on!" Mrs. Peachey exclaimed while keeping a careful eye on the furniture passing beneath her nose. Since none of the ladies had ever inspected the bedroom pieces, it proved illuminating. Jane had acquired several lovely articles of furniture, mostly from the attics of her relatives. All were lovingly polished and in excellent repair.

The kitchen table was the last to be carted over and Hyacinthe stood in the road watching as it disappeared around to the rear of the house. She turned as she heard hoofbeats approaching. Certain the bailiff was returning to take a month's rent from her, she was dismayed to see Lord Norwood, with Lord Latham right behind him, bearing down on her. And here she stood with a dust cap on her head and most likely a smudge on her nose.

"Miss Dancy, what is afoot?" He glanced about with curiosity, obviously noting the men who straggled away from the Tudor cottage back to where they had been working.

"Then you do not know?" she said in confusion. Why else would he come here—unless it was to tell her to get off his property forever.

"You are all right? In my desire to reach the Hall, I neglected to see if you had been harmed when I hauled you over that fence. Your gown?" He glanced at the simple green sprig muslin she now wore.

"A few minor tears, nothing serious," she said, unless, she thought, you considered the damage to her heart.

Jane and Fosdick left the old cottage where Hyacinthe had first come. Jane paused to look it over, as though saying farewell to an old friend. Then she turned and made her way to where Lord Norwood now stood beside his horse.

"Here is the key to that cottage, not that it is important any longer, for I expect it will be torn down ere long." She handed the large key to him, then excused herself. Fosdick took a sharp look at the trio remaining, then followed Jane.

"I do not understand this in the least. What has happened? Why are they going over there?" He gestured to the Tudor cottage, revealed in all its old charm with the weeds and grass trimmed, the windows shining. He watched, quite perplexed, as Jane and Fosdick entered through the front door now restored to polished beauty.

"I am renting it," she declared with pleasure. "I intended to give the rent to your bailiff, but you may as well take it instead." She handed the packet to a very bemused Lord Norwood, then watched when he checked the contents.

He looked up at her, clearly puzzled. "For how long a period does this cover?"

"One month, sir," she replied. She would have to write to her solicitor to see that more funds were sent. Perhaps she might arrange to have a bank in Oxford open an account in her name. She would enjoy an occasional trip to that town for a bit of shopping.

The two men exchanged looks, then Lord Norwood turned to her again. "Tell me, what were you told regarding the amount of rent for the new cottages?"

Hyacinthe sensed something in his voice. He was angry. At her? She couldn't help that. She told him the sum that the bailiff had revealed. That look of anger hardened into cold outrage.

He remounted, then gathered the reins, preparing to leave. "I shall return later to deal with this removal you have affected. But know this—the amount of rent for the new cottages is no different from the old, in spite of my teasing you on the matter. I see that I shall have to have words with my bailiff."

She watched, quite frozen, as the two men galloped off along the road to the new village. His words went around and around in her mind. The amount of rent as given her by the bailiff was wrong! He had lied. The rent had not been greatly increased. Hyacinthe had not only acted in the wrong, but dreadfully misjudged Lord Norwood.

It was as though a cold hand clutched her heart. If she thought him indifferent to her before, he would positively scorn her now. But it was a mistake! An honest mistake. Yet perhaps she should have taxed Lord Norwood over the sum directly, and it would have been revealed. Now she would never know. She taunted herself with the knowledge that she was undoubtedly her own worst enemy.

With a resigned sigh she began her way to the Tudor cottage, although she was reluctant to face Jane with the truth of the matter. So many things were the result of that lie. How could she possibly correct everything to what it ought to be?

The dust had settled when Sir Charles approached from the other direction. What now? she wondered while pausing before the gate.

"What has occurred? I heard that Miss Pennington has moved." He was clearly alarmed, almost amusingly so.

"She has," Hyacinthe agreed.

"But she cannot. That is, she said nothing to me about removing from here. Where did she go? Why did she not inform me? I must speak with her. Tell me where I may find her."

Taking pity on the poor man, Hyacinthe walked forward to where he sat on his horse. "Follow me. We do not have a stable, but I trust you may tie your steed to a tree." She gestured toward the cottage. "I have rented the Tudor house. Jane and Fosdick are there arranging our things."

"She is still in the village, then?" His relief was almost diverting.

"Yes, she is. For the moment. You know, Jane is a very pretty woman. One of these days some fortunate man could well sweep her off her feet and carry her away."

Now he looked even more alarmed. "I must see her."

With that he jumped from his horse, looped the reins on a branch, then surged ahead, hurrying up the path to the cottage where a serene Fosdick ushered him inside with the grace of a born housekeeper.

Hyacinthe observed his greeting to Jane with narrowed eyes. The man was a slowtop and would need more nudging, most likely. But Jane clearly loved him as he was, and she should have him. All it would require would be a bit of intrigue.

When he was safely away from the house, Hyacinthe confronted her cousin in the hallway. Jane carried a stack of clean huckaback towels, most likely unaware of what was in her hands from the expression on her face.

"He desires to take me for a drive on the morrow. He is concerned about the ghosts in this house. I told him not to worry." She gave Hyacinthe a distracted look. "You do not believe we will be pestered by ghosts, do you?"

"Not live ones," Hyacinthe muttered. Seeing her cousin's confusion, Hyacinthe assured her, "The ghosts are likely figments of overactive imaginations and little boys bent on mischief. Put your mind to what you will wear on this momentous occasion."

With that happy thought planted in her mind, Jane sailed up to the linen closet, tidied the things already in place, then went off to her new room, larger and sunnier than the one in the old cottage.

Hyacinthe stared after her. She ought to have informed Jane of the awful lie the bailiff had told. Maybe things would quickly work out so Jane could marry Sir Charles and Hyacinthe wouldn't need to reveal all. Knowing Jane, this might be the better course to take. Hyacinthe's heart yielding to the persuasion of this argument, she followed her cousin up the stairs.

The floorboards squeaked as she entered the larger of the bedrooms. Since, in spite of Jane's objections, she paid the bills now she'd chosen this one—and Jane would soon be gone. Besides, she had a sentimental regard for it. But she wondered how sound the building might be. Her groom and coachman had gone over the house, pronouncing it free from bugs and serious decay. Still . . . there was the secret passage that went down from her dressing room.

Crossing to the closet, she went in, pressed the little wooden knot, then watched the secret panel swing open as it had before. Chilly air rushed up to greet her. Rather than go down to the lower level, she studied the upper portion. Could the jewels be here?

"Hyacinthe? Where are you?"

Upon hearing her cousin, Hyacinthe hurriedly closed up the paneled entrance, then pretended she had been hunting through her gowns hanging in the wardrobe brought from Jane's former house.

"In here, dear. I thought I would have the Widow Smith and Mrs. Peachey over for tea tomorrow while you are off gallivanting with Sir Charles. They are bursting with questions," Hyacinthe invented. She figured it was close enough to the truth and she could quickly send a note to the ladies, who would leap at the chance to snoop. "What does one wear when being interrogated?"

"Oh, Hyacinthe, you are so silly." Jane leaned against the paneled wall not far from where the knot seemed conspicuously present. "That pretty green India mull you think so plain will be lovely. They do not expect city elegance."

"You think not?" Hyacinthe shook her head. "I expect they will like me to dazzle them. After all, I owe something to my image."

Jane laughed, then joined her cousin as she went to leave the little room. Before closing the door, Hyacinthe glanced back to where she knew the passage to be. Later on she intended to inspect it inch by inch. Now that she had a perfect right to be here, there was no need to rush. Tomorrow, while Jane was on her drive and before the ladies came to tea, she could search. For she fully intended to find those jewels before Mr. Wayland found some excuse to return.

Then a terrible thought struck her. Perhaps he could enter from below!

As soon as possible, Hyacinthe excused herself from her cousin, making her way to the rubbish heap with the explanation that she needed to oversee the disposal of the trash. That was a patent untruth, but it was necessary to make certain that no one could get inside.

The door proved easily found when one knew where to search. It didn't take long for Hyacinthe to decide that it could be opened with little effort. She hunted around until she located a hammer and nails, then made certain that for the moment there was no way Dudley Wayland could sneak up those secret stairs. And she intended to find the jewels before he found a way, for she was convinced Dudley Wayland had hidden them somewhere in the passage.

14

The evening meal, the very first in their new abode, turned out well, prepared by the Widow Smith's girl, Fanny. Hyacinthe was a preoccupied diner, however, for her thoughts kept wandering alternately to the lie she must keep hidden and her need to explore the secret passage.

She had a truly deep conviction that the old family jewels were concealed in the walls of the passage. But where? She ought to have good light, and there was nothing but candles to be had in this house. What she needed was an Argand lamp with a shade. The efficient tubular wick of this oil lamp burned more brightly—without smoking—and increased illumination tenfold.

Quite unaware that Jane and Fosdick were deep in a discussion of what gown should be worn on the momentous outing with Sir Charles, Hyacinthe broke in. "Does either of you have any idea where I might buy an Argand lamp? I enjoy needlework of an evening and candles are a poor substitute."

Both women stared at her with perplexed looks on their faces for a few moments.

Jane said, "I believe you may purchase one in Woodstock, or if not there, you could go as far as Kidlington."

"I should think you might even order one, if you are in a hurry and cannot find the time to go," Fosdick added.

"That is true," Jane said. "But it ought not take long to run in to Woodstock." She gave Hyacinthe a curious look. "I had not realized that you were so fond of needlework."

"That is because she has been so busy with other things," Fosdick inserted helpfully. "Why, she is one of the finest needlewomen I have ever seen in all my years of service."

Hyacinthe stared at her abigail. Had being persuaded to join them for dinner while in Worthington gone to her head? Though she certainly enjoyed a bit of needlework from time to time, Hyacinthe could hardly aspire to such heights.

"Thank you, Fosdick," she murmured, then resumed mulling over her problem. She would send a message to the coachman first thing in the morning, then dash to Woodstock for the lamp. When Jane went off for her ride and before the ladies came to tea Hyacinthe could begin her exploration.

She supposed she might confide in Jane, but there were two reasons to remain silent—Jane might blurt out the truth at an inauspicious moment, or she might insist upon helping. Hyacinthe knew a fierce desire to be the one who found the missing items. She didn't delve into her underlying motives.

With the problem of a proper lamp solved, she sat back in satisfaction. The other problem—that of the horrid lie told by the bailiff—would wait. It would have to wait. Nothing must keep Jane from that outing with Sir Charles. Hyacinthe prayed the weather would not change. Clouds hovered toward the horizon. They must just go the other way, for rain would ruin everything.

"Pudding, miss?" Fanny inquired.

"What? Oh, yes, I adore pudding—of any kind," Hyacinthe blurted. She really must pay better attention.

The remainder of the evening went normally. Fosdick resumed her more retiring nature and Jane bubbled with delight on the prospects of her future until it was time to retire.

In the morning, Hyacinthe did as planned. Since Jane slept late she was not obliged to prevaricate about her errand, and anyway, Jane knew she wanted a lamp; just not *why* she wanted a new lamp

With a bit of searching in Woodstock, the exact shop she hoped to locate was found and two Argand lamps purchased. Hyacinthe decided that if one was good, two were better.

"Miss Dancy! What a surprise to find you in town."

Hyacinthe swallowed with care, then turned to face the man she feared to see. "Lord Norwood. Fancy meeting you here of all places." She motioned the shop assistant to where her carriage waited, whispering that he should just place the lamps inside.

"Out shopping bright and early, I see." He glanced at the shop, then back at her. "Lamps? You desire to entertain?"

"Oh, no," she said truthfully. "I enjoy a bit of needlework of an evening, and candlelight is dreadfully hard on the eyes." She must buy a bit of canvas and yarn or else look utterly silly, what with telling this tale so often.

She glanced about her, noting that nothing frightful seemed about to happen. Lord Norwood looked perfectly safe. "Well, I had best hurry home. Jane is to drive out with Sir Charles today, and I must not miss this occasion."

"I gather he is finally coming up to scratch."

Hyacinthe grinned. "Jane said that made him sound like a chicken."

He laughed at that and Hyacinthe hoped that perhaps all was not lost between them.

"I gather you are settling in well enough? I find it hard to understand why Miss Pennington preferred that place to a new cottage." He leaned on his cane while watching Hyacinthe with an intent regard.

"Actually it was the misunderstanding that caused it," she confessed, quite flustered and fiddling with the cords of her reticule with nervous fingers. "You did not help, sir, with your teasing," she reminded him.

"I promise I shan't hold it against you," he said. There was no twinkle in those blue eyes and his smile had faded when he met her gaze. In fact, all seemed to dim about them, for she noticed nothing but him.

"Look out, sir!" cried the shop assistant who had lingered before the door.

Before either of them could move, a boy being chased by four others came barreling into Lord Norwood, knocking him off his feet.

Hyacinthe heard the tearing of fabric with a sinking heart. All the poor man had to do was talk with her and he ended in disaster.

The shop assistant rushed to help the gentleman, offering to chase the boys.

"Never mind, I trust they are far from here by now, all much chastened, no doubt," Lord Norwood said wryly. He turned to Hyacinthe, remaining carefully erect. "I must bid you farewell. It seems I must find a tailor immediately."

Knowing she must look guilty when it wasn't her fault in the least, Hyacinthe agreed, then whisked herself into the carriage and bid her coachman to hurry on his way. She peeped from the window to see Lord Norwood entering a shop a few doors from where the altercation occurred.

Bouncing along the rutted road back to the old village, she considered what had been said and had happened. She truly did not know if he would ever forgive her for all the appalling things that had taken place since they met. She could only hope to atone for a few of them by finding those wretched jewels.

Jane was in alt when she viewed the fine lamps. Nothing would do but that they had to be lit and admired.

"I believe I shall take up sewing something other than mending of an evening with this fine light," she declared.

"I noticed that Sir Charles has a pair of them in his drawing room. Be sure you buy sufficient canvas to work a new set of chair seats," Hyacinthe said.

Jane blinked at this forward thinking, then went off to inspect her gown for the tenth time that morning.

Taking both of the lamps, now extinguished, Hyacinthe brought them up to her room. Fosdick took one look and shrugged.

"I gather you have something up your sleeve. I misdoubt you intend to commence all that needlework you spoke of in the middle of the day."

"If you like, you may take yourself off to visit Mrs. Grigson over at Sir Charles's house." Hyacinthe would find it easier to work with the house empty. Fanny was off at her mother's for the day, helping pack for her removal.

"Hmphf," Fosdick said, following this utterance with a sniff of disdain. She left the room and shortly was heard going down the stairs. Bless the good woman, she'd never say a word about Hyacinthe's odd starts.

Once alone, Hyacinthe hurried to the closet after donning a

mob cap and an enveloping apron, then lit one lamp. Quickly pressing the little knot of wood, she entered the passageway, her lamp now lighting up the area far better than a branch of candles ever could.

She began with the left side of the passage, starting at the top, working her way down, pressing every inch. She knew that whatever was concealed here would be in between the walls, for there was little space allotted to the secret passage. But what could be the solution to the riddle of the hidden treasure? Lord Norwood had hinted that more than jewels were missing.

If she could find whatever else had been hidden here years ago, she could at least feel absolved of all the wrongs she had committed, to say nothing of the dreadful things that seemed to happen whenever she drew near the man.

Minutes passed before she heard Jane calling her. Having found nothing of interest, Hyacinthe quickly put out the lamp, then placed it on the little table she had brought into the closet. She pulled off her cap and apron, tossing them aside before scurrying around the corner.

In the hallway, Jane stood with an uncertain look on her face. "Oh, there you are. Fosdick is nowhere to be seen and you appeared to have vanished as well."' She fidgeted with a lace reticule that Hyacinthe had given her. Then she slowly twirled about. "Will I pass inspection?"

Hyacinthe felt guilty for neglecting the all-important drive. "You look better than a dish of comfits. I vow that if Sir Charles is not swept from his feet by the sight of you, the man needs spectacles."

With a soft little giggle, Jane made her way to the front door where she greeted Sir Charles. By the looks of him, he was struck all of a heap. Jane glanced back at her cousin and winked.

With the drive off to such a promising start—not even a sign of rain in the sky—Hyacinthe went to the kitchen to boil water for tea after washing her hands of dust. A tray had been nicely arranged in anticipation of the visit from the village gossips. When a faint rap was heard at the front door, Hyacinthe was ready.

Actually, things went quite well, far better than Hyacinthe had hoped they would. The two ladies revealed that they had embarked on the village history just as Hyacinthe had suggested. They went on to offer details unearthed through a search of attics, the records kept in the church, and the tombstones in the graveyard.

"I had no notion this would prove so fascinating, Miss Dancy," Mrs. Peachey confided. "Why, Eloise and I have scarce had a moment to look out of our windows the past week."

"Have you learned anything more of the woman who lived here?" Hyacinthe inquired of the authors.

"The dashing redhead? Precious little. There are references to ghosts and such from time to time. But it strikes me as odd that although the house was kept more or less in repair, no one has lived here for any length of time," the Widow Smith said with a sage nod. "And whoever lived at the Hall saw to the repairs through the years. What secret do you suppose is hidden in these walls?

She was uncomfortably close to the truth. Hyacinthe forced a laugh. "You have a wonderfully fanciful mind, Mrs. Smith. I doubt if anything sordid is concealed, for I have slept extremely well, and I doubt if I would were something nasty hidden here."

Hyacinthe could almost see the thoughts that ran through the widow's head. Disappointment vied with pleasure that Mrs. Smith was actually having tea with Miss Dancy and in the wicked Tudor house. After all, a kept woman had once resided here!

When the call came to a conclusion, Hyacinthe graciously walked the two ladies to the door, saying, "I wish you well in your efforts. I expect that once you have it completed, Lord Norwood will wish to publish it for the shire records."

This consideration so astounded the two women that they merely gasped, then fled down the front path deep in discussion.

Hyacinthe watched them for a few moments before going out into the garden, or what remained of the garden. It occurred to her that she ought to find the hedgehog and bring

him here. Poor little thing would be frightened half to death
when they tore down that cottage.

With that thought in mind she crossed the green, entering
through the gate to skirt the cottage—now looking quite for-
lorn—around to the rear of the house.

"Whatever you doin' here, Miss Dancy?" Sukey, the Hadkiss girl of the kite episode, asked.

"I intend to find my hedgehog. Would you like to help me?"
Hyacinthe decided that it should be safe enough. Lord Norwood was miles away from here as far as she knew.

In short order the two were prowling through the garden,
poking under piles of moldering leaves, prying up fallen
branches, hunting into any likely spot where a hedgehog might
hide. Hyacinthe thought she had found him when it happened.

"Whatever are you doing, Miss Dancy?" said an unfortunately familiar voice.

Conscious of her now-rumpled mull gown hiked up well
above her ankles and being crouched on the ground in an improper position, Hyacinthe looked up at him. "Good afternoon,
Lord Norwood. It wanted only you, I expect."

"I daresay I'm better off not knowing what that means," he
muttered. "But you failed to answer my query."

"If you must know," she said somewhat ungraciously, "we
are hunting for Harry, my hedgehog. The one you gave me,"
she added for further illumination. "Perhaps you recall
Sukey?" she concluded as an afterthought.

"How could I forget? I trust you have kept your kite from
further harm, Sukey?"

The little girl blushed then retreated at such notice.

"I suppose I had best help you," Lord Norwood continued.
"I was reckoned to be a dab hand at gathering up hedgehogs
when I was a boy. The little things seemed to like me." At Hyacinthe's amused expression, he added, "And please do not
say that it is very apt, for you would be repeating something
that has become trite over the years."

"Well, you can be a trifle prickly at times," she said with a
grin. "I am not the only one," she concluded virtuously.

He removed his coat—placing it carefully to one side—
pushed up his sleeves, and plunged into the garden. He was

not there very long before he emerged triumphant, hedgehog in hand. "Harry, I believe!" he declared with pride in a job well done.

"And so it is," Hyacinthe agreed after a close look at the little fellow. Then she took a look at his lordship and swallowed with effort.

His broad chest covered in fine cambric had become damp from the moldering leaves and now clung to him, revealing a fine, manly chest. He was more muscular than her brother. He was also much closer to her than she deemed prudent. She wanted nothing more than to be enfolded in those strong arms and held close to him.

But, she realized with horror, he was daubed with mud all over that beautiful cambric shirt. With a sigh she rose, the spell broken.

"I fear your shirt must be consigned to the wash, sir. Gardens are notorious for producing soil, and Harry adores grubbing in the dirt."

Indeed, it also appeared the little fellow had no fear of the man who held him so cautiously. Lord Norwood rose, and with Hyacinthe trailing behind him, crossed the green to the Tudor house where he carefully deposited Harry in the garden. The animal quickly disappeared beneath a pile of autumn leaves and debris.

Hyacinthe handed him the coat she had thought to bring along, then watched while he brushed off his soiled shirt before donning the well-tailored coat of a fine gray cloth.

"Have you tended to the secret passage?" he asked, looking ready to depart.

She gave a guilty start, then realized he must refer to the sealing off of the entrance. "Indeed." She turned from the rear of the house, hoping to draw Lord Norwood to the front gate and safety. "I nailed it shut so anyone who wished to sneak up those stairs would find it impossible."

The perverse man would not follow her. Rather, he strode around past the ashes of the rubbish heap, now carefully raked down by Warton. "Where is it?"

Resigned, Hyacinthe walked along the house until she spotted the slit that indicated the hidden door. "I nailed it shut along here." She pointed out where each nail had been driven. To do so necessitated her coming very close to his lordship. He refused to budge and she rejected the idea of admitting she was so strongly affected by him.

So she daringly turned to face him, awaiting his verdict of her efforts. After all, he did own the house, and she supposed she ought to have sought permission to pound nails in the place.

"Hyacinthe . . ." He stared down into her eyes with an indescribable expression on his face. She would have said he looked hungry, except this was not the time of day for a meal.

Nervous, she rubbed her hands together. Licking suddenly dry lips, she answered, "Yes?"

His fingers brushed her cheek, dusting off a leaf she supposed. But his very touch seemed a caress that sent tremors through her. She ought to move. They ought not be here. For although she had red hair and lived a somewhat unconventional life, inside she was a very proper woman.

She might even flirt just a bit, but always with discretion. This was not prudent. She sensed that a strange sort of danger threatened her.

He stepped closer to her. Scarcely an inch was between them. "Hyacinthe," he whispered.

Suddenly she was crushed against him, his lips finding hers in a kiss that was infinitely sweet. Flee she ought, yet she clutched his coat with trembling fingers.

"Norwood," called a voice from around the other side of the house.

Hyacinthe found herself swiftly abandoned as Lord Norwood strolled around to hail his friend.

"Over here, Val. Miss Dancy has been showing me the results of her efforts at nailing shut the passage door."

Hyacinthe stood where he had left her. Another brief kiss, yet more intense than the first. The sweetness and tenderness she'd experienced made her long for more, unfortunately. While she had no one to warn her of the risks involved, she sensed that she flirted with far more than in the past. Was this what that redhead of long ago had known? Was this intense

longing to be close to the man she loved what had compelled
the woman to flout society's laws to be with him?

Hyacinthe knew that she could not follow that path. Either
she was not as strong, or merely more sensible.

"Well, Miss Dancy," came Latham's mocking voice, "you
have many talents."

She wondered what he meant by that.

"So she has," Lord Norwood agreed quietly.

Somehow she managed the next few minutes with far more
aplomb than she would have believed possible. She smiled
and gestured, thought she acted naturally, when all she could
think of was the feel of his mouth on hers and the warmth of
his hands on her arms. She shivered.

"You are cold," Lord Norwood exclaimed. "What thoughtless nodcocks we are to keep you standing here." With that
masterful manner he could conjure up, he swept her along to
the rear door, then inside to the kitchen.

Lord Latham followed. He glanced about the spotless room,
then noted the cinnamon buns on a tray, covered lightly with a
cloth. A teakettle steamed gently on the hob before a banked
fire.

"I believe we could all enjoy a cup of tea with one of those
buns," he observed, apparently oblivious to the tension between his friend and Hyacinthe.

She forced herself to set a tray for them with pretty cups
and saucers, plates heaped with fragrant buns, and crisp linen
napkins. What a sight she must make, her gown stained and
crumpled, hair likely in a mad tangle. Well, when had anything ever been normal when she was around Lord Norwood?

"My mother likes to collect old china," Val said after they
had settled in the sparsely furnished parlor and he had enjoyed
a bit of bun. "Do you like old things, Miss Dancy?"

"Yes, I believe you might say that I do. My mother left me
her Wedgwood and I hope to have it in my own home someday." She gave Lord Latham a curious look. His face wore a
hostile expression when he thought she wasn't watching him.
Why? Did he so deeply resent the things she had done—accidently or on purpose—to his friend? She set down her cup and
drew her shawl more tightly about her shoulders. While as-

suredly never pampered in her life, she had not known antagonism such as this before.

She heard Fanny moving about in the kitchen, a sign that
the packing had been concluded for the Widow Smith.

"More families are leaving here. The Widow Smith goes
soon and the Hadkiss family tomorrow, according to Sukey.
Before long we will be alone." She hoped her smile assured
that she did not mind the loss.

"I almost forgot to tell you—I dismissed my bailiff," Lord
Norwood said. "The man intended to raise those rents, keep
the difference for himself. As it was, Tombler definitely had
been skimming. I surmised that as soon as I saw your rent
packet. It was not the amount I had told him to charge. You
may skip the next month's payment," he added casually.

"My goodness!" she exclaimed. "What a wicked man."

"I intend to set things to right with the villagers. Contrary to
what you seem to think, I am not a monstrous landowner."

No witty reply popped into her head. The only thought that
persisted was that she had definitely ruined her chances with
the man she now loved. Oh, he might dally with her, trifle
with her a bit, but there was nothing serious. Hyacinthe might
be an innocent, but she knew full well that such a flirtation
rarely ended in something more permanent.

At last she said, "I am pleased to discover you are not what
I thought you were." And with that observation she stopped.

A subdued Hyacinthe bade farewell to the gentleman. Jane
was still gone. That could not but offer hope for her. Hyacinthe was grateful that Lord Latham did not quiz her about
her intentions for the future, a future without Jane or anyone
else.

Since she doubted Fanny—busy with preparations for supper—would come hunting for her, Hyacinthe ran lightly up the
stairs to her room and into the closet. What might have been
didn't bear dwelling upon.

Instead she lit the lamp again and returned to her inspection
of the secret passage.

There was a peculiar indentation about ten inches up from
the third step down. Hyacinthe, thankful her already-crumpled
gown could become no worse, knelt to examine it more care-

fully. She pressed the wall inch by inch, a hope growing within her that she might have found something.

Suddenly a panel of wood swung open. Elated, Hyacinthe grabbed the lamp to peer more closely. A painting! What would a painting be doing here? Replacing the lamp, she removed the landscape from where it had been concealed for likely many years. A bucolic Dutch scene met her scrutiny. She blew off a film of dust, then marveled at the detail, the colors. Surely this must be one of the "treasures" Lord Norwood had hinted at.

Eager to uncover more, she set to work with renewed zeal. Aware that the indentation meant something, she searched for another. In twenty minutes of intense examination she located another such spot.

She excitedly pressed along the same pattern as before. As before, a panel opened to reveal a second painting. She withdrew this larger oil with an awed gasp, for while she might not know the artist she recognized the quality of the work. It was truly magnificent.

After she carefully placed this painting with the first, she set to work with determined intensity. A third indentation was found about a foot below the other. Another panel opened to reveal still another painting.

She studied this one slowly, for it was of a redheaded woman. Clearly a work of great merit, it had an intimate warmth about it as though the artist painted this on a commission. Could this be a painting of the woman who had lived here so long ago? Green eyes seemed to tease her. There was no way to tell. No clue existed.

Hyacinthe sat back on the top step. Jane had still not returned. There was yet time to continue her exploration. With lamp in hand Hyacinthe inched her way along, almost nose to wall.

At last she thought she saw a difference in the wood. Heart pounding, she pressed a knot similar to the one that opened the panel to the passage. At first it appeared she had been wrong. Then slowly, ever so slowly, a small piece of the paneling opened.

"Hyacinthe?" The voice came from below.

Drat. Jane was home. Hyacinthe could not stop now, and indeed if she was right, didn't need to stop. She wrapped trembling fingers around the parcel that had been hidden and withdrew the square box.

"Hyacinthe, whatever are you doing?" It was a measure of Jane's excitement that she did not realize the significance of what Hyacinthe had found. "Come, I have important news," Jane declared with excitement ringing in her voice.

Hyacinthe had already guessed the news, but would never destroy her cousin's joyous moment. With the dusty box concealed in the folds of her skirt, she hurried up the few steps to the top, turned off the oil lamp, then faced Jane with what she hoped was deserved interest.

"Sir Charles has made me the most happy of women! We are to be married as soon as the banns have been read. And if the work continues apace, we shall be married in the new church." Jane fairly danced in her joy.

With great fondness, Hyacinthe kissed her cousin on the cheek. "I can but wish you happy, dearest Jane."

"You will write that distant cousin you mentioned," Jane said, considerate of Hyacinthe even at this time.

"Of course," Hyacinthe promised. That didn't say *what* she might write.

Once the glow had dimmed a trifle, Jane looked around the closet, then frowned. "Whatever is going on here? I do not recall those stairs before. Where did those dusty paintings come from?" Then she studied Hyacinthe and said, "Why are you wearing a most gloating expression? I doubt it is for me, for you must have guessed the outcome of this drive."

Slowly Hyacinthe withdrew the box from the folds of her skirt. Holding it up before her, she opened the lid. Both girls gasped at the contents.

"This is it!" Hyacinthe chortled with glee. "The missing jewels!"

"Oh, my," Jane whispered as she retreated. "You had best send for his lordship. I'd not wish to be responsible for them. Not at all."

"I shall. Oh, I shall with great pleasure, you may be assured." Hyacinthe stared down at the glittering gems, the necklace that must have graced a lovely neck so long ago. The gold gleamed softly in the dim light; the emeralds winked and sparkled in spite of the years.

This would surely atone for all that had happened these past weeks. Perhaps . . . just perhaps. . . .

15

"I take it you can easily explain that dirt-smudged shirt you wear," Val said on the ride back to Worthington Hall.

"Of course," Blase replied with his jaunty grin, one that tilted up at a corner of his mouth and was called rakish by any number of ladies. "I put my expertise at hedgehog snabbling to work—to catch Harry."

Val closed his eyes and shook his head in disbelief. "Every time you go near that redhead it ends in disaster. I fail to see why you must bother with her. Or is it impossible to leave her alone?" Val gave his good friend a speculative look.

"A fatal attraction? Hmmm, I doubt it. Think on this, each time the disaster lessens—witness that I only soiled my shirt this time, and that was my own fault." He thought for a moment, then continued, "And you can scarce blame Hyacinthe for that lad who careened into me while we were in Woodstock."

"What were you doing there, by the by?"

"Checking up on a few things. I need a new bailiff what with dismissing Tombler. I heard of a well-qualified man and wish to interview him. Sent off an express from Woodstock."

"So what do we do in the meanwhile?"

"There is a race on at Newmarket this weekend. Prinney's supposed to enter one of his nags. I believe I should like to see that race," Blase said in a musing tone.

"I can see where you might feel in need of funds, what with all this building. You aren't short, are you?"

"The new church is costing more than I expected. Blast it, everything has gone up in price." They rode over the final hill that offered a splendid view of his ancestral home in all its autumn splendor. Blase paused to survey his domain for a moment, content he was pursuing the right course.

"With your incredible luck you ought to acquire enough blunt while there," Val said encouragingly, seeming anxious for a diversion.

"Trouble is, they all know me," Blase muttered. "Odds will change if I bet on a particular horse—the one that Frank Buckle is to ride. I believe I shall ask Sir Charles to join us, place my bets for me. Better odds that way, you know," he said with a perceptive look at Val.

Val sighed with pleasure. "I don't mind telling you it was becoming dashed dull around here, what with you conferring with Repton and his son and clashing with Miss Dancy every other day. I'll wager Smithson will welcome the respite from the afternoon baths." He grinned at the irritated look from Blase but ceased his teasing.

They clattered into the stable yard and handed over their horses' reins to the head groom before strolling out to the terrace in front of the house.

"It is beginning to take shape as I had hoped," Blase said to Val.

They stood gazing at the nicely altered view for a few minutes, then both strode into the house.

In the library Blase penned a brief missive to Sir Charles requesting the pleasure of his company for a short trip to Newmarket. He sent it off immediately, requesting his groom to wait for a reply.

Val ran up the stairs to alert Smithson and his own valet that they best pack for more than several days, just to be on guard against accidents. The new coats Blase had ordered from London had yet to arrive. Both valets were all too aware of his frequent misfortunes and would be eager to fend off catastrophe.

Across the gentle hills splashed with autumn colors of gold and russet, Hyacinthe sat in the front parlor at a little desk she had seen in Woodstock and ordered delivered immediately. Designed for ladies, it had a hinged front that folded down flat to make a writing board. It had bookshelves above to hold the little novels that Hyacinthe enjoyed. Her hot-pressed and lightly scented paper could be tucked inside the single drawer. It was from here she took a sheet to write her momentous summons to Blase Montague, Lord Norwood.

"How best to persuade him to come without revealing all," she wondered aloud to Jane after nibbling on the end of her pen for some minutes.

"Why not simply inform him that you have found the missing heirlooms?" Jane said with irrefutable logic, glancing up from her now ever-present sewing.

"No." Hyacinthe rejected that idea immediately. "I wish to see his face when I tell him what has been here all these years. I believe he will be very pleased." She wondered if that painting of the redhead would provoke some interesting debate.

She thought on for some moments, then shook her head. "I can think of nothing else but to request the pleasure of his company as I have some information for him."

"That is certainly obscure enough," Jane said with a frown. "What makes you believe that he will pay any attention to such a request?"

"He must," Hyacinthe declared, but without a great deal of conviction.

Before she could summon Warton to deliver the message, she decided she had best have tea. Perhaps she might think of something better while sipping Bohea and nibbling one of Granny Beanbuck's buns.

Fanny had just brought in the tea tray when a rap was heard at the front door. Shortly, Fanny ushered Sir Charles into the parlor. He wore a distressed look on his face that brought Jane to her feet in dismay.

"What is it?" she cried, crossing to his side in a flurry of muslin.

"Now, now," he soothed. "It's nothing terribly serious. It is just that Lord Norwood has urgently requested I join him and Lord Latham on a jaunt to Newmarket for the weekend. I feel I must go along, given the wording of the missive." He gave Jane a fond look. "I had especially wished to attend church this coming Sunday when our banns are first read."

Jane offered a forgiving smile. "I quite understand. You

know, there are some who think it bad luck to be present at this time."

"Well," Hyacinthe inserted, her positive feelings for Lord Norwood suffering at this revelation, "I think it wretched. If the dratted man wants company he can surely find it there."

Sir Charles directed a serious look at her. "You do not understand in the least, my dear girl. I think it important that I spend this time with his lordship. I am dependent upon his good will for a number of things."

"It is an excellent idea, Sir Charles," Jane added with a scowl at Hyacinthe.

Retreating from what was, after all, none of her business Hyacinthe considered the matter from her point of view. This meant that she must shelter and protect those valuable jewels and priceless paintings for the weekend. What if Mr. Wayland took a notion to prowl about in search of them? She dare not leave the house for anything!

She owned a gun. Her brother had purchased a fine pistol from Manton and trained her in the use of it. She could hit a wafer dead center. Whether or not she might have the courage to aim that same gun at a villain she didn't know. But, she thought optimistically, she might frighten him with it. He wouldn't know she had never shot at a person before.

With a murmured excuse, for she could leave the lovers alone now that they were engaged to be married soon, she hurried up to her room to prowl through her trunks.

"I might be of help were I to know what you look for, without your tearing things to bits and pieces," Fosdick said dryly from the doorway.

"My gun," Hyacinthe informed her.

"I see. You intend to shoot his lordship over them jewels?" the maid said, walking over to a small chest beneath the window and near the secret panel.

"Fosdick!" Hyacinthe said, looking askance at this bit of plain speaking. "You are pledged to secrecy. And besides, I may think his rakish lordship a sad scrambler, what with his dashing off to Newmarket for the weekend, but I would never go so far as to shoot him for it. No, I must protect the jewels and paintings until he claims them. What if Dudley Wayland comes sneaking around here?"

The abigail rubbed her chin at this idea, then knelt to open the little chest. " 'Tis in here," she said quietly. "You will have to oil it up some, perhaps test it out back at some sort of target. You have not fired it in some time," she reminded Hyacinthe.

"With his lordship gone away, there is no need to fear I shall accidently hit him," Hyacinthe joked softly.

"Pray you need hit no one," the maid said, a sober look on her face.

After finding the bullets and all else she needed, Hyacinthe went downstairs. Jane was out in front of the house at the gate, saying a tearful but brave good-bye to her betrothed. Hyacinthe swiftly walked to the rear of the house, then out to the garden.

Warton was there, raking up some debris and in general making himself useful.

Hyacinthe rapidly explained what she wished to do. Knowing her expertise, the groom hurriedly set up a sort of target for her, then watched—after seeing to it that she didn't forget one bit of preparation.

Her aim had not suffered in the least, in spite of the elapse of time since her last attempt. Of course the noise brought Jane scurrying to the rear of the house, peering from behind a shrub at the sight of her cousin taking aim at the makeshift target.

"Heavens, Hyacinthe! What a racket you make," she said when her cousin paused to reload.

"It is my duty to protect what is not mine," Hyacinthe reminded her.

"Oh, dear, I had not thought it would come to this." Jane continued to watch, then urged her cousin back to the parlor so they might discuss the matter at greater length. "We need to plan," she concluded.

Deciding that her ability had not diminished, Hyacinthe cleaned her gun properly, then joined her cousin in the parlor, with the gun now safely in its case.

Jane eyed the gun case with misgivings and said, "You are certain you must have that thing handy?"

"Mr. Wayland may be desperate; we do not know."

"Well, I hope no one paid any attention to all the noise over here," Jane said before sipping her replenished tea.

"How could they, what with the demolishing of the cottage along the road? A gun shot is not much different from a tumble of stones," Hyacinthe reassured her with confidence.

They plunged into a plan for the defense of the house. Hyacinthe decided to reinforce the fortification of the door to the secret stairs. Jane prudently decided that the less she knew of the matter the safer she would be.

When Warton had returned to the Cock and Bull—which had already partially removed to a new location—Hyacinthe began.

She pounded more nails along the edge of the door, then dragged—with Jane's reluctant assistance—a barrel over to nudge in front of it. Once that was completed, she stood back, most pleased with her efforts.

"I misdoubt if he can sneak in past that barricade," she declared. Brushing off her hands, she found a rock to tote inside. From within the passage, she placed it so that were Wayland to manage entrance somehow or other, he would trip on the rock. If nothing else, it would serve as a warning, enabling her to meet him at the top of the stairs with gun in hand.,

All this work was tiring, but oddly satisfying.

The days passed in quiet activity. With Sir Charles and Lord Norwood away, not to mention the cynical Lord Latham, there was no social life at all.

Jane worked at a steady pace assembling a proper wardrobe. She embroidered and added lace to petticoats, sewed a sheer shift of finest cotton and trimmed it with delicate lace from a supply Hyacinthe offered.

Hyacinthe also sewed for her cousin, wishing they had time to send to London for a proper wedding dress. Jane elected to be married in a palest blue Gros de Naples trimmed with yards of Bruges lace. It was a dress Hyacinthe had brought her cousin from London and never been worn as yet. Jane thought it excessively beautiful.

When she tried on the gown, Hyacinthe had to agree, but she would have wished for better.

"You are blooming, Jane. I have never seen you in better looks. Sir Charles is a most fortunate man."

"I shan't have the sort of wedding clothes you might find in the City, but I shall do well enough," Jane replied with a hint of complacency. "And I do intend to take your advice on the chair seats."

Having completely forgotten what she had uttered about the needlework, Hyacinthe gave Jane a blank look.

"I will purchase canvas and yarns on my first opportunity. When last I looked, those chair seats appeared prodigiously dreary."

Murmuring something suitable, Hyacinthe set aside her sewing, thankful for the light from the Argand lamps this evening, and went to the windows. There had been no attempt to enter the house by any means last night. She'd taken the precaution of requesting Warton to sleep belowstairs after Fanny went home. There was comfort in knowing a man, even one as old as Warton, was in the house.

She had silently acknowledged that Wayland might attempt to enter from the front door. A surreptitious inspection of both front and rear doors did not offer a great deal of comfort. He could force entry at either—or even enter through a window. The knowledge did not console her.

The next morning Hyacinthe saw Mr. Wayland on the green. At first it looked as though he was inspecting the demolition of one of the remaining cottages. Then she observed him staring in her direction. Or did he peruse the Tudor house instead?

"Good day to you, sir," she said after crossing to meet him with what she hoped to be an agreeable manner.

Flattered to be noticed, he smiled. This sent his angular face into peculiar contortions, rather amusing ones. "You are not displeased with your temporary abode?"

"Temporary? Why do you say that? We find it most congenial." She watched his changing expression with interest. Wherever had he acquired the notion that she would be moving shortly?

"Well," he blustered, "with Miss Pennington shortly to wed Sir Charles, I assumed you would move on. Perhaps join a cousin or an aunt." He smiled again, but this time Hyacinthe felt not the least amused.

"For the present I intend to remain here. I may invite a cousin to join me. I do not care for London in the winter, much preferring the charm of the countryside."

He paled. "You plan to go with your cousin on her honeymoon?" he ventured, hope clear in his voice.

While she knew it was fairly common for a bride to have a companion along, she had no intention of leaving here, and said so. "I have not been asked, and besides . . . I think they will do well enough without me."

"But Miss Pennington is a very gently bred woman; she might find need of your company," he put forth in a persuasive manner.

"Nonsense," Hyacinthe snapped back, quite out of patience with the man. "She will have Sir Charles. Besides, I intend to do a bit of decorating, with Lord Norwood's permission, of course." Dare she hint more? "I should like to enlarge the window in the closet, for the light is dreadfully poor in there."

He frowned and in a hatefully superior voice said, "As an architect, I would not recommend that. You are likely to encounter all sorts of problems in an old place."

"Rubbish," she countered, sensing she might be hitting close to the bone. "In spite of a certain neglect the place is sound enough. I will also order a bit of painting and certainly some more furniture." With that observation she left him, returning to the garden that she and Warton were laying out along one side of the house. She well recalled the plan she had seen among the papers Lord Norwood brought.

The effect of this was one of permanence, of settling in for a long stay, precisely what she intended.

Once in bed that night it was not long before she heard noises, her room being toward the rear of the house. She slipped from between the sheets and tiptoed to the window, taking her gun from its case on the way.

Down below her room and to one side, right before the secret-door location, a shadow moved. Hyacinthe returned to her room to load her gun, don her green velvet robe, then cross to the closet. In the improbable event that Mr. Wayland did enter the passage, she would be prepared to defend the priceless heritage that belonged to Lord Norwood.

She had not closely examined her reasons for such fierce determination. Except . . . she had always been intensely loyal to her family and friends, and she supposed she might classify him as a friend. She had no other designation for him, goodness knew.

She placed an ear against the paneling, but could hear nothing. Perhaps he had been thwarted? Hearing nothing more, she returned to the window to search the grounds below. A shadow moved across the future garden, stumbling from time to time. She deduced that Mr. Wayland had given up, for she recognized his lanky, angular form immediately. But for how long? He must have counted upon her moving away from here, hoping to leave the jewels in the passage until the house again stood empty and he could retrieve them at will. She wondered if he even knew about the paintings. She doubted it. They had been very dusty and looked not to have been touched in ages.

Once again in her bed, she wondered just why Lord Norwood had to leave *this* particular weekend.

On Sunday she remained home from church, explaining to an annoyed Jane that this was precisely the moment when Mr. Wayland might break into the house, figuring that everyone would be at worship services. Jane accepted that justification, but with obvious reluctance. Jane never missed divine services unless she was seriously ill.

It was therefore quite understandable when Jane chided Hyacinthe on her mistake.

"Mr. Wayland came to church this morning. Albeit he entered rather late," she added conscientiously.

"Well," Hyacinthe replied, heroically refraining from permitting a smug note to enter her voice, "he came snooping around here shortly after you left. I was right to send Fosdick along with you. He saw two figures leave and thought it us. He was ever so shocked when I came around the corner of the house. I never saw anyone disappear so quickly."

"Oh," Jane said, much subdued. She didn't argue with Hyacinthe again regarding leaving the house, other than to remark that she hoped Lord Norwood appreciated the sacrifices Hyacinthe was making on his behalf.

As to that Hyacinthe could not speculate in the least.

The three men who cantered along the road to Worthington Hall were in the best of spirits.

"I say," Sir Charles declared with enthusiasm, "I have the greatest respect for your knowledge of horses. I can see where you earn your reputation. Well done, old chap."

"It helped a good deal to have you serve as a front for me. Wouldn't have had a chance at half the blunt had you not assisted," Blase said amiably.

"We were rather clever, if I do say so," Sir Charles replied with a grin. "Had them all fooled. Good idea to separate before we entered town and only meet by chance at the races. Shrewd bit to slip me your wagers on paper when we shook hands. No one suspected a thing. I wagered a little myself, trusting you not to let me down. Appreciate the extra sum, what with wedding costs and all."

"Miss Pennington does not come with a large dowry?" Val said without his usual wry manner.

"No, but it does not matter. I'd have her were she penniless." At that he lapsed into contemplative silence.

Val exchanged a look with Blase, then quietly said, "You will be well set now, I presume."

"Aye," Blase replied with satisfaction clear in his voice. "I can finish the church and village, complete the gardens about the house, and turn my attention to finding the jewels and paintings with no concern."

"And Miss Dancy?" Val probed.

Darting a cautioning nod at Sir Charles, Blase shook his head to indicate he'd discuss that matter later.

"Well, at least you did not have one accident to ruin your clothing," Val concluded as they rode up before the Hall.

Sir Charles took his leave shortly after. Suspecting the gentleman wished to see his Jane, Blase thanked him again for his part in the plan to increase the sum for the rebuilding of the village.

"I have a vested interest in the village, you must know," Sir Charles said as a disclaimer. "We all prosper in proportion."

Val and Blase entered the house to be met by a grave Barmore, a crisp white missive in his hand.

"What is it?" Blase asked. "You look unusually serious."

"As to that I do not know. Miss Dancy sent this message up by her groom, who said it was most urgent. It came several days ago."

"Blast!" Blase said softly. He broke the seal, unfolded the paper to read the message, then looked at Val in puzzlement. "She requests the pleasure of my company."

"That sounds innocent enough," Val replied, slapping his gloves against his thigh with impatience. "I shall leave you to decide just how urgently she desires your company while I go to my room to clean up. I feel in urgent need of a bath myself."

"I'll do the same," Blase said, somewhat abstractedly. He turned to Barmore, who looked as though bursting to say something. "Do you know anything else about this mysterious request?"

"Miss Dancy was not in church last Sunday. One of the workers told one of our grooms that he had heard something that sounded like gunshots at the Tudor cottage on Saturday."

"Zounds!" Blase exclaimed. He dashed up the stairs and into his room.

"Sir?" Smithson said, when he observed his master's haste in removing his garments.

"I'll merely wash up, for I've no time to wait for a bath. I must get to the village immediately."

In less time than he could have believed, Blase washed, changed garments, and hurried out of the house. He vaulted on a fresh horse that stood awaiting him—thanks to orders sent down by Smithson—and rode off toward the old village without a thought to Val.

He went straight to Hyacinthe Dancy.

"My lord, what a surprise," she said demurely when Fanny ushered him into the front parlor.

"You sent for me," he replied bluntly, standing before her while waiting for her explanation.

Rising gracefully from the chair where she had been sewing, she motioned him to follow her upstairs, holding one finger to her lips to urge silence.

Blase watched the slim figure before him ascending the steps with a gentle sway of her hips. Very womanly, was Miss Dancy.

They entered the closet, Blase first noting the feminine aspect of the bedroom; cheerful fabrics and bedhangings, a warm rug on the floor. Yet it appeared sparsely furnished compared to most homes he had been in, particularly ladies' bedrooms.

She crossed the closet to open the secret passage, then removed each painting from where she had again concealed it. "I believed it safest to keep them here," she said over her shoulder. After he had exclaimed over the treasures revealed—with no comment on the redheaded lady of one painting—Miss Dancy again returned to the passage and retrieved the gems. Her satisfaction in handing this box to Blase was marked. Not that he could blame her, once he opened the box.

"They are all here," he said softly, draping the necklace over his arm to admire it. "Did you encounter any problems? Someone reported he thought he heard gunshots here. I see you are not injured, so may I assume another poor soul got shot?"

"I only tested my aim, sir," she replied with a twinkle in her fine green eyes. "But I would have shot Mr. Wayland had he been able to move the barrel, then force entry to the secret passage."

"By Jove," Blase said in admiration.

"Fortunately I was at home when he came snooping around. However, I was prepared for anything."

"How may I ever thank you, Miss Dancy . . . Hyacinthe? . . . for I feel that we are far too good friends to be so formal." He cast her a speculative look.

"I should feel better were Mr. Wayland captured and sent away from here. Surely someone else could finish the project he has begun?" She did not comment on his use of her given name.

Blase rubbed his chin with his free hand. "I imagine that

could be done. I fancy Repton could recommend someone.
But how best to capture Wayland?"

"Well," Hyacinthe Dancy said in a musing tone, "Sir
Charles and Jane are due to wed soon. Perhaps you might give
a betrothal ball for them up at the Hall? Mr. Wayland would
assume us all to be there. But *I* could remain here. If he
comes, Warton and I could handle him."

Brave words, indeed. But Blase observed that her confident
words were not reflected in the way she said them. He thought
for a few moments, then offered his own plan.

"We could leave Warton on guard, as it were. The jewels
and paintings will be safely up at the house, but we will tell no
one. Once the ball is in progress we can slip off here—first
making certain that there is good music, not to mention ample
food and drink, for the celebrants. With Sir Charles and Jane
as the center of attention, I believe we might manage that.
What do you say?"

She gave him a cautious nod. "I believe it might very well
work." This was followed by a shy grin. "I am pleased I was
able to find your missing things for you."

"Dashed amazing bit of detective work. Val will be crushed,
for he fancies himself a bit of a sleuth."

Hyacinthe offered a sack for the box of jewelry, then
showed Lord Norwood how to cushion the paintings with a
length of velvet so they'd not be damaged in route to the Hall.
It made an unwieldly parcel, but she doubted if anyone would
comment. For one thing, few strangers strayed onto Montague
land and his own people would not think to question his behavior.

When she met Jane belowstairs, she countered any quizzing
with the announcement of the coming party. "He is sending invitations to everyone in this area—all who know you both. It
is to be right away, for he feels it important to show his approval of your match."

"Oh, my," Jane breathed in excitement. "A ball! It has been
ages since I last attended one. To dance with Sir Charles . . ."
She drifted upstairs to plan on a suitable gown, eyes full of
dreams.

Hyacinthe hied off to the tavern where she found Warton in the stables with Tom Coachman.

Quickly explaining what was to come, she secured the support of both men. They knew so much she didn't need to explain the necessity for secrecy.

Alone on the green, Hyacinthe looked about her. So many houses were gone, with scarcely a hint of a wall remaining. How sad, she reflected. Future generations would not know this place, save for the records being compiled by the Widow Smith and Mrs. Peachey. And all to satisfy a whim of the landlord.

But she had to admit in all fairness that he had told her he would not raise the rents. She did not wish to interfere in his business in this regard. His new bailiff would obey his wishes in this respect and inform the villagers.

Hyacinthe also reminded herself that she had misjudged him badly.

He had behaved with perfect fairness according to his own standards. And, what's more, he had refrained from a retaliation for her deeds. He would certainly have been justified to order her far away, off his land forever.

Instead he had been most forgiving. But he was hardly loverlike. He had been so terribly correct when he thanked her for restoring his heirlooms.

What had she expected? A warm kiss and embrace? her heart wondered. She would have welcomed both. Instead she was rewarded with a plan to catch a thief.

Still, she wouldn't give up yet. She had a few ideas.

16

"It is a lovely house when all lit up for a party," Hyacinthe admitted while the coach made its way to the front entrance of Worthington Hall. "Not that it is unacceptable otherwise, mind you. But the candlelight shining forth is especially nice."

"Well," Jane said after a sigh of great satisfaction, "I think it prodigiously kind of Lord Norwood to have this ball for Sir Charles and me." She gave Hyacinthe and Fosdick an anxious look. "Will I do?"

Assessing her cousin's glowing looks above the plum taffeta gown trimmed with falls of delicate Point de Venise lace, Hyacinthe replied, "You resemble nothing more than a delectable comfit, the sort one has at Christmas."

"You are in best looks," Fosdick confirmed in her proper way.

"Well, were it not for your excessive kindness in giving me this splendid gown, I should look a dowd. I can never thank you enough for all you have done, dear Cousin."

"I am pleased to see you settled and off my hands, if you must know," Hyacinthe said with a gay laugh.

"We must have a serious chat about your future one of these days. You insist upon avoiding the matter, but I shan't allow that forever." Jane studied Hyacinthe with a penetrating look, one that probably saw more than Hyacinthe wished to be seen. She was relieved when the coach stopped and Warton opened the door for the women.

Jane went on ahead to greet Barmore and discuss last-moment arrangements with him. Fosdick retired to the end of the hall, pleased to greet someone she knew.

Hyacinthe paused by the coach. "All is in readiness? You are to return to Tudor cottage. I doubt if you need hide, but just remain inconspicuous, perhaps?"

"His lordship told us just what to do, miss." Warton touched his hat in a respectful gesture, then stood stiffly at attention while Hyacinthe walked up the steps to the open door. She wondered what his lordship's instructions had been.

Lord Norwood walked up to greet her just inside the large and glittering entrance hall. The gray walls took on a warm tone from the myriad of candles; tall arrangements of autumn flowers and leaves graced the corners, adding to the appeal. Pleasant fires burned brightly on either side of the room. But Hyacinthe noted little of her surroundings in her concern.

"I trust you are prepared," she said in an undertone.

"Once the ball is well in progress I shall drop our little bomb in Wayland's ear. When he leaves, Val and I will be right behind him."

"You are far off the mark if you think I intend to be left behind in all this," she whispered vehemently. "I will be one of that party as well."

He gave her one of those amused, superior looks that men tend to bestow upon a woman when they believe men know better. Hyacinthe fumed, but silently, for she would do nothing to spoil Jane's happy moment. However, she intended to join those two men. She could shoot a gun as well as either of them, and they could use an extra person were Wayland to become violent.

When she entered the long gallery she could see that nearly everyone from the village was already present. The Widow Smith wore a rustling black taffeta gown of simple elegance that amazed Hyacinthe. Her graying curls showed from beneath a fashionable turban.

Mrs. Peachey wore a plain gray sarcenet cut in modest style and adorned with a pretty cameo pin to match her earrings and looked years younger.

If there was a faint aroma of camphor in the air, it was shortly banished by the scent from the flowers. It seemed that his lordship had emptied his conservatory of every decent bloom to be found.

Hyacinthe was quite touched by this gesture. He was giving this little ball, which consisted of the villagers and local gentry from nearby manor houses, mostly to catch a thief. But he was doing it with a grace and style that surprised and impressed her.

He had hired—Jane said all the way from Oxford—a musical group that now played softly in the background. Servants hovered along the edges of the growing throng.

She turned to face her host and admitted, "I could not have done better. This is something Jane will remember with fondness forever."

"But will you, I wonder?" he murmured, then walked away to greet new arrivals.

Blase thought she looked ravishing in the pale green taffeta gown. The neckline bordered on the scandalous, but even so it served as a foil for her exquisite skin and magnificent hair of rich deep red. He smiled. She couldn't quite hide those few freckles on her nose, in spite of what he suspected was a discreet application of rice powder.

Somehow those tiny specks of brown only served to make her more appealing if she but knew it. He greeted the guests, then turned them over to Val, who in turn guided them to where he felt they would be comfortable.

"She give you a bit of trouble?" Val muttered when he returned.

Not bothering to inquire who "she" was, Blase looked after Hyacinthe and shrugged. "She insists she is coming along with us. Why, I can't imagine. How does she think she will get there? I can't quite see that delectable gown perched on a horse, in spite of her determination."

"I would not make the mistake of underestimating her, my good friend," Val advised.

Mr. Wayland came from the rear of the house where he now stayed alone, Mr. Repton and his son having been called elsewhere. He wore a coat in a violent shade of puce over biscuit pantaloons. When Blase saw Wayland's patterned waistcoat in bright orange, he shuddered with horror.

"Good grief!" Val murmured. "It wanted only that."

"Look at it this way, we shall be doing the world a kindness by eliminating him, at least from English shores. For it will be transportation for him, I feel certain."

"I see your local Justice of the Peace is present with his good wife." Val studied Squire Knowler, then went on, "Looks to be a rather shrewd fellow. You intend to bring him in on this?"

"He has already been apprised of what has happened. I showed him the original papers, then the restored jewels and paintings. How fortunate that the next Sessions comes in Michaelmas, not too far away. Although I doubt if Wayland will like his stay in the jail until then."

"He'll like his trip to Botany Bay even less," Val said with evident satisfaction.

"The squire agreed that Wayland cannot be permitted to go free to practice this sort of thing again. Next time he might not have a Miss Dancy about to thwart his designs."

"Ah, yes. Miss Dancy. How do you intend to keep her here?" Val gave Blase a mocking smile, then added in an ironic tone, "I cannot see her standing idly by while you have all the fun. Be careful, she'll probably end up shooting you!"

Blase listened to his friend laugh and not for the first time wondered precisely why Val remained so bitter—or perhaps jaundiced would be a better word—toward women. Saying nothing, for he knew he'd receive no reply to any query, Blase merely shook his head, then wandered into the throng of happy guests.

It was not long before Blase chose to toast the betrothed couple, offering them his felicitations and hopes for a good future. The Justice of the Peace extended his good wishes as well, noting that Sir Charles was acquiring a wife who was well liked by all and who promised to be a fine helpmeet. Then the musical group struck up a joyous waltz and Sir Charles led his chosen lady into the dance to the gentle applause of the assembled.

Blase positioned himself close to where Wayland stood. The man was eyeing Mrs. Peachey's unexpectedly simple elegance.

"Amazing how a woman can bloom given the chance, what?" Blase commented to the angular architect.

They watched as Ambrose Clark led a blushing Mrs. Peachey into the dance. Then Wayland said, "Your curate is behaving unseemly, I think."

"Ah, perhaps he is merely celebrating his acquiring the title of vicar with greater things to come, once he has settled into his living."

"Vicar? The old one die?" Wayland said with a sneer.

"No. He failed to do the job he was supposed to do. I do not tolerate fools about me, once I uncover them. Crooks or cheats either," he added softly. "Witness my ex-bailiff, Tombler."

Wayland did not reply, but Blase observed that the chap's collar seemed to have become excessively tight all of a sudden. A sheen of moisture glistened on his forehead.

"By the by, did you know that I have decided to tear down the Tudor cottage after all? Miss Dancy has other plans for her future." That was no lie if Blase had his way. He would inform her later that she must alter her way of life considerably.

"Really?" Wayland said with distinct alarm. "How soon?"

"Quite soon. Miss Pennington will marry in two weeks and until then the two ladies are sure to be busy day and night preparing for the wedding. Once the wedding is over, the place comes down." Blase noted Wayland's worried frown with satisfaction. He believed what Blase said was true.

"But," the architect sputtered, "I thought you said Mr. Repton agreed it was a most picturesque house and added to your view."

Blase gave a negligent wave of his hand. "I changed my mind. The church spire is enough."

"I think Miss Dancy will be unhappy to leave there," Wayland said, obviously attempting to insert a bit of controversy.

"Miss Dancy," Blase said sharply, "has nothing to say in the matter."

"Excuse me," Mr. Wayland said, clearly agitated, "it has become somewhat warm in here. I believe I shall catch a bit of air on the terrace."

He turned to leave the room. Blase gave a nod to Val, then caught the squire's eye before sidling through the crowd to the main doorway. It was time for action and he felt primed as though for battle.

With the strains of music drifting down the stairs, he silently followed Wayland. Fortunately the chap was in such a tearing hurry he never looked behind him. He most likely believed his host content to entertain his guests.

Blase waited in the shadows of some drapery while Wayland slipped from the house to the terrace, then followed before the door could shut. Val and Squire Knowler were close behind him. Blase paused after letting the other two out of the door, thinking he heard something.

A rustle of taffeta clearly reached his ears. Miss Dancy sailed down the stairs, her soft kerseymere cloak billowing about her.

"I suspected you might try a trick like this," she fumed quietly when she confronted him. "If you think you will go without me, think again."

"And what could you do if I chose to leave you behind, my sweet?" Blase reached out to suggestively trail a finger down one petal-soft cheek in a most daring manner.

"I shall scream the house down, and most likely alert Wayland to trouble!"

Blase gazed into those fiery green eyes, eyes which promised trouble if not a great deal more. Could he resist their appeal? Knowing he would likely regret this, he nodded.

"Good," she said with a snap. "Let us be gone before Wayland stumbles into the trap set for him and we miss the entire event."

Blase couldn't fail to admire the way she whisked herself around the corner and dashed across the terrace, not making a sound in her soft slippers.

When they came up to his waiting horse, she merely turned to face him, an expectant look on her face. "Well?"

Resigned to his fate by now, Blase lifted her to the horse, then leaped up behind her, holding her as close to him as could possibly be allowed.

"Sir?" she questioned, turning her head to look up at him. She was just tantalizing inches away.

"All things will be explained in due time," he said, knowing he must sound obscure, but she couldn't be allowed to have everything her way.

The horses' hooves had been wrapped in sacking, as though they were highwaymen set on a robbery. They followed Wayland just close enough to see the fellow, yet distant enough so he should not hear them.

Hyacinthe nestled snugly against the man seated behind her. His arms came around her—to hold the reins, nothing more—but he had such a manly form and such comforting arms. She balanced as best she could, given the jouncing ride.

The oddest sensation that his lips touched her hair assailed her. But that was preposterous. The man detested her; she was certain of that. Although there had been recent moments when she had hoped. But no more.

Blase. What an appropriate name for a man who had started an unquenchable fire within her. It was a fire she must douse, however. She refused to pine for him once this was done and he went on his way. And considering the state of her fragile heart, that had best be soon.

They tore through the night, Hyacinthe relishing her closeness to Blase. Faint shadows cast by the half-moon crossed their path. She leaned into his strength.

They halted and she found herself abruptly hauled to the ground. Once certain Wayland had reached the Tudor house and tied his reins to a limb, Blase, Hyacinthe, and the others silently stalked toward the house on foot, leaving their horses tied near the green.

Tom Coachman hurried forth to take charge of them.

Unwilling to break the silence to deliver Blase a deserved scold for the rough treatment, Hyacinthe contented herself with giving him a dirty look.

"Follow me . . . and try to stay out of trouble, please?" The pleading note in his voice indicated he did not hold great hope of this.

"I never get into trouble of my own making," she whispered back at him. She thought she heard a derisive snort, but it was very faint.

Deciding they intended to trap Wayland at the base of the secret entry, Hyacinthe left them and ran to the front door, slipping inside without a sound. Even in here she could hear

Wayland frantically at work prying the door open. One by one the nails popped out.

Hyacinthe crept up the stairs and into her room. In her drawer she found her loaded gun, then prepared to wait at the top of the secret passage in her closet. She propped open the panel, but Wayland couldn't know that someone waited there for him. If he had naught but a candle, he wouldn't see beyond the immediate area he searched. He was in for a surprise.

At last the final nail was pried out and the secret access slowly opened. Wayland paused, as though to see if he had been detected. Since Fosdick had made herself conspicuous in the entry of the Hall, Wayland must feel certain the cottage now stood empty.

Hyacinthe heard his footsteps coming up toward her and she raised her gun, hoping he'd not hear her cock it.

The light of his lone candle wavered and flickered in the draft. He shielded the flame with his other hand, thus having no defense should someone rush him.

All was silent save for his steps. Then he reached the spot where the jewels had been hidden and stopped.

Hyacinthe backed away a trifle lest the shimmering green of her skirt be seen. Her gun remained aimed at her target.

He tore at the paneling, having no regard for the fine old wood. When he had removed the last panel he grabbed the box within, little knowing that it contained mere trumpery.

"Stop where you are, Wayland," Blase ordered from the bottom of the secret stairs.

Wayland immediately turned to flee to the top. Here he came face-to-face with Hyacinthe and shrieked in fright, seeing no more than a hooded cloak in the shadows.

In the ensuing minutes nothing was clear except that they could have used some light. Dudley Wayland dropped his candle, which was immediately stomped on by Hyacinthe to prevent a fire.

Then she fired her gun in the direction of his footsteps, hoping to hit the villain even with poor light, and was pleased to hear a man cry out.

But . . . the voice did not sound like Wayland's in the least.

"I've got him," Blase shouted with satisfaction from the far side of the room.

Hyacinthe quickly located her lamp, lit it with trembling fingers—for she suspected she might be in for a scold—then turned about.

"Oh, no!" she cried in dismay. She beheld a sobering sight.

Blase did indeed hold Wayland and was in the process of binding him up with the aid of Squire Knowler. Lord Latham slumped against the far wall, his hand clamped around his arm. Blood seeped between his fingers.

Hyacinthe felt ill.

"I did not know I displeased you so greatly, Miss Dancy," Lord Latham managed to say between gritted teeth.

"*I* did not know that you trailed behind Wayland, sir. I am most sorry," Hyacinthe said, hoping she sounded as regretful as she truly was. She found a stack of linen cloths and made a pad to place over the wound. Warton, who had entered from the hall, assisted her. He located a tin of basilicum powder, then went for a basin of warm water from the kitchen. He returned shortly.

While Blase informed Dudley Wayland of what he knew about Wayland's theft of the jewels, Hyacinthe worked over a now-seated Lord Latham. She removed his coat with difficulty, then—after a moment's deliberation—tore off the sleeve of his shirt. It appeared to her in the lamplight that the wound was but a graze. Nevertheless, it ought not have happened and she felt remorse that she should be the one to hurt him.

Within a brief time she had cleaned the wound, sprinkled on a bit of basilicum powder, placed the pad over it, and tightly bound his arm. When done, she gathered up the torn sleeve and his coat, then waited.

"I fancy Blase is safe enough now," Lord Latham said in his more familiar wry manner. "It is his friends who must take care."

"I did not hurt you on purpose, you know," Hyacinthe said, quite on the verge of tears.

"I shall turn this fellow over to my deputy," Squire Knowler announced. "I doubt if he will like his imprisonment, but he

ought to have thought of that before he ventured forth on a life
of crime," the squire added, prodding Wayland in the back
with a not-too-kind finger.

"And we, with a few adjustments for Val, will return to the
ball," Blase replied. "I had hoped that none would be the wiser
regarding our absence. Pity you had to get yourself shot, Val."

"I suspect it is time for me to leave your house, Blase. If
Miss Dancy is turning her dangerous attentions in my direction, I dare not remain." The old familiar mockery could be
heard along with another, almost pensive note.

"Nonsense," Hyacinthe declared briskly. "I shall take great
care to stay out of your way, sir. And as to the future, who
knows what may happen? I may throw myself on my dear
brother's mercy."

"Poor fellow," Lord Latham muttered ungraciously. He
winced when Hyacinthe placed his coat over his shoulders,
then they all straggled down the stairs.

Tom Coachman insisted that Miss Hyacinthe ought to ride
in the coach to keep an eye on poor Lord Latham.

And so she did. She kept a nervous watch on his skeptical
lordship, maintaining a dignified silence all the way. He said
nothing, staring out of the window into the dark of the night as
though he saw something of interest.

It said much for the food, drink—especially the fine drink—
and the company that the conspirators had not been missed.

Hyacinthe handed her cloak to Barmore, smoothed her curls
from her face, then braved the stairs to the gallery. Warton assisted Lord Latham, with Lord Norwood on his other side.

"Not much of an injury," Lord Latham insisted, although
somewhat weakly.

"Good thing you won't be missed from the celebrations,
then. For you, my friend, are to retire with a splitting
headache. Or do you have another ailment in mind?" Blase
said in a jovial manner only a trifle forced.

"Make me sound like a dashed wetgoose," Val complained.

"I shall say an old wound is troubling you if anyone asks,"
Blase said. "Something from our Oxford days."

"Fine," Val muttered, "just fine."

Blase ran lightly down the steps to where his guests still

mingled. Excellent music drifted toward him as he entered the room. Knowing he did not show any damage—save a faint aroma of horse, which would scarcely be detected, here what with the perfumes, sweat, and scents of food and flowers—he felt safe.

And then he saw Hyacinthe.

She stood quietly chatting with the new Vicar Clark, listening for the most part. Those pert freckles stood out in bold relief. She appeared fashionably pale.

Wending his way through the appreciative throng of increasingly happy guests, Blase found a path to her side.

Ambrose Clark exchanged glances with his lordship, then found he urgently required a glass of negus.

"Are you all right?" Blase clasped her elbow, guiding her along to a sofa close to the door.

"Yes, indeed. I drank some of your excellent champagne when I came in here, then found the good vicar. You were not gone very long." She blinked several times.

"No one has commented on our absence?"

She grinned at him, a small parody of her normal dazzling smile. "I have received two hints that I was away with you too long to be quite proper. I fear you have another shocking tale added to your list." She waggled a finger at him in a mock scold.

"Blast," Blase murmured, distressed that she would be harried in such a way. "You realize that you simply cannot remain in the cottage, gossip being what it is."

"You mean that the locals may link me—a redhead—to the lady your great-great-grandfather housed there? And what is more link you to him?" She smiled wanly. "I do not believe I should like to become your mistress, sir, even if you are a handsome brute. I suppose you could make me an offer. Perhaps I may find it irresistible." She giggled.

"How much champagne did you consume, anyway?"

"One, two, perhaps three glasses. I was very thirsty," she explained carefully.

"Hyacinthe, I hope you do not make a practice of driving a man mad." Blase wished he could whisk her out of here to a more private location.

"Never," she proclaimed somberly. "How is Val?"

Surprised at her use of his name, Blase replied, "He will do well enough. You saw to his care so he ought to mend, at least his arm. Do you fancy him as well, Hyacinthe?" he said boldly.

She merely blinked, then said, "Not at all. He needs someone who can gently nurse him from his misery. I want a man who can offer me a challenge, but of a different sort." With that she ceased to speak, turning aside to look where Jane danced with Sir Charles. "She is as happy today as she may ever be, unless you count her wedding day. It was kind of you to give her this. You are a very good man, I believe."

With that pronouncement she slid gracefully from the sofa to the floor. Or would have had Blase not caught her in his arms and carried her from the gallery.

He found Fosdick lurking in the hall.

"I think it best we see that Miss Dancy return home," he stated, defying the maid to comment.

"Aye, she has sustained more shocks this eve than a gently bred lady ought. But then, her father always said she's as tough as old boots." With that, the maid disappeared down the stairs. Blase could hear her giving Barmore instructions.

If ever a man had been more frustrated than Blase at that moment, he couldn't imagine who he might be. He stood alone with a deliciously beautiful woman in his arms . . . and she had to be unconscious. Or asleep. He didn't know which was worse.

Fosdick returned with the cloak Hyacinthe had worn on the dash across the hills to the old village. "The coach will be in front of the house shortly, my lord. Come."

It was not long before Blase deposited Hyacinthe in her coach, then watched Tom drive it off toward the old village. Well, he thought, so much for carefully laid plans that called for soft music, moonlight, and well-rehearsed words.

The following morning Hyacinthe woke feeling tired and out of sorts. She was not permitted the luxury of suffering in silence.

"Are you awake? Poor dear. Lord Norwood sent you a vast

array of flowers. Warton explained everything." Bearing a tray, Jane tiptoed into the room.

Hyacinthe eyed the contents of the tray and consented to a cup of tea and some dry toast. "I am well enough. *You* had a lovely evening, I believe."

Jane went into raptures over her splendid evening, the likes of which had never been known to anyone before. When she had praised everything from the music to the food, the lovely guests and all else, she became silent a moment.

"I think we need to talk. I will be leaving this house before long. You have avoided explaining what you intend to do with yourself. Did you actually write to anyone?"

"I suspect you know that I did not," Hyacinthe admitted, pushing herself up in bed.

"Well?"

"I believe I shall visit my brother in London after all," Hyacinthe said at long last.

"In spite of the mummies?" Jane asked with a smile.

"Bother the mummies. I need a change. Who knows when his whimsical lordship may decide to tear this place down?"

She faintly recalled saying some shocking things to Lord Norwood last evening. Words about his great-great-grandfather and his mistress. She groaned at the very idea.

"Did you see that the painting of the beautiful red-haired lady was hanging prominently in the gallery? A few people think you resemble her."

"Merely the red hair," Hyacinthe grumbled. She pushed aside her covers and left her bed. "I intend to dress and go for a stroll on the green. Will you join me?"

"Too much to do. But you go; the fresh air will do you much good," Jane observed sagely.

Hyacinthe rapidly did as intended, then slowly made her way along the pond with a bleak heart. She had come here with such noble purposes. Yet, in spite of all her mistakes, Jane had found a gentleman who truly cared for her and she would have a happy future with him.

This left Hyacinthe alone, on the shelf, no one to turn to other than a brother who really didn't wish her presence in London and a grandmother who was likely up to her ears with cousin Lady Chloe. It also left Hyacinthe yearning for a gentleman she could not have.

"Do you intend to fall into a green melancholy?" said a curious male voice from behind her. "If so, you had best douse yourself with tinted powder, for I have it on good authority that you look far too delicious."

Hyacinthe whirled about, teetering on the edge of the pond, waved her arms to regain her balance and lost. She knew she'd end up in the pond and shut her eyes against that slimy green water.

Instead she found herself captured in strong arms and drawn close to a manly chest that smelled faintly of costmary and spice. "Blase," she whispered. When he refused to put her on her feet, she tilted her head. Below her was the pond. He wouldn't, would he?

"We have some unfinished business, my love."

She blinked at the endearment. "I owe you an apology, at least I think I do. Something about your great-great-grandfather and the redhead?"

He drew her even closer. Hyacinthe grew worried at the gleam in his eyes. Did he mean to tease her, then?

"He had the right idea, only she came along too late for him. I do not intend to make the same mistake. Will you marry me, my love? Say you will, or I will drop you in the pond. Only fitting, considering our past."

Hyacinthe threw her arms tightly about his neck and plastered herself against him quite firmly. "Before you acquire any notions, I agree to wed you whenever you wish."

"I already have the notions, my dearest," he murmured, then kissed her with all the fire he possessed.

Behind them a couple watched in fond contentedness. Her red hair had faded, as had her Tudor-style gown. The gentleman, garbed in doublet and hose, gave his lady a pinch on her posterior and grinned. "They'll do fine now, I believe." The redhead winked saucily in response. And then they vanished from sight with naught but their laughter remaining.

Lord Dancy's Delight

Chapter One

Amelia Longworth picked her way with great care along the filth-strewn street of Lisbon. Her pelisse was travel-strained and worn. She had no desire to bring it to further grief by a careless misstep on the wretched cobblestones. Remnants of garbage tossed by residents and discarded by dogs not only left much to be desired, but were hazardous as well.

She turned to her companion, Chen Mei, and addressed her in Cantonese. "Mind your step. Those dogs look wild to me and certainly not to be trusted." Amelia gestured to the dogs that swarmed toward the Praça do Commercio, noting a pack of the most vermin-ridden, ill-tempered, nasty-looking beasts she ever recalled seeing.

"The cautious seldom err," the Chinese woman replied in agreement, looking at the dogs with disdain.

Ahead of them the square, open on one side to the Tagus River, was surrounded by government offices with an arcade beneath. The Custom Office stood on the far side of where they paused while looking about the square, supposedly one of the more splendid sights of the city.

"This is not as fine a city as I had hoped," she commented. Not waiting to see if Chen Mei followed, Amelia strolled forward to study the scene.

She did not care for what she had found so far, but was so thankful to be on solid ground once again that she could tolerate the uncleanliness. After all, other ports they had seen on the way to England from Macao were little better.

The trip had been a tedious and extremely long six months. She understood why her father had sent her off to London, for she suspected she had a great deal to learn about the ways of society. The English in Macao tried to retain hold on the manners and the mores of society, but to make a proper come-out, a girl needed London.

Besides which, Amelia had been raised by a Cantonese woman and imbued with many of the attitudes of the Orient. Amelia suspected she might find a shade of conflict between the two cultures.

But she missed the only home she could remember. There had been strolls along the sweeping promenade of the Playa Grande, which curved along the edge of the sea. White baroque buildings had glittered in the sun while she enjoyed her amble, with the young clerks of the East India Company vying for her attention. The ground rose sharply from the sea and the water front, where Amelia had been forbidden to stray. Chen Mei had scolded her at the mere mention of that area.

When Mama died things had changed. Papa was gone more, traveling to Canton to supervise trading for the East India Company. He worried, she knew, about the whims of the Chinese. They viewed the British as foreign devils and considered the goods brought for trade with utmost contempt. Papa—Sir Oliver Longworth to others—feared Chinese reaction to the opium trading sanctioned by the British government and the East India Company as an important revenue. Papa thought the Chinese might get angry enough to wage war against the British, not that the poorly equipped and trained Chinese soldiers could succeed. But it could get nasty.

Papa would have reaped a great fortune by this time had he participated in the opium trade. Each shipload brought immense profit. Still, Amelia possessed excellent letters of credit, for he had done well enough with his investments, and she expected to have all the money she required for her come-out once she reached London.

There were a few things she would like to purchase, but the shops held little of interest for her. An apothecary shop had yielded tooth powder. A milliner to produce a truly pretty bonnet seemed beyond possibility. It would have been lovely to find a pretty straw confection so her aunt wouldn't think her too provincial. Amelia sighed.

A group of soldiers sauntered across the square, ignoring the Gallegos, or water carriers, who, Amelia had been informed by the captain of her vessel, brought water to each of the houses from one or another of the thirty-one fountains in the city. As the ship had neared the quay where they were to dock, she had glimpsed an aqueduct that came down into the city from mountain springs. In the pleasant February sun the sight of even one of those fountains would be most welcome.

Just then four of the dogs attacked one of the Gallegos, causing him to trip and drop his precious cask of water. The crash and fearful cursing in fluent Portuguese brought Amelia to a frightened halt. She froze as the cask bounded across the square and directly toward her. Behind her Chen Mei burst forth in angry Cantonese, denouncing these hapless foreigners.

Then Amelia was captured up in strong arms and held tightly to a broad chest. The sensation of a man's arms cradling her legs and upper body ought to have rendered her speechless. Shocked, Amelia cried out as she was rushed to the shadows of the arcade at the side of the square.

The barrel rolled past them to smash against the wall of stone, water erupting in a fountain that cascaded everywhere. It was, Amelia considered, a peculiar way to see a fountain even if she had wished to do so. Fortunately she and her rescuer were spared a wetting. Her bonnet was quite shabby-looking as it was, and it the last of her original five.

The man who had so abruptly snatched her from the path of the barrel checked the square behind them, and Amelia wondered if he intended to cart her farther. He smelled pleasantly of eau de cologne, although Amelia could not truly appreciate it at the moment.

Behind them the square was in total chaos. The Gallegos water carrier cursed the dogs, who barked loudly in response, their numbers augmented from a side alley. Barefoot fishwives, dressed in black and carrying trays of fish on their heads, hurried to loudly offer their advice. Bakers, bowed by the enormous weight of bread slung over their shoulders, prudently avoided the mob and skirted the square. The other soldiers laughed at the melee, offering their own pithy observations on the accident.

Geoffrey placed the young woman on her feet in what he deemed a safe enough spot not too far from the remains of the broken barrel. Then he studied the slender damsel who had frozen from fear, and in so doing, had endangered her life.

"I suppose I ought to thank you, sir, but I fear it is quite beyond me at the moment." She didn't appear to appreciate the rough handling, even if he did sweep her out of the barrel's path.

Her pelisse was out of date, but well-made and of a becoming color. That bonnet, now somewhat crushed, lacked style from what he had seen here in Lisbon. But when she raised her head to stare at him, he received a shock.

The girl possessed a fine pair of speaking blue eyes the color of the sky on a summer's afternoon—an English blue of a heavenly color in a face framed, by what glimpses he could detect, with hair like finest corn silk, a rich golden yellow. Her oval face was unbecomingly tanned however, and he wondered at her being allowed to wander about the city alone, with only that improper Chinese woman to chaperon her. Not gentry, he suspected, in spite of her cultured accents. She spoke Portuguese, he recalled, and wondered at that, for she wasn't a local girl. He'd seen what Lisbon had to offer, and few English resided here what with the war and all.

He scolded, "If you had any sense, you would have remained in your abode, out of harm's way. Young ladies do not wander unprotected about the city." His voice carried all the anger he felt at a young chit off without adequate protection.

Then he glanced down at a sudden movement by the Chinese woman and found a curved dagger pointed at his heart, while the woman gazed up at him with a menacing smile.

"You muchee bad man. You no talkee Tian Li." She gestured with the knife that Geoffrey ought to back away.

"Forgive me." Belatedly he remembered his manners and swept his hat from his head. "I am Major Dancy. I am only too happy to be of service to the young lady, who I trust is about to retreat to her inn." He bowed to both women, then waited to see what the blonde would do next. She did not reveal her name, but the companion appeared to be satisfied at his identity.

The dagger disappeared beneath the sleeves of the full frock the Chinese woman wore. The curious garment billowed about her knees above the baggy black trousers drawn together at the ankle by tasseled ribbons. Her incredibly tiny feet were compressed into black high-heeled slippers. He suspected that behind those dark eyes a suspicious mind worked at full speed, witness the swiftly produced knife. Even the long silver bodkins that were fixed into the wealth of black hair screwed up on top of her head appeared to be lethal weapons.

"Well, Major Dancy," the young lady observed in cultured accents, "I thank you for your kind rescue. I might have been injured," she admitted. Her face pale, eyes downcast, she dipped the faintest of curtseys before warily backing away from him. Then head bowed, she glided along the edge of the square, her curious-looking companion tottering along close behind her.

The chit was not at all to his standards, however. She exhibited precisely the sort of behavior he'd not have in a wife: adventuresome, bold, impetuous, although she did appear to be a resolute thing. And she had lovely eyes. But she was not the girl he'd choose. Not in the least!

While Geoffrey stood staring after them, his friends came up to him, still laughing over the incident of the dogs and the water-carrier. After months in battle it was a relief to find something to amuse.

"What ho, Dancy?" said Peter Blandford, the closest friend Geoffrey had made while in Spain and Portugal.

"Nothing much," Geoffrey replied absently. "A schoolgirl slipped the leash and received more than she bargained for, I'm sure. She could have been killed, silly chit." He clapped his hat back on his head, then brushed down the plain jacket he had designed for his peculiar role while serving his government. His uniform was largely civilian in appearance, for he cared not for the fancy dress others affected, all gold tassels and braid.

"Or at the very least a nasty injury." Peter added, looking after the disappearing figures. He motioned with a hand,

and the group set off in the opposite direction, bent upon finding a decent meal.

Once around the corner Amelia rested against the cool stone of the building to catch her breath. She had not wanted to admit how the feel of those strong arms about her had affected her emotions. She'd not been close to any man before. Clerks dare not touch the daughter of the supervisor, and there were few unwed officers around that Amelia had been permitted to meet.

At the speculative glimmer in Chen Mei's eyes, Amelia hastily moved to set off down the street once again.

"Soldier save your life," Chen Mei observed while shuttling along at Amelia's side.

"That does not make him a good man, however," Amelia replied a bit more sharply that customary. "Come, we had best seek out the inn where the captain said we are to await the sailing to England. I shall be grateful for a night in a real bed. We can only pray it does not have bugs."

Her companion agreed, having a more philosophical opinion about those creatures but not wishing to disagree with her precious charge. When the dainty blonde had first appeared, casting her smiling blue eyes on all around her, Chen Mei had fallen victim to her charm. Dubbing the infant Tian Li, or Celestial Delight, because of her remarkable blue eyes and good nature, Chen Mei had attached herself to the Longworth household and remained. Nor would she permit her girl to sail away to heathen parts without Chen Mei to guard her. From what had been observed, her Celestial Delight would need every trick in Chen Mei's bag. No dragon would defend its treasure better.

At the inn designated by the captain as being suitable for a daughter of an East India Company official, Amelia used her accomplished Portuguese to smilingly command a lovely bath and an excellent meal. Such ability with the language was rare in a foreigner, and it brought forth amazed compliance along with a desire to provide the best for the English lady who actually knew the language.

If the serving girl cast dismayed glances at the peculiar "Chinee" who stood glaring fiercely at her each time she entered the room, it mattered not. For the first time in ages

Amelia was able to luxuriate in a decent slipper bath and partake of a truly good meal.

She chattered to Chen Mei all the while she bathed, then ate in subdued thoughtfulness. She had grown accustomed to Portuguese dishes while in Macao, and the flavor of her dinner made her rather ache for her father and the home she had left. Best not to dwell on the matter, hence the murmur of conversation.

"Eat something, Chen Mei," Amelia scolded gently. "It is not like what you prefer, but until we reach my aunt's home you will have to make do with what we have at hand."

Gesturing to the dish of prawns and rice with vegetables mixed in, Amelia nodded again. "It is quite good."

Obviously horrified at the thought of eating while her mistress consumed her own dinner, Chen Mei reluctantly heaped food on a plate and awkwardly fed herself with a fork while kneeling on the rug. As lovely as the day had been, the evening grew cool and the small fire was most welcome. It cheered the room while Chen Mei scowled at her plate.

"You do not like to use a fork yet," Amelia observed. "I know you carry your sticks. Why not use them?"

Her companion hastily rooted about in a capacious bag, and with a pleased smile pulled out a pair of ivory sticks. The remainder of her meal was enjoyed with relish.

Once Amelia was ensconced in her bed for the night, with Chen Mei unhappily settled in the adjacent room instead of at the foot on Amelia's bed so as to guard her charge, she was free to consider the day's activities. Chen Mei considered these parts of the world quite heathen and was determined to guard her charge from foreign devils.

The shops in Lisbon had little to offer. It was a pity, for it would be quite dreadful to appear before her aunt in her sadly crushed remaining bonnet.

Which thought brought her to the event that lingered in the back of her mind. The memory of being carried in those strong capable arms, cradled so close to that broad chest haunted her. Could she even sleep this night? She doubted it. Having pushed the subject away the remainder of the day, she could not prevent it from filling her mind now she had nothing else to occupy her.

He had smelled of eau de cologne, she recalled. Odd. She couldn't recall that any of the naval men who came to meet with Papa had worn such a pleasing scent. It was light, yet sharp; pleasant, yet most masculine. Maybe it was only the army men who preferred to smell of something besides soap and boot polish.

He had been handsome, too. In spite of the tart words she had uttered to him and to Chen Mei, she had noticed everything about the man. His lean, sun-burned face held unusual green eyes that had made her think of palace jade once viewed in Macao. Auburn hair had curled nicely about his well-shaped head. His uniform fit him splendidly, which told her that he could afford an excellent tailor. She couldn't place his uniform, but then, she was not well-acquainted with army uniforms.

He was undoubtedly a dangerous man. Surely any man who possessed such quick thinking, such manly attributes, along with a form that was more than breathtaking could only be such. He looked to be the sort that stole hearts as easily as smiling in that lop-sided manner he'd used when she had scolded him. Oh, he had been so amused with her! And she had been such a hen-witted creature.

On this unhappy reflection, Amelia drifted to sleep, determined to forget the handsome major and concentrate on her coming splash in London society.

Early the following morning, she and Chen Mei made their way down to the quay where they were to reboard the ship that would take them the final lap of their long journey to England and her father's sister, Aunt Ermintrude Spencer.

During the stop at Lisbon the cargo destined for Portugal had been removed, and port and other wines had been loaded, along with lemons, oil, cork, and leather among other goods the English wanted.

In the pale pink light of the early morning, Amelia glanced about her, taking in the sight of the men bustling about the quay, looking important as they ordered goods toted on board the ship.

The ship appeared to be fully loaded. Amelia's own

small portmanteaus and bits and pieces of baggage were a
mere nothing in view of all the rest of the cargo. A sailor
came up to her, respectfully requesting that she come
aboard. He swung her belongings up with ease, then
marched off to the ship, leaving her to follow. She dawdled, fascinated with the scene about her.

There was an altercation somewhere behind her. Amelia
paused, then turned to see what was going on. Lisbon was
quite as noisy and smelly as any other port, and she held a
scented handkerchief to her nose as she looked about to discover what the trouble might be.

Down the quay she espied the man from yesterday, the
major. Again he wore the rather new-looking uniform, if
that was indeed what it was. It had never seen battle, for
certain. Unspotted, unfrayed, it bore no traces of duty unless duty involved nothing more than dancing.

His boots possessed great shine, but there was no sign of
the gold tassels so beloved by most military men. The dashing red tailed-jacket seemed plain when compared to that of
his friend. A discreet touch of gold braid at his collar and
wrist made her suspect his tailor insisted upon the fancy addition, for it seemed unlike the major from what little she'd
observed. Simple white pantaloons clung to strong legs.

Then she was struck with the notion that he had bought
the garb to replace one ruined in war. He turned, walking
along with his friend, and Amelia noted that he had a slight
limp. She was assailed with dismay that she had harbored
such doubts about this man. Of course he was a true soldier, and she was a ninny to believe otherwise.

She wished she might apologize for her graceless thanks
of the day before. What he must think of her did not bear
considering. But then, when she had examined her appearance in the speckled mirror at the inn, she had admitted she
did not present a fetching picture. He most likely was
happy to be rid of her presence. And that thought rankled
the girl who had twirled her parasol and flirted with gentlemen while strolling on the Playa Grande—in far better
looks than what the major had seen.

Instead she ought to avoid the major, boarding the ship
with all due haste. And this could be none too soon. The
characters who strolled about the area appeared most unsa-

vory as they twirled black mustachios and glared at her
from beneath black hats. In fact it seemed to Amelia that
the throng had increased quite suddenly. She was pushed
and jostled about with most disrespectful lack of care.

Impulsively she turned to seek the major. He had saved
her yesterday; perhaps he might take pity on a rather unim-
portant girl, out of duty if nothing else.

The press of the crowd grew, and a flutter of fear rose
within her. Where was he?

Then she caught sight of his trim form and blessed his
distinctive, if plain, uniform. She slipped through the
throng, Chen Mei not far behind. She had reached him, albeit his back, when she felt a distinct shove. Someone had
pushed her.

Panic began to creep over her, building as she sought to
catch the major's attention. She did not like this crowd in
the least. The sooner she boarded the ship, the better off she
would be. Why had she dawdled?

"Sir?" she began hesitantly, speaking up so as to be
heard above the noise of the crowd.

This time the thrust was harder, and she lost her footing.
Unwittingly she had come close to the outer side of the
quay. Below her dirty water waited to receive her body as
she teetered on the edge of the quay, desperately trying to
regain her foothold. She'd never learned to swim, and with
her heavy skirts and pelisse she'd not have had a chance
even if she did know how. She stretched out a hand toward
the major. In the distance she heard Chen Mei cry out.

"What the—" The major had whirled about at the sound
of her faltering call to pull Amelia into the safety of his
arms.

Amelia found herself caught once again against his firm
body. They teetered for what seemed like endless seconds,
then Major Dancy regained his balance and pulled her back
with him in the direction of the ship.

"You again!" He glared at her with a most peculiar expression on his face, one she did not recognize at all.

"Please forgive me, Major Dancy," Amelia said in a
shaky voice, summoning all her reserve of dignity. "I beg
you will assist me to the ship. The press of the crowd be-

came too much and I lost my balance. I did not intend to bowl you over like a tenpin, sir."

She feared her feeble attempt at humor had failed. Then he half smiled at her and nodded, much to her relief.

"I fear your bonnet will never be the same again after seeing Lisbon. Where is your companion?"

Geoffrey clasped her elbow in a firm grip as he searched the area about them, taking note of the unusual throng of men crowding the quay.

What was going on here? He hadn't expected to see so much activity so close to sailing time. All the cargo ought to be stowed by now, with only the last-minute parcels and luggage of passengers coming on board. In fact, if the young miss he steered before him truly intended to sail this morning, she ought to have been on the ship some time ago.

Once on board, Amelia pulled free of that tight clasp, then sank into a proper curtsy. Chen Mei bustled up, smiling in relief at finding her charge safe.

"Please accept my deepest appreciation, Major Dancy. I cannot begin to tell you how that crowd frightened me."

"You ought to have been on board long ago. Were you not informed of the sailing time? Or perhaps you had a last-minute delay, as I did?"

Even as they spoke, the sails began to billow out. Amelia could sense the now-familiar feel of the ship slowly moving out into the channel and underway. The wind was good, and they would have no trouble navigating along the Tagus and out to the ocean.

With the usual creaking of wood, the flapping of the sails, the shouts of the sailors, and the cries of the gulls that wheeled and dove about the stern of the ship as background, Amelia stared at the major, puzzled.

"I received no word from the captain, if I was to have been called. It has been my custom these many months to either remain on board—when the port looked unsavory— or present myself as early as possible. I trusted it would be the same here." She gave the major a speculative look. "Is there a problem, sir?"

"No, none," he assured her, hoping to calm any fears she might have. After seeing her walk apart and converse with her companion, Geoffrey turned to stare back at the quay. Something didn't set right with him.

Why the devil would a Portuguese want to push a strange female over the edge of the quay, most assuredly drowning her if not rescued in time. Why she had been shoved so forcefully that she had nearly taken him with her.

Then Geoffrey stiffened as possible implications struck him. Was the real target himself, and the young woman merely a means to the end? He turned his head to study her. Tian Li, the companion called her. What was that in English, he wondered.

When the moment presented itself, he inquired of the captain as to the girl's identity. They chatted briefly, then Geoffrey properly excused himself and returned to his place at the railing.

Amelia Longworth was nowhere in sight. She must have retired to her cabin. After six months it must seem almost like home to her. Well, he had no need to worry about the chit. She was safe now. After they landed in Portsmouth, he most likely wouldn't see her again.

What a drab little thing she was, although she did have promise, he admitted. He too vividly recalled the feel of that lissome body in his arms. Pity she had such an unlady-like tan, dreadful clothes, and the inclination to be where she should not.

Geoffrey utterly forgot that tan can fade, mantuamakers existed to properly dress unfashionable young ladies, and that this particular one would likely go where she pleased no matter what.

The trip to Portsmouth was uneventful. Given the indication that things tended to happen wherever Miss Longworth appeared, he was grateful for the quiet.

"You will be glad to return home, Dancy?" Peter Blandford inquired as the two stood by the railing again, wondering when they would sight their homeland.

"I should have come home long ago to take over the reins of the household. It is too much to expect that my sisters can manage the estate. Now," Geoffrey said with a grimace and a glance at his injured leg, "I have no choice but to obey the command to sell out and tend to my family business again."

"Your father died not too long ago. What about your sisters?"

"Julia is widowed, you see, and has returned home to keep an eye on Victoria and Elizabeth. But they all need a man in the house to take care of things. You know how women are, can't manage without us." Geoffrey rubbed his chin, while contemplating the task before him. He knew his father had employed a good steward, but an estate needed the owner's interest to keep matters in line. He had the house in town to care for plus the estate in the country.

Peter nodded sagely, readily agreeing to the lack of capability among females in general.

"I shall have to report immediately, and hope there is nothing more they wish me to do," Geoffrey continued. "Then see to my sisters. Victoria is nearly on the shelf, and Elizabeth ought to be nearing the age for marriage."

"How long has it been since you last saw them?" Peter inquired.

"A few years," Geoffrey admitted.

"Given the mails, what makes you think they are still awaiting your guidance?" Peter grinned as his friend glanced up in frowning dismay.

"They wouldn't proceed without me."

"Would you like to bet on that?"

Since gentlemen would bet on nearly anything and everything, Geoffrey abruptly agreed, then stared moodily at the water. Would they? He'd wagered they were still at home, dutifully awaiting their brother to come to assist them in arranging their lives.

Landing at Portsmouth was as hectic as landing at any other port, Amelia decided. However England had the advantage of being her new home, and so she eagerly leaned against the railing, searching the shore to see what her England looked like.

"I fancy you are happy to arrive at long last, Miss Longworth."

Amelia turned to see the major moving closer along the rail. Just then the wind caught her bonnet, tearing at the worn ribands, and it went sailing over the side. Her hands flew to her head in utter dismay. How dreadful. He would think her quite the frump having one old bonnet to wear, and now that gone. For some reason she didn't care to examine she wished for the major's good opinion.

"I fear it is gone for good. It will give you an excuse to buy a new one," he said with a teasing note in his voice.

"Oh, dear," she wailed softly. "It is the fifth bonnet I have lost on this journey. Between rain, wind, and other things, travel is very hard on bonnets."

Geoffrey stared at the delicate-looking girl at his side and felt as though he were losing his grip. Beautiful thick blond hair curled about her face, framing her now-rosy cheeks with incredible beauty—even if she dressed like a dowd and needed a proper London wardrobe.

Pity he would most likely never see her again.

"Do you intend to stay over to take the morning coach? Or do you plan to hire a post chaise to reach your destination, Miss Longworth?" Then he found himself adding, "If I may be of any service to you, please do not hesitate to call upon me. I shall be staying at the Star and Garter." He had named a pleasant inn not far from where the coaches departed for London.

At the sight of her frown he cursed himself for being stupid. How could a young woman arrange for a carriage, or for that matter see to her coach fare?

"If there is no one else to assist you, I shall take care of everything."

Amelia stared in amazement, for she had thought he would be gone the moment the ship docked. The information that the captain was to see to her arrangements somehow was forgotten as she blushed and nodded.

"I would be grateful for your help, sir."

With that blush came common sense. Geoffrey Dancy wondered if he had taken leave of his mind.

Chapter Two

The Star and Garter proved even better than Geoffrey had recalled. The host hurried forward to greet him, and when informed that the daughter of the East India Company official Sir Oliver Longworth also needed rooms, he efficiently arranged everything to their satisfaction.

"I shall write Papa to tell him of your many kindnesses," Amelia said, holding out her hand in a desire to touch Major Dancy for a final time. Her eyes twinkled with a hint of mischief as she added, "He promised me that English gentlemen were truly noble in character and most trustworthy. He will be so pleased to know I have found his assessment correct."

A glimmer of worry crept into the major's eyes. "Do not be too trusting, Miss Longworth. There are a few men who might take advantage of your innocence."

Before Amelia might inquire precisely what that might involve, they were interrupted by the host.

"My lord, your rooms are ready if you wish. I have ordered a bath for you. Possibly the young lady wishes one as well?" It had been chilly when the ship docked, and the host knew they would want fires in their rooms and a hot bath to remove the stains of travel and warm them.

Her mind whirling, Amelia could only nod, frowning at Major Dancy while he made further arrangements with the host of the inn. Had she heard aright?

"He is, you know," Peter Blandford said softly from behind her and to one side.

"Oh?" Amelia turned her head to listen to an explanation if one were forthcoming, while still keeping a wary eye upon the major.

"He is Baron Dancy now his father is gone aloft. I believe Geoff finds it difficult to remember his status has changed. Does it make a difference to you?"

"Why should it?" Amelia replied in an equally soft voice. "Once we leave here, I shan't see him again most likely." There was no clue in her voice she regretted that circumstance. Only her eyes grew wistful.

"I would make a wager on the likelihood of that, but I fancy you are not inclined in that direction."

Amelia smiled at the amusement in his voice, banishing the frown from her face. "No. I only bet on very sure things, sir. And I have learned that life is too unpredictable to take this sort of chance."

"A philosopher at your tender age? Astonishing." Mr. Blandford chuckled.

"What is astonishing?" Major Lord Dancy inquired as he joined them once again.

"I suspect that being raised in the East has turned Miss Longworth into a philosopher. She views life as highly unpredictable so is unwilling to bet on her future."

Major Lord Dancy was clearly puzzled, but merely nodded to Amelia, then gestured to the stairs located directly behind where they stood.

"Your room awaits you. I imagine your companion has already gone to inspect the place. Is she to remain with you in England?"

If Amelia thought his question intrusive, she made no indication. She imagined that quite a few people might wonder about her companion as days went by.

"I doubt Chen Mei would return to Macao if I ordered her to go. She insisted she come along to guard me from the heathen, as she views the English. You may think me unprotected, but she rarely leaves my side."

As though to emphasize that point, the Cantonese woman emerged from the shadows of the inn entry to glide up to her charge. "Missee go now."

"I shall bid you gentlemen good day. And Major"—she paused before mounting the stairs—"I shall be extremely grateful if you can perform one last service and assist me in arranging for a post chaise for the morrow."

Geoffrey watched her disappear to the upper regions of the large inn.

"Pity about the poor girl, all alone in a strange country. Someone ought to look after her better than that Chinese woman. Fancy her thinking *us* a pack of heathen." Peter nudged him in the ribs and chuckled.

"You failed to see the dagger Chen Mei carries up that sleeve of hers. I wonder what else she has up her sleeve." Geoffrey speculated on this for a moment. Then he clapped his good friend on the shoulder and suggested they repair to their rooms. Later they would meet in a private parlor for their dinner.

He contemplated inviting Miss Longworth to join them for dinner, then recalled he was back in England now and could not do such things. But he regretted that he must bid her good-bye. Perhaps he would call on her once in London. The poor little thing would most likely be grateful for a gentleman caller. What her aunt might be like he couldn't imagine, not having had much to do with aunts. His sisters talked about visiting their Aunt Bel, but implied she was a bit strange with peculiar superstitions.

Dismissing Miss Longworth from his mind, he relaxed in a welcome bath, then took his ease with Peter, discussing the meeting he faced with Hardinge once they reached London.

"I believe he will be pleased with what has been accomplished. Not that we shall need all those maps I drew anymore, but I think we have shown that we can gather intelligence with the best of them."

"Meaning the Russians?"

"And the French, at least in Germany. They are meeting at Châument this week, and it will be interesting to see how it all ends."

"Surely Napoleon must admit his defeat? He is being hard pressed on every side." Peter took a sip of the excellent port provided by their host, easing back from the table following their meal.

"I believe he is not one to accept defeat willingly. If I may borrow from Miss Longworth's philosophy, never bet on anything unless it's a sure thing."

"Like your sisters?" Peter teased. "What is your Miss Longworth's destination—since you arranged for her post chaise?"

"She is not *my* Miss Longworth, and she goes to London, the same as we do. The captain informed me that she is to stay with her aunt, presumably until the aunt will arrange a suitable marriage for the girl."

Peter fiddled with the empty glass in his hand, studying Geoff's face as he spoke. "A poorly endowed girl, then? She'll have difficulty in firing her off?"

"You make her sound like a gun." Geoff grinned at his friend, then sobered, reflecting. "Actually, our good captain hinted that Miss Longworth has a generous portion, being an only child of a very prosperous East India official."

"She might look a bit unfashionable, but she seems demure enough to pass the dragons of society."

"It will depend upon her connections, I suppose. I thought I might drop by her aunt's place one day. Just to see how she goes on, you know." Geoffrey waved a hand in the air in a negligent manner, then poured them each another glass of port.

Peter nodded, his eyes downcast so his expression was concealed. "I think that would be kind and most noble of you."

"Are you roasting me?" demanded Geoffrey, slightly insulted by his friend's tone.

"I? Roast you? Never. Now when we arrive in London, I might have a thing or two to say about your sisters." He paused, then added, "You could introduce Miss Longworth to them. Just a thought. She won't have any friends in the city. Apt to be lonely for a bit, you know."

"Good thinking, Peter. By the bye, need a place to put up for a time? House has plenty of room in it for another chap." He gave his friend a searching look, for Peter rarely spoke of his family, and then only in brief terms.

"I'll take you up on that kind invitation if necessary. My, you are turning over a leaf, becoming a regular saint." He chuckled at Geoffrey's expression, then added, "It's only to look over those sisters of yours. Who knows, I might take to one of them?"

"Ha!" Geoff replied, thinking he would very much like to have Peter for a relative. But even he knew he could not order one of his sisters to marry where she didn't want to.

Down the hall Amelia curled up in the good bed, tucking

a wonderful down pillow behind her, then contemplated her companion who refused to be banished to the next room.

"Nothing will happen to us, Chen Mei. This is a perfectly respectable English inn, not like those others we saw. That inn in India might have been full of thieves, but once they saw your dagger, they left us alone."

"Missee have need of mo' than dagger. I feel. I know." Chen Mei nodded sagely, then prepared for the night ahead when she would guard her precious Celestial Delight. Remaining fully clothed, she camped close to Amelia.

Secure in the knowledge that before long she would be with her aunt in London and on the way to acquiring an English husband, Amelia settled to sleep.

She was greatly annoyed when Chen Mei shook her awake in what seemed like the middle of the night. The room was warm, the fire still burning faintly in the grate. She could see nothing out of the window, just a hint of the dawn to come.

"Chen Mei, I hope you have a good reason for this," she scolded softly, so as not to disturb others.

"I hear noise."

"You heard a noise and woke me to tell me that?" Amelia frowned. It wasn't like Chen Mei to do something like this. Quickly slipping from beneath her covers and wrapping the heavy satin Oriental-style robe about her, Amelia crossed the room. At the window she could see that the hour was more advanced than she had realized. Down in the inn courtyard, she spotted Major Dancy supervising the loading of his carriage. What was wrong? She sniffed the air, testing it.

"Stow that last bit of baggage in the boot and we are ready to leave," Geoff instructed the groom. To Peter he added, "I think a bit of breakfast will not come amiss."

Geoffrey wanted to have another look around. When he had come down the stairs this morning, he could have sworn he saw a face he had last seen on the quay in Lisbon. He wanted to search about again.

"Do you smell smoke, old chap?" Peter inquired with the languid air of a London dandy, apparently one he intended to cultivate once he shed his uniform for good.

"Just the chimneys, I suppose. This time of year everyone wants a fire." Geoffrey pulled his coat about him, then gestured toward the inn.

"Not the same, Geoff. I could swear I see smoke rising up from that side of the inn. Look."

Concerned, Geoffrey allowed himself to be pulled along until they were on the far side of the building. Sure enough, the faintest trace of smoke curled up from the eaves. Wasn't that where Miss Longworth had a room? He tossed a worried look at Peter, then made a dash for the inn door.

"It may be nothing at all, but I believe I will investigate. Miss Longworth is in that section of the inn."

Peter following closely behind, the two men ran into the inn and dashed up the stairs. The smell of smoke was stronger here. There was silence, as most of the occupants of the rooms still slept. At the far end of the hall, where Miss Longworth slept, the smell of smoke grew stronger.

All at once flames burst forth from one of the doors, revealing the room behind it on fire. Flames seemed to shoot everywhere at once. Turning to Peter, Geoffrey shouted, "Rouse everyone you can. I'll find Miss Longworth."

The two began pounding on doors, alerting the people before hurrying on to the next rooms. Geoffrey had begun to wonder if he had misunderstood the direction of her room, when he met success.

Amelia opened her door, staring with confusion at Major Lord Dancy even as she wrinkled her nose at the acrid scent of burning wood and fabric. With a call to Chen Mei, she held out her hand to the major.

"There is a fire. I trust you will take us out of here?" She placed her slim hand in his large capable palm, then bravely followed as he led them down the hall.

Chen Mei, her arms loaded with bags, darted past them to check the safety of the hall for her charge. At the corner where the stairs were located, she paused then said, "Velly bad. You carry missee. She no make it otherwise." Then she disappeared from view in the thickening smoke.

Chaos now reigned as the various occupants peeked out of the doors in horror, then pushed and shoved past Major Lord Dancy and Amelia with total disregard for their safety.

Angered as one buck nearly jostled Amelia into the path

of the fire, Geoffrey swung her up into his arms and stalked past the flames, burying his face in the wealth of blond hair to keep from inhaling the smoke overmuch.

"Hold your breath," he ordered as they reached the staircase.

The sound of crackling flames, feeding on old and very dry timber, grew louder. Amelia closed her eyes, shrinking against her rescuer as the blaze flared up and little flames darted out as though to grab her. One hand clung tightly about his neck and her head burrowed snugly against his shoulder as they raced down the stairs.

He was all that was strong and heroic—most noble. Her *preux chevalier*, although it was as well he was not wearing shining armor at the moment, for it would have been most uncomfortable and he would have been roasted with heat. But he gallantly came to her rescue like knights of old. Even in her terror Amelia could not help but know a thrill of elation.

Then they were outside and breathing fresh, cold air. Around them people shivered and coughed, complained and worried aloud as to the fate of their belongings. The stable lads tossed buckets of water on the fire, but it looked to be a hopeless cause. They evidently decided the same, turning their attention to saving the stables. Horses were hurried away from the scene, out to a field behind the inn.

The host of the inn marched about, checking and counting to see all were present, muttering under his breath, "Terrible, terrible, I am all undone."

The boor who had nearly pushed Amelia and Geoffrey into the flames stomped about denouncing with equal temper the innkeeper, the other guests, and whoever had started the fire.

Chen Mei uttered something in Cantonese. At a lift of his lordship's eyebrows, Amelia hastened to translate. "She says that human affairs are always changeable. How can you tell whether what today is a misery may not turn out to be a blessing tomorrow?"

"Dashed hard to see how this might prove to be a blessing," Peter observed, looking back at the blazing inn.

"We had best get on our way before our coach is claimed by someone intent upon travel," Geoff said quietly to Peter.

Then with a concerned expression, he said to the girl, "Was Chen Mei able to rescue some clothing for you, Miss Longworth?" He observed that the companion wore her customary attire, with not a hair out of place in contrast to the disheveled appearance of the others from the inn.

The blonde, her bedraggled plait of hair slipping over her shoulder as she moved, turned to consult briefly with Chen Mei, then replied, "I have what I need to reach London. Thank you for your concern, sir." She again curtsied to him, nodded to Mr. Blandford, then turned as her companion spoke once more, this time in her faulty English.

"Tian Li safe. You save her life again. Three times you save life." Chen Mei nodded emphatically even as she brushed down the once beautiful satin robe, restoring a semblance of order to her charge.

"Do you truly think . . . ? Oh, no! Must I?" Miss Longworth said in obvious amazement and consternation combined.

"Missee know." Chen Mei tucked her hands up her sleeves, giving Miss Longworth a reproving look.

Dropping a lovely curtsy, the girl raised her eyes to meet his puzzled gaze. "It is written, my lord. You have saved my life three times. I am now yours."

Stunned, Geoffrey stared at the girl who bowed her head submissively before him. In her smudged Oriental robe of deep blue satin embroidered with flowers and dragons, she looked far out of the common way. Her blond hair remained in a long somewhat untidy plait, draped over one shoulder in a childish way. There was nothing childish about the softly curved figure, nor the feelings she had stirred within him when he carried her in his arms, however.

"I say," Peter muttered quietly.

"Quite so," Geoffrey replied to his unspoken words. "Most remarkable."

"You aren't serious, are you?" Peter queried Miss Longworth hesitantly, keeping one eye on Chen Mei, who hovered behind her charge like the dragon he suspected she was.

"Most assuredly. I would lose face were I not to become yours, Major Lord Dancy." She half turned to issue soft commands in Cantonese to her companion. Within moments the two women had gathered up what belongings Chen Mei had taken from the inn.

"Lose face to whom?" muttered Peter in confusion. "I don't understand a bit of this."

"That makes two of us, but we can't just stand here in the bloody courtyard of the inn in a freezing chill to discuss it." Geoffrey looked about him for the groom he'd hired yesterday.

"Mind your language, Major Lord Dancy," Amelia rebuked, looking back at him while she walked across the inn courtyard.

"Sorry, Miss Longworth." Geoffrey rubbed his neck in a gesture of frustration, wondering what in the world he was to do now. The glance he exchanged with Peter revealed he had no ideas to offer. He looked equally bewildered.

"You had best call me Amelia, if I am yours. And could we not set out for London? I do wish to get on our way."

"Our way?" Geoffrey echoed, a feeling that things had just taken a peculiar turn hitting him with full force.

"Naturally. If I am to be your chattel, I must be at your side." She calmly walked to where his coach awaited him, then climbed inside.

"I do not believe any of this," Geoffrey declared in an undertone while watching Chen Mei follow suit. "It is a strange sort of dream, no doubt from those mushrooms in the steak and kidney pie last night. I told you they were off."

"Not mushrooms, old chap. Just one determined young lady who has been living in the Orient for most of her life." Peter motioned to the coach where the driver patiently awaited his command.

Geoffrey started toward the coach, after giving some instructions to one of the servants of the inn regarding the post chaise that had been ordered for Miss Longworth. He discovered that two of her trunks had been in the stables, awaiting the post chaise, so a delay occurred while they were loaded on his coach.

Amelia, she had instructed him to call her. Did she have any notion of how this all might be viewed in London? He groaned, then gave Peter a dirty look when he laughed out loud.

When he climbed into the coach after Peter, he discovered that the two women sat facing the rear, leaving the forward-facing seats for Peter and himself. He protested this arrangement.

"It is not seemly, my lord," Miss Longworth, that is, Amelia replied smoothly. Perhaps too smoothly? She stared at the folded hands in her lap instead of flashing those blue eyes at him, as he suspected she must yearn to do.

"What do you mean?" he said while the coach lurched forward to commence its trip to London.

"As your chattel, I must consider what is best for you and act accordingly. Also, I would have Chen Mei sit beside me. I truly believe this to be the best for all." She glanced at him. "Perhaps we may pause at one of the inns so I may change into a gown. There may have been no time to find another inn at Portsmouth, but I am dressed most improperly." She touched the blue satin robe.

"Well," he said, determined to have the last word, "this is to be a fast trip. I wish to make London today. We shall make a stop for a meal, and I suppose you would like to change clothes before we reach the City." This last was not said grudgingly, for Geoffrey was most impressed by her lack of fuss. Any other woman of his acquaintance would have been up in the boughs, demanding they stop over so she might regain her sensibilities. It seemed that Miss Longworth was down-to-earth. Her practical nature seemed providential to him if he was indeed to be saddled with her.

A glance at Peter revealed that his friend was equally at a loss. The coach dashed along the Portsmouth Road, with only murmured comments between the two women, and an occasional remark between the men.

The stop at Horndean went rapidly, the coachman passing along the news of the fire at the inn at Portsmouth with relish. Then he swung up, and they were off once again, barreling along the road at great speed.

Chen Mei stared out of the window at the passing scenery with curious intent.

"I say, those must be some of Featherstonhaugh's race horses. Can't be far from Uppark at this point," Peter said, leaning forward to study the animals as they raced past them. "They look as though they might give us a good run."

That brought up the subject of horse racing, which kept the gentlemen entertained all the way to Liphook.

As they entered the small town, Amelia took note of the attractive inn where they were to pause while the horses were changed. With its ivied walls and sparkling windows it made her long to leave the coach for a bit.

"Might I change my clothes here, Major Lord Dancy?" she hesitantly inquired. Since she and Chen Mei had thrust themselves upon this gentleman, she hated to put him out, especially when it seemed he was in a tearing rush to arrive in London.

"I can't imagine what the proprietor will make of you two in your most unusual garments, but I expect this place will be as good as any." He ushered the two women from the coach, arranged for a room to be placed at Amelia's disposal, then joined his friend. Looking over her shoulder as she walked up the stairs, Amelia could see them plunge into conversation.

It was the first time she had found a chance for a private talk with Chen Mei since the dramatic outburst at the inn following the fire.

The blue satin robe quickly fell to the floor. Chen Mei untangled the plait of blond hair and rapidly brushed it while Amelia bathed her face with a soft cloth, trying to refresh herself after feeling embarrassed for her disarray.

"Major Lord Dancy was most kind not to object to my appearance," she observed while watching Chen Mei work wonders with a gown that had been carefully rolled up in one of the portmanteaus.

"He good man," the Chinese woman observed. She held out the blue sprigged muslin for Amelia to slip over her head.

"Chen Mei, are you quite certain I must do this thing?" She didn't define the matter, for they both knew what was meant. Wiggling into the gown, then holding still while Chen Mei fastened the tapes and adjusted the dress took but moments. Once that was accomplished, Amelia folded her blue robe to place in the portmanteau so they might leave the room.

"Hold faithfulness and sincerity as first principles," the companion stated in Cantonese with a nod of her head. "You know what written. He save your life three times, now you his." A crafty look flittered across her face. "Fire no bad thing, for it give you him. Now you have family." It was obvious that Chen Mei considered family to be of first importance.

Amelia sighed, wondering how she was to make Chen Mei understand the more complicated ways of the West. In both cultures a young woman had a father, or older relative who arranged a good marriage for her. But other matters could be involved. Not that Amelia had one thing against the major, who was handsome, titled, wealthy—if his actions gave any clue—and kind as well.

"I shall obey, for I have no desire to have the fates punish me." While not precisely superstitious, Amelia had seen too many instances where retribution followed failure to follow the old sayings. Unless . . . Chinese sayings lost their power once she was in England. One glance at Chen Mei decided that question. Amelia had no desire to find out. Chen Mei would heap dire predictions on her head until Amelia yielded.

"Missee be sincere, faithful to him. Good come." Chen Mei bustled their things down the stairs and out to the coach.

Amelia sought out the men to tell them she was ready to depart. A glance at the large clock in the common room revealed she had changed in record time. At the quiet sound of their voices on the other side of a partition she halted, not wishing to intrude on a private conversation.

"I tell you Peter, it was the same face I saw in Lisbon. The more I think on it, the more certain I am. Why he would want to start a fire at the inn I can't fathom, but start it he did. I'm certain of that as well. A hunch, if you will, but *that* I'd bet on."

"You believe he'll follow you to London? Is that why you are in such haste?" Peter replied softly.

"The sooner I report to Hardinge the better. We have received information from the royalists and others disenchanted with Napoleon that is to our advantage to use. And Hardinge is dashed clever in utilizing it. Wellington will be prepared for anything Napoleon can think up."

"Well, we best see if your Amelia is ready to leave here. I suppose it's too much to hope for, but we can look."

She heard the sound of chairs scraping against the stone floor, so slipped back toward the stairs. What she had heard them say needed to be considered at length, and she did not wish them to know she had overheard their conversation. It seemed that Major Lord Dancy needed someone to look after him. Amelia had a task to perform.

Well, she thought as the men started in surprise when they saw her waiting for them, he would have her—and Chen Mei as well, for that matter.

"Gentlemen, I await your pleasure." She curtsied, then hurried to the coach where she resumed her place.

"She's a rare one," Peter observed quietly.

Geoffrey contemplated those words from Amelia and what it might be like to have her pleasure him. One look at the Chinese dragon and he put it aside. No one would touch the Celestial Delight as the captain had translated for him, until the dragon gave permission.

It was late when they clattered past the Robin Hood gate hard by Richmond Park. Shortly after that came the Vauxhall and Newington gates before they raced across London Bridge into the City.

"Glad to be home?" Peter inquired as the coach drew up to the Dancy residence at No. 15 Berkley Square.

"Yes," came the fervent reply.

Few lights showed from the house other than the entry. The door opened in response to the groom's urgent knock. Geoffrey hurried from the coach and up the steps to the house leaving Peter to cope with the ladies.

"Evenson, my sisters around? I have guests for them." It had been decided that the ladies from Macao would stay with his sisters until he could locate Amelia's aunt.

"Oh, my Lord, your sisters are from home."

"From home! Where?"

The portly butler rubbed his chin, then said, "Miss Victoria, now Lady Hawkswood, has been in Switzerland on her honeymoon after marrying Sir Edward, you see. Lady Winton has gone to visit at the home of Lord Temple, painting. And I believe Miss Elizabeth is to shortly marry Lord Leighton with your Aunt Montmorcy's blessing."

"The devil you say," Lord Dancy breathed, feeling Peter's not so gentle nudge in his back.

"I ought to stay here with you," Amelia said in a small voice, "but I daresay it would not look at all the thing. We had best find my aunt. Do you know where Mrs. Ermintrude Spencer resides?" she inquired of Evenson. "I lost her address in the fire."

"It wants only that," Geoff murmured. "Come, have a cup of tea while I sort things out. We shall have you at your aunt's home before you know it."

"Jolly right, Geoff, or else," Peter muttered with a knowing arch of his brows.

Chapter Three

"Do you recall anything about your aunt's address in London? The area, perhaps? Or the street?" Geoffrey studied Amelia Longworth with a narrowed gaze. Dash it all, he couldn't have the chit staying here now, what with his sisters gone. Why, if word seeped out about it, he was as good as wed to the girl.

He considered the crumpled appearance of her garments, her tanned skin, the unfashionable hair style, not to mention her strange ideas, and shuddered. Not that he was so top-lofty as to judge by appearances alone, but the girl stirred something within him. She bothered him. And her blasted Chinese companion with all those peculiar notions did as well, in a different way. His chattel, indeed. Nonsense.

Miss Longworth sat demurely upon the brocade sofa, apparently mulling over his questions. At last she nodded and replied, "I believe she lives on Brook Street. Do you know where it is? Would that be terribly far from here?"

Geoffrey exchanged a relieved look with Peter, then smiled at Miss Longworth. "It is quite close, actually. There ought to be no problem in locating your aunt, for it isn't a very long street at all."

At that moment Evenson entered bearing a large silver tray upon which reposed not only the requisite tea, but also coffee, sandwiches, biscuits, and thick slices of poppy seed cake.

He placed the tray on a large table, then straightened, looking at Lord Dancy with a softened expression. "May I say on behalf of the staff that we are pleased to have you home again, milord. We are certain that your sisters will be very sorry to have missed your homecoming. They eagerly awaited news from you while you were gone."

A slight guilt at not having written more often assailed Geoffrey before he recalled that for much of his stay on the peninsula he was unable to write because of his location and fear that his identity might be revealed.

"War does not often permit us to do as we please," he commented. "It is very good to be home again. I fancy I shall catch up with my sisters before long." Then he glanced at Miss Longworth, his problem for the moment, and said, "How can we best find out the address of Miss Longworth's aunt, Mrs. Spencer? She lives on Brook Street."

"I shall consult James, the first footman. He frequents a small tavern not far away where the servants frequently gather in their time off." Bowing correctly, Evenson quietly marched from the room and down the hall.

"We might as well enjoy the contents of this tray. Will you pour, Miss Longworth?" He offered Peter a slice of poppy seed cake.

"Coffee, I suppose?" she said, looking at him with a smile in her eyes.

"Please." From the corner of his eyes he could see Chen Mei fussing in one of the bags she had refused to relinquish to the groom, preferring to carry it herself.

"Chen Mei, here is your tea. I believe you will like the cake," Miss Longworth said softly to the Chinese woman at her side.

The cup of China tea was accepted and a small parcel placed on Miss Longworth's lap at the same time. She ignored it for the moment, taking care of Peter's beverage, then pouring a cup of tea for herself.

For a few moments silence reigned while the hungry travelers consumed the food so providentially brought by a conscientious Evenson.

When Amelia had consumed sufficient sandwiches and cake to appease her hunger, she studied the packet in her lap. After a searching look at Chen Mei, who nodded solemnly back at her, Amelia rose from the sofa. She walked to stand before Lord Dancy, wondering how he would accept her gift.

"Yes? What is it, Miss Longworth?" His face was inscrutable: no clue to his inner feeling showed on that handsome countenance or in his eyes. They weren't precisely cold, more like wary, perhaps.

"Since society will not permit me to share your home so that I may look after you as I ought, I wish you to have this, my lord." She bowed most correctly as Chen Mei had taught her, then offered the slim packet wrapped in yellow silk.

Her eyes followed his hand as they picked up the little parcel, examining it with obvious curiosity before beginning to unwind the silk. There were several layers of fabric to undo before he found the item inside. A long, thin piece of silver slid into the palm of his left hand. Several pieces of yellow silk drifted unheeded to the floor while he studied the characters inscribed onto the surface of the object.

He glanced at Peter, then returned his gaze to Amelia. "What is it?" With a finger of his right hand, he traced the characters, frowning as though he sensed something from them, but didn't know what it was. "It's most curious, for the silver feels cold and yet warm. Very peculiar."

"That is very good." Amelia shared a smile with Chen Mei before continuing. "This is an amulet that will protect you. You must wear it always, my lord. The characters will guard you from evil influences and accidents. That you sense the power of them means that you will find it most superior." She bowed once again, then backed to the sofa, seating herself with demure grace.

Geoffrey gave Peter a helpless look, then turned his gaze back to the amulet in his hand. Oddly enough it was true that he did feel something when that silver piece had slid into his palm. He couldn't explain it to anyone so that it would make sense. But he could not shake off the feeling that Miss Longworth had placed some sort of spell on him. *Something* must explain the way he felt, the awareness that crept through him.

"You must wear it at all times," she reminded him. "Even in bed." She looked at her companion, who produced another little packet from her sleeve. "Here, I believe you will be able to use this."

Placing the amulet on the table, Geoffrey opened the second packet to find a silver chain. It was obvious she intended him to thread it through the loop on the amulet, and so he did. At her gesture he then placed the chain over his head, feeling dashed silly. Men didn't wear necklaces of any sort. For instance, how could he go sparing at Gentleman Jackson's with this thing dangling around his neck?

"You wear it next to your skin," Miss Longworth further instructed. "It is very important, my lord." She approached him again and appeared to be about to tuck the amulet under his collar when Evenson entered the room.

Geoffrey breathed a sigh of relief at the rescue, yet a part of him wondered what it would be like to feel the touch of Miss Longworth's gentle hands on his skin.

"Success, milord. James is well acquainted with the butler from the Spencer household. Mrs. Spencer resides at No. 45." Turning to Miss Longworth, he added as though to reassure her, "It is a fine, large house with an excellent garden in the rear. Mrs. Spencer is praised by her servants as a kindly woman."

He had apparently observed the frightened look that had flashed into Amelia Longworth's lovely blue eyes at the mention of a large house. Had she feared it would be too grand or imposing, and that her aunt would be haughty and cold?

Geoffrey frowned as he considered the worrisome thoughts that had just popped into his head. Miss Longworth was a gentle girl, demure and perhaps too trusting. Would this Mrs. Spencer take advantage of those qualities to align her with whomever happened to be available, not seeking to find someone deserving of Amelia? This would not do in the least. He would see to it that the girl was happy before turning to his own affairs.

He had wanted to find his sisters and tend matters at his estate, but he would not be so heartless as to abandon poor little Miss Longworth to an unpleasant fate. Another look into her celestial blue eyes intensified his determination. He would champion her, perhaps help find a fellow who would appreciate a tanned, unfashionable, but obedient and demure little miss. He totally forgot that stubborn streak that had emerged on more than one occasion.

"We had best take you to your aunt immediately, before the hour is too late." A glance at the long-case clock near the door confirmed his belief that they must hurry along.

"Thank you, Evenson, for your kindness in seeing to it we were fed so nicely," Miss Longworth said to his butler, causing the usually unflappable man to turn red in the face. "My lord is well served by you, I believe. Keep an eye on him while I am gone." With these peculiar words said in the most gentle and confiding manner, the young woman drifted from the room with a dignity far beyond her years.

Geoffrey watched Chen Mei scurry after her mistress, then gave Peter a puzzled look.

"I don't understand any of this, but I'll wager any amount you wish to name that you haven't seen the last of that girl," Peter said in an undertone.

"No wager, for I fully intend to see that Miss Longworth is safe and content with her aunt. I could hardly do otherwise. She may think she is my chattel, but really, it is my place to see that she is all right, isn't it?" Geoffrey sent Peter a rather top-lofty look, one that proclaimed him superior to a mere woman, and a girl at that.

"This situation ought to be interesting." Peter shook his head, then strolled from the room after Amelia and Chen Mei, out to where the Dancy carriage now awaited them.

In moments Geoffrey had joined the others, first giving his coachman instructions on their destination.

The carriage rumbled off, then shortly turned a corner. Within a very brief time they had presented themselves to the Spencer butler. This august gentleman escorted them all to the salon upstairs, then disappeared from sight.

"Amelia, my love?" A dainty woman paused in the doorway, her long draperies and several scarves fluttering around her so it was impossible to tell if she was plump or merely surrounded by yards of pink fabric. Soft gray curls framed her face beneath a modest evening cap of lace and pink satin. Beringed fingers waved at them all as she crossed the room to greet her niece with an enveloping hug.

Amelia dropped a proper curtsy, then smiled shyly at her newly found relative, sister to her papa. "I am pleased to be here."

"How like your dear mother you are. Oh, we shall have a famous time of it. And who are all these people, my love?"

"This is Chen Mei, my companion, who raised me after Mama died. The tall gentleman is Major Lord Dancy, who saved my life three times and has taken very good care of me since. The man next to him is Mr. Peter Blandford, a friend."

Mrs. Spencer scrutinized the gentleman who had saved her niece from serious harm. "I am much in your debt, Major Lord Dancy."

"Just Dancy, if you please. I am to sell out and will no longer use my military title."

"I see." She smiled, then tilted her head like a small bird. "Your sister pulled a coup when she up and married Sir Edward Hawkswood. Every chit in Town had been chasing him. And Lady Winton is off to visit Lord Temple. Wonder what that dragon of a mother of his will make of that. She's been trying to push him into a second marriage for ages. Miss Elizabeth has sensibly taken herself off to your Aunt Isobel's place in the country, I hear. Odd that Lord Leighton absented himself about the same time for the same part of the country. Oh, your family has provided society with such marvelous tidbits. I do hope you intend to follow suit?"

Lord Dancy looked rather stunned at the aunt's outrageous statements by his expression. "I shall endeavor not to disappoint you, madam."

"I should hope not," she murmured with a flutter of eyelashes. "I'm accounted a shade eccentric, but after all these years, I feel I'm entitled to live a stimulating life. With dear Amelia here I shan't be bored this Season."

Amelia darted an inquiring look at Lord Dancy, wondering if he was to be a part of her Season in London. She had no intention of losing trace of him. He needed her protection, for she had not forgotten one word of the overheard conversation regarding the menace from Lisbon.

"I am certain Miss Longworth would appreciate a night's sleep. Perhaps I may call upon you later?" Lord Dancy said, as though in answer to Amelia's unspoken plea.

"We shall look forward to seeing you, although don't rush your fences. Between the mantuamakers and milliners, and what-all-not, we should be exceedingly busy for some time." Mrs. Spencer nodded regally, then accepted his parting words and bow with serene good nature.

Once they were alone, she bustled Amelia and Chen Mei

up the stairs to a large room in the front of the house. Blue silk curtains hung at tall windows and draped the wall behind a pretty cherrywood sleigh bed as well. Two comfortable-looking chairs and a cherry dressing table with a bench covered in the same blue comprised most of the furnishings. Through an open door Amelia could see a small room with a neat bed and small table, most likely for a maid. Chen Mei would take that if Aunt Ermintrude had no objections. She was unable to prevent a yawn from overtaking her.

"Now I must hear all about this rescue business. I suppose you are far too tired to explain tonight, but be assured I shall want all the details in the morning." She surveyed her niece, frowning as she walked around Amelia.

"The skin is good but the color is not. I cannot believe you should so forget yourself as to allow the sun on your face, my love. Had you no parasols? But then, I imagine you found it difficult, all those months on board ship."

"I have lost five bonnets and four parasols for one reason or another. I finally gave up," Amelia said with a shrug.

"Quite so. Well, in the morning we shall begin our attempts with cucumber solution. Sleep well."

Most bemused, Amelia watched her aunt float out of the room. Did her aunt intend her to eat the concoction or was it merely to place on the skin?

"Leave all things to take their natural course, and do not interfere," Chen Mei intoned solemnly in Cantonese. Then in English—for she was sincerely trying to learn that language—she added, "Aunt velly kind. Good woman."

"I am worried about Lord Dancy, Chen Mei. He is in trouble, and I fear he will not wear the amulet."

Amelia divested herself of her garments, then allowed Chen Mei to undo her hair to brush it in the usual evening ritual. Their eyes met in the mirror, both concerned.

"While times are quiet, it is easy to take action; ere coming troubles have cast their shadows, it is easy to lay plans," Chen Mei said, reverting to Cantonese once again.

"Of course," Amelia said, while trying to hide another yawn. "Tomorrow we shall put our heads together and devise a plan. I wonder if Aunt Ermintrude will help?"

"Good lady," Chen Mei repeated. "You desire to help others, you will help yourself in the end."

"You know I don't wish to help Lord Dancy just to improve my lot," Amelia protested after donning a dainty white cambric nightgown delicately embroidered with flowers. She slipped beneath the covers, then pulled them up to her chin while giving Chen Mei a solemn look. "You have taught me to care about others more than myself. Therefore I must see that Lord Dancy comes to no harm."

"It is so," Chen Mei agreed before silently tottering off to her own bed.

Amelia hoped that her unusual aunt would see it from the same point of view, then fell into a deep sleep.

"Wake up, wake up, there is much to be done," Aunt Ermintrude sang out as she floated across Amelia's lovely bedroom. She jerked aside the draperies to allow the pale light of the February sun to shine in, with the hope of encouraging her new niece to arise.

Following a modest breakfast of rolls and chocolate, Amelia's face was covered with a cucumber mixture to whiten her skin. Then she sat with her aunt to plan for the forthcoming shopping trips.

"Once we wash your hair with chamomile to bring out the color, you will see that delicate hues will suit—pale blue and violet, and pretty pinks. And I think you ought to wear lily of the valley scent."

At that point Chen Mei brought a silken bundle to place in Amelia's lap. Giving her aunt a hesitant look, Amelia unwrapped the bundle, revealing a string of perfectly matched pink pearls, along with ear bobs and a ring holding one perfect pearl.

"Exquisite!" exclaimed her aunt with a pleased smile. "Your father did well by you. He wrote me that his solicitors will handle all your expenses. Once we succeed in whitening your skin, we shall proceed to the mantuamaker. There is a great deal to do before we reveal you to Society. How fortunate you have already made the acquaintance of two charming gentlemen."

"You seem to know his family well," Amelia said with a glance at Chen Mei.

"I know everyone who is anyone in London. I have already spoken to Maria Sefton about you. I feel assured you will have the required vouchers for Almack's when needed."

"Almack's," Amelia murmured, somewhat bewildered. "I shall learn what I need to know, I suppose. I would like to employ a dancing master to learn the new dances. The rest of my come-out I will leave in your capable hands, dear aunt."

"As is fit and proper. I am so relieved to see you are such a pretty-behaved girl. You will prove to be no problem at all with such lovely manners."

"Aunt Ermintrude, there is something you ought to know," Amelia cautioned.

"Ah, yes, your story. How did Dancy rescue you? I wish to hear all." Aunt Ermintrude settled on her chair to listen to the tale. Her eyes watched carefully as she listened to what Amelia had to say.

With a commendable brevity of speech Amelia related the tale of the wild dogs in the square, the pushing throng on the quay in Lisbon, the terrible fire in Portsmouth, and her conclusion—that she owed him her life.

"Of course you do, my love. Such appreciation is only proper."

With another look at Chen Mei Amelia continued, "It is not just that. In China when your life is saved three times by an individual, you *owe* him your life. I am his."

There was utter silence while Ermintrude Spencer digested this remarkable statement. After a time she said, "And what does this mean?"

"He is in great danger. I heard him tell his friend that he fears a man from Lisbon who followed him to England, and who set the inn on fire as well. Chen Mei agrees with me that it is my duty to protect him from danger. After all, he saved me from death!"

"How in the world can a slip of a girl protect Lord Dancy from harm!" Aunt Ermintrude quite obviously found this task to be beyond Amelia's capabilities.

"If one is clearheaded and intelligent, can one be without knowledge?" Amelia said, repeating one of Chen Mei's bits of wisdom.

"Knowledge is one thing, to protect him is another."

"I shall go where he goes, follow discreetly, and so learn much about him and his enemies. You will see. With Chen Mei at my side he shall be safe. I shall keep my ears alert, my eyes open. It is surprising what one may learn when others think you do not exist."

Somewhat aghast at this extraordinary side of her niece, Aunt Ermintrude merely stared.

It took several days of skin treatments before her aunt would dream of permitting Amelia out of the house. Dressed in the best of her outmoded gowns and wearing one of Aunt Ermintrude's more girlish bonnets, Amelia faced the first of her trips to Madame Clotilde's establishment with commendable calm.

"I trust your Madame is not one of those haughty women who look down their noses at a girl?" Amelia said while twisting the cords of her reticule.

"I doubt she will treat you with other than utmost respect," Aunt Ermintrude replied.

While it was true that Madame could depress the pretensions of upstart mushrooms, Amelia possessed a rather special quality, one that would intrigue Madame. Also there was the matter of Amelia's generous allowance. Even though Mrs. Spencer was not the least purse-pinched, the presence of ample funds filtered through Society rapidly, often from the mantuamaker.

When the Spencer carriage stopped before the discreet gray building with a bow window picked out in gold, Amelia exchanged a wary look with Chen Mei.

Once inside they found Madame occupied in fitting a young lady for her come-out ball gown. Amelia perched on a dainty gilt chair, content to page through a fashion journal. Her aunt did likewise while Chen Mei sat quietly listening to what she heard.

At last Madame Clotilde floated into the front area of her establishment with every appearance of genuine sorrow at having kept them waiting.

"I do not mind, Madame Clotilde, for I know you will give us the same undivided attention—especially when you see the young lady I have brought to you."

Madame Clotilde studied Amelia until she felt acutely uncomfortable. Then with a whirl of skirts, the mantua-maker beckoned to Aunt Ermintrude. "Come with me, for I wish to show you the latest fabrics and do the final fitting on your peach sarcenet. Then I will devote the rest of the day to your niece. I believe I can find just the right way to make her unique, for her hair and those lovely eyes deserve special treatment." To Amelia she also beckoned. "I trust you would prefer to wait in a dressing room. One of my girls will bring you a cup of tea. Your companion, as well," she concluded, giving the elegant long silk garment Chen Mei wore a speculative look.

Amelia and Chen Mei dutifully followed the mantua-maker, settling in the little dressing room on two of the dainty gilt chairs with resignation. After the months of sailing it seemed odd to merely sit to await the ministrations of this peculiar little woman with her fake French accent and improbably colored red hair.

The tiny room had an assortment of fashion plates on a small table and the requisite looking glasses. Amelia wondered how long she would wait when she realized that she could hear the conversation coming from the next room. Ordinarily she would not have strained to listen, but she heard a familiar name.

"Chen Mei, do you hear what I hear?" she whispered.

Chen Mei nodded, her eyes narrowing with displeasure.

Amelia shifted closer to the partition, trying to hear better.

"It is carefully planned, I tell you," said the woman. "Nothing will go wrong, so stop worrying your silly head about it. Mama is very particular about the matter. She discovered Lord Dancy has an excellent estate with abundant funds. It will be a pleasure to become engaged to him."

"But I still do not understand. You are in love with Thomas Sands. How can you even think of someone else?" The second voice sounded exceedingly perplexed.

"It is absurdly simple," said the first voice. "I shall contrive to arrange the engagement by means of a compromise. After all, he has been off on the Continent for some time and cannot be awake on all suits when it comes to the wiles of young ladies."

"You love Thomas but will become engaged to Lord Dancy. Outrageous," declared the friend.

"But you still do not comprehend the beauty of it all. Once we are safely engaged, I shall endeavor to give Lord Dancy a disgust of me, by whining, or merely making myself utterly impossible. Mama has explained just how to do it. Then he will break the engagement, for what man like Lord Dancy will wish such a wife?"

"And?" queried the second voice.

"And we will sue him for breach of promise. Is that not a wonderful plan? Then I may marry my Thomas. He is going to do the same thing. That will bring us two sums, which properly invested, ought to last for a time. Only, I believe Thomas intends to attempt an elopement with the intent of her guardian buying him off. He is exceedingly handsome, you know, so he ought not have the least difficulty."

"That seems highly improper to my way of thinking. Who is Thomas going to deceive?"

"I understand there is a new girl in town, the daughter of an East India Company official who has pots of money. Mrs. Spencer is her chaperon, and you know how silly she is. A solicitor is her father's London agent and would have less interest in the matter than a gentleman. He would likely join the aunt in depressing any account of an elopement. And you must know that Thomas, as handsome as he is, would utterly bowl over a green girl from nowhere. Why, just the thought of his blue eyes twinkling down into mine as he requests a dance is enough to make my heart flutter."

"That does sound utterly delicious. What a naughty girl you are, Clarissa."

The sound of an opening door brought the conversation to a halt. Before long, farewells were made and the two wicked young women had left the establishment.

Once assured they might not hear her, Amelia turned to face her companion. "Did you understand what that girl intends to do? Poor Lord Dancy. As for the other, I will be on the lookout for a blue-eyed man named Thomas. I believe *he* will receive a great surprise."

Chen Mei withdrew the curved dagger from her sleeve, and smiled while she inspected it.

"I doubt it shall come to that, Chen Mei. But you and I will have to take care of Lord Dancy. That terrible girl must not be allowed to get her way!" Amelia declared in Cantonese.

The two plotters put their heads together, then self-consciously drew apart as Aunt Ermintrude and Madame Clotilde entered the fitting room.

In spite of the improbable hair color, Madame proved to be a kind and talented woman.

"I shan't want white gowns, although I know they are proper for young ladies making their bows to Society," Amelia instructed. "White is the color of mourning in China, and I'd not offend Chen Mei."

The Chinese nodded her agreement to the matter, settling back to watch her adored girl.

After that bolts of delicate pastels in blues and violets, raspberry and pink filled the room as Madame cleverly took charge of the challenging young miss. Once her skin achieved the suitable paleness required of young Society ladies, with her magnificent blond hair and incredible blue eyes, she would take the *ton* by storm.

If Amelia was not quite as attentive as might have been expected, it was not noticed by her aunt or the mantua-maker. Young girls were easily tired by this sort of business.

But Amelia and Chen Mei communicated with little nods and shared looks. They were considering something else altogether. First to find out who this Clarissa might be and then to convince Lord Dancy he must take great care.

The meeting with Clarissa proved a simple matter. It was a collision, actually. Amelia's skin gleamed with the results of days of skin treatments, and she wore a pale pansy blue jaconet gown. When she heard someone mention a Clarissa Filbert, Amelia contrived to bump into her, quite by accident, of course.

"Oh, I do apologize. Such a dreadful crush," Amelia cooed, refering to the Abvile rout they attended.

Clarissa stared with narrow eyes, as though not quite accepting Amelia's wide-eyed gaze as genuine. "I do not believe we have met."

"How sad," Amelia replied, fluttering her lashes in a helpless manner. "I am Amelia Longworth, lately of Macao and come to London to enjoy my come-out, sponsored by my dear Aunt Spencer. You are Miss Filbert. I have heard such things about you." Amelia waved a delicate lace and ivory fan about in the air, having recognized that voice at once.

Clarissa's change of expression revealed to Amelia that the girl recognized her name immediately. Good. Amelia forced herself to chat, becoming less and less pleased with what she found.

"Tell me, Miss Filbert, are you attached to a gentleman? There is such a vast number of fine young men here in London. Such a contrast to Macao, I vow."

"No," Clarissa admitted. Then a feral gleam lit her eyes. "But I expect to be promised any day now."

The expression that glittered in Clarissa's eyes utterly repelled Amelia. It was the predatory focus of a cat about to pounce. Poor Lord Dancy. Amelia's butter-soft heart went out to the man. She must prevent his becoming entangled with the cattish Miss Filbert at any cost!

Chapter Four

Geoffrey gazed about the dining room of his club while making an assessment of the occupants. The meal had been good, by peninsula standards. White's had improved since he had last been in London. He wondered what sort of meals Miss Longworth had enjoyed while on her trip to England. Six months was a long time to travel. The food must have been tolerable, or else she would have weighed even less than the delicate bundle he had carried from the inn that morning of the fire.

One of these days he would have to stop by to chat with the girl, poor thing. It was to be hoped that her aunt might find some chap who would need the dowry and not mind the lamentable appearance. And then, perhaps, Geoff might be able to get her out of his mind.

"Hello, old boy. Good to find you at last. Been trying to hunt you down for days." Peter Blandford gave Geoffrey a cheerful smile. To any who watched, the two appeared to have not a care in the world.

"Sit down, sit down," Geoffrey said with a mild irritation. "Settling in well, I take it now that you've decided to open the house for your parents?"

Peter flopped down carelessly on the opposite chair, assuming the pose of the ultimate dandy, that of sophisticated boredom. He leaned forward as though to inspect the bottle of wine that sat on the table.

"What did Hardinge say when you reported? Haven't had a moment to discuss it with you." Peter helped himself to wine at a gesture from Geoffrey while speaking so quietly as to be barely heard.

"He was pleased, just as we expected," Geoffrey replied with equal discretion. "I fancy that the proper lads were informed before the cat had cleaned its whiskers and all will be in place. No surprises—at least for our boys?"

"Well, I won't go so far as to agree with you there. But I daresay the more Old Hookey knows, the better things will go. No general likes surprises." Peter eased back in his chair again, but still tense as though he had more information to impart and merely awaited the right moment.

"Better open your budget, old chap. I can see you are about to burst." Geoffrey gave him a wry look while twirling his wineglass between his fingers.

"Tell me, have you visited our fair Miss Longworth?" Peter's expectant expression deserved more than a terse yes or no reply to the odd question.

"I thought I'd give her another week to settle in. It's past Easter and the Season is just coming into full swing. Do you mean to say you have heard something? I thought you went out of town to see your parents." Geoffrey took a sip of wine, frowning at his friend.

"I've been back in Town for a few days. She is the loveliest creature, Geoff. I saw her last evening at the Sefton's. Her tan is gone, as are the frumpy clothes and hair. She has, ah, filled out a bit as well," Peter declared with unusual relish.

"Do tell," Geoffrey murmured, for some reason furious that Peter should have seen this vision before himself.

"Well, if you had not been so busy reestablishing yourself with certain ladies of the opera, I would not need to tell you a thing. I heard her say she and her aunt intend to attend the opera this evening. If you spent more time in the audience instead of the green room, you might see for yourself."

"Would that I had been involved in something so pleasurable. I've been busy with my man of affairs. Lawyers can be the most bloody- fools at times," Geoffrey said in disgust. "But at least I have the matter of my sisters' inheritance, and portions straightened out, and Julia is well set. Poor girl, her husband was a rascal, make no mistake. He left her with a pittance, but I corrected that."

"Think that she'll marry that fellow she's visiting with at the moment?"

"Have you heard anything beyond what Mrs. Spencer

said?" Geoffrey frowned with concern, for he'd had no news from his absent sisters, although Evenson assured him they were likely quite well with nothing to worry him about.

Peter shook his head, then gave Geoffrey a grin. "She's a charmer, that old lady. Has the fellows eating out of her hand. Why, Thomas Sands hangs over her as though she were the one making her come-out instead of Miss Long-worth."

"Sands? Don't think I know the chap. Is he someone I ought to know?" Geoffrey gave a narrow-eyed look about the room, wondering if the fellow was present.

Peter pursed his mouth, glancing up to the ceiling as though the answer might be written there.

"Well?" Geoffrey revealed a trifle of impatience, rare in him.

"If you really want to know, I suggest you present your-self at the house on Brook Street tomorrow during calling hours. He is to be found there every day, from what I un-derstand."

Geoffrey digested this information with an impassive countenance, then invited his friend to enjoy a game of cards for the low stakes they played when together.

The following day found Geoffrey presenting himself at the front door of the house on Brook Street a trifle before the customary hours for visiting. The same starchy butler showed him up the stairs into the same salon as the night he had brought Miss Longworth here. Geoffrey paced about the room, wondering just how much Amelia Longworth had changed.

"Lord Dancy!" cried a soft, delicate voice from the door-way, sounding enormously pleased.

He slowly turned about, standing utterly still as he ab-sorbed the transformation of Amelia Longworth from a dowdy frump into a shimmering butterfly, a true diamond of the first water. Peter had not done her justice. Why, the chit stunned the eye. His hand unconsciously crept up to where the amulet rested against his chest.

"Amelia? It *is* you, is it not?" He took a step toward the vision in fragile mauve muslin. Her simply cut round dress—trimmed only with a delicate frill at the neck and a flounce at the bottom of the skirt—hung to her ankles, below which he could see black Roman sandals of the latest design. In her hair silk lilies of the valley artlessly nestled amid her tousled blond curls. She was quite the loveliest girl he could recall seeing.

"I had hoped to see you before this, Lord Dancy," she chided gently, as no Society miss ought to scold a gentleman she found interesting. Come to think of it, her smile was most sisterly. He discovered he didn't find that pleasing.

He smiled gravely at her, a note of reserve in his voice as he replied, "I have had the pressure of business, else I would have been here long ago. May I say you look very well. And are you enjoying your visit to the city?"

"Are we to be as strangers, then," she said politely, clearly disappointed. "I have so much to tell you. Indeed, there is a good deal you ought to know about. Come, we shall discuss what is to be done."

Amelia beckoned to Lord Dancy to join her on the satin striped sofa after summoning the footman to request tea.

"Now, I wish to know if you have had any troubles," she inquired with that direct manner she possessed. He had forgotten how she tended to look a fellow straight in the eyes when asking questions. It was only when being paid compliments that she lowered her eyes, or when trying to conceal something that Miss Longworth had failed to meet his gaze.

"No serious troubles other than my lawyer, who is the dreariest man alive," he said with a smile, then recalled the man from Lisbon. The fellow must be biding his time, for Geoffrey had not caught a glimpse of him so far. But he would not relax his guard. Now that he was caught up with his desk work, he'd be out and about and need exercise more caution, he supposed.

"And you wear your amulet as promised?" she asked with the same directness.

"I do." The weight had been distracting at first. Now he found its warmth pleasant. "Is your aunt not to join us? I would not wish to compromise you."

He gave her an amused look, then glanced up as Chen

Mei tottered into the room, her soft-soled shoes making no sound. She stared at him, nodded, but said nothing.

"Oh, you shall not compromise me, I promise. But tell me, have you met a young woman named Clarissa Filbert as yet?"

He shook his head in bemusement. "No, I cannot say I have. Should I seek her out?"

"No. Absolutely never." Then Amelia revealed what she had heard in the dressing room from the girl named Clarissa. When introduced to the girl at a recent rout Clarissa had not proved more agreeable face-to-face than in the overheard conversation.

"You must be jesting," Lord Dancy stated when Amelia concluded her recital of the overheard conversation at the mantuamaker's establishment. "I cannot believe such an outrageous scheme."

"Well, that odious Thomas Sands has been hanging about for days and days. I am excessively tired of him, and he pays more attention to Aunt Spencer than he does to me. I believe he is trying to get into her good graces. Any moment now I expect him to suggest that to save expenses a Gretna Green marriage would be just the thing for a girl. As though I would partake in anything so havey-cavey. Why, a girl could be ruined." Amelia gave Lord Dancy an indignant look, hoping he would understand that he ought not take this lightly.

"I suspect that wouldn't bother Mr. Sands."

"You do believe me, then? I would not jest with you about something so serious. Oh, how I would like to teach them both a lesson they'd not forget in a hurry."

"Does your aunt know about this?" Lord Dancy said, his charming smile once more back in place.

Amelia was most grateful to see him relax against the sofa. She did as well, feeling as though an old and valued friend had come to call instead of the dandies and bucks who frequented her aunt's salon most days. Having odes written to her eyes and poems praising her curls seemed excessively silly.

"I doubt she would accept that anything was amiss with Mr. Sands, for he flatters her shamelessly, you see." Amelia sighed as she considered the foppish Mr. Sands.

How he thought she might be attracted to someone so lacking in good *ton* was beyond her.

"So you and Chen Mei have contrived to obtain the background on the two of them?" Lord Dancy shot a look at Chen Mei, then returned his attention to Amelia.

She felt warmed by his regard. Even though he apparently had not thought of her often in the past weeks, he was here now, and she hoped to make the most of it.

"It is not difficult. Chen Mei learns much, for people assume she cannot understand English and are quite free with their speech even when she is around. She is most useful, for her English improves daily." Amelia gave her dear companion a fond smile.

They went on to chat about the places Amelia had gone, the parties attended. However the more they talked, the greater her unease grew. Something was not right. Lord Dancy did not seem to consider the Filbert girl to be a genuine threat, and it appeared to Amelia that he totally dismissed Mr. Sands as a menace.

When sounds of people were heard below in the entry, Lord Dancy arose, bowing over Amelia's hand just like one of the dandies might. "Do not be overconcerned about this business with Miss Filbert and Mr. Sands. I'm certain you misunderstood the entire matter." He smiled into her eyes, and for one precious moment Amelia felt enormously drawn to him. Then she recalled his foolish dismissal of her concerns, and she sighed inwardly.

Amelia watched him depart with a feeling of great frustration. While she thought he had understood the danger, he had merely been placating her, intending to do not one thing. Rising from the sofa to await the approaching guests, she looked at Chen Mei with her disquiet plainly revealed.

"It is up to us, then. We shall have to save him from his own folly." Amelia gave a determined nod, for she felt her obligation deeply.

"A man without thought for the future must soon have sorrow," Chen Mei observed from her corner of the room.

Amelia turned a now-composed self toward the door, but said over her shoulder, "Knowing what is right, without practicing it, denotes a want of proper conduct. Never say that I fail to do what is right and proper."

The remainder of the afternoon was tedious for Amelia. She was impatient to closet herself with Chen Mei and plan the downfall of Miss Filbert and Mr. Sands. Instead she had to listen to the tiresome Mr. Sands simper over Aunt Ermintrude's new lace cornette with its satin trim. Amelia thought the moss roses that wreathed the edge a trifle much for an older woman, but Mr. Sands praised it to the skies.

What a pity that Lord Dancy considered the threat to his marital status mere moonshine. Amelia had *heard* Clarissa, *observed* the unctuous ways of Mr. Sands as he poured the butter boat over her aunt's head. There was little doubt in Amelia's mind that those two were malicious troublemakers. Perhaps were Lord Dancy to see them as she did, he might change his mind.

Once the callers had left, including the dubious Mr. Sands, Amelia urged her aunt to have a nice quiet rest on her bed.

"You do not wish to be too tired to enjoy the opera this evening, dear Aunt," Amelia gently scolded.

"Dear love, how considerate you are. I will take myself off to bed at once. You intend to rest as well?" Her aunt paused by the salon door, giving Amelia a speculative look.

"Chen Mei and I plan to retire to my room. We shall be fine."

With that her aunt disappeared to enjoy a pleasant respite in her bed.

"Come, we must plan." Chen Mei joined Amelia in a hurried flight up the stairs to her room.

Amelia closed the door behind them, then motioned Chen Mei to be seated. The Chinese woman preferred a low velvet hassock, finding it most comfortable.

"I have considered it from many angles," Amelia began. "I believe we ought to find some way to allow Miss Filbert to think she has engaged Lord Dancy's interest. Next, perhaps we could lure her to a house, or a room at one of the parties she attends? And then," Amelia continued, "see that she is definitely positioned in what might be a compromising situation—were a gentleman to join her. Only . . . instead of Lord Dancy, why not have Mr. Sands be the man to appear? That will effectively put paid to his intentions to elope with me as well."

Chen Mei applauded, then cautiously said, "A plan is fine, but how you get them to do as you wish?"

"Since Lord Dancy did not believe he is in danger of being forced to marry that odious Clarissa, we must enlist the help of someone else, I suppose."

"His flend?" Chen Mei suggested, still unable to cope with the sound of *r*.

"Of course, his friend Mr. Blandford. I shall send off a note to him at once. Perhaps he will join us at the opera this evening?" Amelia was not entirely delighted with the opera. The only circumstance that made it palatable was that the noise was so great one scarcely heard the music anyway. It seemed to her that everyone was either dying or in some tragic situation, not precisely her notion of entertainment. But everyone who was anyone attended, and the social consequence of merely being there in an excellent box was enormous.

Her aunt liked to glean the latest gossip, and the opera was a place where a great deal went on, and not necessarily on the stage.

Peter Blandford presented himself with delightful promptness when he received the note from Amelia. Once he heard she wished for his company and wanted to involve him in a plan to rescue the foolish Lord Dancy from a scheming hussy, he immediately agreed.

"I must confess that I consent to help you so that I shall know the pleasure of your company, Miss Longworth."

"Why, Mr. Blandford!" she exclaimed with genuine delight. His shy smile was most endearing to Amelia, particularly since the man who intrigued her had failed to appreciate her in the least.

That evening Amelia dressed with more than usual care. Her peach lace dress over a peach satin slip had a pretty drapery of peach lace entwined with pearls around the bottom of the skirt. Once dressed, she picked at the tight—and minuscule—bodice of the dress where it dipped very low so as to reveal perhaps a trifle too much.

"A silk rose here do you think, Chen Mei?" she asked. "I vow I feel as though there is nothing to this gown but a skirt. Even the sleeves are tiny."

Chen Mei shook her head, for she had been going over

the fashion plates and knew precisely what was to be worn. Rather, she clasped the pearls around Amelia's neck, then placed a pretty evening hat of peach satin and lace just so on Amelia's head.

"Now go, and do not forget what you are to do," Chen Mei reminded. She would not go along for she thought the English music very bad on the ears and declared the singing to be more like the screeching and yowling of a cat.

"If all goes according to plan, we shall set things in motion tonight." Amelia gave herself one last inspection in the mirror before joining her aunt and Mr. Blandford in the entry.

Had she not been so preoccupied with the plan to save Lord Dancy, she would have more fully enjoyed the appreciative expression on Peter's face when he first saw her. As it was, the three set off for the opera with Aunt Spencer chattering away about the latest scandal and Peter replying with great courtesy. Amelia smiled and nodded, clearly distracted.

Once settled in the box that Ermintrude Spencer considered an absolute necessity during the Season, Amelia searched the interior of the theater.

Mrs. Spencer welcomed a crony of hers to the box, and they commenced to share all the latest news.

"Do you see either one of them?" Amelia whispered, leaning close to Peter. She waved her fan languidly before her while her eyes methodically took note of the occupants in each box.

"Amelia, I trust we are doing the right thing. I'd hate to set this up only to have it rebound on Dancy or you." Peter ignored the patrons to fix a troubled gaze on Amelia. The neckline of her gown distracted him greatly, had Amelia paid the least attention. The vast expanse of creamy skin above the delicate swell of her rather nice bosom had quite an effect on a susceptible male.

"Do think of a way that you can cross over to the far side of the theater so you may discover if they are to either side of us. And do not worry about me . . . or Lord Dancy, for that matter. These scoundrels must be taught a lesson, and how better than to use their own plan?"

"What a clever girl you are. I wonder if Dancy fully appreciates your consideration for his future."

"I doubt it. But then, one must do one's duty."

"You believe he is your duty?" Peter said in amazement, tossing a glance at his good friend who had just entered a box directly across from where Peter sat with Amelia. Surely no woman had ever placed Dancy in such a light.

"For the present," Amelia replied somewhat obscurely.

Just then Mr. Sands presented himself to Mrs. Spencer and her crony, flattering the older lady outrageously. Peter surveyed the fellow with obvious distaste, then set about cultivating his acquaintance to learn what he could.

According to instructions, Peter managed to find out what the man's plans for the week were before he left the box. Amelia drew a sigh of relief when the door safely closed behind Thomas Sands.

Then Peter went on his errand of inquiry. Amelia had espied Miss Filbert in a box close to where Lord Dancy sat.

Within minutes she had the satisfaction of seeing Peter converse with a smirking Clarissa. Without seeming to, Amelia watched as the chat appeared to go as Peter desired.

She had not paid any attention to Lord Dancy during all this and was quite startled when he entered the box, seeking her side after bowing correctly to Mrs. Spencer.

Amelia's heart fluttered in that alarming manner again, just as it always did whenever he hovered close to her.

"I am surprised to see Peter Blandford with you this evening."

"Did you expect me to have Mr. Sands as escort? I vow, sir, that is a rather harsh judgment upon your part."

"Peter is a fine man, but you must know he has a very small estate."

"I do not choose my friends because of their money. He is a very kind man, and he does not treat me as a silly girl."

"You still believe that nonsense about Sands and Miss Filbert? By the bye, I met her as I came into the opera this evening. She seems a nice enough girl."

"I understand some poison mushrooms are utterly beautiful," Amelia responded obliquely.

"She can scarcely be labeled poison."

"Truly, I did not say that she is such. Perhaps I cannot

forget the words I heard her speak. But you are free to do as you please."

"You have abandoned your determination to see their plan foiled? You agree with me that it's all a hum?"

Amelia turned her head to discover that Lord Dancy was alarmingly close to her, bending to speak softly in her ear so their speech might not be overheard. Her eyes sought his, and for several moments she absorbed his look. Concerned? Alarmed? Irritated? Whatever his emotions might be, they were hardly ardent.

Somehow Amelia survived the remainder of the opera. Lord Dancy returned to his box when Peter came back from his errand of inquiry.

"I say," Peter whispered while the soprano warbled on about her tragic love, "I hope Dancy isn't angry with me. Near froze me with that glance of his."

"No, I doubt it, more's the pity," Amelia replied. "I cannot see him being jealous of anyone, especially not one as nice as you."

Peter seemed highly gratified at her kind regard of him and sat with a smug expression for the rest of the opera.

When she retired that evening, she related the furtherance of the plan to Chen Mei with less than might be expected relish.

"You upset. If you think things should go easy, they sure to be difficult. Best to anticipate trouble, then things not so bad," she counseled in Cantonese.

"Well, Peter said that Miss Filbert and Mr. Sands are both to be at the Twysden soireé Thursday, Lord Dancy as well. I convinced Aunt Ermintrude that we simply must attend. So, we go to Almack's tomorrow night, then the Twysden affair the next. By that time I ought to have everything well in hand."

Chen Mei looked rather dubious, but was far too fond of her charge to point out the large holes in her plan.

The following morning found Amelia at the little desk in the morning room, nibbling on a pen while she contemplated what to put in the note to Mr. Sands so it would be convincing. After all, she had avoided the man whenever possible. It would be difficult to suddenly declare she was most intrigued by him. But then, perhaps the man's conceit would ignore that fact.

At last with a bit of prompting from Chen Mei the note was written. Amelia signed and folded it with hope that her plan to save Lord Dancy from Clarissa Filbert could succeed.

"Missee write to Filbert next," Chen Mei reminded.

Once that onerous task was completed, Amelia faced the day with a lighter heart. That evening at Almack's she found Lord Dancy in attendance and her pleasure increased tenfold. When he made his way through the crush of people to her side she found it difficult to speak, so flustered was she with his nearness. He bowed over her hand, with that charming smile Amelia found so delightful.

"I sought to request permission to dance the waltz with you only to discover you have already been approved for the dance. It seems Lady Jersey thought you a very pretty-behaved girl."

"Well," Amelia said judiciously, "I did say that she was much younger and prettier than I had expected. And that I was not surprised to see most of the men sighing in her direction."

"Minx. Sally adores flattery from all I have heard. However, it enables me to beg the next waltz." His lazy grin sent Amelia's susceptible heart into a near frenzy of pitter-pattering.

"Of course. I am yours to command, my lord," Amelia said with a sincerity that shook Geoffrey to his toes. He had grown accustomed to the coquetry of the young women who frequented London during the Season. Forthright behavior as Amelia displayed when with him was most unusual. He intended to watch carefully to see if she behaved like this toward other gentlemen.

He guided her onto the dance floor, slipping his arm about her with a sense of the familiar. After all, it had been mere weeks since he rescued her from the fire, carrying her to safety in his arms. He had not forgotten the sensation she created within him when she snuggled so trustingly against his chest, her arm so ingenuously curved about his neck.

Now he gathered her as close to him as proper manners permitted, enjoying her lightness in his arms, the delicate scent of lilies of the valley that wafted to his nose when he twirled her about the room.

He saw Clarissa Filbert staring at them from one of the chairs along the end of the room. Even in the light shed from the crystal chandeliers her antagonism was clear. The narrow-eyed gaze chilled Geoffrey to his bones. Could the chit actually harbor such silly notions in her head as Amelia had suggested? It seemed so absurd he would have dismissed it out of hand had he not caught sight of her countenance.

Mr. Sands was not in evidence this evening, and suddenly Geoffrey wondered if the man was out arranging for the traveling coach to use while absconding with Amelia. Then sanity returned and Geoffrey dismissed the whole as too utterly fantastic.

Once returned to her aunt, Amelia watched with regret as Lord Dancy fell into the trap of inviting Miss Filbert to dance. Or . . . did he merely seek to allay her jealousy, or possibly encourage her plans?

Amelia had not failed to see the anger in Clarissa's eyes when Geoffrey had squired Amelia for the waltz. She told herself he asked Clarissa to perform the country dance with him only because it did not require intimate contact.

The remainder of the evening was less than delightful. Lord Dancy left early, as Mrs. Spencer made a point of noting.

"Lord Dancy has gone. What a pity. A man who has such exceptional legs and dances as well as he ought to remain to show the others how to get on."

"Perhaps he has an early appointment?" Amelia replied, glad to see her aunt gathered her belongings in preparation to departure, even though the hour was not terribly advanced.

"We shall see him tomorrow at the Twysden affair. I asked him if he intends to go and he said yes. That lovely Mr. Sands will be there as well. You will have a wonderful time, my girl."

Amelia considered the odious Thomas Sands and barely repressed a shudder. She and Chen Mei would have to ensure their plot would prevail. They must. The alternative was unthinkable.

Chapter Five

Aunt Ermintrude did not receive guests on the day of the Twysden's soirée. Instead she took Amelia shopping along Bond Street early in the morning before the Bond Street loungers took over, planning to rest that afternoon.

It was unthinkable that a lady should present herself on Bond Street at an hour when the fashionable gentlemen left their lodgings and hotels to saunter along to the circulating libraries and bookshops in the area or perhaps to enter Mr. Truefitt's establishment for a session of barbering. An hour or two in the morning was all a lady might hope for in shopping time, and Aunt Ermintrude intended to make the best of her morning.

"I do so hope to find a lovely new evening hat or some appealing trifle," she said with a wistful sigh. They strolled along, peering into shop windows, discussing all they found on display with keen interest.

"Come along," Mrs. Spencer said at last when convinced there was nothing tantalizing to be seen. "I wish to go to Savory and Moore for I require some Daffy's Elixir and perhaps some distillation of willow bark. Oh, and I need more lavender water. When one has the headache there is nothing better than a soothing application of that after taking a bit of the willow bark liquid."

Obediently following her aunt up the street, Amelia made discreet glances about her, taking note of who was out and about this day. When her aunt entered the apothecary shop, Amelia gladly followed, for she had caught a glimpse of Mr. Sands exiting Long's Hotel and had no desire to have him latch on to her aunt's company. She lingered in the rear of the shop while her aunt made her purchase, hoping that Mr. Sands would continue on his way without glancing in the shop window. Perhaps, considering his garb, he was on his way to play a game of tennis at the Royal Tennis Court, which was not far away in James Street. She hoped so.

"We shall stop at a perfumer's shop. There is one on Oxford Street I favor," Aunt Ermintrude declared, her wrapped purchase tucked into the depths of her large reticule.

Relieved at escaping from Bond Street without having seen more of Mr. Sands, Amelia immediately agreed.

Additional stops on Oxford Street produced a pretty fan with ivory sticks, and pink roses painted on the silk gauze.

"I wish you to have a new trifle for the Twysden soirée this evening. I believe Mr. Sands will be attending," Aunt Ermintrude said with a flutter of her lashes, for all the world like a young girl. "You must contrive to make a better impression on him, my love. He is a most elegant and well-mannered young man."

"Is he?" Amelia murmured. "I thought he hinted that a Gretna Green elopement was not a thing to deplore when he visited the house the other day. Surely you cannot consider that well-mannered."

"I do not recall such a remark," Aunt replied, visibly confused. "He seems such a nice person I can scarce think he actually believes *that*. Perhaps you misunderstood him? Your dear Papa desires you to make a suitable marriage, and I confess that Mr. Sands is quite appealing. You should do more to attract his attention, my love."

Amelia felt a shade guilty, for she well knew that Mr. Sands had not made such a remark to her aunt. However Amelia knew he felt that way, yet she could hardly reveal her source of information, nor how she intended to deal with it that very evening.

While her aunt took her afternoon rest, Amelia sent off a note to Peter to remind him that she depended upon him to be present at the Twysden affair.

Some blocks away Lord Dancy eyed the note delivered by Mrs. Spencer's footman with barely concealed curiosity. He watched Peter unfold it, scan the contents, then toss the note aside on a table.

"A love letter, Blandford?" Geoffrey said idly.

"Actually, it is nothing of the sort. Miss Longworth reminds me that I am to attend the Twysden soirée this evening." Peter added, "You plan to go?"

"Now that you mention it, I believe I did send an acceptance to the lady." Geoffrey fidgeted with the signet ring he wore, shifting on the chair, his manner edgy.

"Are you having difficulty with a woman, Dancy?" Peter inquired lightly. "You know that girls, and servants as well come to think on it, are the most difficult people to handle. If you treat them familiarly, they become disrespectful; if you keep them at a distance, they resent it. Dashed hard for a fellow to know what to do at times."

"No, no. Merely at loose ends for the moment." Restless and annoyed at the amused glance Peter sent him at his interest, Geoffrey rose from the chair where he had lounged and chatted with his friend, making a barely coherent excuse to depart.

Out on the street Geoffrey debated on what to do. He had not planned to attend the Twysden soirée this evening at all in spite of his assurances to Mrs. Spencer. They usually had the most boring of parties. But he knew he had received an invitation; it languished somewhere at the bottom of the pile of social correspondence that had accumulated of late.

Somehow Geoffrey found his feet directed to his residence, walking faster and faster the closer he came. Once there he plowed through his stack of gilt-edged and nicely lettered invitations until he found the one for the Twysden thing. Even the invitation looked boring. However he felt compelled to attend. He must know what was going on between Peter and Amelia Longworth.

He had seen their heads together too often to suit his taste. Amelia had seemed to turn to Peter ever since they had arrived in London. Yet she had declared that she belonged to Geoffrey Dancy, no one else. Never mind that he had refused her bizarre claim, he felt strong reluctance to permit anyone else to have her, either.

In short order he sent off a missive by his man to the effect that he begged Lady Twysden's pardon most humbly for being so late and prayed that he be allowed to attend her party that evening. He rather doubted that she would be annoyed, for single men were always in demand, especially for Lady Twysden.

Later that day at the house on Brook Street Amelia dressed for the evening with the greatest of care. She wanted to look seductive, yet demure; alluring, yet reserved. That was not an easy matter, she discovered quickly enough.

"It is your heart that is disturbed," Chen Mei advised. "Nothing seems fitting when you upset. Let the root be good and the fruit shall not be evil," she quoted in Cantonese from her endless store of wisdom. She often managed to avoid her *r* problem by resorting to her native language when faced with the use of the troublesome letter.

"You know well and good that my motive is the purest. I can only pray that the fruit of my efforts will be as good as you seem to believe." She flashed a minatory glance at her companion, then turned to the looking glass again, hoping to improve her appearance a trifle more.

At long last Amelia left her room, assured by Chen Mei that she was as well turned out as might be, considering she dressed in the English style rather than an elegant silk gown such as worn by the ladies of the Chinese court.

A quick check in the looking glass on the landing revealed to Amelia that her delicate turquoise gown of sheer sarcenet over a white satin slip and trimmed in pale peach silk roses and rouleaus of turquoise satin was all the crack. The neckline seemed shockingly low, but she knew it fashionable. Her gloved fingers touched the dainty sleeves puffed out and slashed with turquoise sarcenet over white satin. A pale peach rose nestled at the front of her bodice. Although Amelia thought it drew attention to her bosom far too much, Chen Mei muttered something about setting bait to catch a rat. After that Amelia kept silent.

"Amelia, my love, are you coming? I wish to leave early, else it will be impossible to draw near the house. The street is narrow, and I detest sitting in the carriage for an hour while my gown becomes horridly rumpled."

"Coming," Amelia replied and skimmed down the stairs with as much haste as seemly, followed by Chen Mei arrayed for once in a simple black gown. It was Chinese in style and made of elegant lustrous silk.

It was fortuitous that they arrived early for it presented Amelia with an opportunity to set the stage as it were. She was able to station herself so she knew precisely when Clarissa Filbert arrived and observed the hurried consultation she held with Thomas Sands. When Peter Blandford came, Amelia had little trouble catching his eye.

Aunt Ermintrude had settled herself at a card table early on, leaving Chen Mei to keep an eye on Amelia, which suited the two of them to a tee.

Since there often was no dancing at a soirée, Amelia contented herself with joining in a game of charades. She was curious to know what the surprise might be that the hostess promised her later in the evening, but having been warned by Aunt, had no high expectations. Lady Twysden apparently had no great reputation as a hostess.

Amelia and Peter Blandford had just stumped the entire group with a charade depicting the abdication of Napoleon, which Peter felt due any moment, when she sensed that someone watched her. Looking about, Amelia discovered that Lord Dancy had come. Peter had assured her that he knew how to lure Dancy into coming. He'd succeeded. She edged her way until she stood next to an elegant Lord Dancy.

"Good evening, sir." His eyes widened slightly as he studied her, and Amelia wondered if he also found the neckline of her gown to be just a trifle shocking.

"You and Peter make an excellent combination when it comes to charades. I have the feeling that you have had more than a bit of practice."

Amelia attended to his words with one ear while she watched Clarissa Filbert signal to Thomas Sands.

"Ah, I wonder what Lady Twysden has planned for her surprise." Amelia knew what she intended to do. If she could just get Lord Dancy to cooperate, all would go well and she could teach Clarissa a lesson that she would not forget in a hurry.

"Having just arrived, I could not imagine what her ladyship intends to dazzle us with as entertainment."

Amelia noted the biting tone of his voice and glanced back at him. "I gather you do not care for Lady Twysden's games, sir. Perhaps you ought to stick to cards?"

"Oh, there are games I enjoy," he said with a highly provocative tilt to his brows. Those eyes, the color of precious jade, danced with an intimacy that Amelia found bone-melting in intensity.

"I do believe you tease me, sirrah," Amelia said, batting her lashes as she had observed Aunt Ermintrude do, while hoping that she might survive his bedevilment.

"There are a number of things I should enjoy doing with you, my dear. Did you have a particular game in mind?"

"As a matter of fact, I did." She gave him what she hoped was a flirtatious look. "Would you meet me in the first room down the hall—on the right side?"

She didn't blame him for his hastily concealed look of astonishment. It was most unlike her usual circumspect behavior to beg his company.

"Now?"

"Most definitely now."

He studied her with that inscrutable assessment as he had once before. Chen Mei had commented that he would have made an excellent Chinese, as he could so well conceal his thoughts if he chose. Then he bowed most correctly, sauntering off down the hall just as she had hoped.

Across the room Clarissa watched his departure with an avid gaze before signaling Mr. Sands once again.

Amelia caught Peter's attention by wiggling her fingers at him to bring him to her side.

"Yes, my goddess," he teased. "You summoned me? I noticed you in conversation with Dancy a bit ago. Things coming to a head?"

"It is so simple I fear something may go astray. Quick, follow him to the first room on the right, get him to hide behind that screen by any means you can. I checked there earlier, and that is an excellent place to eavesdrop on all that happens. If you must, tell him that you have a surprise for him."

"Will do," Peter replied with commendable brevity. He circled the drawing room, then paused in the adjacent card room before slipping along the hall to where Lord Dancy waited.

Fortunately Clarissa had not noticed Peter Blandford's departure. She was undoubtedly so intent upon timing her

arrival at the room where she suspected Lord Dancy was
that she missed all else. She conferred a few minutes with
Thomas Sands before nonchalantly walking toward the
hallway.

Amelia watched, drawing Chen Mei to her side so to be
poised to pounce at the proper moment. For one frustrating
moment Amelia thought she would be drawn into the game
of charades again, only to be reprieved by Lady Twysden.

"I want you all to meet the famous Dr. Spurzheim," she
gushed with enthusiasm. "He lectures on the new science of
phrenology and is going to demonstrate how one can deter-
mine much of the character of a person, his disposition,
even his chance of success in life by the shape of his head."

The good doctor bowed most correctly, then drew one of
the young men forward to begin his demonstration.

Amelia gave thanks for the diversion offered. Although
it might be interesting to hear the opinions of this man, she
was wary of such fatalistic views. Why, it would seem that
no one had any control over his destiny if what the man
said was true. And what if a gentleman was hit on the
head? A new bump might change his entire future!

She stationed herself in an alcove just outside the drawing room, ostensibly admiring a small sculpture of a horse
with Chen Mei properly at her side and making snide observations on the poor quality of the supposed Ming piece.

Clarissa walked to the first room on the right after peering into those on the left side. Amelia slipped around the
corner, leaving Chen Mei positioned to watch the door.
Giving a message to a footman, she then watched as
Thomas Sands marched around the corner and along the
hall, pausing cautiously at the first door on the right before
entering.

Behind the screen Geoffrey had given his friend an exas-
perated look. "I daresay you have a reason for your hare-
brained behavior, but I'll be dashed if I can see what it is."

"Patience, my good fellow. Only a few moments more."

At that the door to the room opened and Peter made a
cautioning gesture.

"Lord Dancy? I must speak with you, sir. Lord Dancy?"
Clarissa called again, this time more loudly.

When Geoffrey gave Peter a questioning look, his friend

merely shook his head, raising a finger to his lips. So Geoffrey kept silent, wondering what this was all about and why Miss Filbert thought she must speak with him.

"Oh, bother," Clarissa muttered. "I made certain he was in here. Where else could he be? The other rooms are all empty." She turned as though to depart when the door opened.

"Clarissa! What are you doing in here alone? I thought you had Dancy with you. That was the idea, if you recall," he said in a voice that dripped with sarcasm. "In case you have forgotten, you are to lure him in here first, *then* summon me."

"Well, doubting Thomas, I did not summon you here, nor did I find Lord Dancy here as I'd expected. He cannot disappear, after all. He must be nearby. Quickly, you must go before someone finds us here alone. If you recall," she hissed with matching sarcasm, "I am to be compromised with him, not you. You have no money, my darling. He has pots of it. Speaking of which, why are you so slow with that twit Amelia Longworth. I thought you would have that matter taken care of by now. Or had you forgotten that we need a goodly sum of money upon which to live? Neither of us has common tastes."

"True, my love. I shall flee here immediately. But before I go, allow me one small boon?" With that he stole a lingering kiss.

Precisely at that moment the door flew open and Mrs. Spencer stood, utterly aghast at the sight before her. She cried out in horror, and in moments a cluster of people gathered about to stare at the well-compromised couple, Clarissa Filbert and Thomas Sands.

"Well, I never," Mrs. Spencer declared to the sorely afflicted Mr. Sands. "And to think I believed you such a gentleman. Such behavior is not at all seemly!" She turned her gaze from him to Clarissa and back again. "I wish you well, sir. And you, Miss Filbert. I trust the wedding will occur ere long?"

There were titters of unkind laughter among the *tonnish*, gossipy gathering that flanked Mrs. Spencer. That good lady was not amused, however. She glared at the culprits through narrowed eyes.

No doubt knowing that his goose was well and truly cooked, Mr. Sands bowed, then bestowed a somewhat sickly smile on the lady who accused him with her gaze, not to mention a regrettable tongue. "May you be the first to know that Miss Filbert had done me the honor of accepting my suit."

Clarissa was speechless. In fact it seemed to Geoffrey from where he stood behind the safety of the providential screen that Clarissa looked as though she had been hit over the head with a blunt instrument and merely waited to collapse.

Things were soon sorted out, with Mr. Sands escorting Clarissa to her fond mama's side. The three left shortly after that, Mrs. Filbert looking as though she was about to rupture her stays.

Geoffrey eased from behind the screen, followed by Peter. "I gather this affecting scene is what you intended me to hear, if not see?"

"Yes, well, we thought it best to handle it this way. Sands was becoming a shade too particular in his attentions to Amelia, and Miss Filbert had determined to entrap you this very evening. Amelia thought this would wrap things up quite neatly."

"Amelia *planned* all this?"

"I suspect that Chen Mei had a devious hand in it as well. She is devilishly good when it comes to plotting."

"Really?" Geoffrey controlled his temper with difficulty until he began to see the funny side of it all. "Do you realize that she has paid me back one? For that Filbert girl would have been the figurative death of me, had I been forced to wed her."

"Oh, she didn't wish to marry you. Have you forgotten? All she wanted was your money. She planned to give you such a disgust of her that you would cry off, whereupon she would take you to court with a breach of promise suit so fast it would make your head swim."

"I'd heard of men doing something like this, but never truly expected it of a woman. And"—he gave Peter a rueful look—"I cannot say it does much for one's dignity to be considered merely as a potential source of income."

"Oh," Peter said after chuckling at this sally, "I fancy

there is some woman about who will have you. The trick is
to know where to look."

"And I suppose you know just where that is?"

"No need to come over the lord with me, Dancy. We
have been through far too much together."

The two men strolled from the now-deserted room with
rapport reestablished, intent upon finding a drink with
which to seal their strengthened bond.

"Just a moment, Blandford. Find me a glass of wine. I
see Miss Longworth over there and wish to speak with
her."

Peter nodded, a knowing grin crossing his face before
heading in the direction of a servant from whom wine
might be obtained.

As he approached Amelia, Geoffrey stared at her. That
gown just bordered on the proper. Never mind that many
other women wore similar gowns this evening or other
evenings, for that matter. All he could think of was that
Amelia ought not be revealing quite so much skin.

She seemed part angel, part devil, no doubt because of
that Chinese woman's influence upon her. Certainly her
aunt would never think of such connivance. What was
Amelia's aim? Did she seek to ensnare him?

"I see you are quite safe from harm, my lord," Amelia
said demurely.

"If you mean Clarissa Filbert, I daresay you are correct.
Blandford tells me I owe my deliverance to you?"

"No, it is I who owe you a debt, or had you forgotten?"

Geoffrey stared at her. Forgotten that he had carried her
in his arms from the blazing inn, cradled her close to him,
learning the delicate shape of her with amazing intensity?

"No," was his totally inadequate reply.

"I think you ought to consult Dr. Spurzheim." She gestured to the man who continued to fascinate his audience.
"Perhaps he may be able to tell you about your character. I
believe you are noble and kind. I hear things, of course.
But . . ." Her voice trailed off in a suggestive manner that
irritated Geoffrey.

"Amelia, my love, let us depart. My nerves are utterly
shattered that Mr. Sands would prove to be such a naughty

man. I declare, he quite deserves that frightful Clarissa Filbert and her mama."

After bestowing a twinkling smile on Geoffrey, Miss Longworth gracefully drifted after her aunt. He watched as they made a properly reluctant farewell to their hostess. Then they disappeared from view.

Within moments Geoffrey followed suit, quite forgetting about Peter and the wine, declining Lady Twysden's offer to introduce him to Dr. Spurzheim. The notion that another female thought he needed help of any sort was entirely too much and he went home to bed, thus shocking his valet.

Geoffrey had paused outside of the Twysden house, taking note of the number of men clustered about in the shadows. Unusually prudent, rather than walk as he had intended to do, Geoffrey took a chair home. There was something about the men that bothered him. Bah! He was turning into an old woman, thanks to that Longworth chit and all her fears. But she *had* saved him from a great deal of expense, not to mention notoriety that could have cost him a respectable marriage—when he finally chose to wed.

Just who that lady might be, he truly had no idea. But, he determined, she would not be an angelic blonde with positively wicked blue eyes.

Across London Thomas Sands paced back and forth in his lodgings with furious mutterings against the same young woman. To his friend and confidant, John Pringle, he declared, "She was behind it all, of that I am sure. It is all her fault that I must be forced to wed Clarissa without two shillings to rub together when I'd counted on piles of nice shiny guineas."

"Nothing you can do about it now, Sands."

"Oh? You think not?" Mr. Sands came to a halt, rubbing his chin with a reflective gesture. "I disagree. Wouldn't you say that aunt of hers would give a bundle to save her niece from a scandal? Just because Clarissa's part in this affair has gone amiss don't mean that my plan need fail. I shall proceed as soon as able."

"By Jove," breathed Mr. Pringle in reply, all admiration.

* * *

Aunt Ermintrude was in such a state that she declined to leave the house for a day, claiming an indisposition.

Since no one suspected she had nurtured plans for Mr. Sands, no connection was drawn. At any rate most of the *ton* knew Sands to be without a feather to fly with, so of course no provident parent or guardian would consider him as a potential *parti*.

Amelia did not find the enforced quiet unpleasant. She persuaded Chen Mei to take a stroll with her, intent upon the peace and greenery of Hyde Park.

When Mr. Sands came into view, she gave Chen Mei a dismayed look before casting about to see if she might turn aside and avoid the man. They were truly hedged in. It seemed there was no help, unless she did an about-face and went the other way. No coward, she elected to see what he had to say.

"Ah, the fair Miss Longworth of the celestial blue eyes and exquisite blond curls."

"Miss Filbert is not with you this morning? I am sorry not to see her, for I had no opportunity to wish her happy last evening."

"You were not present when I made the, er, announcement, then?" Mr. Sands frowned as though trying to recall if he had seen her or not.

Amelia retreated slightly at his intense gaze. For just a moment it had seemed most malevolent.

"It looks to rain, sir. We had best make our way back to my aunt's house. I would not ruin my bonnet." The clouds were of the type that could possibly bring a shower.

"Oh, my dear Miss Longworth, permit me to take you up in my carriage," he replied with thoughtful promptness. "I would not forgive myself if your bonnet is ruined because I detained you merely to chat with so charming a lady."

Amelia gave Chen Mei a wry look. A rumble of thunder gave her earlier remark most unwelcome support. "Well, I truly would feel horrid if I jeopardized my new bonnet simply because I do not trust the man," she murmured to Chen Mei in Cantonese.

"The struggle for rare possessions drives a man to actions injurious to himself," observed Chen Mei in the same language as she studied the impatient young man now awaiting them next to his carriage. "I think we walk."

A light mist of rain began to fall.

"Allow me to take you both home. It might be a shade crowded, but I believe we can manage." Mr. Sands hastily put up the top on his cabriolet. Although intended for two, he obviously sensed the Chinese woman would not permit her charge to go without her.

Annoyed at the weather, Amelia felt she had no choice but to accept his fortuitous offer. She quickly climbed into the cabriolet, then watched as Chen Mei scrambled up with near-unseemly haste to perch close to her.

"I not trust the man," she said softly in Cantonese.

"We shall be on our guard," Amelia murmured back, then gave Mr. Sands a demure look. "It shall not take long, sir? I would hurry."

He set off at a commendable clip, the hinged leather apron protecting their clothing from the falling mist. At the corner where Amelia knew he ought to have turned, he went straight ahead out of the city.

"Precisely where do you think to take us, Mr. Sands? We wish to go home," she said firmly, her worry increasing with each block.

"Oh, you shall get there . . . eventually."

Amelia did not think his laugh at all amusing, nor had she any inclination to join him.

"I had planned for us to take the air at Barnet," he said casually, referring to the well-known stage on the road north to Gretna Green. "This rain requires we change to a closed carriage, but I fancy that will do us even better."

Her protests fell on deaf ears. If anything his speed increased. They drove madly though the countryside that stretched from Hyde Park to the village of Barnet at a pace Amelia found frightening. Trees were but a blur, and had it not been for the carriage hood behind her, she was certain her bonnet would be long gone.

When they arrived at Barnet, he pulled his winded team to a halt, obviously intending to switch carriages and cattle here. Amelia tensed as he turned to face them.

"I want you to take a hackney back," he said to Chen Mei. "Give this message to Mrs. Spencer immediately."

Amelia snatched the note from his hand and scanned the contents. "You intend my aunt to ransom me from you for a handsome sum? What a cad you are, sirrah!"

At Amelia's side Chen Mei smiled and pulled her little dagger from her sleeve.

Chapter Six

"You out, Mista' Sands," Chen Mei said, bringing the dagger swiftly to Thomas Sands's throat. "We go home now. You velly bad man. Tian Li no like you. You want too muchee money." Chen Mei had quickly moved from her side of the cabriolet to appear half-crouched before Mr. Sands as though conjured out of the mist.

The astounded man gave a croak of anger and shock. His hand dropped from Amelia's arm. The reins fell uselessly against the hinged leather apron, now pushed aside by Chen Mei, when he dropped them in his surprise.

An ostler ran forward to pick up the reins just as a familiar figure came into view around the side of the carriage, a pistol held unwaveringly in his hand. The ostler held the horses, his eyes wide at the strange doings of the Quality.

"Amelia, are you all right?" Lord Dancy held out one hand toward her with a side nod to Chen Mei.

"Oh, Lord Dancy," Amelia wailed, clambering hastily down from the carriage and flinging herself against his broad and welcome chest. His free arm wrapped around her, offering splendid comfort, hugging her against him with an intensity that Amelia found most agreeable.

"Not trust Mista' Sands," Chen Mei repeated. "Lord Dancy know what do with him. Send message this day." Obviously satisfied that a true gentleman was here to deal with the blackguard, Chen Mei removed her little dagger from the spot against Mr. Sands's throat, then sat back, arms folded, to watch Thomas Sands reap his punishment.

"I am reckoned to be a dead shot, Sands, but if you contest that opinion, I should be happy to demonstrate my aim." Peter Blandford stepped from the other side of the carriage, a pistol trained directly at the hapless Sands.

Mr. Sands, now faced with two pistols aimed at his head and heart plus a quixotic Chinese woman at his side ready to slit his throat with a wicked-looking dagger, swallowed with difficulty and appeared near fainting.

Amelia withdrew from Lord Dancy's protection after that most comforting embrace, suddenly aware of the impropriety of her behavior. It had been an instinctive move on her part to turn to him, for he had saved her before and she trusted him implicitly. She tossed Mr. Sands a dark look.

"That miserable creature did not give up his dastardly scheme to swindle money from my father by kidnapping me as I thought he must," Amelia cried. She glared at Mr. Sands. "He intended to abduct me so he could obtain the money he needs to marry Miss Filbert. Surely there is a fine for kidnapping an heiress? I recall reading something to that effect not long ago."

At this information Mr. Sands turned even more pale. He clambered down from the carriage with dispatch, then stood uneasily while casting a wary eye on Peter Blandford and Lord Dancy, both of whom looked more menacing than his future mother-in-law. She was certain to give him a wigging for mismanaging this affair.

The mist eased and a pale March sun peered from behind a cloud. Amelia shivered, wishing she was anywhere but involved in such a frightful mess.

"This is too much. You gentlemen may do as you please with this creature. Chen Mei and I intend to go home." For no reason she could think of, Amelia felt like crying and she hated to have anyone see her dissolve into a watering pot, particularly Lord Dancy. She had tried to be brave all the while the carriage had racketed from London to Barnet. She had remained calm when Chen Mei thrust her dagger at Mr. Sands's throat. Now that it was all over, her knees felt thoroughly unreliable, and she longed for her bed and a cup of tea, not necessarily in that order.

There was hasty conversation between Lord Dancy and Peter Blandford, who managed to keep their guns trained on Mr. Sands all the while. Chen Mei planted herself close by, her dagger again in evidence lest Mr. Sands take a notion to do something unpleasant.

In short order Amelia found herself being assisted into Lord Dancy's curricle, with Chen Mei sharing the small seat behind with the affronted groom, Hemit. Since she was tiny, if intimidating, it truly did not inconvenience him. Perhaps he too vividly recalled that dagger?

"You have saved my life again, sir," Amelia said in a wavering voice. She settled back on the seat, accepting the small rug that Lord Dancy placed over her lap and legs with a nod. She admired the manner in which he gave the horses the office to start, the carriage taking off with a smooth motion. The leather hood remained up, offering them a modicum of privacy.

"I hardly think so," he replied blandly while he skillfully guided the two horses along the road back to London. "Chen Mei had things well under control. I should say that you merely completed your task of delivering me from the clutches of Clarissa Filbert. My, what a heartless little thing she is."

"But I do not believe we could have managed without you," she stubbornly persisted.

"No? The sight of Chen Mei with a dagger at Thomas Sands's throat would most assuredly have drawn sufficient attention for you to get all the help you need."

Amelia gave him a thoughtful look and subsided. It seemed he did not want any part of her gratitude for rescuing her from the dastardly hands of Thomas Sands. Dancy didn't want her thanks, nor did he wish her to feel obligated to him. It seemed to her as though Geoffrey, Lord Dancy did not appreciate her devotion. Pity, that, for Chen Mei had taught Amelia well. One fulfilled one's duty, and Amelia's duty was to look after Lord Dancy.

He competently guided the carriage through the press of city traffic until they reached Berkley Square. Here he drew up, then handed the reins to his groom, who still looked as though he had been sucking on a lemon.

The short-lived shower had moved on to the east, leaving the streets freshly washed; a lovely spring sun beamed down upon London. Refreshed by the rain, daffodils and primroses bloomed from pots and window boxes. Indeed, the city was beginning truly to come to life. The square bustled with others who had braved the uncertain weather to sample Mr. Gunter's rightly famous fare.

"I thought you might enjoy an ice from Gunter's. Or perhaps tea, if you are chilled." Lord Dancy signaled to the young waiter who came dashing across from the shop to take the order. "Well? Which shall it be? Ice or tea?"

Amelia was chilled, but she had yet to enjoy an ice in the comfort of Lord Dancy's curricle. You did not have to be in London long before learning that this was one of *the* places to be seen. Her earlier malaise seemed to have vanished. Lord Dancy had a wondrous effect upon her.

"An ice, please. Lemon, I believe." When the waiter sprinted back to the shop, she gave Dancy an artless smile, then added, "I have not been here before, and I have longed to sample the ices."

"You mean none of the sprigs who have been lingering in Mrs. Spencer's salon have taken you to Gunter's?" he said in mock horror. "What poor-spirited things they are."

"Oh, I doubt that, merely that they are leery of being too particular in their attentions," she replied with surprising honesty. "I suppose that were the amount of the dowry Papa has settled on me or the size of his fortune be revealed, I would be flooded with requests to drive out, not to mention attend plays and see Astley's Amphitheater." Her cynicism was temporarily ignored when Dancy fastened upon one detail that worried him.

"I'd not wish to see you go to Astley's without adequate protection." He frowned so that the young waiter looked apprehensive when he hurried up with their ices.

"If you feel I must, then of course I must," Amelia said simply, not including the information as to where she intended to acquire that extra security.

At that moment Peter Blandford drove up in Mr. Sands's carriage. He leaped out, giving instructions to the badly shaken young man who took over the reins without so much as casting a glance at Lord Dancy and Amelia.

"You are allowing him to go free?"

"What charges could we bring against him without doing you a great deal of harm in the process?" Lord Dancy argued.

"I see," she said, thinking back to the note. Thomas

Sands had calculated that her aunt would rightly desire to prevent all gossip and scandal from touching her fledgling niece. Even though they foiled his attempt to extort money, they could not prosecute without damaging Amelia's reputation. There were so many who would titter behind their gloved hands, speculating on what had happened, had she cooperated, and to what extent.

The two men chatted while Amelia consumed her ice in silence. Peter Blandford explained what he had said to Sands, then launched into another matter dealing with a horse sale at Tattersall's.

It was most thoughtful of Lord Dancy to order an ice for Chen Mei also. But then, Amelia had observed that he was a remarkably considerate man. Fancy his charging after her when he received Chen Mei's message. It said much for that sense of duty she had observed in him before.

Amelia allowed her thoughts to wander, contemplating on what her aunt would say when informed of this escapade. Then another gentleman came up, placing his foot on one of the wheel spokes of the curricle while he spoke.

"Heard you are about to race Taunton? Think that wise? The man's a bit of a goer."

Amelia pretended not to have paid the least attention to this remark when Lord Dancy glanced her way. She looked across the square while concentrating on what was said.

"One of those things, old fellow. You know how it is."

"Ought to be a dashing good time of it."

From the corner of her eye Amelia could see Lord Dancy shake his head at the two men, effectively silencing them regarding the upcoming race.

Knowing that she would not hear anything of value from now on, Amelia turned back to the men, then briefly touched Lord Dancy's arm. Placing her hands most properly into her lap, she smiled, then said, "I expect I had best return home. Aunt Ermintrude might become worried that I am gone so long."

"Of course, Miss Longworth," Dancy replied correctly, for all the world as though he had not rescued her while she was wearing nothing more than a nightgown and robe, carrying her to safety while clutched tightly to his chest. That was a secret between them, and Peter Blandford, of course.

Amelia tended to discount that young man, for although he was kind and pleasant, he was not Lord Dancy.

Leaving the two gentlemen gazing thoughtfully after them, Lord Dancy drove Amelia through the streets of London until he reached Mrs. Spencer's home.

With a glance to the rear where she knew Chen Mei sat, Amelia faced Lord Dancy with pleading eyes. "Could you come in for a few minutes, sir? I would have you explain all to my aunt. She is inclined to the vapors, I suspect, and I fear that Chen Mei may frighten her. If you are present, my companion will remain silent, for she holds you in great respect."

"And your aunt would not listen to what you say?"

"Well, listen, but perhaps discount it."

Geoffrey handed the reins to his groom, who looked somewhat relieved to see the Chinese dragon disappearing into the house. Geoffrey smiled with amusement at the reactions of the man who had been with him for years. Very few things frightened Hemit. Chen Mei not only frightened him, she rendered him speechless.

Geoffrey assisted Amelia from his curricle, considering all the while her comments on how Mrs. Spencer and Chen Mei so greatly respected him. He wondered precisely how Amelia felt about him. Perhaps for the first time in his life he really wished he knew how a young woman regarded him. Respect? He was beginning to hope for something stronger than that. She had flown to him, nestling against his body in terror. He found her trust overwhelming in a way. It placed such responsibility on his shoulders. And yet . . . it also gave him the sensation of being ten feet tall, for she had gazed at him with what almost amounted to adoration in her eyes.

It was most likely the thing of a moment, the situation being highly charged with anxiety. Still, he found her dependence in his ability to right all wrongs very satisfying.

They found Aunt Ermintrude in her salon, for once alone, for it was not her afternoon to receive callers. Apparently Chen Mei elected to go up to her room, and Geoffrey felt the slim figure at his side give a sigh of what was most likely relief.

"Lord Dancy, Amelia, my little love!" Mrs. Spencer exclaimed with relief.

"I feel I owe you an explanation for keeping Miss Longworth so long. You see, we went for a drive, then to Gunter's for an ice where we met friends. You know how time can fly."

Mrs. Spencer gazed at the two with a dubious look on her face. "Ices? I was told that Amelia went haring off along Park Lane with that odious Thomas Sands in that dashing cabriolet of his. At least two people saw it."

Geoffrey exchanged a look with Amelia, who bloomed a lovely tint of pink at the uncovering of her deception.

"It threatened to pour, as you know it eventually did, and Mr. Sands insisted upon taking Chen Mei and me up in his carriage. Only he did not take us home, but rather to Barnet with the intention of holding me for ransom. He wanted a hideous sum of money to have me released."

Here Geoffrey interposed his comments. "Chen Mei sent me a message to the effect that she worried about Mr. Sands, that he might attempt something while she and Amelia walked in Hyde Park. Fortunately it came as I was about to go out for a drive. I merely guided my horses in the direction of the park to see Sands heading up Park Lane. I followed him, thus saving Amelia the fate intended for her."

"We are greatly indebted to you sir. I know Amelia will say that she owes you yet another obligation."

"No, no," Geoffrey hastily inserted into what he feared would be a long recitation of his merits. "It was something any gentleman would have done. Blandford was there and Miss Longworth is as indebted to him as to me."

"Aunt, Lord Dancy held a gun on Mr. Sands, as did Mr. Blandford. I believe they quite frightened him. I doubt if he will present himself to me again." She turned to face Geoffrey, offering him her hand. "Thank you, sir. You are a true hero."

"Your servant, Miss Longworth." He found the steady, trusting gaze from Amelia to be prodigiously unnerving. "However, I do not think we can discount the watchful eye and faithful service of Chen Mei. She held Sands in place with a dagger, after all."

"Amelia, I cannot like the thought of that woman carrying a dagger about with her, even if she does conceal it up one of those enormous sleeves." Aunt Ermintrude frowned in consideration of the things she had to endure with that foreign woman beneath her roof.

"But Aunt, it undoubtedly made a great difference," Amelia argued.

Sensing that this disagreement might continue for some time, Geoffrey begged to be excused and went on his way with the repeated thanks of both ladies ringing in his ears.

He gave his groom a nod, at which the fellow jumped up beside Geoffrey. "Good going, Hemit. All in all it's been quite a day."

"Think the young leddy heard that business about your race, milord?" Hemit inquired after a bit.

"Hard to tell. She appeared to be looking rather intently on the near carriage. That woman in the awful hat, you know, the one with the lime green cabbage roses and fuchsia ribbons on that enormous straw."

"Rather," Hemit agreed, but looked dubious.

Amelia removed her pelisse, feeling as though she had been from the house for days instead of a few hours.

"My love, you do seem to get into the most remarkable situations," her aunt said, obviously wondering precisely where Lord Dancy stood in all this.

Amelia waved a hand as though to dismiss past events from discussion. "I heard something ominous today."

"Never! What?"

"While we were sitting across from Gunter's and consuming our ices—and they certainly are delicious, by the by—some man came up to Lord Dancy to inquire about his upcoming race with a man called Taunton. The way he referred to this man made me very curious. I believe I shall try to find out something about this Mr. Taunton. Or Lord Taunton, as the case may be."

"Name is familiar. I seem to recall a Lord Taunton of some years ago, which must be this man's father. Gambled away his estate, or as near as may be. Nasty creature as I recall. I wonder if his son has managed to bring his estate about?"

"All the more reason to find out what I may about him, do you not think?"

"Oh, by all means," Aunt Ermintrude agreed with a firm nod. The dainty roses on her daycap quivered, possibly in anticipation of another interesting series of events. Life was never dull with Amelia about the house.

Amelia left her aunt to saunter up the stairs to her room. Once there she consulted with Chen Mei.

"Mista' Blandfo'd, he know race man," Chen Mei offered.

"Then we had best send for him, for I have very bad feelings about this, merely from their voices, you understand. That, and the interesting fact that Lord Dancy did not wish me to know about this race."

"Maybe ladies not attend races? Not ploper?"

"Perhaps. There are a great many things considered first rate for gentlemen but not proper for ladies. It is all very confusing."

"Send message to Blandfo'd," Chen Mei advised.

"I believe I shall," Amelia replied, crossing her room to sit down before the pretty little desk. She drew forth a sheet of pressed paper that was lightly scented. It took but a short time to compose the note for Peter Blandford. If she knew the young man at all, he would be here as soon as he possibly might.

It was some time after tea that Mr. Blandford presented himself at Mrs. Spencer's front door, requesting to see Miss Longworth, stating he was expected.

As indeed he was and the butler had been so advised.

"Mr. Blandford," Amelia caroled as she gayly floated down the stairs to where he stood in some bemusement at the sight of her.

"Miss Longworth, you continually amaze me. Where another woman would take to her bed with potions and lavender water, you appear untouched by your ordeal. In fact, you look like a veritable sprite in your green sprigged gown and the crown of flowers in your hair. Very lovely, if I may say so." He bowed correctly over her hand, then waited for her to speak.

"What a dear you are, to come to my aid like this. As to being untouched by the day's events, well, I find it best to put the unpleasant behind me, for it does no good to dwell upon it. Come ... we had best join my aunt in the salon where we shall confer."

His curiosity piqued, Peter followed her up the stairs after she had requested refreshments for Mr. Blandford from the stern-faced butler, a fellow aptly named Grimm.

"Now," Amelia began once Grimm had departed after placing a tray with tea and biscuits, and an excellent canary wine for Mr. Blandford on a table close by, "I wish to know all about the gentleman who intends to race against our Lord Dancy."

She handed Peter the wine, poured tea for her aunt and herself, then passed biscuits. Grimm would have been delighted to do all this, she knew, but since no one would speak while he was still present, she was happy to send him along.

"I gather Benedict, Lord Taunton is the man you mean," Peter replied, thus confirming Mrs. Spencer's guess.

"Indeed, Lord Taunton," echoed Aunt Ermintrude. "Knew his father. What a nasty little man he was, too. Gamester, as you may know. Lost nearly everything. Would have lost the rest, but he stuck his spoon in the wall in time to prevent it." She studied the far wall with a reflective expression on her face.

"Taunton is no great shakes, either. Oh, he does not sail quite as close to the wind as his father did, but close enough. Still has his estate, but barely, I suspect. He gambles, but with amazing success. I'd not say he cheats, for I scarcely wish to face him in a duel, but I have my doubts about his incredible luck with cards or anything else he tries." Peter took a fortifying sip of his wine, then leaned back against his chair while waiting for the delightful ladies to astound him with whatever they intended to do.

"That puts a seal on my fears," Amelia said, then firmed her lips with determination. "I have this peculiar feeling, you see. I believe Lord Dancy is in danger."

"Hardly likely in this race, Miss Longworth," Peter said with a smile at the young lady sitting so demurely on the sofa. "Dashed difficult to do as Hemit—he's Dancy's groom—will oversee everything, and he is as loyal as they come. I expect he will sleep with the rig just to see nothing happens to it."

"Do things *happen* to carriages that are raced?" Amelia asked with deceptive mildness.

"Yes, I fear so," Peter confessed. "Why, I've seen any number of disasters, axles sawed into, wheel pins dislodged, a lot of things can go wrong with a carriage. Even the horses can be tampered with, you see. But in this case with Hemit on the job, there is no likelihood of danger. Dancy will be as right as rain." Peter assured her with confidence.

"Forgive me for doubting you, sir. I am nothing more than a curious female, wanting to know about something I suppose most ladies do not attend?" She gave Peter a wistful smile that would have melted the heart of a marble statue, if a statue could have a heart.

Since Peter's heart was closer to butter, he rushed to persuade her otherwise.

"Miss Longworth, let me convince you this is not so. Any number of ladies watch such a contest as this. While it would never do for a lady to take part in a race, it would be acceptable for you to sit in your carriage to watch the event. Dancy is certain to win, for his matched pair are prime goers."

"Yes, I had noticed the horses this morning. They are beautifully matched chestnuts, Aunt Ermintrude," she explained in the event her aunt was unaware of the excellence of Lord Dancy's horseflesh.

"You see, Miss Longworth, it is difficult to find a perfectly matched pair that also work together so well. Dancy and Hemit have turned this pair into a superb team. There is no way that Dancy can lose," Peter added with supreme assurance in his friend.

"I expect there will be a prodigious amount of betting on the race?" Amelia said.

"I fancy so," Peter assured her.

"Then if Lord Taunton has such an incredible ability to win when he bets, would it not seem likely that he does something to ensure that he wins this particular wager?" she demanded in her practical manner.

"I say," Peter protested. "That wouldn't be cricket."

"Cricket or no, I shall not idly sit by while Lord Dancy may be in danger," Amelia declared.

"But, dash it all, I fail to see what you can do."

"I have Chen Mei," Amelia reminded her friend. "You would be surprised at what the two of us can manage."

A disturbed expression settled on Mr. Blandford's face as he considered what this might entail. "I say," he began.

"Do not worry about it in the least, sir. We shall do no more than investigate, perhaps ask a few questions." She spoke in a soothing manner, but for some reason Peter Blandford did not appear assured by her words.

He chatted about other things, confirmed that Miss Longworth was indeed not harmed by the morning's expedition, then left.

Chen Mei entered the room through the connecting door to the adjacent room, normally opened when there was a great deal of company.

"You listened?" Amelia asked.

"Man very foolish. No trust bad man in race. Dancy will lose," Chen Mei concluded succinctly, again resorting to Cantonese.

"That is precisely what I believe," Amelia said with a narrowed gaze. "What utter nonsense to be sure. How in the world did Lord Dancy come to make a wager with such a man, I wonder?"

"And why would Lord Taunton desire such a race if Dancy's horses are such prime goers?" Aunt Ermintrude tossed out to the two others. "Something mighty fishy here."

Chen Mei nodded vigorously. "Tian Li take care of Lord Dancy," she said with supreme conviction.

"Oh, I must, mustn't I," Amelia agreed with a resigned look at her aunt.

"Well . . . " Aunt Ermintrude looked to where Chen Mei sat on the round ottoman, the picture of Oriental implacability.

"I fear he does not welcome my intervention, but dear aunt, he has saved my life so many times it is incumbent upon me to do all I can for him."

"I suppose so," Aunt Ermintrude said doubtfully. "Still it seems to me that you go rather far, my love."

"Nothing is too much for Lord Dancy," Amelia concluded, this time with greater spirit and utter devotion.

"I fail to see how you will ascertain whether there is anything havey-cavey about this race." Aunt Ermintrude looked first to Amelia, then to Chen Mei.

"Where there is determination, a way will be found," Amelia declared fervently.

"We keep ears open," Chen Mei said thoughtfully.

"True," Amelia added. "We can make a point of listening wherever we go. Perhaps I may be able to bring the race into conversation by some means."

"I shall help as well by doing the very same thing," Aunt declared with a delighted smile. "I do so love intrigue, and this seems as interesting as my days ever get. I am very pleased your father sent you to me, my love. Think how dull this Season would have been otherwise."

Amelia sent her dear aunt a grateful smile. She was not certain how she was to find out what she needed to know, but learn she would. Whether Lord Dancy liked it or not, she would do all she could to protect him from harm. And as far as she could see, this Lord Taunton was out to queer the race by some dastardly means. My, London was not so unlike Macao after all, where shady characters abounded.

All that remained was to discover which shady character in London intended to do Lord Taunton's dirty work and how.

Chapter Seven

"We shall have to find someone who is an expert at carriages to inspect Lord Dancy's for us, Chen Mei," Amelia said thoughtfully.

"Bad man velly watchful. No want evil found light away," Chen Mei said with shrewd insight.

"It is *right*, not light, Chen Mei," Amelia said patiently. "And yes, we do not need to search the carriage immediately. Lord Taunton may wait until the last moment to do the damage. We must find out precisely when the race is to be run. Mr. Blandford failed to tell us that. I hope he comes to visit soon, or else I shall have to call on him for his help."

Chen Mei murmured something in Cantonese that Amelia decided she would rather not hear. The companion was sitting on her favorite ottoman in the salon, embroidering a tiny peony on one of Amelia's plainer gowns. By the time she was finished, the gown would have an entire garden of dainty flowers embroidered here and there. Amelia felt very fortunate to have so talented an embroiderer with her as her own work, while not displeasing, couldn't compare to Chen Mei's.

An hour or so passed in peace. Amelia had just finished a letter to her dearest papa when she heard sounds from the hall.

Curious, she went to the landing to see what was going on for it was not the time for society callers to present themselves for tea and gossip.

Peter Blandford glanced up to see Amelia, then waved a hand as he murmured something to Grimm before dashing up the stairs. "Good, you are home this morning."

"We usually are, except for days when we get abducted

to be held for ransom. Come into the salon. Shall you like anything to drink? Coffee?" She tucked her hand comfortably in the crook of his arm, tugging him along with her so they would be less apt to be eavesdropped upon. Aunt Ermintrude had loyal servants, but one never knew.

"Coffee sounds wonderful."

Chen Mei placed her embroidery on the hassock, then slipped from the room to order the coffee for their guest. In moments she returned, picking up her embroidery and seeming to fade into the wallpaper.

Peter and Amelia chatted about the weather, which looked to be warming, and Napoleon, who looked to be fading, until one of the maids brought a tray bearing coffee and biscuits.

Once she had left, Peter took a sip from his cup then set it on the saucer with a loud clink, giving Amelia what she considered a desperate look.

"Tell me what is on your mind, Mr. Blandford."

"Please make it Peter, for you are like a sister to me. And that's the trouble." He stared morosely at his loosely folded hands held before him.

"That you feel brotherly toward me is a problem?" Amelia replied, quite confused.

"Oh, no. 'Tis my sister who's the problem. She and m'mother came to town yesterday. She wants to attend Astley's. I am supposed to get up a party. Trouble is, I don't know any young girls suitable to present to my sister. Ain't been to Almack's; I avoid the chits who are looking for a husband. But I do know you." Here he grinned at Amelia. "Would you set aside your plans for the evening to join us at Astley's?"

"I should be pleased, but naturally I would have to consult with my aunt. Allow me to find her. I suspect she would enjoy a gala evening. I saw in the newspaper there is to be a special performance this evening that I believe would be quite wonderful to see," she concluded shyly.

When Amelia left the room Chen Mei suddenly spoke. "You know good blacksmith? We need one to see Lo' Dancy's coach all right," she said with care. "Race come soon?"

"The end of this week, I believe," Peter replied, quickly,

following Chen Mei's enunciation carefully. "I believe I know of a good fellow out near where the race is to be held. Unless Taunton wants the route changed to a different road. Since he challenged, Dancy chooses. I will look into it. You truly believe there will be something underhanded?"

"I do," Chen Mei answered, clearly pleased that the intelligent young man would listen to her opinion.

Peter shook his head in dismay. "I know Taunton is not the best of *ton*, but it's hard to accept he'd not act like a gentleman."

Aunt Ermintrude was quickly found and proved most agreeable to the change in plans. She and Amelia bustled into the room, both wearing pleased smiles. Chen Mei returned to her embroidery.

"For we had planned to take in Mrs. Evesham-Fowler's card party," Aunt Ermintrude explained. "I truly would enjoy a visit to Astley's, for I have not attended in years. And it would be a pleasure to see your mama once again. I met her a year or so ago with Lady Sefton, I believe." If Mrs. Spencer believed that the Royal Amphitheater, as Astley's was advertised, to be more for children, she gave no indication. Amelia wondered if she thought Peter might have an interest in her, hence Aunt's willingness to accompany the heir to the baronetcy of Blandford.

"Quite so, I imagine. They are good friends. I am ever so grateful to you both," Peter beamed a smile at them. "Mean to persuade Dancy to join us if he can tear himself away from . . ." Peter clamped his mouth shut and turned slightly red.

Amelia wondered what it could be that caused his embarrassment, deciding it must be a woman Lord Dancy liked. Why the thought of Lord Dancy involved with some woman should cause Amelia a distinct pain in her heart, she couldn't understand. But, pain it did. To cover her peculiar reaction, she offered Peter another cup of coffee, then turned the conversation to what might be expected while at the evening performance.

"Chen Mei will most likely admire the horses, and a new song is to be introduced, 'Knowing Jerry'," he added with a mischievous glance at Amelia.

"I scarcely *know* what to make of that," she replied primly. She joined him in a shared smile.

"There will be a lot of dashing fellows about that you must take care to avoid. A pretty girl like you is bound to attract attention," Peter cautioned.

"It is nice to be thought pretty," Amelia allowed, "rather than be considered for my dowry."

"Most of the fellows know to a penny what every young lady is worth. If they can find one who is pretty *and* well to grass, all the better," Peter observed with brutal honesty.

"I gather Lord Dancy is not particularly interested in finding a wife," Mrs. Spencer said pensively.

"More's the pity. After what he's been through these past years, he needs the comfort of his home. His sisters are away, and the middle one married while he was gone. Wouldn't surprise me were the other two to marry within the year. Both of 'em are dashed pretty from all accounts I've heard. His parents were killed while on a trip to France to visit the *Bibliothèque Nationalè*—a trip authorized by Napoleon himself. Someone accused them of treason when all they wished to do was examine a manuscript. Before anyone could rush to their aid, they were dead. Murdered, if you ask me. Why, no one knows." Peter cleared his throat, then took a restoring sip of coffee. Since it had cooled considerably during his revelations, it lacked a certain something.

"How tragic," Amelia murmured, her heart going out to the gentleman so alone in the world. At least she had her dear papa and Chen Mei. Aunt Ermintrude, as well.

"Well, I must be off. Want to catch Dancy before he is out and about." Peter rose from his chair, waiting politely for his dismissal.

"Is Lord Dancy inclined to sleep late?" Amelia wondered. She rose from her place on the sofa to walk with Peter to the door.

"Actually he tends to business in the morning—correspondence, messages from his estate's steward, that sort of thing. His steward tries to persuade Dancy to come out to inspect the place he inherited. For some reason"—and here Peter looked a bit self-conscious,—"he's reluctant to leave London."

Although Amelia said nothing, she suspected that whatever kept Lord Dancy in London wore skirts and perfume.

They agreed upon a time to depart for the Royal Amphitheater in time to be present for the eight-thirty overture, then Peter clattered down the stairs and out to the street where his groom had patiently been walking his horse and curricle.

Amelia ran to the window, peering down to the street below. She observed that Peter drove off in the direction of Lord Dancy's home. Dropping the curtain, she stood a moment, wondering just who the lady was that had captured Dancy's interest. Most likely she would be slender, dark-haired, with shining black eyes and perfectly white skin. She would wear the most dashing gowns in seductive red satin and brazen black lace. Amelia thought she might hate the woman given the slightest provocation. And then she wondered about her intense reaction to this bit of news.

"Come, my love," Aunt Ermintrude trilled, "we had best decide what to wear this evening. Were it later in the year, we might have gone to Vauxhall Gardens, and that, I may tell you, is a wondrous place. When the weather turns warmer, we shall make up a party. It is something I know your dear papa would wish you to see."

Chen Mei watched as the two women left the room, then she sank into a reflective silence. In a short while she went to the butler's pantry and, after making sure he was not around, sharpened her little dagger. One never knew. At long last she hastened to Amelia's room to see what she might do to help.

"It will not be easy, to persuade Dancy of bad man," Chen Mei observed for no apparent reason.

At a curious look from Amelia, Chen Mei said in Cantonese, "It is easy to convince a wise man, but to reason with a fool is a difficult undertaking."

"You do not believe that *he* is a fool, do you? Rather believe that Taunton is the stupid one. He is the one who hopes to win by harming another," Amelia argued.

"In your acquaintance with a man you may know his face, but not his heart. His mind is as hidden from you as by a thousand mountains. Who knows what is in Dancy's heart?"

Since Amelia would like to know that very thing, she said nothing to the topic, reverting to their foe. "Taunton is the enemy. He cannot be considered as trivial."

"There is no sin greater than ambition; no calamity greater than discontent; no vice more sickening than covetousness. He who is content, always has enough," Chen Mei quoted from her store of Chinese proverbs. It never ceased to amaze Amelia how the woman could manage to think of a proverb that covered nearly every situation.

"Since Taunton gambles heavily on the race, I imagine he qualifies for nearly any one of those. He truly is an evil person, for Mr. Blandford said he's not a good person. We must find a way to keep Lord Dancy from this unprincipled man," Amelia replied.

"What did she say?" Aunt Ermintrude said with curiosity, obviously not wishing to be in the dark.

"She believes the man who opposes Lord Dancy, Lord Taunton, to be a fool," Amelia said, arranging the facts to suit what she contended to be true. "But even fools can win by evil measures, if only for a time." Amelia refused to accept the notion that Lord Dancy might be thought a fool, even by Chen Mei.

"What a wise little thing you are, my love," Aunt Ermintrude observed. Then she turned to sort through the gowns in the wardrobe in search of one that would dazzle the group this evening. She settled on a delicate blue sarcenet with silver threads woven through it. Silver ribbons enhanced the tiny puffed sleeves and the low neckline.

Amelia took one look, acquiesced, deciding she had best bring along a shawl else she might have to endure the sort of attentions Mr. Blandford cautioned her against.

Later that evening they joined the Blandford trio in the commodious town chariot that the Blandfords used when in London. Evidently they were a large family, for Mary mentioned how delighted her younger sisters would be to hear her account of a visit to the famous equestrian attraction.

The crowd was far greater than Amelia had anticipated. Suddenly she was pleased that Chen Mei hovered at her side and that Lord Dancy had agreed to meet them later in the evening.

Lady Blandford audibly regretted that her husband, the

baron, had not joined them this evening. "He must go off to his club, I know, but I would feel better in this crush were he at my side."

"The second spectacle this evening is promised to be unusually special, with a small bit of fireworks. Everyone is looking forward to it," Mary Blandford said, giving a happy bounce as they made their way through the crowd to find their box.

"We had wonderful illuminations in Macao. The Chinese invented fireworks, you know. They do marvelous things with them; Catherine wheels, figures, cascades, even dragons," Amelia said to Mary, rather liking Peter's enthusiastic sister.

"How wonderful to have traveled as you have. I should like to go to an exotic place someday. Have you never been in China itself?"

"English women are not permitted to enter China. I suspect the gentlemen are quite satisfied to keep it that way, for Papa has told me of the elegant dining room where they gather to eat after the day's business is over. There are servants in long robes and caps behind every chair, and the silver on the table glitters beneath the light of the chandeliers. Papa fears that nothing would get done were ladies to come. Chen Mei said English ladies are not wanted by the mandarins. They would most likely stop doing business if one of us popped up in their precious factories." Amelia chuckled, revealing that she didn't mind the banishment in the least.

"How much you have seen," Mary said wistfully.

"Not all is good. There is much you would rather not see, believe me," Amelia replied, thinking of the unsavory side of Macao and the ports along their route to England.

Green curtains concealed the stage to one end of the theater, below which the orchestra sat tuning up. Around the circular performing arena people thronged in the tiers of boxes. A magnificent glass chandelier containing fifty patent lamps hung from the center, or so declared an awed Mary, who'd read up on the place. Along the second tier smaller chandeliers contributed to the excellent lighting.

With a roll of the drums and the blare of a trumpet, a silver-garbed gentleman began a rather extraordinary performance on a tightrope.

Mary clutched Amelia's arm as she stared up at the daring feats executed above them. Below in the center of the arena, two clowns in outrageous costumes presented silly skits when the tightrope performer was between his audacious tricks.

"How perfectly lovely," Mrs. Spencer exclaimed with a sigh.

"Oh, look!" Mary cried as the tightrope walker retreated to thunderous applause, and a young fellow in a sailor suit appeared on the stage at the far end of the theater. She checked her program. "He is to sing."

The crowd listened with more attention than Amelia thought the song called "The Sailor's Land Voyage" deserved. It was amusing, she admitted at the conclusion. She suspected that it served to prepare for the next performance, that of the Equestrian Troop, according to the program.

That it was a trial of skill seemed to be an understatement. The men seemed to defy all reason in their fearless and bold riding exploits. She was glad when the segment came to an end and no one had been injured.

Again the young man came out to sing, this time a silly ditty called "Timid Johnny O." Amelia's mind wandered from the song. She looked about her, wondering where Lord Dancy could be. Perhaps he would not appear, as he had told Peter. This fare was pretty tame for a man of his background and apparent tastes.

"Dancy ought to be along by now. I said we'd meet him here." Peter craned his neck, looking over the audience to see if his friend had arrived and not found them. "I think he'd find the next item on the program quite amusing."

Amelia noted the dry note in his voice and wondered what could be amusing about "The Heroic Battle of Salamanca" to one who had most likely been there.

She saw Lord Dancy first. She espied him in a box across the central arena deep in conversation with a strikingly beautiful woman—dark eyes, sleek dark hair, gowned in palest gray satin that, while it hung simply, revealed a superb figure.

Amelia said nothing, preferring Peter to either say something or overlook their presence. If he did that, she would know that this woman was the one who had captured Lord Dancy's interest.

Yet she could not keep her gaze from returning to him. He looked superbly handsome in his rich coat of dark blue over a pearl gray waistcoat and pantaloons. Hints of red gleamed in his auburn hair from the light overhead. The conversation must be fascinating, for he didn't even notice the man who had drawn near him. The boxes in front were quite low, and there was ample space to circulate behind them. This was where Lord Dancy elected to chat with his lady friend.

Then the man behind Lord Dancy moved so that a shaft of light struck his face. Amelia stiffened as she recognized him.

She glanced at Chen Mei, then excused herself to slip from their box, murmuring something about the necessary to her aunt. Chen Mei followed her as Amelia raced along the hall that circled the tier of boxes.

From the stage she could hear the sound of battle, the blare of trumpets, and booming of guns. No doubt flags were waving madly in the smoke-filled air with heroic soldiers dashing madly about the arena on their steeds.

That shadowy man she recognized meant danger for her lord. Chen Mei had spotted him as well, which was why the two of them scurried along, ignoring the spectacle that was supposedly the highlight of the evening.

At last they reached the area where Lord Dancy hovered close to the beautiful lady. They stood near the rear of the box behind the rest of their group. Why he had promised Peter he would join them when it was plain he intended to escort this lovely woman Amelia did not know. However she knew her duty, and that was to protect Lord Dancy no matter how painful it might be.

"He is a fool," Chen Mei whispered, repeating her earlier opinion. "That man—"

Amelia darted forth through the open doorway to brush against Lord Dancy, throwing him off to one side just as a loud boom came from the stage. Once he regained his footing, she apologized profusely when she saw a dark flush of anger cross his face. He stared down at her with what appeared to be utter contempt.

"Miss Longworth, may I present Lady Catherine Beaton. Lady Catherine was just telling me about my sisters." His voice was correctly polite—polite and icy cold.

"How lovely, my lord." Amelia blushed under his reproachful glare. "Lady Catherine, I feel so foolish to lose my balance like that. A fold in the carpet caused me to stumble. How dangerous for a thing like that to be permitted."

Amelia knew she was babbling like an idiot. But how could she convince Lord Dancy that a man had stood behind him with a gun, most likely with the intention of shooting him? She had glimpsed it just before throwing herself between the Portuguese man and Lord Dancy. Chen Mei was correct. He was a fool. And Amelia thought it a pity that she was bound to serve him, for he was far too blind to recognize her devotion for what it was.

"I believe you came with Peter and his family." His voice could have frozen cream.

"Then you observed our party," Amelia said with equal hauteur. "I was delegated," she lied, "to inform you that we shall partake of refreshments after the performance. But I see you are quite absorbed. Forgive me for disturbing you, my lord." With that she slipped away and along the passage, following the direction she had seen Chen Mei go after the stranger when Amelia had pushed Lord Dancy out of harm's way.

Up ahead she caught sight of them in the shadows near the stairs. Chen Mei had the man back against the wall, her dagger to his throat.

"Oh, good. Perhaps we can dispatch this man once and for all. Then his lordship need not be bothered with him ever again," Amelia whispered.

Chen Mei glanced around her as though to see if there might be a place where they could dispose of the body when they heard footsteps.

Amelia half turned to see who might be approaching. Lord Dancy bore down on them in a furious stride.

Chen Mei let forth a spate of Cantonese that would have curled the lank hair of the Portuguese had he understood.

"My lord," Amelia said with affected calmness, although her heart was pounding madly. "What is it you wish?"

"Did this man accost you?" He glared at the man who cowered against the wall, his fright at the assault against him by the Chinese dragon clear.

Seizing upon the plausible explanation for Chen Mei's dagger at the man's throat, Amelia nodded. "Yes, I was returning to our seats when he popped up demanding money. As though I would carry a handsome sum upon me."

Lord Dancy looked suspicious. "Another abduction attempt, Amelia?" Then he caught sight of the gun tucked in the fellow's belt. With one motion, Dancy pulled it out to inspect it. "This has been fired recently. Who is going to tell what has been going on here?"

Chen Mei looked at Amelia, unconsciously relaxing her dagger a trifle. At this the man wrenched himself free to dash furiously down the stairs.

"You fool!" Chen Mei spat at Lord Dancy to Amelia's embarrassment, although she quite agreed.

"What . . ." Lord Dancy looked from one angry woman to the other. "I think I deserve an explanation."

"You fool, milor'," Chen Mei repeated less angrily than before. "That man try kill you. Tian Li save your honorable life. He mean to shoot you." She had waved her dagger around in the air, finally pointing it at Lord Dancy when she concluded her remarks.

"Good God," Geoffrey whispered, things rapidly falling into place. He had been so absorbed in what Lady Catherine had been telling him that he had paid not the least attention to that fellow who had crowded against him.

"Now he is free again, he may try once more. Why does that Portuguese man wish you dead, sir?" Amelia asked with commendable composure, considering what she had gone through the past few minutes. "He is the man we saw at the Lisbon docks. I believe you saw him once more in Portsmouth, am I not correct? And I doubt that is the only other time he has drawn near you. I repeat, why?"

"I cannot tell you that," Geoffrey said in reply to a reasonable question, given the amount of information she had either seen or deduced. When she drew herself up to her full five feet and six inches, glaring at him in offence, he hastened to add, "You see, I truly do not know why. Unless . . ." He paused to think for a few moments.

"Unless what?" Amelia demanded.

"Unless he has been sent to assassinate me for some peculiar reason," he said softly.

"You were a spy in Portugal. In France as well, perhaps? Also in Spain?" Amelia crossed her arms before her, tapping her foot in growing indignation, he'd wager. The silver riband on her gown glimmered in the dim light of the hall, and her eyes sparkled with outrage. Her cheeks were delightfully flushed, and that soft rose mouth was now firmed into a line.

"I believe we could have used you with us, Amelia," Geoffrey murmured at her clever conclusion. "Your guess is close enough to bring you problems, however."

He felt her attraction all the while he fought it. She was not for him, no sir. He wanted a demure little thing who wouldn't dream of doing what Amelia did.

"Chen Mei was right. You *are* a fool. You ought to have some sort of guard. There is a distinct limit to what I can do for you, my lord."

Affronted that a slip of a girl who looked more like a fairy princess than an avenging angel should think to constitute herself a guard for him, Geoffrey firmly clasped her arm with his gloved hand. "I believe you had best return to your aunt. The theatrics of this place has affected you far too much."

He marched her along, Chen Mei trailing unhappily after them. He paused in the open doorway leading to the Blandford box.

"Perhaps it would look better were we to enter with pleasant smiles on our faces, and not as though *we* had been at daggers drawn?"

"If you wish," Amelia said, not wanting to make him more angry with her than he already was.

Below them on the stage and in the arena the so-called Persian Festival was in progress. Not one person in the box turned to see who had entered. All the pomp and ceremony believed to exist in that part of the world together with exotic costumes and dances whirled about in a frenzy of color and pageantry.

When the players had retreated, Mary sat spellbound, unwilling to move.

"Come, sis, we had best go," Peter urged with success.

Mary rose, smiling broadly at Amelia.

Peter noted Lord Dancy had joined them at long last and gave his friend a disgusted look. "I thought you were to meet us here earlier."

"Something came up," Geoffrey murmured while wondering how he would see to it that Amelia and her Chinese dragon got home and stayed there. "Why do we not adjourn to Claridge's for a light repast? From there I shall see you ladies"— nodding to Mrs. Spencer and Amelia—"safely home."

Since Mary gasped with delight at this offering, it was quickly concluded that they would meet at Claridge's, which was just along Brook Street from where Mrs. Spencer lived.

Lord Dancy elected to join them in the Blandford carriage, sitting close to Amelia. Chen Mei perched with the Blandford groom, who appeared to relish her company no more than Hemit.

Amelia was not overly pleased at this particular development. His lordship could have taken his own carriage, or he and Peter might have ridden up with the coachman.

Fortunately it was not a long trip. They assembled in the hotel, then enjoyed an elegant repast that left Mary with stars in her eyes and Amelia wishing that she did not seem to incur Lord Dancy's anger every occasion she chanced to save his life. Alas, he simply did not seem to understand that it was what she must do, like it or not.

It was becoming increasingly clear that Lord Dancy didn't like it at all. Nor her, either.

Later she climbed the stairs to her room with a lamentable droop to her pretty shoulders, dangling her blue and silver reticule from limp fingers. At her door she looked at Chen Mei.

"We shall find that blacksmith tomorrow. I wish to make certain that Lord Dancy will be all right." She gave a tremulous sigh. "Being a chattel isn't what I had hoped it would be."

Chapter Eight

"I say, old chap, you were rather hard on Amelia last evening," Peter said. "She looked at you as though you were going to eat her."

"I could," Geoffrey muttered into his coffee cup. "That blessed girl is behind me everywhere I turn. I was having a very nice chat with Lady Catherine Beaton last evening when Amelia and Chen Mei catapulted into the box area, nearly knocking me over in the process, then nattering on about the carpet tripping her."

"You ought to be honored that she cares about your somewhat worthless head, my good friend," Peter retorted, looking not at all pleased with his companion.

"I would be more pleased if she adored me from a distance." Geoffrey took another sip of coffee, grimacing at the bitter taste. He set the cup on its saucer, then contemplated his unhappy friend.

"She does adore you, I suspect," Peter admitted. "More's the pity. You know, if you do not take care, she will finally have quite enough of you. I hope she does," he declared, "and you will find you have lost something very precious."

With this succinct pronouncement, Peter rose from his chair and stomped from the room.

Geoffrey heard the front door slam shut and picked up his cup, taking another swallow of hot coffee in hopes the near-scalding liquid would make him feel less a cad.

That girl had rescued him again. What was he going to do about her? No other man had a delicate-looking blonde trailing after him and pulling him out of one disaster after another. It was downright humiliating. He couldn't reveal to Peter all the events of last night before he had joined the happy group at Astley's. Peter would think him daft.

Geoffrey thought *himself* daft, and he knew all the circumstances. Better that Peter merely think Geoff was a cad and let it go at that. If Peter knew that the Portuguese fellow had been so hotly on his trail and nearly succeeded in shooting him, Geoffrey would find Bow Street in his pocket before he could sneeze.

If only she wasn't so lovely. That's what made it so deucedly tough to put her where she belonged. Last night when he had been with Amelia in the hall at Astley's and she had stared up at him with those celestial blue eyes so full of trust, he had almost forgotten all else that was going on—even the elegant Lady Catherine, not to mention the fellow who had intended to do him in.

What was it that the Chinese dragon lady called Amelia—Tian Li? Which he understood meant Celestial Delight—appropriate. Only she was not quite what Geoffrey would call a delight at this point.

She looked ethereal, those wide blue eyes gazing at him with such lack of guile and total faith. And he supposed her frank and open manner with him might be called delightful by some.

But ... dash it all, a man didn't want some female—even if she was a lovely creature—to be saving his life every time he turned around.

Now Peter hinted that Amelia worried that the blasted race might be rigged in some way. Well, Geoff supposed that it might; it was not beyond possibility.

He rose from his chair and wandered along down the hall until he could stare out of his rear window at the little splash of green that constituted his garden. Meditating on his problem might bring a solution that would keep Amelia's nose far away from it all.

Taunton had the very devil's own luck. Geoffrey had yet to figure out precisely how he had been tricked into the race, for it had not been of his choice. When one is challenged, one accepts or looks a fool. Geoffrey had had quite enough of feeling like a fool without this added to his plate.

He would take care to be on his guard. Hemit had gone over his curricle inch by inch and pronounced the carriage safe. Curricle races were common enough. It seemed that

every week a couple of idiots were tearing along the high-
way to somewhere, like a pair of demented geese.

Since Geoffrey had the pick of routes, he had selected
one that seemed sound enough, given the condition of most
roads at this time of year. It was a road that had traffic, yet
not likely to be overwhelmed with drays and wagons from
the farms as the major turnpikes might be. He had thought
they could travel north out the Tottenham Court Road past
Primrose Hill and Chalk Farm as far as Spaniard's Inn.
Even though the road went along Hampstead Heath, the
highwaymen didn't bother that area during the daylight
hours. And anyway, it had been some time since one had
last attacked a coach, much less curricles in a race.

It wouldn't be a long race, for Geoffrey had no desire to
injure his grays. Taunton drove a pair of roans that, while
they didn't match in color—one a blue, the other a straw-
berry—did well enough in hand.

But the entire business bothered him. As if he didn't
have sufficient to plague him—Amelia and that chap from
Lisbon who seemed to think he had to put a period to Geoffrey's existence. Was ever a man so ill-fated.

Having spent a restless night, Amelia was pleased to be
called to the salon to receive visitors. She was in no mood
to sit contemplating her own foolishness, or what other
people considered her silliness. She had kept the details of
last night secret, even withholding them from her aunt. Her
behavior had not been easy to explain, and so she found
herself held at a distance this morning.

She floated down the stairs until she arrived at the door
to the salon. Once there she was delighted to discover that
Mary Blandford, accompanied by her mother and brother,
had arrived for tea and a comfortable coze. At least they
didn't consider her beyond the pale.

Mary rose when Amelia entered the room, a welcoming
smile on her sweet face. The afternoon sun brought out
pretty highlights in Mary's dark hair and revealed a happy
gleam in her gray eyes.

"Mary," Amelia said with real pleasure, for the attractive
girl was the first woman her own age Amelia had been at-

tracted to since arriving in London, "how lovely to see you."

"And after such a long parting, too," Peter grumbled good-naturedly.

"Do not mind him. He has been in a grumpy mood since this morning." Mary drew Amelia with her to a cream striped sofa at the far end of the salon.

Amelia glanced at Peter to find him studying her with disconcerting thoroughness.

"What a pity," she said lightly. Could it be that Aunt Ermintrude was right? Could Peter Blandford entertain a tendre for her? It seemed unlikely, but then Amelia tended to concentrate on Lord Dancy, which did make her somewhat blind to others.

"Well, it is when there are so many things I long to do while in London," Mary replied, then sighed at her brother.

"I suppose you intend to visit the mantuamaker?"

"Did that this morning." Mary twinkled a gamin smile at Amelia from beneath a stylish cottage bonnet.

"And you wish to go driving along Rotten Row in that awful crush of smart carriages and horses?"

"Peter has promised faithfully that he will take me in his curricle tomorrow." Mary turned a hopeful look at her older brother.

Amelia smiled at Peter, amused at his resigned look. "Silly boy, your sister will become the toast of the town. Her dark curls are quite in fashion at the moment, and her liveliness of manner is sure to inspire devotion in some gentleman's heart."

He looked cheered at that promise, then grew wary at the speculative look Amelia sent him.

"Have you seen Lord Dancy today?" she inquired in a nonchalant manner.

"This morning."

"I take it that you two disagreed about something?"

"You might say that." He had a closed expression that warranted silence on the subject.

Amelia could see that she would get absolutely nowhere with Peter, so she turned her attention back to Mary. "What else do you wish to do while in town, other than have your presentation and come-out?"

"Did your aunt mention to you that we might share a ball? Mama spoke about the terrible cost of parties in London, and when Mrs. Spencer agreed, they talked about puffing us off together." Mary bestowed a hesitant, somewhat shy look at Amelia.

Having dreaded putting her aunt to the bother of a London ball or anything resembling a come-out party, Amelia immediately saw the benefit of joining forces, as it were.

"My aunt has been involved in a domestic crisis this morning. The cook discovered that the second footman has been walking out with the upstairs maid and she is now in the family way," Amelia said in a near whisper, for young ladies were not supposed to know about such things.

"How dreadful," Mary replied, wide-eyed at such goings-on, although they were common enough.

"He is going to marry the girl, and they are to go to my uncle in the country. Uncle does not know it yet, but Aunt believes he will accept them. She is more tender-hearted than most of the *ton*."

Dismissing the domestic predicament as something beyond her, Mary continued, "So we shall plan on a modest ball? Before too long?"

"Agreed," Amelia replied. Glancing to where her aunt sat with Lady Blandford, heads together and smiles of satisfaction evident, she added, "I believe they have come to the same conclusion."

Peter rose and restlessly walked to the window to stare out.

With a look at Mary, Amelia rose to cross to his side. "Something is bothering you today, for you are not your usual cheerful self. May I help?"

"Ain't that just like you," he said with admiration. "Always wishing to be of help to a fellow. Pity some don't appreciate it."

"What brought this on?" she said, not knowing whether she ought to laugh.

"Dancy. Fellow won't listen to reason. Still going to do the race. Of course, I understand—a chap doesn't like to back off, you know. But dash it all, he will do the damndest things."

"Mind your tongue, Peter," Amelia scolded absently.

"One of these days it will be someone you truly wish to impress, not your sister."

Seeing her affront, he muttered, "Sorry. I tend to forget around you. I know you ain't my sister, but you seem like one."

Amelia smiled, thinking that any hopes Aunt Ermintrude nurtured were far and away off the mark.

"Well, we intend to plan for a lovely ball, and I believe we shall hire Almack's for the occasion. It's nice that such a place is usable for those of us in need. Aunt Ermintrude does not have a ballroom, and I gather you don't either?"

"True. M'father thought it a lot of nonsense. But won't Almack's be . . ." He hesitated to finish the sentence, for it was most impertinent of him to inquire about finances.

"My dear Papa wrote me that he especially desires me to have a lovely ball, and I think that place will do quite well. I found out that when not in use for the Wednesday evening subscription balls, it is available for hire. And it will have such smashing cachet."

"You have evidently thought it out quite well. I daresay Mary is a clever puss to have you for a friend."

"Is that Lord Dancy approaching?" Amelia inquired softly, her eye caught by a carriage coming up the street. She looked again, more closely, and was quite certain it was his curricle.

"Dashed if it ain't. Wonder what brings him here?"

Geoffrey drove just fast enough so he did not hold up traffic, truly a snail's pace. Why he found himself approaching the Spencer home, he did *not* know. The chit irritated him. She drove him utterly mad, one way or the other. And yet, here he was, meekly trotting up to her door as though he had no will in the matter. Maybe that silver amulet he wore around his neck had peculiar powers?

The trouble was that while she nearly drove him round the bend, she also beguiled him with her honest and direct manner. Loyalty such as she revealed was rare today, not to mention her devotion. He didn't know what he was going to do about Amelia, but one thing for sure, he couldn't keep away from her. However he was not going to allow her to stop his race.

When his groom rapped at the front door, Geoffrey discovered that he was welcome. After last night's business, he wasn't sure, but he marched up the stairs after Grimm. When he entered the salon, he found the Blandfords sans his lordship, Mrs. Spencer, and Amelia. He held his hat and gloves in one hand, bowing to greet the ladies.

He avoided speaking to Amelia until the very last. What did he expect to see? Certainly not that expression of amusement on her face when she met his eyes.

"And how are you today, sir?" she said in that soft, almost husky note he enjoyed hearing.

"As well as a chap can be who expects to eat crow. I trust you have one suitably boiled with a good sauce?" He spoke softly for her ears only and, without realizing it, held her hand far longer than polite.

"Oh, stuff and nonsense," she replied irrepressibly with a charming twinkle in her fine blue eyes. "What a lowering reflection to think that you have dreaded to come this afternoon because of a mere altercation last evening. I trust you have not seen that man since then?" she inquired in a guarded manner.

"You save my life, almost nab the fellow, then pass it off lightly? Doing it much too brown, my dear."

"Well, and so I do, I suppose. What a piece of work about nothing. Well," she amended at the tightening of his hand, "almost nothing." She glanced pointedly at her hand, then let it fall to her side when he belatedly released it.

"Well, I behaved like a veriest shatter-brain. I do apologize, my dear." Geoffrey searched her face for some sign she accepted his tardy excuse for shabby behavior.

She laughed lightly. "I imagine Lady Catherine considered me a very silly girl, nattering on like a magpie like that."

"My senses were quite confused. I scarcely knew what to think when you cannoned into me like that, then Chen Mei dashed off down the hall as if chasing a dragon."

"I only hope that wretch comes by his just desserts."

"He will, he will. One of these days." Geoffrey fingered his quizzing glass absently. "By the bye, I have not mentioned anything to Peter about that business with the gun and all. Dratted fellow would have Bow Street hovering over me as though I were a damned tulip."

"Mind your tongue, Lord Dancy," she admonished. With that, she turned aside to draw Mary into what had become a rather longer conversation than was seemly, given the circumstances.

"Hullo, Geoffrey," Mary said with the ease of one who has known another since childhood.

"I hardly recognized you with that dash of town bronze," he rejoined, grinning at her in a way that made Amelia swallow rather hard. Wretched man.

"Amelia and I are to have a ball together," Mary said. "Will you come? I shall be crushed if you do not, for you are the very kindest man I know."

"Hush," he reproved. "Never let others hear you say that. I'm supposed to have a great deal of consequence, you know."

"How excessively droll," Amelia murmured, but loud enough for him to overhear.

"I say," Peter inserted, "I think it's dashed clever that the girls will have Almack's for their ball. No fuss at all. Should be simple."

The two girls exchanged looks, then smiled.

"I suspect it will not be quite that simple. If I know aunt, she will find a great deal to do," Amelia said.

The gentlemen excused themselves at that point, Peter assuring his doting mama that he would see her later.

Amelia went to the top of the stairs when they ran down to the front door. She listened to their lighthearted comments while wondering where they were actually going—to discuss the route for the race? She couldn't bear to consider the dangers Lord Dancy would be exposed to on an open road. She wasn't unmindful. Anything might happen.

The days passed in a rush of preparation. Once Lady Blandford and Mrs. Spencer ascertained that Almack's was available for their ball, they plunged into the undertaking with great relish. Gunter's was secured to cater the party, and Mrs. Spencer discovered a clever little shop that did decorating for just such an affair.

Amelia and Mary allowed as how the older ladies knew

precisely what they were doing and had little to say on the matter—except that Amelia insisted the punch would be a pretty pink and delicious. She agreed that she and Mary ought to have similar gowns, but in different colors.

With so little to do, Amelia found plenty of time to worry about Lord Dancy and his race. On the morning she suspected it was to take place, she persuaded Mary and Chen Mei to go with her. Peter had let slip just where the route was to be when quizzed by his sister.

They rode in the Blandford landau in tense silence, exchanging looks from time to time. Mary wore an apprehensive expression that revealed only too clearly she had more than second thoughts about the advisability of this outing.

"We must go, for I cannot like the nature of this race," Amelia said at last. "Whenever I have queried someone about Lord Taunton, I have heard that he is a good-for-nothing Jack Straw, a coxcomb. How can you trust a man like that to be honest in a race? I ask you!"

"Geoffrey will not thank us for interfering," Mary cautioned. "Gentlemen are rather fussy about things like races and wagers and the like."

"Rubbish," Amelia exclaimed, ignoring the frown from Chen Mei at such language from a young lady. "Chances are there will be the devil to pay, but I must own that I don't relish a dressing-down from him. I must see that he is safe. You see, I owe him my life." Amelia prudently did not mention the startling fact that she considered herself Geoffrey's chattel.

"Missee mind tongue," Chen Mei scolded, sounding something like Amelia.

The carriage approached the Tottenham Court Road, and both girls fell silent again. Across from them Chen Mei appeared lost in thought as well, although Amelia noticed that Chen Mei was fingering her dagger. Most fortunately Mary did not recognize its pretty sheath and was spared the knowledge of what Chen Mei was prepared to do if necessary.

In the open landau Amelia found it a simple matter to look over the selected course for the race. The road was a busy one, and they soon found it a far different world from Mayfair. Poverty existed in abundance from the look of the buildings and people. Few private carriages traversed the street, rather drays, wagons, and hackneys. They passed by the Tottenham Street theater, giving it a curious glance for it was not one frequented by the *ton*.

The turnpike gate stood at the top of the road, and the coachman paid the fee from the money Amelia had handed to him. Then they were headed along toward Primrose Hill and the wildest part around London, Hampstead Heath.

It was a pretty prospect, and if Amelia had not been so upset about the stupid race, she would have quite enjoyed the view. She recalled a verse she had read lately. "A steeple issuing from a leafy rise, with farmy fields in front and sloping green." There had been more, but she was not that clever at memorizing. She had also read that a number of poets preferred to live in this area and decided that if they thought it a lovely place, it could scarcely be dreadful.

Primrose Hill—the place she'd heard was so popular with duelists—turned out to be a charming rise of some two hundred feet to the left of the road not far past the sign to Chalk Farm.

Across the field she could see laundry spread out to dry on the broom and the gorse bushes. With a gentle sun it was sure to dry quickly and have a fine fresh scent for the nobility and gentry who sent their clothes to be washed in the clean Hampstead water. Even Mrs. Spencer sent her linen to a woman out here.

At the village of Hampstead she looked about with a curious gaze, then spotted Hemit on the far side of the road in front of a blacksmith shop. With a questioning glance at Mary, Amelia requested the coachman to stop. Once down from the carriage, she approached the groom without the faintest notion of what she intended to say.

"G'day, miss," he said with a bob of his head.

"Is everything as should be?"

"Aye, nobut there might be trouble."

"You mean *you* believe me?"

"Lord Taunton be known as one what allus wins. I'm thinkin' he may not be too careful as to *how* he wins." His rather speaking look concurred with the way Amelia felt.

"The course is all right?"

"Aye. What can he do in such a public place?"

Still uneasy, Amelia left Hemit to return to the landau.
Mary insisted they return home before someone they knew
saw them off in such a precarious place without a gentleman to protect them.

Amelia immediately agreed with her friend, although pri-
vately she would rather have Chen Mei than most of the
dandies she had seen in London.

"What did you learn?" Mary said, most curious about her
unconventional friend. The coachman set a goodly pace
back into the city, evidently in agreement with his mistress
as to the atmosphere.

"Nothing more than I already suspected. Since your
brother will not tell us the time, we can only return to my
aunt's house and wait."

At the other end of Tottenham Court Road, unseen by
Amelia and Mary, Geoffrey and Peter prepared to give the
curricle its final inspection prior to the race.

"Hemit is in Hampstead, checking with a blacksmith he
knows there to see if anyone has been nosing about."

The two men exchanged looks, then motioned to the
blacksmith Peter had hired to look over the carriage as
well. Dancy might ignore Amelia's suspicions, but Peter
felt just as strongly as she did by now.

There was silence for some time as the burly man went
over the curricle, using his hands to feel and test. Finally,
when Geoffrey was about to dismiss the fellow, the blacksmith straightened and gave Geoffrey a peculiar look.

"You intend to drive this today?"

"I drove it here from the mews behind my home. Why?"
He drew closer to where the leather-aproned man stood.

"See that?" He pointed to the bolt that held the pole in
place on the carriage. "It's been loosened. A few more
miles and you would have parted ways."

The thought of what might have happened to his fine
team, not to mention his head, brought his eyes to meet the
blacksmith's in shared consternation.

"Saw that happen once," the blacksmith said. "Curricle
tipped over, fellow had his hat smashed and his coat cut to
ribbons by the horses, but he survived all right. Pretty

shaken, though," the blacksmith observed in what must have been an understatement.

Geoffrey turned to Peter and said one word. "When?"

"Dashed if I know. With Hemit out in Hampstead, all that was needed was for us to turn our backs a trifle."

"Aye," the blacksmith agreed. He listened to Geoffrey's instructions, then accepted a coin from his lordship before returning to his shop.

"This gives us the excuse we want. It will be interesting to see what Taunton makes of this. Once we have it out in the open, we can get that blacksmith to do the repairs. I'll not drive it another yard until then, nor do I ever intend to race against Taunton."

At that moment the man they sought drove up with a flourish, looking for all the world as though he fully expected to make the dash to Spaniard's Inn.

"Taunton," Geoffrey hailed. "Bit of a dilemma, my friend."

At his side Peter snorted in disgust.

Taunton oozed surprise and astonishment when Geoffrey explained what had occurred to his curricle.

"Surely you don't intend to call the race off!" he exclaimed in affront.

"The blacksmith insists that the bolt could not possibly have worked its way out. Someone had to do that bit of work. Since the carriage can't be driven, I fear the race is off."

Taunton glared at Geoffrey, but there was little he could say with so many others around listening to every word.

"Sorry, old chap. My days are rather full at the moment. Perhaps later?" Geoffrey gave Taunton a grim smile, then turned away to greet the blacksmith again. The horses slowly walked the curricle to the shop where the blacksmith unhitched it, then removed it from the street. Geoffrey found stabling for the horses not far away next to the skittle-ground.

Once in a hackney the two men breathed a sigh of relief. "I can't understand how I got into that mess in the first place," Geoffrey grumbled.

"Neither can I. You're usually the cool one, Dancy. Not like you to be tricked. Although from what I've heard,

Taunton makes a practice of manipulating fellows into his schemes. I doubt you had a thing to say about the matter."

"Amelia will say 'I told you so,'" Geoffrey added with a grimace.

"Aye," Peter agreed with a laugh, "that she will."

Chapter Nine

"Well, I would never do anything so shabby," Amelia declared in what appeared to be a miff when the two gentleman had presented themselves in the drawing room of the Spencer home.

Amelia and Mary had wisely returned to the house to await the outcome of the wager, wondering and hoping that all would be well.

What with all that was going on in London at the moment, their concerns had seemed rather trifling. The Grand Duchess of Oldenburgh was to arrive from Russia on March the thirty-first, and speculation was running wild as to her appearance and behavior. Mrs. Spencer was of the opinion that the haughty duchess would snub the Prince Regent. Amelia could scarcely credit such manners, or lack of them. But Russians were deemed rather wild people, so anything was possible.

When Peter had informed Amelia that the rig had been tampered with, she had merely nodded in a knowing manner, then remained silent about her dire prediction.

"I say," Peter said with admiration, "I am surprised. Thought you would come all over righteous."

" ' I told you so' is not a very kind thing to say, even if it is well deserved," Amelia replied prudently with a side glance at Lord Dancy.

"As long as you do not take to looking over my shoulder, I do not mind what you say," Dancy observed in the most wry of tones. He had crossed to glance out of the window, presumably to see if it threatened to rain.

"Why?" Amelia said. "Would I be likely to see something I ought not?" She looked at Peter and noted his amused expression. "Most probably I would discover how you spend your evenings in wild dissipation. Gambling, I daresay. High stakes, I suppose? Shame on you, both of you, wasting your time and money in such foolishness. Have you never learned that in the long run the gamester loses?" Amelia offered her scold in a gentle, teasing voice, but no one doubted that she meant every word of it.

From her seat on the drawing-room ottoman Chen Mei observed, "Superior man satisfied, composed; the mean man always full of distress."

"Then I am neither superior nor mean, for I feel no distress nor do I reek satisfaction and composure." Lord Dancy sent the Chinese woman a narrow look. "However, I am full of gratitude that I have so genteel a shadow to follow me about, *rescuing* me from my follies. I vow it is what every gentleman wishes he possessed, a female deliverer." The implication of this caustic remark could scarcely be missed.

"Take note if someone praises you with no occasion, he sure to have reason fo' doing so," Chen Mei added with a wicked gleam in her eyes. Her mastery of the "r" sound had progressed, although at times she regressed.

"I believe Lord Dancy wishes that I would return to Macao, Chen Mei. He does not appear to appreciate his deliverance from Clarissa Filbert nor that nasty man at Astley's Amphitheater nor what could have been a disastrous curricle race." Amelia admirably concealed the hurt she felt at what she perceived was a lack of appreciation from Lord Dancy. Or did he hold his life in so little esteem?

Mary glanced at each face in turn, then commented, "I do wish you would all stop this quibbling. I do not like it in the least."

"Perhaps I had best speak plainly then. Miss Longworth, while I appreciate your feeling of obligation to me, it is not necessary for you to perform repeated acts of rescue in order to redeem yourself," Lord Dancy said abruptly. "Besides, three good turns on your part make us even. I hereby absolve you of any indebtedness you may think you owe me."

"In other words, you do not wish to see my face popping up at every inconvenient moment?" Amelia managed a smile, but just barely.

He had the grace to look uncomfortable, but did not refute nor deny her charge.

"What an odious man you are," she said in a considering way. "I shall try to respect your wishes, sir."

He looked as though he wondered what sort of reprieve that might bring. Amelia had no intention of enlightening him.

Mrs. Spencer entered the room, all aflutter and waving about one of the morning papers that contained an account of a balloon ascension to come about in two days.

"I believe you girls would enjoy seeing this. I shall take you myself as it has been an age since I last observed one of these ascensions. They are most colorful and so thrilling to see. When the balloon rises so majestically in the air, your heart nearly stops." She sparkled with delight in offering such a treat to Amelia and Mary. "I believe this is going to be an unusually festive spring what with the foreigners visiting and all."

"What a famous suggestion," Amelia said, happy to have the matter of her watch on Lord Dancy dropped. "Mary, you must promise to join us." Then Amelia looked at the gentlemen and said, "I shan't request the pleasure of your company for I suspect there are a great many places you'd rather be than at Green Park on a sunny morning to watch a balloon go up in the air."

"You had read the article earlier?" Lord Dancy said.

"Indeed. I'd hoped to persuade my aunt to take us, and she has anticipated my desire wonderfully." Amelia gave her aunt a fond smile, then crossed to the window where Lord Dancy had gazed out not long before. She noted what he must have seen, that the man from Astley's loitered about across the way, keeping an eye on this house. At least, it appeared to be that same man. It was hard to tell.

Dancy peered over her shoulder, seeming to follow the direction of her gaze.

"I would wager that is a familiar face to you, were you to see it closely," Amelia murmured.

"I thought you agreed to suspend all interest in my doings, Miss Longworth," he replied in an equally soft voice.

"Quite so," she replied, but prudently did not tell him whether she intended to keep to her agreement.

Mary and Peter were quietly arguing about whether he ought to go along or not. Mrs. Spencer persuaded them both that it might be rather nice to have an escort, particularly if Peter could find a suitable escort for Mary, thus escorting Amelia himself. She also reminded Peter that the day of the ball drew closer, and a young lady could not have too many promising gentlemen about her.

Amelia turned from the sight of the three settling just who was to be invited on the outing.

"She ought to broadcast the amount of my dowry. So far she has refused to do so, saying it is better for me to be accepted on my own merits," Amelia said in a mocking voice.

"Cynicism doesn't become one so young. And you must admit she has a point. Most women in the *ton* would be in alt if their *protégés* had such a prodigious dowry."

"What you do not want done to yourself, do not do to others," Amelia quietly observed. "I would be foolish beyond permission to argue with my aunt's plans. She has my best interest at heart, I feel sure. It is that I feel like a commodity to be auctioned off to the highest bidder, and once my value becomes widely known, I fear I may not be best pleased with the offer."

"Yet you will obey your aunt, even though you might have different feelings within."

"You are perceptive about me, sir. Would that you developed the same ability regarding your enemies." Amelia's gaze returned to the man who lingered in the street.

"You think I have so many? What a lowering reflection." Now it was his voice that held deep amusement.

"I only hope you will not regret . . . " Amelia did not complete her thought, for she hated to give voice to the words that lurked on her tongue.

Shortly after that conversation the gentlemen left the house, both in a peculiar mood. Peter wondered aloud where he was to find someone to escort his young sister and whether his old friend Denzil Warwick was around and available. Although he himself was clearly delighted to accompany Miss Longworth. He said this with a sidelong glance at Dancy.

Geoffrey felt mixed emotions. While he might be freed of Miss Longworth's attentions, he confessed he had rather enjoyed her concern in a way. He suspected that any number of good ladies looked after their particular gentlemen with secret anxiety, yet took care not to be discovered doing so. Amelia didn't merely worry, she became entangled in his life. He admitted, although only to himself, that he would miss the intriguing Miss Longworth from his life.

The morning of the balloon ascension dawned reasonably clear, with only a few clouds to mar the serene blue of the sky. Peter gallantly told Amelia that the sky reflected the color of her eyes.

Amelia smiled at the pretty encomium, thinking that her sky blue pelisse of kerseymere trimmed in deep blue velvet had more to do with her looks than the sky. She reached up to pat her new bonnet of the same blue velvet interlaced with levantine, with blond lace peeping from beneath the brim. Deep blue-dyed ostrich plumes curled over the crown of the bonnet in a rather fetching manner she thought. Peter was a dear, but her interest quickly turned to the scene about them instead of her escort.

The balloonist and his assistants worked diligently to inflate the massive balloon while Mary and Amelia looked on with more than a little curiosity.

"Do you know," Amelia confided, "I would adore going up in a balloon."

"I should hope not," the more cautious Mary replied. "But I suppose that after traveling half way around the world through storms and the like, a balloon does not appear so dangerous to you."

"Well, any number of women have ascended," Amelia said having read a bit on the topic. "Elizabeth Thible, Jeanne Labrosse, and a great many others."

"I should think they were more like circus performers, ascending for profit, not merely because they liked it. I doubt if any *lady* should attempt it," Mary said sagely.

Denzil Warwick, the chap Peter had persuaded to escort his sister, looked at Mary with approval at her modest and retiring behavior.

"Indeed," he agreed with a near-pompous attitude. "Although I think it is admirable that a young lady displays an interest in the new and curious things to come our way."

Mary beamed a pleased smile at him. They began conversing in quiet voices about the strange and wondrous things to be viewed in London. The panoramas were declared most intriguing, and they decided it would be lovely to view one or two of them. Plans were made for a few days hence.

Amelia gave them an impatient look, then turned her gaze on the balloon once again. Murmuring something particularly vague to her aunt, she slipped from the carriage where she had been sitting with Mary, her aunt, Peter, and the proper Mr. Warwick to draw closer to the balloon.

By means of careful questioning and a remarkable ability to glide through the throng seemingly without any effort, Amelia gained her objective, . . . the balloon.

The balloonist was a pleasant-looking man of about thirty, Amelia guessed. When she approached him about riding along as a passenger, he gave her the most horrified look she recalled receiving in her life.

"No, miss. 'Tis impossible."

"I do not see why," Amelia argued. "You may leave something or someone else on the ground and simply take me instead." It seemed quite logical to her.

The man threw up his hands, then turned to walk away from her with a haste Amelia found irritating. Why shouldn't a lady be able to go up in a balloon just as well as a performer of sorts?

"I suspected I would find you here. Contemplating stowing away in the basket? I fancy there might be a few objections to that," came a familiar and most irritating voice from behind her—close behind her.

"Lord Dancy!" Amelia exclaimed with dismay.

"Indeed," Dancy replied, looking down his nose at Amelia with that infuriating smirk some no doubt called a smile. "Caught you out, did I?"

"You have no notion as to what was in my mind," she snapped back at the man she had been unsuccessfully trying to dismiss from her mind for two long days. How could society go into such a dither over the man. While he was handsome, wealthy, and possessed any number of other attributes, he was exasperating to the point Amelia longed to box him on the head and ship him to Macao on the slowest possible boat.

"Well, I daresay you are too much of a pudding heart to make such a passage, but I vow I would like to go," Amelia said wistfully.

"Pudding heart!" Geoffrey said in disgust. "Young woman, I'll have you know that I have engaged in all manner of deeds deemed dangerous by a goodly number of people. A balloon ride is a mere nothing." With this affronted comment he stepped to the side of the basket, surveying the interior with an assessment as to the safety of the craft. That he feared heights he unwisely failed to mention.

Amelia laughed, thinking he looked rather silly in that pose of the offended expert.

"Oh, sir," she trilled at the balloonist. "Since you will not consider me, perhaps you will permit his lordship to ride with you?" She quite ignored the sharp inhale behind her, suspecting Dancy was more of a pudding heart than he'd let on.

Since the balloonist had been devoutly hoping for some sort of aristocratic recognition, he swooped on Lord Dancy with an enthusiasm Amelia found extraordinary.

"Of course, my lord. We know that females of the gentry are too full of sensibilities to risk taking such dangers. Gentlemen dare anything." He beamed up at Geoffrey with a broad grin, then urged him into the basket, explaining all the while what was contained inside.

One of the assistants ran up to hurriedly consult with the balloonist who then turned to Lord Dancy.

"Well, my lord. We go aloft."

Amelia distinctly heard Lord Dancy mutter, "I do not like the sound of that," as he leaned his hands on the railing, glaring at Amelia so fiercely that she was suddenly glad he was there and not beside her again.

"I shall bring you a full report, Miss Longworth. I trust that the next yearning you have in my presence will be a good deal milder." Lord Dancy tipped his hat at her and the gentlemanly action brought a cheer from the crowd.

The last words were carried down to her from a distance, for the ropes had been released one by one and the supporting poles withdrawn. The purple and gold balloon rose majestically above the park and slowly drifted off into the distance.

"This is terrible," Amelia murmured to Hemit, who had sidled up to her as the balloon rose into the sky. "He ought not be up there. He hates it, I could see that. It is all my fault, for I goaded him into doing something he would never do otherwise. Oh, what a terrible girl I am. Hemit," she declared fervently, "we must do something."

"Yes, miss," He gazed at the slowly departing balloon. "But what?"

"Follow that balloon!" she cried dramatically, pointing at the road that ran in the same direction. She dashed to the Dancy curricle—now completely restored to proper repair—and would have taken the reins had Hemit not understood she might just do such a thing and scurried after her.

"Here we go, miss. Hang on." With a flick of the reins he directed the curricle away from the park.

Without a glance at her aunt's carriage where all occupants waved frantically at her, Amelia clung to the side of the carriage. At her side Hemit urged the horses to a full gallop along the street and out the road to the north.

Fortunately Amelia had her reticule and could toss the sum of money required to the keeper at the toll gate as the curricle raced through behind another that preceded them.

Craning her neck this way and that she managed to keep the balloon in sight. "I do believe we are gaining on it," she said to Hemit in encouragement.

The road was anything but smooth, and dust rose in the air behind them. With one hand clutching the side of the carriage and the other firmly attached to her bonnet that threatened to fly off at the least additional gust of wind, Amelia searched the sky.

"Trailing after that balloon is not the easiest of things, is it, Hemit? I believe we shall have to turn at the next road to the east. It appears that the wind is sending it that way."

"Yes, miss," Hemit muttered, his hands full with controlling two very prime bits of cattle.

They feathered the corner with the proper amount of dash, then charged along the country road with more fury than grace.

"Oh, he will kill me. I know he will," Amelia murmured

to herself, tugging on the ribands of her bonnet in hopes of tightening them.

Hemit threw her a wry grin, looking as though he suspected otherwise, but he said nothing.

After what seemed like an age, although it was a more reasonable time, it appeared the balloon drifted closer to the earth.

"Oh, it is coming down. Faster, Hemit. I only hope he isn't killed." Amelia blinked away the moisture that suddenly gathered in her eyes. "It is all my fault if he is injured. Oh, Hemit will he ever forgive me? I doubt he will," she replied to her question. "How can he? What a miserable wretch I am."

"I think you be too hard on yourself, miss," Hemit observed mildly as he skillfully guided the horses along the lane. Their course appeared to parallel the path of the balloon which looked to be heading toward a large plowed field.

Now that they were closer, Amelia could see Lord Dancy helping the balloonist with something. It appeared they stowed away gear, and a rope dropped over the side of the basket. Hemit muttered something that sounded like, "I believe the guv has need of a hand."

The carriage bumped across an access to the field, then came to a halt with a jolt. Amelia tumbled off the seat to land in a heap on the floor, her bonnet all askew, pelisse a tangled mess.

"Come on, miss, if you wants to help." The tired horses were not likely to budge an inch and were left standing where they halted.

Hemit tugged at her free hand, and without regard to her appearance Amelia struggled from the curricle, then ran along with Hemit to catch the rope.

The basket nearly touched the ground. Amelia could see Lord Dancy studying the lay of the land, yelling something to the balloonist who appeared to agree.

The basket hit the ground quite hard, bumping and dragging along while the balloonist pulled a cord to spill the air from the bag. Hemit caught the rope that had dangled over the side of the basket, Amelia joining him to pull on it in an assist to stop the forward movement.

The bag gave a sigh, collapsing on the ground as it continued to deflate, looking very much like a limp sail.

Lord Dancy leaned on the now-settled basket for a moment with both hands, then climbed from it, not appearing as shaken by the landing as Amelia suspected he ought to be.

The three men were quite occupied for a short time until the crew that had assisted with the balloon ascent rumbled up in a wagon. A group of men piled out and ran across the field to give the final assist.

Amelia retreated to the curricle, feeling definitely out of place here.

She was at the point of wondering just how she would manage to return to London when Lord Dancy approached. She wanted to shrink against the carriage, but her pride refused to encourage such craven behavior.

"Good day again, Miss Longworth."

He tipped his hat in greeting, but she detected the grim note in his voice and trembled in her half-boots. Even his hat had stayed in place, she thought balefully.

"I am pleased to see you are in one piece, my lord. Did you enjoy your flight?" Amelia had decided that she might as well be audacious. Otherwise, he might be even worse.

He said nothing. Rather he walked to her side to stare down at her face before taking one gloved finger to trace the skin below her eyes.

"Were you worried about me, Miss Longworth? I'm touched," he said quietly. Then he undid the mangled ribands of her bonnet, smoothed down her hair, and replaced the bonnet with judicious attention to its tilt.

Amelia gulped. This was far worse than anything she had anticipated. She suspected he longed to strangle her, a feeling reinforced when he tied the ribands rather tightly under her chin.

"I am sorry," she said with downcast eyes. "You must be wishing me to perdition by now."

"Oh, I wished you even farther than that, Amelia," he replied. "I rather thought it would be nice to see you on a boat back to Macao."

"I shall leave you immediately," she said totally dispirited and wondering just a little how she would manage to walk back to London. She turned away from him to walk along the curricle toward the country lane she had jounced upon not long before.

At least there were trees along the lane, and the weather was not so hot as in summer, she consoled herself.

"Ahem," he said, reaching out to take hold of her elbow. "You asked if I enjoyed the ride. Well, I did. Enormously. I owe you a great debt of gratitude, Amelia. I'd always longed to try one of those things, and never quite had the courage. You cinched that for me. Allow me to express my appreciation."

With that he tilted her face up to his, then kissed each eyelid smudged from her tears of concern with dust from the road. After that, while Amelia held her eyes tightly shut for she was certain this was a dream, he touched her lips ever so gently. Then he released her.

Amelia opened her eyes to give him a highly bemused look.

"And if you ever do anything like that again, I shall forget that I am a gentleman and beat you, my dear."

She stood uncertainly in her tracks, debating whether or not he was serious. She decided he was. His eyes told her.

"I will try to avoid you if possible, my lord," she croaked. Her voice broke when she tried to speak. With the most dejected heart in the world, Amelia turned away from the man she suspected she loved rather deeply and began her trudge to the road.

"Where do you think you are going now?" came a dangerously quiet voice from behind her.

Amelia stopped, but did not turn. It hurt to look at him standing there so disgustingly handsome with his hat still in place and gloves scarcely smudged. She was quite certain that she looked a veritable sight, all rumpled and dusty. One thing about air travel, it didn't leave you looking as though you'd been through a dust storm.

"You will ride back to town with me, unless of course you prefer to walk. I daresay some enterprising chap will be delighted to offer you a lift, although to where I couldn't say. Hemit will ride behind. You will sit next to me and not do one blessed thing all the way back to town."

She swirled around, her temper flaring. "You enjoyed the

flight in the balloon, so I fail to see why you are acting as though it was the end of the world. Men! Lords, in particular!" Her dainty fists balled up, then settled upon her hips as she glared back at him. Why had she been so broken-hearted? This man was enough to drive any sane woman to drink!

"That's more the thing," he pronounced cheerfully. "Now before your aunt has a permanent attack of the vapors, I suggest we depart." He scooped her into his arms and plopped her onto the seat of the curricle. He looked over his superb team as he walked around to the other side of the curricle, then joined her.

He waited a few moments until Hemit had climbed up behind them, then guided the team carefully over the rough ground until they reached the lane. Even there the surface was rough, and the curricle jounced along until Amelia thought her teeth would come loose.

"The horses are fine, no doubt to Hemit's splendid driving."

No thanks to you, was implied. Amelia considered ways and means of doing him serious harm. It was no use, for her brains seem scrambled. A bit more of this road and her eyes would no doubt cross permanently. Why had it not bothered her when they came? Hemit's driving skills? Or had she concentrated so on Lord Dancy that nothing else in the world mattered? Foolish girl, she admonished herself.

At last they made the main road into London. Thanks to Mr. MacAdam the road was reasonably smooth and the dust somewhat less. No water from the recent rains puddled in the road for MacAdam had decreed a crown to the road so it might drain well. Amelia decided she preferred the jouncing. At least then there was a reason not to speak.

The silence stretched on for an hour or so until they reached the toll gate where Amelia handed Lord Dancy a coin.

He glared at her, but took the coin and drove on most assuredly in a miff, she decided.

"I can pay my own tolls, thank you."

"No trouble," Amelia replied airily. "I happened to have the coin in my reticule. That's the advantage of heiresses, you know. They are far more apt to have some of the ready to hand."

She thought he was grinding his teeth, but wasn't sure. The contact of the cobblestones with the wheels of the carriage, plus the clip-clop of the horses, plus the myriad other noises of the city quite well covered what sound he might make.

"I will say one thing, my dear," Lord Dancy said in the mildest of tones that made her wonder if she was right about the grinding teeth business. "Being around you is never dull."

Slightly affronted, Amelia nevertheless took the remark philosophically. "I have three precious things that I hold fast and prize," she quoted from her store of Chen Mei's teachings. "The first is gentleness; the second is frugality; the third is humility, which keeps me from putting myself before others. Be gentle and you can be bold; be frugal, and you can be liberal; avoid putting yourself before others, and you can become a leader among men. Or woman as the case may be," she amended.

"I might have known the woman would influence you. Do you carry a dagger as well?"

"I wish I did," Amelia retorted darkly. She smoothed the skirt of her pelisse over her knees then leaned forward in anticipation when the carriage turned onto Brook Street.

When they drew up before her aunt's home, she turned to give him a considering look. "You are not really so bad off, you know. You had an interesting trip that you enjoyed very much, I suspect. Your carriage was not damaged in the least, thanks to Hemit's skill at driving. All in all, I believe you ought to count your blessings, the least of which is that the man who again leans against the post over there has not been able to take a shot at you yet. I trust you will be most careful, my lord."

With that parting gibe Amelia climbed down from the curricle and marched up the steps into her aunt's home, firmly shutting the door behind her.

Chapter Ten

Geoffrey stared after Amelia, his mind in a whirl. A glance revealed the man, who was obviously trying to melt into the stonework across the street.

"Hemit, go around to the rear of Mrs. Spencer's house. I may be some time, but I trust these nags will welcome the rest. They've had a hard day."

With that understatement Geoffrey handed over the reins, then marched up to the front door. A firm rap brought Grimm's face to view when the door opened.

Without so much as a by your leave, Geoffrey smoothly brushed past the butler to enter the front hall. At the bottom of the stairs Amelia paused, looking quite startled. One hand clung to the oak banister. Her pretty blue bonnet, the plume on it slightly crushed, dangled from the fingers of her other hand. Her glorious blond hair was tumbled into appealing ringlets. However her eyes blazed with a blue fire that made Geoffrey distinctly uncomfortable.

"You were right," he said promptly. "That fellow *is* lurking outside. I suspect he wants to put a period to my existence. Why, I still can't imagine." Geoffrey glanced at her, then crossed the hall, going into the small parlor at the front of the house. From here he could see where the fellow now lounged beneath a tree as though he hadn't a care in the world. Although he hadn't told Amelia, he'd consulted with Hardinge's office. They had no lead on the man, either.

"You obviously have not put your mind to work on the matter. There must be any number of reasons someone might wish you finished." She had followed him into the room, conspicuously leaving the door wide open. "Think again."

"He can bloody well find someone else to murder in any

event. I'm not about to please the chap." He studied the man, trying to figure out who it was that wished him booked. While almost everyone had someone who might dislike them, what brought about murder?

"Mind your tongue, Lord Dancy," she reprimanded quietly.

He whirled around to stare at her, suddenly recalling the moment he had kissed those pretty tear-smudged eyelids, touched her sweet mouth with his, and wondered if he were losing his senses. With an effort he managed to control the most peculiar urge to stride across the room and clasp her in his arms. To his regret he would very much like to kiss her again, and that would never do. Not in the least. If he succumbed to necessity and married, it would be to a demure, biddable creature—certainly not the young woman who had hoodwinked him into taking that balloon ride.

Never mind that he had found it delightful once he had conquered his fear of the height. No fellow wanted a harum-scarum woman as a bride, dashing around to pull his chestnuts out of the fire. He fancied the Chinese dragon would accompany her charge when Amelia married. He wished the fellow well who acquired the pair of them. He would have his hands full.

"Oh," Mrs. Spencer trilled from the doorway, "You are safely home. My love, I nearly had the vapors. You have been gone for hours! What a naughty girl to dash off like that." She waggled her finger at Amelia, but her face did not appear to wear a harsh expression to match.

"I apologize, dear Aunt," Amelia said contritely. "There was no time to explain, you see. I had most stupidly challenged Lord Dancy to that balloon ride. Poor man, I called him a pudding heart. He took that ride as a dare. And then I feared he might be killed, so Hemit and I chased after him to see what we could do."

"I doubt if you could have saved my hide were the balloon to have caught fire or become tangled in trees," Geoffrey inserted, for she made him sound bird-witted.

"But you must admit it was exceedingly brave of the girl," Mrs. Spencer said with a frown at him. "Come along, for you must tell us all about it. No doubt it will be a second hearing for Amelia, but we are all in suspense to learn the details." She paused at the bottom of the stairs to add, "What was it like?" She looked to Amelia as though she expected some sort of reply from her.

Amelia gave Geoffrey a rather poisonous look that he supposed he deserved. "I have yet to be regaled with his tale, as he chose to remain silent on the matter. I would also like to hear of the horrors endured by our brave aeronaut."

"That is what they now call them," Mrs. Spencer agreed with a nod. "It sounds so dashing." With a dramatic sigh she led the way up the stairs.

The others sat in the drawing room, expectantly awaiting them. Peter and Mr. Warwick leaned against the fireplace surround, a glass of sherry in hand. Mary sat on the sofa, her tea cup placed on the low table close by. All eyes were fixed on those who entered the room.

"The adventurers return," Mrs. Spencer cried in her fluting voice. "Lord Dancy is going to tell us about his experiences in the balloon." She crossed over to join Mary, who sat perched on the edge of the sofa like a child awaiting a treat.

"Yes, Lord Dancy," Amelia said, looking at him with a curiously unfathomable expression. "Do tell us all about your trip."

If the chit thought he was going to confess to those stolen kisses she was far and away out. "Actually, it was most interesting. They fill the balloon with the hot air that's produced when they burn straw, as you may have noticed. Once aloft, I helped feed the fire until the chap spotted a likely place to land. It seems they prefer an open field away from trees and such." Geoffrey bestowed a cautioning look on Amelia, but had no clue as to what went on in her mind.

"But," Mary gently queried, "what was it like? What did you see? I should have been terrified."

"The perspective was quite fascinating," Geoffrey said, recalling his trip. "Everything looked very tiny, the carriages and people seemed like mere specks on the ground. I could see off to the west where the Thames winds about like a snake through the city, then the green fields and on south toward the sea. To the north I could almost think I saw Windsor. The wind felt surprisingly gentle. I saw Holland House and the Bath Road off to the west."

Mrs. Spencer gasped at this revelation, for it seemed far too fantastic. It was evident that she doubted the validity of his claim.

"How about the landing, Dancy?" Peter said, raising his glass in a toast of sorts as he spoke.

"Once the fellow decided to land, we extinguished the fire. Then he kept watch on our landing site while I made certain the rope went down on the opposite side so those who followed might grab a purchase and assist us in the landing."

"And what did you do, Amelia?" Mrs. Spencer asked her niece with a stare that seemed rather intimidating even to Geoffrey.

Amelia looked at Lord Dancy, wishing she might push him out a convenient window or something equally dire. Oh, he positively enjoyed all this fuss over him, the odious man.

"Why, Hemit and I followed the course of the balloon as best we could. And it is a good thing we did so, for the assistants were ever so slow in arriving at the field. Their wagon was no match for Lord Dancy's curricle and splendid horses."

"Weren't you frightened?" Mary asked, her hands clenched in her lap, revealing her own apprehensions just thinking of such a mad dash.

"I fear that I was too engrossed in keeping the balloon in sight to be afraid for myself. I did feel a shade guilty for teasing Lord Dancy into taking the ride," she confessed, again with a sidelong glance at his elegant lordship.

"What could you do when you arrived at the field where they landed?" Mr. Warwick inquired with the narrowing of one eye in a highly speculative manner.

Amelia couldn't have met Lord Dancy's gaze to save her life at this point. She felt almost as though the words would be emblazoned on her forehead . . . *I allowed that fool man to kiss me, that's what I did.* Fortunately, Lord Dancy came to her rescue.

"She and Hemit ran across the field in our direction. The basket thumped along the ground, bounced a few times, then skidded toward the end of the field. At the last moment the basket toppled over on its side, and I was more than a little shaken when I crawled from it," he revealed with a look at Amelia. "Hemit grabbed hold of the rope, as did Miss Longworth. Once the balloon settled on the ground, Miss Longworth quite properly retired to the curricle, leaving Hemit to assist the . . . er, aeronaut, did you call him, Miss Longworth?" He met her gaze with no hint that he recalled that enticing kiss. Amelia wished she might know how he felt about it and her.

"Sounds smashing to me," Peter said with a wistful note in his voice. The others began to voice their opinions all at once.

"I don't know," Mr. Warwick said in a momentary lull. "I should think that if man were intended to fly, he'd be born with wings."

"Then why do we take ships rather than swimming when we wish to cross the Channel?" Amelia wondered aloud. "It seems to me that anything man can invent or develop to make our life easier or more interesting is certainly to the good."

The others fell into a casual debate on the topic while Lord Dancy walked to the window to survey the scene on the street below.

Amelia followed him, keeping a proper distance, yet able to speak without the others overhearing what she said.

"He is still loitering about." Amelia gave the fellow a disapproving look. "Someone ought to shoo him away, for he certainly does not improve the neighborhood."

"Does your aunt have a carriage house? Is there a way out of the back to a mews or something?"

Although Lord Dancy spoke in an undertone, Amelia could hear him surprisingly well. "Yes," she quickly replied.

"I shall simply avoid the fellow until a time when I am better armed to meet him."

"Would you shoot him? A dagger is so much quieter," Amelia offered prosaically.

"What a bloodthirsty one you are. It must come from growing up in the Orient. I feel a contest is much better when the odds are a bit more even, if you know what I mean."

Amelia nodded, wondering a little at the feeling of camaraderie that had sprung up between them. She felt shy with him, yet oddly comfortable if such a thing were possible. She could not dismiss that gentle kiss at the curricle in the middle of a plowed field, right out in the open where anyone might have seen them. However, she'd wager that everyone present had their eyes on the balloon. She and Lord Dancy had escaped censure by means of a better attraction being around.

"Good-bye, sir," she said at last, holding out her hand for a final contact with him. "Perhaps I shall see you round and about. Society being what it is, it is difficult to avoid people you know."

"I shall take great care to refrain from any actions that might require my rescue, Miss Longworth." He paused, then continued, "You are a surprising creature, gentle and mild-mannered, yet fierce as a tiger. You are not a comfortable sort of woman," he said.

Amelia noted the twinkle in his jade eyes and replied in a properly demure voice, "Chen Mei says gentleness brings victory to him who attacks, and safety to him who defends. Those whom Heaven would save, it fences around with gentleness."

"That obviously explains why you are still with us, Miss Longworth. You would no doubt have been strangled long ago had it not been for the wise guidance from your companion," he said in a sardonic voice.

"Are you contemplating something hazardous in the near future, Lord Dancy? Perhaps I ought to make you a loan of Chen Mei so you might also be protected."

"A bit of gaming will scarcely be deemed as dangerous."

"White's this evening? Peter said something about a match with Lord Taunton. Did you not have sufficient warning of his character before, my lord? I can scarce believe my ears."

"What I do with my time is hardly any concern of yours, the debt you feel you owe me notwithstanding. I absolved you of that long ago, if you recall. As to Taunton, it is of no consequence if we have a congenial game of piquet. The chap insists we must have the match to compensate for the cancellation of the race."

"Why is it that I doubt if any game of cards could be

congenial with Lord Taunton? You must give me leave to doubt you there, my lord."

Amelia withdrew from the window, returning to the others to join in the discussion of their plans for the next day. It seemed she was being caught up with the other three. And although she liked Peter Blandford very well, she knew it could never go beyond a mere liking.

"Well, I am off. I shall see you this evening, Peter?" Lord Dancy said in the most off-hand manner.

"You may depend on it, Dancy," Peter said bracingly.

Amelia walked to the landing to see Lord Dancy lightly run down the steps, then consult with Grimm for a moment before disappearing down the hall that led to the rear of the house.

She drifted back into the drawing room, absently agreeing with the others as to the plans for the morrow. Peter decided to take Mary home, and Mr. Warwick left with them.

"Well," Aunt declared, "all in all it has been quite a morning. I believe we ought to have our luncheon before we both collapse for one reason or another. You look rather pale, my love. Why do you not rest for a bit after we have eaten. We are to go to the Wyndham's ball this evening, and you will wish to be fresh."

Amelia blessed her aunt's thoughtfulness and joined her in a light meal. Before she entered the breakfast room where the two of them pleased to eat when alone, Amelia slipped into the front parlor to check the street. The man was gone.

When her aunt retired to take her rest, Amelia went to her room, not to rest, but to consult with Chen Mei.

"We are to go to a ball this evening. I doubt if Lord Dancy will be there, as *he* contemplates a game of cards with Lord Taunton, no less. Foolish man. He thinks that he can deal with a cheat."

"Tiger and deer do not stroll together," Chen Mei observed from her hassock.

Amelia gave her a nod of agreement, then restlessly wandered about the room.

"What you do?"

"Oh, go to the ball, I suppose. Ladies do not frequent gambling establishments, except the ones specifically set up for them. Can you imagine what it would be like were a woman to try to gain entrance to White's? She would not only be barred from the club, but society as well, most likely."

"Let every man sweep the snow from before his own doors and not trouble himself about the frost on his neighbor's tiles," Chen Mei said in Cantonese with a curious glance at Amelia.

"Infamous," Amelia snapped back. "I owe him my very life, or do you forget? He may be the most infuriating man on earth, but I know what my duty is."

"Mr. Blandford help, maybe?"

"Of course." Amelia sent Chen Mei a triumphant grin. "Lord Dancy asked if he would see him there, and Mr. Blandford agreed. I will write him immediately."

"What you going to say?" Chen Mei placidly resumed her embroidery work.

"Oh . . . I shall urge him to keep watch most carefully, for I do not trust that Lord Taunton."

"Lord Taunton most skillful cheat. No one caught him out all these many years. How Mr. Blandford catch him?"

"What a pity you could not be there. You'd see it right away. We must think on this, Chen Mei. I have heard that Lord Taunton has fleeced many a lamb of his fortune. We cannot allow that to happen to Lord Dancy."

Chen Mei rubbed her chin in reflection. "We see," she concluded. "I find way."

With that small comfort Amelia had to be content. She carefully penned a letter to Peter Blandford, sealing it with wax while worrying all the while. Peter was not the most observant of souls. She feared that he would miss something.

The Chinese doted on gambling, and Chen Mei had quickly learned all the English games of chance from Amelia's father. Chen Mei had incredible ability to detect hand movements. She had explained about card cheats once when Amelia had wondered about such—how one might skillfully manipulate the deck so he could see the top card, or perhaps deal from the bottom, or fake a shuffle. Marking a deck of cards might be cleverly done, especially if the light was not the best. Oh, if only they could smuggle her

into the club so she might watch the cheat at work. She
would soon see how he managed to win so often.

Into White's? Absurd. Amelia wondered how it would
be done. For she well knew that to Chen Mei precious little
was impossible.

Amelia dressed for the Wyndham's ball with more than a
little preoccupation. A gown of sheer peony crepe over a
peony sarcenet slip with the short full sleeves trimmed in
silver crepe made her feel considerably more the thing. Silver chenille was vandyked across the low front of the
bodice and on the border of the skirt just below two rows of
white silk roses. It was a lovely gown.

"I do believe this bodice is trifle skimpy, Chen Mei,"
Amelia complained quietly to her companion.

Chen Mei adjusted the diadem of white and silver silk
roses on Amelia's hair, then stood back to inspect her
charge. "Three-tenths of good looks due to nature; seven-
tenths to dress. You wish to look best this night to Mr.
Blandford, no?"

"No," Amelia replied with a heart-rending sigh. "What I
wish I cannot have, it seems."

The companion draped a delicate wisp of a scarf over
Amelia's shoulders. The richly worked embroidery of silver flowers reflected Chen Mei's fondness for them, not to
mention the touch of silver in the gown.

"This is the crowning touch," Amelia said, fingering the
delicate silk fabric with delight. "Thank you so much, my
dear Chen Mei. Without your help I fear I would look a
sight."

"Falling hurts least those who fly low," Chen Mei observed with approval at Amelia's modesty.

Amelia glanced at the clock on her dressing table. "Oh
dear, the hour is late. I had best hurry downstairs." At the
door she paused. "What about Lord Dancy?"

Chen Mei bowed, then crossed over to withdraw a very
elegant but plain man's suit of clothes from the depths of
the wardrobe. All was black but for a plain white waistcoat.
Small black shoes and black hose were also produced along
with a nutmeg wig.

Leaning against the door Amelia gasped with excitement. "You will go! But how? One must be a member."

In less time than Amelia had dressed, Chen Mei was transformed into a funny little man, somewhat Oriental looking in visage, with the nutmeg wig confusing it all. When the cravat was tied and affixed with a superb pin of jade, Chen Mei bowed most correctly to Amelia.

"You no go, so I go. Mr. Blandford take me. He member."

"I only hope he holds to his promise to escort me this evening," Amelia cautioned darkly.

"I meet you at Wyndham's. No ploblem," Chen Mei concluded. "I fix all things."

Leaving the transformed companion to work further magic on her face, Amelia drifted down the stairs in a highly bemused state.

"I say," Peter Blandford said, "you look like a peony this evening." He chuckled at his own bon mot with Mrs. Spencer adding her trill of laughter.

Lord and Lady Wyndham gave glorious parties, and this ball proved no exception. Amelia was pleased to note that peony flowers had been brought from the famed Wyndham greenhouses to decorate the ballroom. The fragrance added to the beautiful appearance of the room. Cream walls elegantly trimmed in gold with looking glasses reflected the light from the hundreds of candles in the crystal chandeliers. The flowers merely enhanced what proved to be excellent background for the colorful gowns of the ladies present. Gentlemen provided a punctuation of black and even more vivid colors.

"Miss Longworth, you must have known Lady Wyndham's intent. You carry out her theme of peony most admirably."

"Lord Dancy! But I thought, that is, you said," she sputtered, hope rising that Chen Mei would not have to attempt the precarious masquerade.

"I could not slight my dear friends, Miss Longworth. I see you have Blandford in tow this evening."

"Yes, well, he and Mary and Mr. Warwick make up our party along with my aunt."

"Quite frequently, I understand." He nodded to Peter, and the amused expression on Dancy's face was quite enough to make Amelia wish to kick him. Except she would likely hurt her toes more than his leg.

The dratted man looked superb. Black from head to toe but for a cream marcella waistcoat and a single diamond in his cravat. He put every other man in the shade. The candlelight caught fiery sparks in his hair, but his green eyes glittered at her with that look of knowing that was nearly her undoing. *What was he thinking?*

"To set your mind at ease, I intend to go on to White's sometime later. Taunton will be there, I feel sure. He has made quite a thing of it, you see I could not retreat now, Amelia." He gazed directly into her eyes, a bit of the facade he habitually wore when in public slipping, so Amelia was able to see his uncertainty for but a moment.

She ignored his use of her given name, and merely nodded in understanding.

"Blandford? May I count on you?"

"If Amelia don't mind my leaving her." He looked first at Lord Dancy, then turned to Amelia.

"As if I could. Were it possible, I would go as well, just to wish you luck, my lord."

"Then I would be certain to have a disaster!" He laughed after this remark, but Amelia felt a stab of hurt.

"One thing I ask, Blandford. A dance with your partner before her card is overflowing with names."

"Amelia?" Peter said, refusing to be drawn into any discord that might arise. It would take a man who was deaf and blind not to see there was something between these two. Peter might be a trifle slow, but he was not stupid.

The opening notes of a familiar waltz floated across the room from where the musicians sat. Lord Dancy bowed to Amelia and held out his impeccably gloved hand.

"Shall we, my dear?"

"By all means, if you can manage to mind that odious tongue of yours," she said in a tight little voice.

He merely laughed and swept her away from where Peter and Mrs. Spencer watched.

"For a man who declares he detests the chit he shows a remarkable interest, I should say," Mrs. Spencer observed.

"Indeed," Peter agreed.

From the dim shadows of the room a small peculiar-

looking little man watched the proceedings with a rather
pained expression on his face. Whether it was the English
music or a tight pair of shoes one couldn't say.

"You waltz very well for a young woman who has come
all the way from Macao," he said while spinning her about
at a dizzying pace.

"You waltz very well for a gentleman who spends his
time dashing about foreign countries being chased by spies,
racing in curricles, ballooning, and whatever," she replied
in a remarkably calm manner.

"A direct hit, I vow," he acknowledged with a bow of his
head.

"They have balls in Macao, you know. As matter of fact,
life is not so very different there," Amelia reflected. "It is
an attractive place, with the ground rising sharply from the
Playa Grande up to where the shops and houses, convents
and the Senate House are located. There are pretty trees in
the bishop's garden. In the summer there are numerous parties, dances and fancy-dress balls, musical soirées, fetes,
and theatrical performances. The receptions in the Portuguese governor's mansion are quite grand. I rather miss it
all," she concluded wistfully.

"I am surprised you left the place," Dancy said with a
hint of puzzlement in his voice.

"Papa wished me to have a proper English come-out."

"And he is one person you obey?" Dancy said, amazement ringing in his voice.

"Obedience brings joy," Amelia said with a demure flutter of her lashes.

"I wish you would desire joy when around me," Lord
Dancy muttered without considering what it might sound
like to Amelia, obviously.

She debated whether she ought to comment on this statement, then decided that prudence was a better course.

"What? No clever little quote?"

"Think twice—say nothing," Amelia snapped back.

Lord Dancy laughed in delight. Other gentlemen about
the room noted his obvious enchantment with his partner
and resolved to snatch a dance with the beguiling blonde
who had attracted the interest of the notable Lord Dancy.

It was well that she had that first dance with him, for

Amelia scarcely saw Dancy after that. She was besieged with partners.

It was well into the night when Amelia sensed that Lord Dancy had left the ballroom. Pleading fatigue, she begged her aunt to leave. Since Peter Blandford had also disappeared, Aunt Ermintrude was disposed to go before the night became too dangerous. It was well known that thieves lurked about to filch jewels from party-goers when possible.

Fortunately they reached Mrs. Spencer's house without incident. Amelia ran lightly up to her room to discover a suit of men's clothing laid across her bed. Closing the door with care, then bolting it, she stared at the black garments with satisfaction.

There was a note of sorts in Chen Mei's crabbed writing. Amelia deciphered it with growing delight. It took some time to ease her way out of her gown. Even in her hurry she set the flowers on the dressing table, draped her gloves over her chair, and placed the precious peony gown carefully on her bed. Chen Mei would give her a horrendous scold if she failed to give them proper attention.

It was no easy matter to dress in the men's garb. Only years of helping her papa with his cravat enabled her to tie that creation with any credibility. Then she released the bolt of the door, opened it, and upon hearing silence tiptoed from her room.

It was remarkably simple to slip from the house, hail a passing hackney, and get to White's on St. James's Street. When she stepped from the carriage, she faced another matter entirely. How did she gain entrance? The door opened and she glimpsed a pleasantly lit hall. No doubt the porter's stall was right at the opening, and there would be no way she might slink past him; he would be too canny to allow that.

A carriage drew up, then two gentlemen came out of the club discussing something in a heated manner.

"Fancy, Capel bet Brummel five guineas that Napoleon will not be head of the Frenchies within ten days."

"Ponsonby has bet Raikes one hundred guineas to fifty that Boney enters Paris as a conqueror on or before May the first," countered his friend as they entered the waiting carriage. "Place is abuzz with the talk."

Amelia took heart and sidled up to the front door, peering through the still-open doorway to the entrance hall beyond. It seemed to her that it was empty. Just when she was about to attempt to slip inside, a somewhat tipsy man approached and clapped his hand on her shoulder. "Don't dawdle, my man. Move."

Amelia found herself propelled past the porter and into the dimly lit card room. The room was hushed. At one of the tables near the center of the room Amelia could see Lords Dancy and Taunton seated at a small square table. Lamps with shades were placed in opposite corners of the table to shed light on their hands.

Chen Mei and Peter stood behind Lord Taunton. Amelia marveled that no one had challenged either her or her companion, yet. But she knew all those present concentrated on the game at hand.

All of a sudden Chen Mei nudged Peter, and he cried out, "I say, the man is a cheat!"

Confusion broke loose.

Chapter Eleven

A round of gasps were followed by outraged murmurs from the members clustered around the table.

"That's a dastardly thing to contend, Blandford," Sir Humphrey Elson said. He had lost two hundred pounds to Lord Taunton not so long ago, yet he did not like to think the club housed a cheat.

"I demand you retract that charge, sir," Lord Taunton said, not releasing his hand of cards. He slowly rose to face Blandford, staring at him with cold eyes.

The room grew silent as the members held their collective breath. All gazed at the two confronting each other by the side of the small table.

Peter bent his head to confer with Chen Mei, then straightened. His hand darted out to snatch the cards from Taunton's hand, followed by those on the table, then he took the cards in Lord Dancy's hand. He examined the cards with his quizzing glass, eventually nodding in satisfaction. The murmurs grew as members discussed the charge, most of them looking at Lord Taunton with hostile eyes, for he was not well liked.

Geoffrey had not said a word, merely staring at his friend with a perplexed frown. He presumed his friend had reason to issue so daring a challenge. Then his gaze shifted to Chen Mei, and lastly to Amelia, who had edged close to her companion, retaining her hat and keeping to the shadows. Not by a flicker of an eyelash did he reveal he recognized them. If they were discovered in White's, they might as well board the next boat to Macao, for they would be ruined. He clenched one hand as he considered what he would like to do to that minx, Amelia Longworth. Then, at the change of expression on Peter's face, he returned his attention to his friend.

"Look! I'll show you how he does it," Peter said with a certain triumph. "See the pattern on the back of this deck of cards? The outer line is thickened near the top on the back of an ace. The line on a king is a bit lower, the queen lower still. By concentrating on the back of the cards, he can tell just what is to come up and what his opponent has if he can see those cards."

"By Jove, I see just what he means. Look at this, Sefton. Scandalous!" Sir Humphrey handed two of the marked cards to Lord Sefton, who in turn passed them along to Thomas Creevey, who shared them with Lords Alvenley and Worcester. All used their quizzing glasses to examine the cards closely.

The Duke of Beaufort declared, "I believe we have a serious charge before us, my friends."

Earl Gray, known and greatly respected for his honesty in all dealings, concurred. "It will ruin the club if it is known that we tolerate a cheat in our midst, member or no. I say he must go."

All were in agreement, to judge by the nodding of heads and indignant glances exchanged.

"I refuse to issue a challenge to a duel, Taunton," Lord Dancy said quietly. "Shooting you would be far too kind. I suggest that to save your face you consider traveling abroad for a long period of time, such as the remainder of your life." The look he gave Taunton held a silent menace that would have intimidated a stronger man than Taunton.

Geoffrey reached over to scoop up all the counters that Taunton had amassed. "And since these are mine, albeit fraudulently won by you, I shall keep them."

There was absolutely nothing Lord Taunton could say to the charges other than to stalk silently from the room. The evidence was there, if one knew what to look for and examined the backs of the cards most carefully. There was no doubt in the mind of anyone that Taunton would be driven not only from London, but from the country, by his dishonesty.

"Blandford, we owe you a great debt," Lord Sefton said

fervently. "To think that one of our members should be such a blackguard as to consider cheating all of us."

"Indeed," Sir Humphrey chimed in, "I have lost a goodly sum to that scoundrel. Pity there isn't some way we could recover it."

"If one had known what his ruse was, I suppose it would have been possible to switch decks on him, then fleece him in return. He'd have been ruined, of course," Geoffrey said, rising from the table and moving slowly in the opposite direction from where Chen Mei and Amelia had half hidden behind Peter. He drew Blandford with him, his very action attracting others.

The other gentlemen followed, no one seeming to notice the two strangers, one oddly dark, the other rather young, who now edged out of the door of the room.

Mr. Raggett, the proprietor of White's, then entered, passing that duo with scarcely a glance. "What's this, gentlemen? Lord Taunton expelled in disgrace? Explain, please."

Lord Sefton assumed the role of narrator, deferring to Peter every now and again, then suggested they all join in a toast to Mr. Blandford for saving the club from disgrace.

Chen Mei and Amelia slipped along the hall amid the ensuing confusion and loud discussion. In the room behind them they could hear champagne called for; the waiters scurried about arranging trays of glasses and opening bottles of champagne.

Attempting to walk nonchalantly down the curving stairs with past members staring down from their frames, proved rather daunting, Amelia discovered. Somehow they managed.

The porter saw nothing amiss in their departure. He merely nodded at the two strangers, and before long Amelia and Chen Mei were out on St. James's Street once again.

"Chen Mei, you did it," Amelia crowed with delight, just barely refraining from giving her companion a well-deserved hug.

"Feel good," Chen Mei admitted. "We best hurry home. Lord Dancy no looked too pleased, missee."

Amelia agreed and hailed a passing hackney.

She scrambled into the hackney that drew up before the

club, followed quickly by Chen Mei. They drove in contemplative silence until they reached Mrs. Spencer's house. Here they ran into problems.

"The door is locked," Amelia observed in a dismayed voice.

"Grimm think we asleep," Chen Mei explained. From the sleeve of her borrowed coat she withdrew her little dagger and within minutes the lock clicked. They slipped inside the house, then relocked the door.

"You are certainly a handy one to have around," Amelia whispered while they hurriedly climbed the stairs.

They tiptoed along the hall, then into Amelia's room. Once there she bolted the door behind them and collapsed in a heap on her bed. This didn't last long. Her companion had other notions.

"Missee look not too bad in those pantaloons," Chen Mei observed as she nudged her charge to her feet, then began the removal of the also-borrowed clothes.

Amelia surveyed her slim figure clad in the boyish black pantaloons in her cheval glass and grinned. "They are shockingly comfortable. I would not mind wearing them more often, I vow."

"Chinese women know this already," Chen Mei said with a smile, referring to her usual daytime garb.

"Sensible custom, I believe," Amelia mumbled as her nightdress was tugged over her head.

At last she was settled in her pretty sleigh bed with her covers drawn to her chin.

"Do you think he will be angry with us again?" She gave an enormous yawn as she settled her head on her pillow.

"Maybe. Men funny. They like to think they know all. A man who knows that he is a fool is not a great fool," Chen Mei concluded in Cantonese from her store of knowledge.

"What makes you think that Lord Dancy would admit he is a fool?" Amelia murmured, already half asleep.

"The day will come," Chen Mei replied, then blew out the candle to retire to her own well-earned rest.

The following morning Amelia slept far later than usual. When she finally drifted down to the morning room, she discovered her aunt all atwitter at the breakfast table, deeply absorbed in one of her morning newspapers.

"You will scarce credit this."

Amelia tensed, wondering how in the world the news of the cheating scandal at White's could have reached the papers in time to be published.

"Some absurd man wagered that he could walk blindfolded from the Obelisk at the end of Fleetmarket and Fleet Street to the iron gate in front of the Mansion House."

Relieved that she was not to hear about the incident at White's, Amelia inquired with more interest than she felt, "And did he?"

"Indeed. He won his ten guineas on Sunday morning, although it took him an hour and forty minutes to accomplish the deed. The account says there were a great number of spectators who followed him along his path. Fancy anyone doing something so silly," Mrs. Spencer concluded.

Amelia nodded her agreement while popping a bite of buttered egg into her mouth. Utterly starved, she managed to make a tidy meal of her eggs, crisp bacon, and toast with jam. Once her plate was clear Amelia sat back to reflect on the past evening.

Aunt Ermintrude broke into her thoughts. "Your ball is nearly upon us, my love. Another two days and you shall make your bows to society with Mary. It is a pity there isn't a Drawing Room to be held at the Palace for ages. But be assured that Lady Blandford is sponsoring both of you girls so you may make your curtsy to the Queen."

It was a jolt for Amelia to be brought back from all her mental wanderings to reality. "I hope my dress will be nice. I think Papa would like to have a painting done for him, perhaps in that dress? I daresay it does not have to be a grand one, just so he may see how I look. He is so very far away," Amelia concluded on this rather wistful note.

Immediately after this Grimm entered the breakfast room to announce in a most disapproving voice that Lord Dancy awaited Miss Longworth in the drawing room.

"Oh, dear," Amelia murmured as she rose from the table. "I cannot think what brings him here this afternoon. We saw him just last evening. Is there something I do not know, my love?" Aunt Ermintrude asked in a soft, most curious voice. "Do you wish me to come with you?"

"I expect it is a mere nothing, dearest Aunt. Enjoy your papers while I tend to Lord Dancy. Chen Mei shall come with me."

Chen Mei awaited Amelia in the hallway, and together they marched up the stairs to the drawing room. Amelia paused at the threshold, attempting to assay his lordship's mood.

"Come in, come in. And close the door behind you, if you please. I should not wish to have this business nosed about town."

Amelia resolutely crossed the room while Chen Mei did as bade and shut the door as quietly as possible. She came up behind Amelia and said quietly, "In every affair retire a step, and you have an advantage."

Unsure what her companion meant, Amelia nodded, then took a final step to meet Lord Dancy. "You wished to speak with me, my lord?"

"I ought to beat you, you impossible girl! Yet you and Chen Mei succeeded where others have failed, so how can I? But do you have any notion of the risk you took last night? Many of the premier lords of the land were there. If they had gone home to tell their wives of this amusing bit of tittle-tattle, you would not only have put paid to any hope of a respectable offer of marriage, you might as well leave the country. It simply is not done for a young woman—a woman of any age, for that matter—to enter one of the gentlemen's clubs in London. You ought not even drive down St. James's Street after noon, for pity's sake. Amelia, what am I to do with you?"

She clasped her hands before her in an attitude of meekness, although she seethed inwardly. Small thanks they got for saving his hide.

"Amelia?" He looked just a trifle unsure of himself when she peeped up at him.

"I do not know what can be done now, sir. Lord Taunton must by now be packing to leave the country. I have no desire to go with him."

"Good lord, I never suggested that!"

"Well," she said prosaically, "my ball at Almack's is the

evening after tomorrow. I look forward to it with great enthusiasm. I would not wish anything to spoil my aunt's pleasure in that event, sir. Perhaps if I promise never to do anything like this again, it would help?"

He gave a derisive sniff. "That's easy enough. There will never *be* anything like this again. I thought you were to leave my life?"

Amelia tightened her clasp on her hands a moment, before allowing them to drop to her sides. "It is written: A speck upon your ivory fan you soon may wipe away; but stains upon the heart or tongue remain, alas, for aye."

"And you nearly tossed it aside. You charged across the country to fetch me from the balloon, last night you dared to enter a club where no woman has ever gone. What ever am I do?" he repeated in his evident frustration.

"Why, nothing, my lord. Chen Mei restored your fortune and your blessed club. I went only because I longed to see that all went well for you." A tear escaped from one eye and she angrily dashed it away. "I know it does not help to say that I truly meant for the best, but I did."

He shook his head and began to pace back and forth. He thrust one hand through his hair, disarranging the carefully tousled effect his valet had spent considerable time over.

"Somehow, asking you to refrain from helping me is like adding fuel to put out a fire. Not only is it impossible to accomplish, it seems to have the opposite effect."

"Shall you attend our ball, my lord?" Amelia said in the most humble manner possible.

Lord Dancy paused in his steps to consider her, then reluctantly nodded. "The Blandfords will expect me. I shall request the honor of a waltz with you. At least you've been approved for that dance, and we shan't risk censure for that," he concluded with another sigh.

Amelia allowed herself a tiny smile, then composed her face again. "I shall await your pleasure, my lord."

Her demure curtsy must have had an effect, for he relaxed and smiled at her.

"I'm being something of a gudgeon, am I not? Only when I saw you enter—and you do have the most splendid legs, my dear—my heart nearly stopped. I will see you at your ball, then. Perhaps we could have the supper dance as well? I do owe you something for lending me Chen Mei."

To the Chinese woman he bowed and said, "Many thanks, good lady."

Gratified to be so noticed, Chen Mei nodded gravely, then said, "Better do a kindness near home than go far to burn incense."

Amelia watched his lordship depart, then turned to Chen Mei with great relief. "I suspect he intended to give us both quite a wigging."

"He right," Chen Mei replied in Cantonese. "You must take care to protect your name. As to Lord Dancy," she added, "if your desires and wishes be laudable, Heaven will certainly further them."

"And what do you know of my wishes and desires in regards to Lord Dancy, may I ask?" Amelia queried pertly as she returned to the lower floor in search of her aunt.

"Think twice, say nothing." If Chen Mei was puzzled when Amelia burst out in laughter at this comment, she said nothing.

The following hours saw the delivery of Amelia's ball gown, a confection of silver tissue over the most delicate of pink silk. Later Mrs. Spencer bundled Amelia into her carriage and went to consult with Lady Blandford about the final arrangements. Everything proceeded smoothly.

Too smoothly? Amelia wondered a day later on her way to Almack's. Since it was Friday rather than Wednesday, the usual flock of the *ton* had altered slightly. The acceptances had poured in until nearly all invited had indicated they would be there. Amelia suspected that a few desired to attend merely to see what the inside of Almack's looked like, since they had not managed to obtain one of the precious tickets for the exclusive Wednesday Assemblies.

The canopy at the entrance would protect all in the event of bad weather, but that was the least of Amelia's worries. She had developed a sort of trembling that was most felt in her knees. When she entered the lofty-ceilinged ballroom and gazed up at the huge chandeliers, she wondered if all who had accepted would actually present themselves. It was most frightening.

The musicians tuned up at the far end of the room, with their leader Colnet supervising them all.

Mr. Willis, the guardian of the establishment and nephew of the founder, William Macall, hastened to greet them when Lady Blandford and Mary, followed by Lord Blandford and Peter entered the room to join Mrs. Spencer and Amelia.

"Nervous?" Mary whispered so her mother wouldn't hear.

"Petrified," Amelia murmured back. "I doubt if I shall be able to dance one sensible step let alone make intelligent conversation."

However neither proved true, fortunately. The people thronged into the rooms in a steady flow of gratifying numbers. Before long Amelia was so busy trying to keep all the names straight and noting their faces that she had no time to think of wobbly knees.

And then Lord Dancy was there. Correctly attired in black coat and knee breeches, a white waistcoat embroidered with a delicate silver thread, and his famous diamond in his cravat, he presented a handsome picture. He bowed with commendable poise while holding her gloved hand.

"Miss Longworth, I trust you have saved me a dance," he said with a quirk of his eyebrow when he glanced up into her eyes. A glimmer of mischief lurked within the green depths of those eyes, Amelia noted with apprehension.

Glancing about her to see if anyone was close enough to overhear, Amelia replied, "It is my pleasure and my duty as your chattel to await your every wish."

"Doing it a bit too brown, my girl," he retorted, although softly, still not releasing her hand.

"Well, and you know how I feel about it all," she replied, not quite happy with the role thrust upon her by circumstances.

"I believe I have mentioned more than once that I released you from that silly whatever it was. If it wasn't a vow, it was some sort of Chinese custom? Whatever, we need not heed it."

"But I must, you see. It would be so terribly wrong if I failed to do all I could for you."

"Amelia," Lord Dancy said with a heartfelt throb in his voice, "you totally unman me."

"Oh, I doubt I could ever do that, sir," she replied with such sincerity that he was sent into a fit of coughing.

He drifted away from the receiving line after earning searching looks from Mrs. Spencer and Lady Blandford.

Lord Blandford, a gentleman with surprising grace, escorted Mary, while Peter stood in for Amelia's family in the first dance, a graceful cotillion. This was followed in succession by one minuet, two country dances, a Scotch reel, and a contradance. After which Amelia began to think it would be extremely nice to catch a breath of fresh air.

"Overwhelmed, my dear?" Lord Dancy said when Amelia paused to study her card to see with whom she was obliged to dance with next.

"Lord Dancy, it is you," she replied with relief. At his puzzled expression, she explained, "You are my next partner, sir."

"Of course. That is why I forced my way to your side. Such a crush, my dear."

Amelia thought it a great pity that she was not his dear, but merely extended her hand and mechanically smiled at him.

"This dance will be something to enjoy, then we shall disappear to partake of that lovely supper. Lady Blandford was so kind as to tell me in advance what treats await us. I believe we shall both do it justice."

With those words he drew her into his arms and gracefully swung her into the waltz that had just begun.

"I do not recall we requested a waltz be played," she mused aloud.

"I consulted with Colnet, and he confirmed my suspicion. So I requested one. You could not be so shabby as to deny me this? Now could you? After all you have said about pleasing me?" He grinned down at her, and Amelia laughed back at him, her blue eyes twinkling up into his handsome face with a happy glow.

"I believe you have made your point, my lord," she replied with a charming little giggle.

Geoffrey whirled her about through the respectable throng, wondering what they would think if they knew that the beauty in his arms had dressed in gentlemen's clothing two evenings ago and entered the premises of White's. Oh, there would be a prime scandal, the likes of which would take years to live down. It would rival the doing of Caroline Lamb, no doubt, and she had done all manner of outrageous things.

The music was seductive, he decided. That had to be the reason he felt like drawing her closer to him in a true embrace. Her eyelids fluttered down against those ivory-tinted cheeks that had a touch of peach in them in obvious enjoyment of the dance. He wished he might dare to kiss her again. But scandal lurked too close for comfort. If one of the men present that fateful evening at White's should chance to study Amelia and detect her identity, he shuddered to think what would befall her. Especially when he saw her with Chen Mei and put two and two together.

Amelia bowed her head for a moment at the conclusion of the dance, then tucked her hand into the crook of his arm, prepared to trot along to the blue damask room where refreshments were laid on by Gunter's.

"You know," he said in a mood matching hers, "I believe it was once the custom for a gentleman to claim a kiss from his partner in a dance. Time of Elizabeth, as I recall."

"You were there, of course," she said, followed by a chuckle.

"I am not that old, my dear Amelia. Shakespeare refers to it in *Henry VIII*. Come, wait here while I fetch us plates of the delectables." He stationed her by one of the tables, then crossed over to where a sumptuous buffet quite unlike the Wednesday evening fare of lemonade and stale cakes was offered.

Had he dared to kiss her, Amelia decided she would have made a joke of it. She lived too close to censure to contemplate otherwise. Fortunately he seemed to understand the situation, for he neither behaved with impropriety nor acted as though she had committed a crime.

Others crowded into the refreshment room, and Amelia lost sight of his lordship. People she did not recognize stood close to her, and she guessed they must be friends of the Blandfords. Indeed, most of the people who had come this evening owed more to friendship with them than her aunt.

"Look at him over there, just as though he were not responsible for the death of so many of my countrymen," came a voice not far behind her.

What shocked Amelia was that the man spoke in Portuguese. He must calculate that no one would be likely to understand him, given how few of the English bothered to learn that language. She strained to hear more above the growing din.

"We shall strike soon now. He has been careful so far, but he grows careless. Had that stupid woman not intervened, we could have shot him that day when he took the balloon. Fool. He went sailing off, and we hadn't a hope with her chasing after him."

Amelia's heart grew cold as she realized that she was the woman the man referred to and that Lord Dancy was the man he intended to shoot! She shifted about in order to see if she could take careful note of this person who spoke so boldly of killing an English peer. Dressed in acceptable ballroom attire, the Portuguese did not appear out of place. But his dark complexion was suited to the shadows where he lurked. Amelia wondered just when he intended to strike.

Then the crowd shifted, and she could hear no more, much to her frustration.

"Ah, there you are, waiting for me just as I requested. I must say, if you would behave like that all the time, I would be most grateful," Lord Dancy said, that jade twinkle in his eyes most pronounced.

"My lord," Amelia said as she joined him at the table she had stayed near while he had gathered their feast, "I just overheard a most disturbing conversation."

Before he could reply to this puzzling remark, Peter with Chloe Moore, Mary Blandford, and Denzil Warwick joined them, each carrying full plates and gaily chattering.

"Later on we shall discuss this conversation you overheard, my dear," Lord Dancy murmured to Amelia in an aside.

With that Amelia had to be content, for it would not do to bruit it about that Lord Dancy was the target of an assassin. It was difficult for her to concentrate on the prattle about her. Mary and Chloe giggled merrily about the events of the evening . . . who was seen dancing with whom, the pretty gowns, and who was not paying court to you know who.

It was silly gossip, and normally Amelia would have joined in with the others, but she had too much on her mind—something Peter noticed in a trice.

He edged over close to where she sat with Dancy at one end of the table. "I strongly suspect something is the matter. May I be of help?"

"No," replied Dancy while at the same moment Amelia said, "Oh, yes, please."

"What is it?" Peter's kind gaze darted between his two good friends.

With a cautioning look at his lordship, Amelia said in an undertone, "I overheard a rather dark-complected man say he plans to shoot Lord Dancy. He spoke in Portuguese you understand, and I greatly fear that he meant what he said. We must not leave his lordship alone for a moment. Otherwise his death would be upon our consciences forever."

"Rubbish," Dancy declared, but not very fervently.

"He said he had intended to shoot you that day in the park, but you foiled his plans by going up in the balloon and blew away from him. Had I not torn after you, he would have, I believe. Shot you, that is, for he cursed me for interfering with his plans."

"I say," breathed Peter before turning his attention to his partner as might be expected of him at a ball.

Amelia stared at Lord Dancy for a moment, then dropped her gaze to her plate, where her lovely treats were sitting as they had been for some minutes. "You see why I thought that conversation disturbing?"

"I forbid you to do a thing about it, my dear."

"Of course, my lord," she dutifully replied. And pigs will fly, she added to herself. She knew where her duty lay, and it wasn't in obeying a stupid command like that. But whom could she get to help her this time?

Chapter Twelve

"By Jove," Peter said thoughtfully when he could return his attention to his friend once again, "Do you think it could be. . . ."

"Most likely," Lord Dancy replied quietly.

"Now that I think on it, I do believe his mastery of Portuguese was flawed," Amelia mused. "He sounded more like a foreigner who speaks the language well. I would not be surprised were he to prove a Frenchman."

At that statement Lord Dancy and Peter Blandford exchanged concerned looks, but made no comment.

Amelia knew they felt she must be excluded and that a ball—where anyone could overhear a conversation when you least expected it—was not the place to discuss the matter. But she would very much have liked to know precisely what they were thinking.

"I wonder how he managed to gain entrance?" she continued. "Surely he would not be on my list, and I very much doubt if Mary or your mother would have invited a person of questionable background, a man unknown to you." She threw Peter a quizzical look before glancing at Mary who was immersed in conversation with Chloe Moore.

"That's true. Perhaps he came with someone known to us?" Peter said speculatively before he had to return his attention once again to Miss Moore.

People were filtering back into the ballroom, leaving the small group at the Blandford table somewhat alone.

"This will never do," Lord Dancy declared. "Miss Moore, I believe I may claim this dance. Peter, did you not say you are to partner Amelia?" Lord Dancy whisked Chloe Moore out of the room, taking Mary and the others with him. Peter remained behind with Amelia.

"I say, Amelia, you did promise not to interfere in this business. Could find yourself in a bit of a pickle, you know." Peter eyed Amelia as though he fully expected her to go about inspecting each and every guest to see if they spoke Portuguese with a French accent.

"I shan't involve you whatever I might do, Peter," Amelia said with a fond look. "Indeed, his lofty lordship has made it quite plain that he does not wish my help. But they *had* intended to shoot him that morning of the unexpected balloon ride," she stated firmly, defending what she had done. "You must admit that his life has been in danger."

"And once again you saved his life. Dash it all, Amelia, that sort of thing could truly irritate a fellow after a while. A man likes to think he can take care of himself, you know. Don't want to be having a female look after him. Downright disheartening." Peter gave her a rather comical look of dismay.

"Well," Amelia said, trying not to sound vastly annoyed, "why do we not join the dancers before the ball is over. I suspect that my aunt will be concerned if she does not see me." She rose from the table and watched while Peter jumped to his feet as though scorched.

Apparently realizing that his presence alone with Amelia might be greatly misconstrued, even if they were in an open room with servants milling about, Peter escorted her to the main room where they joined the others in a rousing country dance.

Amelia had found Peter to be an excellent dancer. Not once did he tread on her toes. She laughed up at him, with the hope that Lord Dancy might notice her attentions. Then she caught a glimpse of him going down the line with Chloe and realized he did not pay Amelia the least attention. Indeed, the redheaded Miss Moore seemed to have quite captivated Lord Dancy this evening.

Amelia firmly quelled the rising sensation of envy she suddenly developed for the lovely and very nice Miss Moore. Rather, she turned her mind to the present problem as she viewed it.

This entire matter would require drastic measures. She would have to consult Hemit, to make certain that his lordship was protected at all times. Perhaps it would help to hire a detective, or maybe one of those fighters she had heard spoken about when gentlemen chatted about the boxing world—which they oddly enough called the Fancy.

Then, she must find someone close to Lord Dancy who had his best interests at heart, someone who would be willing to assist Amelia with her plan. Perhaps Hemit would know just who to ask.

"I say, Amelia, you have the most peculiar expression on your face. I hope you are not hatching another one of your schemes." Peter again viewed her somewhat askance, and Amelia wondered what he truly expected of her.

"I only wish I could," she said, smoothing her brow and turning on that polite social smile every girl learned to produce. "Has Lord Dancy heard anything from his sisters as yet?"

"Said something about his sister Victoria being in the family way and not likely returning to London for some time. Far as I know the others are in the country. Elizabeth is still with her aunt while Julia is yet off painting or something."

Drat. Then the sisters were not apt to be of any help. Peter had mentioned something about Victoria and Elizabeth assisting with efforts to foil various French attempts at spying in England. Since Amelia was firmly convinced that Lord Dancy also had associations in that direction, she wondered if the villain wasn't someone who had a massive grudge against Geoffrey Dancy.

How she liked his name. She wished it was proper for a young lady to use a gentleman's first name. But it wasn't. Which brought to mind the numerous times that Geoffrey Dancy had used Amelia's first name. So far no one had commented on his slips. While Amelia had said he might use her first name, she had supposed it to be only on that journey to London. She had soon discovered it would not do elsewhere. London was more stuffy about name usage and all that it implied than Macao. Although she was so young at the time she had left there that people had still referred to her as Miss Amelia, and no one appeared to think a thing of it.

What would a drastic measure involve, she wondered, returning to the problem involving Lord Dancy, while performing yet another country dance. If she were an agent for the government, would she not try to infiltrate his household? Perhaps she could become a maid for a day or two? That would surely be one way to find out the person who best to approach for help.

Chen Mei would offer advice. Goodness knew that she overflowed with that commodity.

The hour was nearing morning when the Blandfords, Mrs. Spencer, and Amelia all left Almack's Assembly rooms together. Mr. Willis expressed himself most gratified at the pleasure of serving them and complimented the ladies upon the excellent refreshments.

Amelia thought he could take a lesson from them, but then, if his wife poured tea and made the lemonade, perhaps they were merely extremely saving. However it seemed to Amelia they might do better than to serve cakes that had become stale.

The next day Chen Mei woke her far earlier than Amelia would have preferred. Rubbing her eyes and yawning hugely, Amelia propped herself up in bed to survey her companion.

"I trust you have a reason for this?"

"You say you velly much want to obtain place in Dancy household. I fix. They need a maid fo day while one is sick. You new maid."

All thought of lolling about in bed left her. Amelia tossed back the covers, then slid from her bed with great haste. She pulled her nightgown over her head, then impatiently said, "I imagine you have found some clothes suitable for a maid. I had best hurry." She scrambled into her underthings and stockings with more haste than care.

"What you going to tell Aunt?"

"I shall tell her . . . " Amelia gave a vexed sigh, then brightened. "I shall tell her that I am playing a trick on a friend—to see if she will recognize me. That ought to do it, for you must know that at least half of the *ton* do not pay the least notice of their servants."

Chen Mei nodded, assisting her charge into a simple

challis print dress with a mobcap to cover her lovely blond curls.

"Is this the sort of thing Lord Dancy's maids wear?" Amelia asked, pivoting about before her cheval glass. "I vow, the fabric may be a touch scratchy, but it is pretty enough."

"His lordship likes to see pretty girls, maybe?" Chen Mei stood back to survey her handiwork. "I think you too pretty. Better turn your back when you see him."

"Oh, indeed. I intend to do that very thing, you may be sure. I can only hope that he sleeps late, then promptly goes out." Amelia slipped from her room and down the stairs to the morning room. As expected, her aunt was nowhere to be found so Amelia sat at the desk to write a letter of explanation. It was to be hoped her dear aunt would not think of too many unanswered questions.

Before leaving the house, Amelia entered the breakfast room to enjoy a good meal. Goodness knew whether she would have such at the Dancy household. She suspected that many London homes might request smashing repasts for themselves with little for the help. Although perhaps leftovers might not be that bad, she decided upon reflection. When she considered all the food that was returned to the kitchen after one of the Spencer meals, it might be that the staff ate reasonably well.

How simple it turned out to be to sneak from the Spencer house. With the butler occupied in his morning duties and all the other servants ignoring her, Amelia felt nearly invisible. She knew they were suspicious of Chen Mei, avoiding her whenever possible. When they saw her with Amelia, they assumed the two were off on some errand, and would rather not question it.

Amelia presented herself at the back door of the Dancy household, hoping no one would have seen her. How she might avoid Evenson, that stately butler, Amelia didn't know, but she would find a way. Perhaps in her new guise he wouldn't recognize her as the same girl who had come here weeks ago with Lord Dancy. She wasn't quite certain if a butler would be one to approach, for all his starch he might prove to be a potential ally. Hemit would know, perhaps.

Using the name of Susan—which happened to be

Amelia's middle name—she neared the housekeeper with hesitant steps. From a distance she appeared formidable.

"Mrs. Hardesty?" Amelia knew the hierarchy below stairs to be inflexible and hated to expose her unfamiliarity with her position immediately.

"You have come to replace Rose for a time?" Mrs. Hardesty replied, less haughty than Amelia expected.

"Yes, ma'am." Amelia bobbed a curtsy she hope resembled that of the upstairs maid at her aunt's home.

"Hm," the housekeeper said, glancing away at something before returning her gaze to her. "Have you served in a gentleman's home before? Or has it been a female establishment?"

"I worked for a lady, if you please, ma'am."

Mrs. Hardesty's look sharpened, possibly at Amelia's speech which was hard to disguise. Amelia breathed a sigh of relief when she questioned her no further.

"You will do the dusting on the ground and first floors. Do not go to the second; only the older maid goes there, for that is where Lord Dancy's quarters are located. I was not here when Lord Dancy was in residence in the past. While he has not bothered any of the maids so far, I don't wish to take any chances. You will also polish the brass, open the shutters, clean and blacken the grates. The looking glasses and windows are due for a cleaning. See to them when you finish the other tasks. Mind you, I do not wish his lordship to discover you about when he comes down."

Paling at the thought of cleaning and blackening the grates, Amelia nodded, then followed the young person summoned along to where the supplies were kept.

"Dusting first," she told the hall-boy. She had decided that she would put off the matter of the grates as long as she could. When he pointed to the necessary cloths, she carried them along to the first of the rooms she was to clean and busied herself. After opening the shutters, she set about her work.

She took great pleasure in examining all the beautiful treasures she assumed that Lord Dancy had accumulated during his travels. Either he or someone in his family had loved interesting and splendid things. She particularly admired the sculpture of a pair of twin girls.

"That's Lady Julia's girls," Evenson offered from the doorway. "Done by Miss Victoria. Sweet little girls, they are." He remained to study Amelia as she worked, making her exceedingly nervous.

"I see. It's beautiful." She didn't know whether to ask Evenson's advice or turn to Hemit. She feared that Hemit might go to Lord Dancy out of loyalty. What she needed to do was to find someone she could trust who would listen to her. So far she had not figured out a way to reach the groom. Not having any reason to be near the mews where Lord Dancy stabled his horses and reluctant to expose herself to possible hazards in that area, she hoped to find him while here. But how?

Evenson watched her as Amelia reverently ran a dust cloth over the sculpture, then went on to the next piece.

"I should like to know what you are about, young miss," the butler inquired in a conversational manner. "It's clear to me that you have had no experience as a maid in your life. Suppose you tell me what this is all about?" He actually wore a somewhat inviting expression on his face, a sort of softening.

Since this was precisely what Amelia had hoped would come about, she smiled at the dignified gentleman, who looked as thought he had served the Dancy family for a good many years and sighed with relief.

"Is there some room where we might talk without anyone overhearing what is said?" She looked about her warily to see if there was anyone eavesdropping.

Not revealing the least bit of surprise at her question, he gestured to his left, then walked silently with Amelia until they reached a small office of sorts. An etching of four children hung on one wall, and there were surprisingly comfortable chairs for the two of them. He busied himself in a small closet off to one side, then brought Amelia a small glass of sherry.

"Sherry? This time of day?"

"I thought after your exertions this morning, you might be in need of a restoring glass of something. If I request lemonade for a housemaid, there might be a few raised eyebrows. We do not wish that, do we Miss Longworth?"

"Oh, you recognized me." She took a sip and liked the

taste very much. "Well," she began. "It is this way. I met Lord Dancy in Portugal when he saved my life twice. He saved it again when we arrived in Portsmouth, carrying me from the burning inn."

Evenson nodded slightly, encouraging Amelia to continue.

"So, I am his." Her simple statement caused the butler to elevate his eyebrows a tiny bit, but otherwise he sat impassively in his oak armchair.

Heartened by this acceptance of her status as Lord Dancy's chattel, she continued to fill Evenson in on all that had occurred to date—from her point of view, naturally.

"I have served the Dancy family ever since I began service as a lad. I would do anything to help them. But I cannot think how to assist you in this." Evenson pursed his lips while he contemplated the problem at hand. "His lordship would not take lightly to having someone interfere with his plans. Somehow I misdoubt he will like having someone peering over his shoulder, as it were."

"Do you think Hemit would go along with our wish to protect Lord Dancy from his enemies? For I know there must be at least two, possibly three of them."

The butler nodded. "I daresay he would take on the task with relish. So . . . what do we do?"

If Amelia felt the least bit peculiar sitting with the Dancy butler in his private quarters, detailing her opinions on the gentleman who was even now most likely abovestairs asleep in his bed, she didn't show it.

"Well, I believe we *must* hedge him around with people to protect him at all times. *Never* allow him to go out on his own. Always see to it that he has a friend or two, an extra groom in attendance, and perhaps not drive his curricle about, but take a closed carriage instead." She gazed at the butler with a hopeful expression. "It should work."

Evenson pursed his lips again, then left his chair to cross the room to where a row of bell ropes hung. He tugged at one; they waited until the door opened.

"What's up?" Hemit said in a surprised voice. "Miss Longworth! You here?" Hemit proved aware that it was not the proper thing for a young woman to enter the house of an unmarried gentleman at any hour of the day. Even a few minutes were enough to compromise her reputation.

"Lord Dancy is quite unaware I am here, Hemit. I tried to think how I might speak with you and Evenson or someone here without Lord Dancy knowing a thing about it. This was the only way I could manage it."

"She is supposedly taking Rose's place for the day," Evenson explained to the groom with a wry twist of his mouth.

"Mrs. Hardesty will be in a rare taking if she finds out she's sent a lady to clean the house," Hemit observed with a look at the prim young woman perched on Evenson's chair.

"That is nothing that can't be remedied. Perhaps we can tell her I did it as a lark, a joke on his lordship or something of that sort," Amelia offered somewhat hesitantly.

Hemit and Evenson exchanged dubious looks.

"See here," Amelia said, "we simply cannot sit about nattering on over this. Any moment now his lordship will come down those stairs and go off into a very dangerous world. You do wish to protect him?"

"Yes, miss," the men fervently agreed.

"Well then," Amelia declared with equal zeal, "let us commence." She took off her apron, then settled more comfortably on the chair.

The three put their heads together, mapping out a likely guide to Lord Dancy's movements for the day.

Once this was accomplished, Amelia leaned back in her chair, polishing off her sherry. "There, if I do say so, he ought to be safe for the day." She saluted the men, then opened the door tb peer out into the hallway.

"'Tis empty," she whispered. "How do I get out of here?"

"Leave it to me." Evenson allowed himself a grin. "Mrs. Hardesty is a bit stuffy. It will come as a surprise to her that the girl she engaged to help has disappeared. Not stolen anything, either. Come, I'll let you out of the front door. No servant would dream of leaving that way, and she'll never see you."

"Oh, you are an angel, Evenson. I can see why Lord

Dancy depends on you so." She bestowed a flashing smile on the butler, her blue eyes lighting up with her delight.

The dignified man nodded to himself for some unknown reason, then ushered Amelia to the front door, allowing her to slip out to a waiting Chen Mei with not the least sound.

Once at the Spencer household, Amelia found her aunt in the front parlor puzzling over the letter written hours earlier.

"Oh, my love, what a muddle this is. Where have you been? From this letter you left, it sounds remarkably like you have been pretending to be a maid. Surely that cannot be true!"

"Only for a little while," Amelia admitted with a grin for her dearest aunt. "I thought I could fool my friend, but my identity was uncovered very soon. And I thought it a very good disguise, too." At this Amelia twirled about in her mobcap and challis print dress. She bobbed a proper curtsy to her aunt and attempted to appear demure.

"I can see you tried hard enough. I hope that is the reason for your charade. You were in such a bemused state last evening that I had begun to worry about you. You do become involved in the oddest starts, my love. I shouldn't like to think you risked your reputation in some mad scheme to safeguard Lord Dancy."

"Lord Dancy is somewhat of a trial, Aunt Ermintrude."

"Is he, now? Fancy that. I daresay you are one of the very few who might venture such an opinion. Most people think he is quite handsome and as a peer, entitled to do anything he pleases."

"It is easy to convince a wise man, but to reason with a fool is a difficult undertaking," Amelia quoted from Chen Mei's store of maxims. "That fool simply refuses to admit he is in danger. Last night I overheard two gentlemen talking—and I do not in the least understand how such dreadful men were allowed to come to our ball. Anyway, they said they intended to shoot Lord Dancy and cursed me for luring him off on that balloon ride that he so unwillingly took. It saved his life," Amelia concluded virtuously.

"Oh, mercy," Aunt Ermintrude gasped, fanning herself with Amelia's letter. "I scarce think Lord Dancy is a fool, my love. He is highly regarded in our circle, you know."

"Well, I hope that his groom and butler will see to it that he is well-guarded. As devoted to him as they appear to be, he ought to be well-watched."

Aunt Ermintrude looked as though she would like to inquire just how Amelia knew all this. Apparently she decided it was well not to know, for she rose from her chair and drifted across the parlor to look out of the window.

"Anything interesting?" Amelia asked on her way to her room so she might change.

"Callers. You must hurry to your room and put on that pretty blue muslin with the clusters of forget-me-nots on the bodice and flounce. It becomes you so well."

"Yes, ma'am. They shan't see my shadow," she caroled gaily as she dashed from the room and up the stairs.

Behind her, Aunt Ermintrude sighed, looked at the ceiling, and muttered something that sounded like, "Give me strength, oh Lord."

"Strong coffee. A large pot, I believe," Lord Dancy ordered in his usual pleasant manner. He rifled through the early morning mail while he sipped from the steaming cup in his hand.

"Morning, Geoff," Peter said from the doorway where he paused for a moment as though to gauge his welcome.

"Come in, come in," Geoffrey muttered none too heartily. "I trust you slept better than I did. I kept thinking of those two fellows at the ball last night. Wish I'd had a chance to see them for myself. Amelia was less than forthcoming regarding their appearance."

"True. If a chap is going to be shot, it would be jolly to know what his enemy looks like. Much better chance to beat him to the draw that way." Peter helped himself to a cup of coffee, grimacing at the bitter taste. He proceeded to add cream and sugar, before pulling out a chair at the table.

"I cannot hide in my room. I refuse to become a recluse merely because of something Amelia overheard—or thinks she overheard."

"Well, she has been right before. And what about that business of the balloon?"

"Sheer luck."

"Well, I believe she is telling you precisely what she

heard. What's more, I intend to stand guard on you today," Peter declared with a diffident air.

"I bloody well do not need a nursemaid!" Geoff roared at his good friend.

"Did you wish something, my lord?" Evenson inquired from the doorway in the blandest of manners.

"Tell this buffle-headed fellow that I left short-coats a long time ago. I do not need a guard." Geoffrey replaced his slice of toast on his plate, looking at it with surprise, wondering how he had come to have it in his hand.

"You can call me a jingle-brained fool if you like, but we had some hair-raising times in Spain and Portugal. If you can tell me that your senses ain't standing on end, I shall drop the matter at once," Peter said shrewdly. "I daresay that you will admit that you know you are in danger and in need of your friends right now. Dash it all, Geoff, what are friends for if not to chime in with a helping hand?"

Geoffrey sighed, then nodded. "Too right, old fellow. I cannot say I like this one bit, however."

Peter grinned at Evenson as though he sensed an ally. "I gather you are aware his lordship has been threatened by some nodcock—Frenchie, most likely. Mean to see to it that my friend doesn't come to an untimely end."

"We are deeply concerned as well, my lord. Hemit and myself, that is. I trust that between Mr. Blandford and your groom, you will have staunch accomplices."

"Hmpf," Geoffrey replied, waving his hand in dismissal. "Do you think there is anyone around who doesn't know about this business?"

"I haven't uttered a word, I swear it," Peter avowed.

"Well, then, since I know that Hemit doesn't come until called, how did my butler become so well-informed about the matter? Pixies?"

Peter frowned, then helped himself to the raspberry jam, which he proceeded to spread on Geoff's toast in generous quantity.

"Wonder how Amelia is this morning," Peter said after stuffing himself with eggs and a slice of ham plus a third slice of toast.

"You ought to wonder what she will think of next to be-devil me."

"Now, Geoff, the girl means well. She has your best interest at heart," Peter argued after downing the last of his doctored coffee.

"I would that she leave me alone. How can I possibly fix an interest with that lovely armful at the opera house with Amelia dropping out of the sky when I least expect her?"

"You know what I think? I think that one day you will miss her."

"As I miss an aching head. If you have finished demolishing the remainder of my breakfast, I suggest we depart. Tatt's is placing some one hundred carriages on view, with the sale to come up in a few days. I understand a rather fashionable landau owned by a lady is up. Says she only used it a few months. According to the *Post* it's painted patent yellow, lined with light blue cloth trimmed in lace, and has yellow morocco reclining cushions, plated furniture, and patent axle trees no less. I think I just might have a need for such a beauty in the not too distant future." Geoffrey grinned at his amused friend.

"By all means. I believe Tatt's to be safe enough. It's driving there that might prove hazardous. Listen to reason and do not take the curricle today," Peter pleaded.

Geoffrey went out his front door, then came to a halt when he viewed his traveling carriage. "I suspect I wouldn't be allowed if I wanted," he commented wryly.

Chapter Thirteen

"Oh, my love," Aunt Ermintrude sang out in her fluting voice as she drifted into the breakfast room, waving one of her many morning newspapers in the air. "Napoleon has abdicated! He is banished to the island of Elba. Peace is here at last."

Chen Mei frowned. She had joined Amelia at breakfast at her insistence so they might better plan the day. It was clear she did not condone so gentle a treatment for the man responsible for thousands of deaths. "Killing a bad ruler is no murder."

"Oh, he will be unable to do a thing from Elba, for he will be guarded most efficiently," Aunt assured them. She looked slightly shocked that Chen Mei would advocate something as strong as murder, even for Napoleon.

The Cantonese woman appeared to think little of that opinion, but she said nothing.

At the end of the table Aunt Ermintrude sank down upon her chair, utterly absorbed in reading the account of all that had occurred and was to take place in the next few days.

"There are to be festivities everywhere," she read aloud. "Oh, dancing in the streets ought to be the order of the day with that hateful man out of the way." She beamed a smile at Amelia, then avidly returned to her newspapers.

"He would be better off dead," Chen Mei muttered to Amelia. "A dead man cannot inspire others to rise up so to overthrow."

"I am not so certain about that, but I suppose you are right," Amelia murmured back. "You realize that this will make protecting Lord Dancy enormously difficult. With the press of people everywhere he goes, one slim Frenchman will have no trouble at all in disposing of a hated Englishman."

"Best lure him away from city," Chen Mei said practically.

"All of London will be heading toward Paris, or so this says," Aunt inserted into the softly spoken conversation. "How I long to see Paris again. Would you not like to travel across the Channel to look the place over, my love?"

"I suppose London will become rather thin of company if that is the case," Amelia replied, not answering the invitation to travel to Paris. While she might enjoy a view of the French city, she dare not leave Lord Dancy. She very much doubted if he intended to enter the dragon's mouth by making the crossing to a free France. Actually the sparsity of people in London would work to their good, for the parties might not be so crowded. She said as much to Chen Mei, who nodded slowly.

"Good thing."

"I must go out to purchase some white cockades to do honor to the Bourbons. And I wish to find that scarf I have that has fleurs-de-lys embroidered on it, for I feel sure that will be all the thing. This is enormously exciting. His majesty, Louis XVIII, is to hold a levee. 'Tis said even women will be allowed to attend. What a pity he is such a fat old man," Aunt concluded with wide-eyed conviction. "I believe the French deserve someone a little younger and more understanding after the tyrant Napoleon. I wonder if Louis has learned a lesson from the revolution that nearly ruined his country."

"Indeed, ma'am," Amelia replied respectfully. She rose in a flurry of blue muslin. "I shall send a note to Mary Blandford to see if she would care to go for a drive. Perhaps we may see something of the festivities in progress."

"Invite her brother as well, dear Amelia," Aunt Ermintrude trilled before returning to the news of the day.

Amelia exchanged a resigned glance with Chen Mei, then slipped from the room and along the hall. It took but a few minutes to dash off her suggestion, adding her hope that Peter might come along. Perhaps they could make a party of it and invite others as well. Amelia did not wish to encourage her aunt's fond hopes regarding Peter Blandford.

He might be heir to the barony, but he did not hold Amelia's interest other than as a friend.

"Dare I invite Lord Dancy?" Amelia wondered aloud to herself. Since Chen Mei had parted ways with her at the bottom of the stairs, there was no one to advise Amelia one way or the other. "Why not? The worst he can do is say no. I hope Evenson will hide all his other invitations for the day so that he feels compelled to accept this one."

When the footman returned, he brought a delighted reply of acceptance from Mary; Peter agreed to go with them. Amelia rushed up to her room to dress for the outing.

"Where you go?" Chen Mei inquired as she riffled through the wardrobe of pretty gowns.

"I believe it would be safe enough to visit the British Museum Gardens. It is on the very edge of the city and although usually much sought out, should not be busy today. Any stranger will be noticed immediately. With Hemit and Peter, and my little dagger in addition, Lord Dancy will be as safe if he were still in bed."

"Ah," Chen Mei replied, nodding with satisfaction. She withdrew a gown of peach-bloom sarcenet having three narrow flounces at the hem, followed by a matching pelisse. Once dressed, Amelia set her bonnet in place, admiring the pretty confection lined in peach satin and trimmed with three lovely plumes. She tied the ribands to one side of her chin in a fetching bow. It was a simpler variation of the Oldenburg bonnet made so popular by the tsar of Russia's sister. Amelia felt quite in style and hoped that his lordship would notice her fetching attire.

She walked slowly down the stairs and was in the act of drawing on her chicken-skin gloves in a delicate peach color when the front door opened.

"Miss Longworth," Geoffrey said with commendable calm after he passed Grimm, considering that Amelia had cautioned him to present himself or risk death.

"You are wiser than I thought, sir," she declared as Grimm shut the door behind his lordship, retreating discreetly to the far end of the hall.

Geoffrey advanced on the dainty bit of peach fluff that stood so sweetly at the bottom of the stairs. How could any woman who looked like a piece of candy cause such havoc in his life? He guided Amelia into the front parlor, hoping to keep what he had to say from the ears of the butler.

"We shall endeavor to take very good care of you," she assured him sunnily. "I feared that if you went out and about on your own, the wicked Frenchman would be able to shoot you very easily. You must know we could not allow you to place yourself in such danger. So we wish you to be with us. We will protect you."

Geoffrey stared at the wicked little dagger she pulled from her reticule and restrained a shudder. The richly engraved sheath fell from it easily, exposing a sharply pointed blade.

"Do you always go about with a dagger on you, Amelia?" he asked in a somewhat strangled voice.

"Of course," came her answer with a straightforward smile directly into his eyes. "Chen Mei's brother taught me to throw this most accurately at a target. One never knows where danger lurks. I must place your well-being first, you know."

What was a fellow to do with such honesty and loyalty? Her notion of protection did not quite match his, but how could he scold her—or tell her that she was making him feel stifled? Or how to explain that a chap would rather handle a menace of this sort without an interfering female? Not when the chit gazed at him with such determination out of the most earnest blue eyes he had ever seen. She looked like an angel, but had proved to be a devilishly irritating one.

Geoffrey sighed with defeat. He had not the heart to *again* tell her not to bother him anymore. Or was it that he fancied the girl? No, he assured himself. How could a man be drawn to this aggravating baggage? Not Geoffrey Dancy—never.

Mrs. Spencer fluttered into the room, her face wreathed in a smile. "Is not the news wonderful? That dreadful man is off to Elba, and we may sleep well again. I shall go to purchase our cockades, my love," she said to Amelia. "Where do you plan to venture?"

"By all means, tell us what our day shall bring?" Geoffrey inquired with an arched brow that usually intimidated everyone in sight. Not so Amelia. This chit merely giggled and patted him on the arm in a pleasant manner.

Geoffrey gritted his teeth and firmly quelled the desire to shake this young woman until she . . . He put that thought aside as well. Once he had her in his arms he feared he would forget all about chastising her. He had not forgotten that taste of a kiss after his balloon ride.

"I propose that we visit the charming gardens behind the British Museum. We do not need tickets for that, and it is a lovely day."

Geoffrey gave her a dubious look. But then, with his traveling carriage that Hemit insisted upon driving and the parasols the ladies always carried, they ought to do well enough. If it rained, they could always go over to the Blandford house.

"Would you care for coffee, Lord Dancy?" Mrs. Spencer said. "Cook has baked some rather nice ratafia biscuits."

"Are we to await the Blandfords here?" he asked of Amelia before assenting to the beverage and biscuits.

"Yes. Mary can be ready in a trice. I fear it is Peter and his cravat that may keep us waiting."

He conveyed his polite thanks to Mrs. Spencer, then watched while Amelia sat down on a backless sofa covered in plum silk. The room had been decorated in a current mode—Greek revival, or whatever it was dubbed. It reminded him of the French Empire style that had raged across that country when Napoleon made it popular. He seated himself rather gingerly in a facing chair, pleased to discover how comfortable it proved.

From this vantage point he had an excellent view of the young woman who had tumbled into his life and caused no end of mischief. He had to admit that she was the most appealing bit of mischief he'd ever seen . . . or held in his arms. Thoughts of holding her once again began to stir within, and he welcomed the entrance of the butler as a timely restraint.

Grimm brought the tea and coffee with such promptness, Amelia suspected he had anticipated the request. She poured, for Aunt Ermintrude was still absorbed in reading snippets from the columns of her various newspapers to them.

Amelia studied Lord Dancy's face while handing him the cup of coffee, then offering the plate of biscuits. He did not appear to be angry, but she sensed an annoyance in him, one she would do well to lessen.

"I trust you are well-pleased that Napoleon has been banished to Elba, sir. Do you think that will somewhat ease the danger to yourself?" Amelia asked when assured her aunt was not paying the least attention to the conversation.

"It all depends, does it not? If the fellow bears ill will toward me for some reason, Napoleon may not enter into the business in the least." Lord Dancy demolished several of the biscuits with his coffee, then set the cup down on the table close to Amelia. He appeared not to notice her nervous start when his hand strayed near her knee.

A stir in the front hall indicated that the Blandfords had arrived. When Amelia rose to greet them, she found Lord Dancy right behind her, disquietingly close. He stirred feelings within her that she tried to ignore, for they interfered with her thinking processes. If she didn't quell these odd emotions, she would soon be in a briar patch, for certain.

"Miss Moore," Amelia said with mixed pleasure, daring a glance at Lord Dancy to see how he reacted to this addition to their group. "Mr. Warwick, what a delight to have you both join us."

Miss Moore was a vision in mint green muslin with a dark green pelerine. Mary wore a pretty dress of jonquil yellow edged in white lace ruffles. The assessing gaze of each young woman when they encountered Lord Dancy standing close to Amelia made her feel uneasy. How much of her feelings did they guess? She hoped they believed her care for the man was motivated purely by kindness.

Within several minutes they had bid Mrs. Spencer farewell, then set off in the Dancy carriage. Fortunately the commodious traveling coach could easily hold them all. Amelia sat by a window where she could peek out at the streets and people as they went.

"I do not see you-know-who," she murmured to Peter, who sat between her and Miss Moore.

"Wouldn't expect such a thing," he quietly replied.

Once assured that they appeared to have given the slip to the man who declared he wished to shoot Lord Dancy,

Amelia eased back on the seat to enjoy the day. After all, it was reasonable that the man had other things to do besides lurking about in Lord Dancy's shadow.

All declared that the gardens were as charming as promised. The six of them sauntered along the paths, examining the flora as they went. There were a fair number of people about on this day, but not so many they had to worry about a crush. Amelia figured that a man could be easily chased in such an open area, and less apt to strike when he was so vulnerable. Lord Dancy could be better protected as well.

"Oh, how I adore the tulips," Chloe Moore exclaimed. "Lord Montague must have been caught up in the tulipmania of some years ago. Look at the vast number that are planted in this garden."

This phenomenon had to be explained to Amelia, who declared it the silliest thing she had ever heard. "But since the tulips are so beautiful, I can well understand how a person might become obsessed with them." She reached over to touch the feathery petal of one striped in red and white.

The garden contained terraces, many carefully tended flower borders, lawns, and gravel walks along which people strolled. The house commanded striking views of the country to the north of London, the fields of Hampstead Heath in particular. A number of trees offered pleasant shade, and Amelia suggested they rest here for a moment.

"What a pity we could not organize a game of cricket. That lawn looks to be perfect for it," she commented as she surveyed the lush green.

"But ladies do never play at such a game," Miss Moore reproved ever so gently.

"Truly?" Amelia had played with the neighbor children in Macao. "What a pity. Perhaps we could play battledore and shuttlecock instead." Then she straightened as she saw a lone individual not far from where they sat.

"Peter," she said in a quiet voice, "does that man appear threatening to you?—the one in the dark green coat with fawn pantaloons and black boots."

"Sorry. No different from any of the others that I can see. Are you sure you recognize him?" Peter wrinkled his brow in concentrated examination of the possible villain.

"Amelia sees villains beneath every clump of shrubbery and behind every tree," Lord Dancy snapped in what Amelia thought a nasty way.

The tranquility of the outing destroyed at this remark, Amelia jumped to her feet and gave him an accusing look. "We are but trying to protect you, my lord. I am so sorry if you feel it is not worth our while."

She whirled about, commandeering Mary and Chloe to walk with her. "Come girls, let us examine those marvelous flowers over there."

"Fat's in the fire now, Geoff," Peter said as he watched the ladies march away.

"You must admit this is becoming a bit tedious, always looking for the little man who isn't there. Besides, I worry about Amelia. Do you know that she carries a dagger with her at all times? I don't want her hurt."

Peter gave Geoffrey a narrow look then turned away to follow the girls.

"What a Cheerful Charlie you are today," Geoffrey said, strolling along after the group with Denzil Warwick at his side. "Perhaps it would be best if we left. There are clouds on the horizon." And that was certainly true in more ways than one.

Amelia scorned Geoffrey's assistance when she went to enter his carriage, preferring Hemit's hand. Geoff noted the glances they exchanged and wondered if everyone he knew was in on this conspiracy to protect him.

The carriage went past the Pulteney Hotel on Piccadilly where throngs of people waited to greet the Grand Duchess Catherine. It had been reported that she had inspected the Whitbread Brewery, which had made the Prince Regent furious. All of the *ton* knew the strong Whig sympathies of Samuel Whitbread, not to mention his extreme opposition to the war with Napoleon. That the Grand Duchess should meet with the Prince Regent's most vocal and radical opponent did not promise well for harmonious relations.

"I wonder what will happen when the Tsar arrives later?" Amelia said to Peter, suspecting Miss Moore would not voice an opinion on anything so ungodly as politics.

"Between the Tsar and King Frederick, not to mention General Blücher and the others, I fear London is in for a spate of parades and festive occasions the likes of which we haven't seen for some time. I wouldn't mind it so much if we could afford them."

Amelia sobered at this truism, wondering how a country could plunge into such debt while allowing its prince such extravagance.

Miss Moore, then Mr. Warwick were deposited at their residences, followed by Peter and Mary Blandford at their house.

Peter exchanged a cautioning look with Amelia when he exited the carriage, but she wasn't sure what it was supposed to mean. She sat in stony silence as long as she could, then turned to face his lordship.

"That was to have been a very pleasant outing for us all," she said in an accusatory tone.

"You are the one who persists in seeing villains everywhere you look. May I remind you," Lord Dancy said in a perfectly odious manner, "that no one else heard that threat against my life."

"Nevertheless, I did," she declared with quiet fervency. "And you shall see for yourself—when you least expect it." Her look was intended to be censorious, then she recalled her mission. "Do you go to Lady Titheridge's rout this evening?"

"Since she is my aunt, I had best put in an appearance, I expect. She also happens to be a very dear lady, so I do not mind. I suppose you plan to go?" Lord Dancy gave Amelia a mocking grin, as though he knew full well she would dog his footsteps if possible.

"I do," she replied sedately, ignoring any implications she may have merely imagined.

The carriage drew up before the Spencer house and Amelia prepared to get out. She sensed Lord Dancy wished to add something to what he had said, so paused for a moment at the open door, looking down into his handsome face. The most peculiar sensations stirred within her when she stared at him like this. It was as though a flock of demented butterflies had taken residence in her stomach. She didn't much like the feeling, although she confessed—only to herself—that she relished the touch of his hands on her waist when he swung her down from the carriage.

"You will like my aunt, I believe. She is a very independent woman, something like you. One never knows what to expect from her next."

Amelia caught his glance at her reticule where her little dagger discreetly reposed. She couldn't prevent a small grin escaping. "I suppose any number of women might surprise you, were you to learn more about their habits."

"Deliver me from such a fate," his lordship said with a comical shudder.

"Until later, my lord. And . . . do be careful," she couldn't resist adding. She noted his grimace and scolded herself all the way into the house.

Up in her room she found the white cockade her aunt had bought her along with a lovely tissue silk scarf embroidered in gold thread with fleurs-de-lys. Chen Mei held up a gown of gold gauze over cream satin for Amelia's approval.

"Day not go well," Chen Mei concluded when she observed Amelia's preoccupied mood.

"He thinks I am but a fool, imagining the threat against him. He appears to have forgotten that man at Astley's. Or is it that he resents my concern?"

"As it is impossible to please men in all things, our only care should be to satisfy our own consciences," Chen Mei counseled. It had not been necessary to ask who the "he" was; there was only one man who obsessed Amelia to the exclusion of most else.

"And that is what I must do. My conscience would never give me peace if something happened to his lordship. I owe him a great deal. I should not have liked to be burned in that horrible fire." She exchanged a look with her companion that met with a nod of total agreement.

"Missee go to party tonight, see him again. Bad man may try then. You be prepared."

"I have my dagger. What else could I bring with me? That I could put in my reticule, that is."

Chen Mei crossed the room to the dressing table to pick up a crystal vial of vinaigrette. She held it up to show Amelia, then removed the stopper. A sniff of the contents brought tears to her eyes, and she hastily replaced the covering.

"This velly strong, throw it at man . . . before you throw

dagger." She dropped the vial into Amelia's golden reticule, then added the dagger along with a comb, a handkerchief, and a few other essentials. "You find?"

"I shall find it, for it has a peculiar shape to it." Amelia sank down upon her bed, gazing thoughtfully at her companion. "Little did I dream when I left Macao that I would be embroiled in an effort to prevent the murder of a man I admire. He must not die, Chen Mei. I do hope he remembers to wear his amulet."

"You take rest for now, be sharp when you leave for party."

At dinner her aunt inquired about the outing, expressing dismay to learn that it had ended so badly. "You may wish to consider forgetting this business about Lord Dancy, my love," she advised. "It would seem to me that the gentleman does not appreciate your efforts on his behalf."

Amelia nodded. "I cannot please him, I know that. However, I must tend my conscience, dear Aunt. Could I ever forgive myself if something terrible happened to his lordship while I merely stood by and did nothing?"

"I suppose you have the right of it, love." Aunt Ermintrude gave Amelia a doubtful look.

Amelia suspected that her aunt was not entirely convinced, but changed the topic to the events of the day that had occupied her aunt for hours.

"I must thank you for the pretty cockade, dear Aunt, and this shawl is quite the most splendid I have ever seen."

"Yes, well," her aunt said in a pleased fluster. "I want us to look our best this evening. 'Tis rumored that the Prince Regent will attend."

Suitably impressed, Amelia thanked her aunt once again for her thoughtfulness, then completed her meal while listening to her aunt's chatter.

The ride to the Titherbridge mansion proved the usual frustrating wait while what seemed like every carriage in London attempted to deposit passengers before the doors.

At last Amelia and Mrs. Spencer left their carriage to walk up the red carpet stretched before the Titherbridge front door. A throng of people clustered to either side, admiring or simply staring at the guests while they arrived.

Amelia glanced at them, wondering if the Frenchman hid

among them, then entered the house with her aunt hoping
to discover Lord Dancy before his enemy did.

Lady Titherbridge had managed to snare Lord Dancy
into standing by her side to greet the guests. If London was
thin of company, it couldn't be noticed here. Gentlemen
clustered about the card room, gossiping, arranging for
games of cards, calling for wine, and in general enjoying
themselves. A few ladies looked vexed, although a good
many of them joined in card games as well.

Amelia greeted Lady Titherbridge with a pleasant smile
and a proper curtsy before offering her hand to Lord
Dancy.

He totally forgot his manners and used her first name
while holding her hand far too long. "Good evening,
Amelia."

"My lord, how pleasant to see you again," she replied
primly. She glanced about her with concern, hoping no one
had overheard his slip.

His aunt appeared to have noticed, but since she said
nothing, Amelia could not be certain.

"Geoffrey, why do you not escort Miss Longworth
about. I am sure you could find something of interest to
show her." Her ladyship turned back to Mrs. Spencer for a
few words before the next arrival came to the top of the
stairs.

"You need not show me about, sir," Amelia protested. "I
well understand how you feel about me." She gave him a
polite look that did not conceal the distress in her eyes.

"You cannot possibly know how I feel about you,
Amelia. Even *I* am not certain at times," he concluded in an
undertone that Amelia barely heard.

He placed her hand on his arm, then proceeded to stroll
about the handsome rooms, pointing out to her any number
of elegant objects collected by his aunt during her travels.

"It is all quite dazzling," Amelia declared while inspecting a series of tiny animals carved from semiprecious
stones. She turned from them to study a tall cabinet. Lord
Dancy opened the doors for her.

"See here, different woods are used on each of the draw-
ers." He gestured to several rare woods.

"Most remarkable," she replied, trying not to notice his warm clasp on her arm when they resumed their walk.

"So here you are," Peter said in an amused tone when he joined them. "Doing the pretty, Geoff? Evening, Amelia. Geoff, your aunt has more clutter in her rooms than even Prinney manages. Wherever does she find them all."

"She collects them on her travels, Peter. How she gets them all back in one piece mystifies me."

Amelia listened to the details of his aunt's fascinating life when she suddenly observed a man acting rather oddly. Instead of simply walking straight up to where they stood, he sidled and edged, quite as though he hoped to move close to them undetected. He might have succeeded but for his dress, which was so boringly dull that he stood out like a weed in the midst of a bed of petunias.

Not bothering to disturb Lord Dancy, Amelia slipped one hand into her reticule, closing her fingers about her vinaigrette. With stealth, she removed the crystal vial, took off the stopper, then waited.

The flash of metal proved what she waited for. Before the Frenchman—for that was who she firmly believed the man to be—could cock his gun and take aim, she tossed the contents of her vial in the villain's face. He sputtered, cried out in distress, and waved his gun about in the air.

"Amelia!" Lord Dancy exclaimed, then immediately understanding what was afoot, dove at the villain, knocking him to the floor.

Peter quickly dropped to the fellow's side, pinning his arm while removing the pistol from his hand. The flow of French was such Amelia was glad she was not accomplished in the language.

"Someone fetch a man from Bow Street," Geoffrey demanded. "I'll tie this chap up in the meantime."

In the distance music could be heard, with an unusual hush from the guests.

"His Royal Highness the Prince Regent has arrived."

"It wanted only that," Geoffrey moaned as he turned his gaze to where Amelia stood prudently returning her empty vial to her reticule.

Chapter Fourteen

Everyone froze, Geoffrey tightly holding the Frenchman with both hands. In the next room the murmurs of the pleased guests could be heard as the Prince made his way through the throng of people.

Peter darted a look at Geoffrey, then said, "I'll go. They most likely won't believe a servant. Who would, with a wild tale like this?" He strode from the room, escaping before the Prince came along the hall that led to the card room.

Amelia took a step in the same direction, thinking to fend off His Royal Highness. Surely there should be someone to warn who could prevent the Regent from straying into this room.

There wasn't time. Before she could accomplish her intent, the Prince had paused in the double doorway, staring in perplexity at the peculiar scene before him. Amelia sank into a curtsy worthy of a royal presence. Then she backed toward the wall, hoping to go unremarked.

"I say, dashed odd behavior, Dancy. What's going on here? We should like an explanation." The portly first gentleman of England advanced a few steps into the room, one of the lovely cedar-paneled anterooms in Lady Titherbridge's London home.

Geoffrey straightened, attempting to keep a firm hold on his prisoner and yet give due respect to his prince. "Please stop where you are, Your Royal Highness. This man just attempted to shoot me. I believe he is a French spy."

The Prince halted in his steps, unsure whether Lord Dancy was being amusing or meant what he said.

A gentleman at the Prince's side murmured something in the royal ear, and the Prince nodded. "Bow Street on its way, I trust?" His Royal Highness inquired as he turned to quit the room.

"May it please Your Royal Highness, I should like to tie this fellow up before they arrive. He's an elusive one." Geoffrey looked about as though in search of a sturdy cord or something else that would serve the purpose.

The Prince merely waved his hand as a signal of sorts that he fully concurred, then left the room, murmuring words to the effect that Lady Titherbridge had invited rather uncommon guests this evening. Not one of the men remained behind to help Lord Dancy, all assuming that he had things well under control and needed no assistance. The wretched man wouldn't ask for help, either. Yet Amelia well recalled how the Frenchman had slipped just like an eel from Chen Mei's grasp when at Astley's.

Amelia waited until the Prince and his party ambled along the hall to the card room, then dashed over to snatch a length of drapery cord from next to the window. "Here, this ought to suffice." She watched from a prudent distance as Geoffrey tried to wrap the cord around the fellow. It was an awkward business at best.

"Maybe I could tie the knot while you hold him still?" Amelia inquired at last.

"No," Geoffrey snapped. "Keep your distance."

Amelia took an alarmed step backward as the Frenchman suddenly wrenched himself from Geoffrey's hold, then lunged for the gun that Peter had placed on a nearby table.

Geoffrey dove after him, but was too late to prevent what followed. The Frenchman grabbed the gun, then aimed it at Geoffrey. In slightly imperfect English he said, "I should shoot you now and be done with it."

Crouching warily, Geoffrey slowly straightened to his full six feet in height. When the other man held a gun, height mattered not in the least. "What do you wait for?"

Amelia desperately looked to the hallway. There had been only the three of them in here and Peter had gone. Now there appeared nothing she might do to save the man to whom she owed her life. It seemed that people either hovered about the Prince Regent or clustered about in the main salons. Not a soul ventured along this particular hall.

"Please . . . do not shoot him. What has he done to you that he ought to die by your hand?" she pleaded.

"He was a spy. Had he not been in Spain, in Portugal, in France, many lives would not have been lost," the man snapped back at her.

"He was so important, then?" Amelia said trying to stall for time, although she had no idea what she might accomplish.

"He drew maps, talked to the people. He is a devil, for he knew when our generals planned to strike next."

"I do not see why you must shoot him for that," Amelia said in a reasonable voice. "You would have done the same thing. In war all is fair, I have heard tell. Put down your gun, and the charge will be less," she coaxed. "I feel certain that plotting against a peer of the realm is not as great a crime as actually killing one."

Geoffrey took a step closer to the man.

"Do you not have a family in France? Someone who will miss you, worry when you do not return?" Amelia pressed. "For you must see that you will die. In England you simply cannot kill a man and then walk off as though nothing has happened. Why do you not hand me the gun?" She spoke in a soft, almost mesmerizing voice.

"Silence!" the Frenchman shouted. "You, woman. Come closer."

With a glance at Geoffrey, Amelia took several hesitant steps toward the madman. At least, he seemed utterly demented.

Suddenly his arm snaked out to clasp her to his side. He sneered at Geoffrey. "I take your lady with me. She will guarantee my freedom. You," he said to Amelia, "you have spoiled all my plans. I will take you along, then maybe I will shoot you when I am done with you."

His little chuckle chilled Amelia right down her spine all the way to her toes. It occurred to her that this lunatic might actually shoot her, and she trembled. What else he might do to her did not cross her mind as yet.

Somehow—and Amelia never understood quite how—the Frenchman—with his gun close to her ribs managed to whisk their way along the hall to the rear of the house where he propelled Amelia down the stairs ahead of him. "*Rapide*," he kept murmuring in their mad scramble.

Once they had gained the narrow street that ran by Lady Titherbridge's home, he forced Amelia into a small carriage that waited for him. A spate of French to his small, wiry companion followed, and then the carriage tore out along the street at such a rate that Amelia figured that no one could possibly have followed them.

Huddled against the shabby squabs of the musty carriage, Amelia listened to the two men discuss what they ought to do with her. It seemed that her interference could cost her life this time.

The carriage turned a corner, and Amelia's heart sank. With so few lights any possible pursuer would have had a difficult time to follow them. Now they had altered their direction, there was no way she could be trailed.

Geoffrey paused at the side gate at his aunt's home, then ran to her stables. He ignored the carriages, for there was no time to harness one. Instead he grabbed the reins of a horse that apparently had been out not too long ago and had not yet returned to his stall.

"Lord Dancy," the coachman cried in some alarm.

"In a hurry, Soames. Explain later." With that terse remark, Geoffrey and his mount dashed from the stable. He urged the horse along the same street that Amelia had been taken not long before, turning where he thought he had seen them turn.

There was but a small sliver of a moon, not enough for much help, but the lights here and there offered a little benefit. Geoffrey persisted. It was unthinkable to just do nothing when Amelia had saved his hide so many times. First there was Clarissa and her scheme, then came the danger at Astley's, followed by the damage to the curricle. That was not enough, but she had goaded him into the balloon ride that had most likely prevented his being shot. Taunton and his card cheating had been exposed, thanks to her, and now this evening. He would be safer if she disappeared, he suspected. She seemed to attract danger.

She also attracted him, but that was all it could be—attraction. Good grief, fancy being married to a woman like Amelia! It was enough to make a strong man turn pale!

The street before him was empty. Not a carriage to be

seen, not even a person moving about, much less a Charlie he might ask. Quite obviously they had turned once again, the darkness covering their direction.

Geoffrey kept going, pausing at each street intersection and alley to stare into the night, searching, hoping to see a clue.

Nothing.

At last he turned his horse toward his aunt's house. If only he'd had something better than a slippery drapery cord to use; the fellow had slithered out of that like melted butter. If only the Prince hadn't arrived at that precise moment, Peter would have been able to help. If only Amelia had not been present, or at least not so close. He suspected that once again she had saved his life at risk of her own. If only he had been able to save her from being dragged along with that lunatic Frenchman.

The thought of just what that man might do to Amelia before shooting her spurred him to action. He tore along the streets back to his aunt's, then up the back stairs, hunting for Peter or a man from Bow Street.

Back in the anteroom he found them both looking puzzled, with the Robin Redbreast sounding annoyed, saying something about a wild-goose chase. Geoffrey plunged into the room, coming to an abrupt halt beside Peter.

"He managed to escape, taking Amelia with him."

Peter cursed the man in several languages.

While none of them were known to the runner from Bow Street, he could guess at the meaning with no effort. He hastily identified himself to Geoffrey as Ben Tobin. "Do you have any idea at all where they might be, milord?" the runner asked.

"Geoffrey," his aunt said upon charging into the room, "I just heard the most astounding thing from the Prince. He said something about a spy being held in here by you, of all people. Poor man. He must have been imagining things." She stopped, glancing from Geoffrey to Peter to the stranger in the red vest.

Geoffrey shook his head, giving his aunt a grim look. "Fear not. Chap has been giving me a spot of trouble. Now he has bolted, taking Amelia with him."

"Dear me," Lady Titherbridge replied. "And I had

thought India to be a dangerous place. What will you do
now?" she demanded. Having traveled about the world
much of her adult life, few things daunted her. She was accustomed to taking charge of events that crossed her path
and looked to be fully prepared to do the same here.

Geoffrey began to pace back and forth as an aid to thinking. He rubbed his chin absently while his mind frantically
searched for a clue he might have missed.

"Nothing. I cannot think of a blessed thing he said that
might give an inkling as to where they intend to go. He said
he will shoot her once he has finished with her," he baldly
declared in spite of his aunt's presence.

"Good grief," the lady said in a fading voice, for she well
understood the implications and the effect on a gently
reared girl.

"You may as well know," Geoffrey said in an aside to
Peter, "that she saved my life yet again. Stepped forward to
argue with the chap, just as though he didn't have a gun, or
wasn't a raving lunatic. Talked him out of shooting me and
ended up being taken hostage. He wants a free passage
from England with no promise that he will give up
Amelia—unharmed or otherwise."

Lady Titherbridge murmured her excuses, for she had a
houseful of guests and the royal prince to entertain. She
promised to inform Amelia's aunt in such a manner that the
dear lady would not have an attack of the vapors.

Geoffrey realized that he had totally forgotten Mrs.
Spencer. He thanked his aunt, then returned to the serious
problem at hand. He, Peter, and soft-spoken Ben Tobin put
their heads together to formulate some sort of plan.

In short order Geoffrey led the two men along the route
the abductor's carriage had gone. They peered into shadows, rode along for a ways down each street, but it was
hopeless. Amelia and the Frenchman had vanished.

To the north of London Amelia warily made her way
along the steep stairs to what appeared to be a loft above
some shop or warehouse, propelled by the Frenchman. His
name appeared to be Claude from what she could make of
the conversation between the madman and his helper.

"Take care," she said in English, not wanting him to

know she could understand his French, or Portuguese, for that matter, although neither of the men attempted it now.

Inside the door at the top of the stairs she discovered a rather stark room with three wooden chairs, one cot, and a small wooden table that looked to have legs of varying lengths. The Frenchman thrust her onto one of the chairs, after which he tied her in place using stout rope that Geoffrey could have used to advantage.

Amelia pressed her reticule to her lap, finding a small comfort in the knowledge that her little dagger reposed within.

Across the room the two men argued about what to do with her.

"I am tired," Amelia said at long last, wishing she'd had the foresight to have eaten something before being carried away. "Permit me to sleep." She glanced longingly at the cot without a thought to what might evolve.

The men laughed and made crude remarks that prompted Amelia to wish she had kept her mouth shut. So, she didn't pursue the matter of sleep. Eventually she nodded from sheer exhaustion, but it was a fitful drifting in and out.

She woke to find one of the men had disappeared, and the Frenchman sat in another chair contemplating Amelia with a look she preferred to ignore. Dismissing it from her mind was better than dwelling upon possibilities.

When morning arrived, it brought her one roll and a cup of bitter coffee, brought up by the accomplice. Apparently they had decided to keep her alive for the moment. Perhaps, she thought with rising hope, they intended to use her as a means of exiting the country. Then she recalled that Claude had also announced he would shoot her regardless. It did not look to be a good day. She wondered where Geoffrey Dancy was, and thanked the heavens he, at least, was safe.

The day seemed interminable. She had begged twice to use a necessary, and had been shown to a closet with a chamber pot within and precious little privacy.

It seemed that Claude and his accomplice—named Henri, Amelia deduced from their conversation—could not agree on the next step in their escape. Nor could they agree on whether they ought to go to France and hope to fade into oblivion, or possibly to assist Napoleon to flee Elba, or if perhaps they ought to find some ship sailing to America. Henri had heard that New Orleans offered possibilities for the French.

But all that day they ignored Amelia. She grew hungry, and she was more tired from the strain than she had ever been in her life. But as long as they left her alone, she would not complain. She listened and watched and remained silent.

When darkness fell Henri grudgingly brought Amelia a cup of bitter coffee and another roll, allowing her the freedom to eat by releasing her hands. Apparently they felt that merely tying her to the chair was sufficient to keep her quiet—that and keeping a perpetual watch on her movements. Where could she go in this neighborhood and be safe? For Amelia suspected she was far from Mayfair.

"I do not see how you allowed that man to simply disappear with my niece, Lord Dancy," Mrs. Spencer declared. "I am glad I have discouraged her interest in you. I doubt you would make a fit husband. No doubt you would lose your wife before you left the church!" She shredded a cambric handkerchief as she perched tensely upon her sofa. Her worried gaze sought that of Amelia's devoted companion.

Chen Mei sat upon her ottoman, her almond-shaped eyes staring at Geoffrey with such dislike that he felt chilled. "I not there when she need me," the Cantonese woman stated in a bleak voice.

"Believe me, I would rather he had shot me than taken Amelia, Mrs. Spencer. With his temper, he might have proved to have terrible aim, and we would both have been spared." His attempt at a bit of levity fell flat.

"But that poor girl," Mrs. Spencer continued as though Lord Dancy had not spoken. "She must be utterly terrified."

Geoffrey recalled the words spoken by the Frenchman and shuddered. "Terrified" would scarcely cover Amelia's reaction if those men lived up to their threat.

"The wise place virtue in thought," Chen Mei offered, then proceeded to follow her own maxim.

Ben Tobin was ushered into the Spencer salon by Grimm. The Bow Street runner appeared to have had a good night's sleep, for he looked fresh and ready to do battle. Neatly attired, his red vest spruce and brushed, he greeted Mrs. Spencer with the kindest of smiles.

Geoffrey wondered how the man could have slept when Amelia was in the hands of that lunatic. Then he realized this was merely a job for the man. Amelia didn't have reality for him other than a name. Geoffrey had fared badly during the night, finally falling into an exhausted slumber, only to have a nightmare about Amelia. She had screamed as those two men reached for her, and Geoffrey had awakened with a heart full of despair. In a city the size of London what chance did they have of finding one girl cleverly hidden away?

"We have been combing the area where the French émigrés tend to congregate," Mr. Tobin informed them all. "There are several men who meet your description, but only two of them are recent arrivals to the area. One has lived there for some years. Nevertheless we shall investigate all three."

"I will go with you," Geoffrey declared. He hated the inactivity and feeling of helplessness.

Ben Tobin eyed Geoffrey, then nodded. "You may as well. At least I'll have you under my feet instead of going off on your own."

Mrs. Spencer rose from the sofa, offering her hand to Lord Dancy in farewell. "I trust you to bring my girl back to me, my lord. I depend on you."

Rising from her ottoman Chen Mei tottered to the door, declaring as she went, "I go, too. Tian Li may have need of me."

Both men gave quick shakes of their heads and began to deny her.

Mrs. Spencer put a hand on Lord Dancy's arm. "Please allow her to go along. She is extremely clever and seems to have an uncanny sense about some things. She may be of help to you. Besides, she will drive me to distraction here with her habits, the least of which are her wails that frighten the maids."

Geoffrey turned his gaze to the runner. "Mr. Tobin?"

"You never know," replied the soft-spoken man. "Let her come."

So when the search continued, it was with the addition of a Chinese lady dressed in her usual outlandish garb.

But two days passed, with the trio growing more and more frustrated when the leads proved futile. Finally they had one hope remaining. A man who delivered coal reported some French chaps had let the loft above a hat manufactory in Marylebone.

Upon that clue the three based their expectations. Chen Mei withdrew the dagger from her sleeve. Ben Tobin glanced at it, shared a look with Geoffrey, then made his way quietly up the steps, one at a time. At last they all reached the top.

"Allow me," Geoffrey said grimly. He reached out a hand to push open the door.

Chen Mei shoved him aside and darted into the room, dagger at the ready and aimed for the man she hated, Claude. In moments it was all over. Chen Mei cut the ropes to free her Tian Li.

It took a few moments for Amelia to regain feeling in her limbs. She bent over to rub her ankles, then rose from the chair. She rushed into Geoffrey's arms, taking refuge there, seeming to relish the feel of his body as he wrapped his arms about her in a crushing embrace.

"Are you all right?" were his first words after he searched her face, as though there might be some indication of the ordeal she had endured written there.

"I am now," she whispered, her throat sounding tight.

Across the room, Ben Tobin efficiently tied up the accomplice while Chen Mei held her dagger to the throat of the Frenchman. She looked determined that he wouldn't be allowed to slip away from her again. Geoffrey wagered that the fellow would have a scar—for as long as he lived—from the pressure of that little dagger.

A second runner joined them and took over the guard on the Frenchman.

"His name is Claude, and he intended to take me with him to Dover. I was to be his insurance." Amelia turned away from the sight and sound of the Frenchman being led from the loft. He raved and ranted against the English, Dancy, and Amelia in particular.

"Your aunt is anxious to have you home."

"It has been days, but it seems like years."

"For all of us. Poor Chen Mei nearly drove Tobin mad with her demands. She will undoubtedly not allow you out of her sight for some time to come."

"And you?" the whispery voice said hesitantly.

"Not now, Amelia. We shall discuss all else later when you have had a decent sleep and food in whatever order you please."

Chen Mei had followed the men down the steep stairs to make certain the chap didn't get free again. Geoffrey and Amelia were now alone in the loft.

"I knew that you would save me. You always have," Amelia said in a tremulous voice.

Geoffrey felt her melt against him and a rush of tenderness overwhelmed him when her slim arms encircled him. Poor Amelia, now safe and in his arms. When she lifted her face to give him a tentative smile, he did what any gentleman of sensibility would have done. He kissed her gently, then more fiercely as he remembered what he had gone through to find her, how worried he'd been, wondering, hoping she would somehow survive untouched and unscathed.

She leaned her head against his chest, then said in a very contented-sounding way, "You may take me home now."

Rather than permit her to attempt the stairs in her weakened condition, Geoffrey scooped her into his arms and carefully carried her to the ground level and out to where the carriage awaited them.

Tobin gave a salute and said something about seeing him later. Geoffrey merely nodded. He had to tend to Amelia.

She nestled in his lap all the way to the Spencer house. Chen Mei kept an eagle eye on the pair across from where she perched. Her eyes missed nothing, not even the rosy glow on cheeks that ought to have been ashen.

Grimm opened the door and gasped, for once definitely shaken. One of the maids sniffed into her apron, then disappeared from view.

Mrs. Spencer hurried from the salon where she had spent most of the days Amelia had been gone, dabbing her handkerchief at her eyes even as she barked out orders to one and all.

Geoffrey carried Amelia up the stairs to her room. Chen Mei had darted past him and now had the bed covers drawn back and awaiting her charge.

"I shall see you when you are fully recovered. I fancy you need sleep as much as I do," he joked.

Amelia studied him, then turned her head away. "As you please, sir. And," she added as Geoffrey turned to leave the bedroom, "Thank you for saving my life . . . again."

He paused at the door, meeting her gaze. "That makes us even, I believe . . . again."

It took two days for Amelia to feel more the thing. She ate a breakfast of tea, toast, and marmalade, then slept around the clock.

On the third day she knew she could not postpone what had to be any longer, and she sent for Lord Dancy.

"My lord," she said when the polite amenities had been observed. "I believe you wished to speak with me." Her heart was so full of hope. Her love for this man had sustained her all through the incredible hours of her capture. But now, looking at that handsome face of his, so closed, so shuttered, she began to fear the worst.

"Dash it all, Amelia, this is exceedingly difficult for me." He rose and began to pace the floor, looking everywhere but at Amelia. Her heart sank even further. .

"Do go on," she replied evenly, giving no hint of her emotions.

"When I saved you from danger while in Portugal, I was performing a rescue of sorts, and while I did save your life in Portsmouth, it was nothing that any gentleman would not have done given the same circumstances. Since then," he plunged on after a moment's reflection, "you have pulled my chestnuts from any number of fires."

Amelia frowned, unsure of what he meant by this expression.

"You have extricated me from several awkward and dangerous situations," he explained when he observed her confusion. "That business with Clarissa was admittedly difficult. The curricle race—now that I might have managed on my own, you know. As to Astley's, the chap ran away and later missed me at the balloon ascension thanks to your coercing me into taking that sail. Not that I didn't enjoy it once I recovered from the height," he admitted. "The affair with Taunton and the cheating, now, well, I might have been able to expose him myself, had you not been so precipitate. But this latest, when you were placed in such terrible danger—Amelia, this must cease."

"I suspected you would say as much, my lord," Amelia replied formally.

"Then you agree? We are settled once and for all. You will no longer dog my footsteps and make my life a terror for fear that some disaster will befall me, and you as well?" He paused, staring down at her from his green eyes with such anticipation that Amelia felt her heart grow cold.

"Is that how you view it? I cause apprehension when you see me?" Amelia repressed a sigh, knowing it might well lead to the tears that were rapidly gathering. She did not want his final sight of her to be one of a watering pot.

"I propose that henceforth we shall be as polite strangers," he suggested in a coaxing voice that nearly finished breaking Amelia's shattered heart.

"By all means, sir." She rose from the sofa, praying that her trembling knees would not betray her. Extending her hand in a graceful gesture, she concluded, "I trust you will excuse me, I am still a trifle tired. Perhaps some country air will improve my spirits. Good-bye, Lord Dancy," Amelia said, firmly controlling those still-threatening tears. "And do take care," she could not resist adding for one last time.

Amelia swept from the room, chin high, legs steady. She marched to the bottom of the stairs that led to the second floor and paused to see him slowly make his way down to the entrance hall and out the front door.

He was gone from her life, forever. He wouldn't change his mind. She had driven him to distraction.

Tearing up the stairs and around the corner, she burst into her room to throw herself on her bed. A good bout of weeping would heal the wounds, Chen Mei had said when Amelia had hurt herself as a child. Amelia felt as though no amount of tears could heal this wound to her heart.

Chapter Fifteen

"You were quite right, Chen Mei. The man is a fool. He does not wish my help, even though I love him dearly and want only the best for him." Amelia leaned against the headboard, scrunching pillows behind her so she might be more comfortable. Her bout of weeping had been brief. Indignation had taken its place.

"Remember," her companion said, "it is the beautiful bird that gets caged."

"You mean there are compensations. Perhaps. Although I fail to see what the compensations might be in this case. You think that I might find someone better?" Amelia considered that idea for several moments, and finally nodded. Her innate honesty compelled her to agree. "I imagine there is a man who might suit me more admirably." Her tone implied that it would be next to impossible.

"The man who fail to appreciate your devotion is not worthy of you," Chen Mei declared with narrowed eyes.

Amelia caught sight of her companion fingering her dagger and hastily said, "You will not do anything foolish, Chen Mei. I have no wish to learn that Lord Dancy has expired of a dagger wound. Besides, I have decided you are correct, and I shall turn my attention elsewhere."

"Good." The Cantonese woman gave a decisive nod, tucking the dagger back up inside her sleeve.

"Remember I have served his lordship as was proper, yet it did not nurture his regard. It is for the best that I forget him. I shall agree that I owe him nothing more."

A soft scraping on the door was followed by Aunt Ermintrude peeking around the corner. "My dear little love, what has been going on here? You look very much as though you have indulged in a bout of tears." She stood near the door, gazing at Amelia with some caution.

"Never fear, I shan't turn into a watering pot."

"Good. I wish you to join me in a theater expedition this evening. There will be any number of important people there, and the program is touted as being exceptionally brilliant." She approached the bed with a hesitant smile, as though uncertain what reaction Amelia might have to her suggestion.

"Aunt . . ." Amelia protested, not feeling much like going out where she could possibly see Lord Dancy. Even if she intended to turn her interest elsewhere, she needed a bit of time first.

"No silliness," her aunt scolded, wagging a finger at Amelia. "I suspect that you have decided that you and Lord Dancy are not destined to make a pair. In that event you ought to be casting about to see upon whom you will decide. For you must, you know." Her aunt plumped herself on the edge of the bed, taking one of Amelia's slim hands in her own soft, pudgy one. "Your papa wishes you to marry well, and to please both of you it is necessary to find a man who has both a proper background and will cherish you, for I know that is what you wish."

"True. I have been rather obsessed by Lord Dancy, have I not? Although not as fatally as Lady Caroline Lamb with Byron, I should hope." Amelia grimaced at the very idea.

"Gracious, no. Now, I suggest we make an expedition to the milliner's shop. Buying a lovely new bonnet is just the thing to cheer a girl."

Determined not to fall prey to the green melancholy, Amelia slid from her bed and permitted Chen Mei to help her dress for the outing. Before leaving her room, Amelia paused to issue a caution. "I shall be fine, and there will be no thought of retribution against Lord Dancy. Is that clear?"

Chen Mei agreed, although most reluctantly.

Joining her aunt in the carriage, Amelia considered the devotion of her companion and hoped that she obeyed Amelia. While angry and hurt, Amelia still cared too much for the dratted man to permit him to be injured or worse.

Later, after a successful trip to the milliner's, Amelia

beamed a smile at her aunt and confessed, "You were right. I am tremendously cheered." And, she added to herself, she had not observed Lord Dancy out and about, although the Spencer carriage hadn't gone anywhere near Bond Street or St. James's, where the clubs were located.

It was with a lighter heart that Amelia dressed for the theater that evening. She wore a pretty gown of celestial blue satin that had an overdress of silvery spider gauze. In her blond curls Chen Mei wove an arrangement of silver leaves and blue silk flowers. While drawing on her long gloves, Amelia glanced at the looking glass, well pleased with what she saw reflected.

The streets around the Drury Lane Theater were clogged with elegant carriages and people pressing to enter the premises. When at last she and her aunt were able to go inside, she found the noise considerable.

Amelia searched the lobby for a familiar face and was relieved when she saw Peter and Mary Blandford with Chloe Moore and Denzil Warwick. She suspected that Peter revealed more than a passing interest in Miss Moore, and if so, fine. Amelia liked Peter. But that was all. Mary appeared attracted to the somewhat stuffy Mr. Warwick, but then, Mary was a trifle on the reserved side herself.

Of Lord Dancy there was no sign. Following a few moments to say hello, the parties went their separate ways. Their boxes were not close, and Amelia did not expect to see them during the intervals. Besides, Mary looked so uncomfortable, as though she wondered about Lord Dancy and feared to inquire.

During the first act of the tragedy Amelia took the chance to study the audience. She had not wished to when they first came in, for if Lord Dancy was there, she was not certain she wanted to know about it. Now she did.

It was as though her eyes were drawn only to him, for she discovered where he sat on the far side of the theater almost immediately. He looked well, she noted with relief. Then she observed that a woman shared the box with him when he leaned over to whisper something into her ear.

Even from this distance she appeared beautiful. Not in the sprig of youth, nevertheless she glowed with a radiance that a woman has when showered with the attentions of a handsome gentleman. Diamonds glittered about her throat above the black gown that dipped low over an ample bosom. She appeared an expert at flirtation, using her fan with skill.

Stupid man, Amelia said to herself. Resolution firmed within her heart. Henceforth he would cease to exist. Amelia would search elsewhere—far away elsewhere.

Calm in her determination, Amelia faced the stage where the drama unfolded. She paid little attention to the acting or anything else for that matter. Plans were formulated in her mind only to be discarded immediately. At last, about the time of the final curtain and just before the farce, she decided.

"I should like to travel in England, dear Aunt," Amelia announced after comments on the drama had trailed off and there was relative silence in the box.

"I suppose you saw Dancy and his lady friend over there and now wish to do something foolish," Aunt Ermintrude said in dismay.

"Not really," Amelia replied judiciously. "But what about my uncle? Could I not visit him? To tell you the truth I have not been that drawn to any of the young beaus I have met in London. Perhaps I might find a country gentleman more to my liking? I think the prospect of a husband who might gamble away my fortune rather distressing. And most all the London bucks gamble."

"On curricle races and cricket matches and the like," her aunt said with a nod. "I daresay what you point out has merit. Not that country gentlemen do not indulge in gaming. Horse racing and other temptations exist there, too, you understand. I fear I shall miss you dreadfully when you depart. You truly feel that you must?"

Ignoring the hopeful look on her dearest aunt's face, it took but a glance in the direction of Lord Dancy's box to firm Amelia's resolve.

"I shall leave once you write my uncle to inform him I should like to make an acquaintanceship."

"Your mama's brother is the Viscount Quainton. Lord Quainton is somewhat of a recluse, preferring plants to people."

"Intelligent man," Amelia said with a final glance at Lord Dancy. "You *will* write to him?"

Her distress obvious, Aunt Ermintrude nodded most reluctantly. "If I must. He took in those servants, most likely he will take you in as well."

During the week it took for an express to reach her uncle and his answer to reach Mrs. Spencer, Amelia packed her belongings, shopped for a very few things, and endured a call to Mary and Peter Blandford.

When Peter left the room to fetch his map of the countryside so Amelia might have a better notion as to where her uncle resided, Mary moved closer to her guest.

"Amelia, you are not leaving because of that dreadful woman Lord Dancy was with at the theater, are you?" Mary reached out a comforting hand to pat Amelia's arm. "Perhaps it is for the best, for I suspect he did not appreciate your concern for him."

"Chen Mei said the same thing. No, I merely long to see a bit of the countryside and visit my uncle. However, you must promise me that you will not reveal my whereabouts to anyone, particularly Lord Dancy."

"What's this?" Peter asked as he returned. "Dancy giving you a spot of trouble?"

"No more than usual. I want you both to promise me that you will not tell anyone where I go," Amelia repeated for Peter's benefit.

"She means Lord Dancy in particular," Mary added.

Both promised to do as Amelia requested, although Peter did not look happy about it.

"Dash it all, Amelia, you and Dancy go well together. He didn't mean anything serious by attending the theater with Mrs. Hawtaine."

Amelia bestowed a level look on her friend. With a half smile she said, "It matters not in the least. I decided I would look elsewhere for a husband. Since Lord Dancy has freed me of the obligation I owed to him, I may search the country."

She studied the map Peter remembered to offer her. The estate was located in Wiltshire. "It is not far from Salisbury, so I shall have delightful shopping and who knows what else? Although I suppose the assembly rooms are not open in the summer." She parted from her friends a bit teary-eyed, but resolved.

When the viscount's reply arrived that he would accept a visit from his niece, Amelia packed the last of her belongings, prepared to set out at once.

"For," she explained, "I wish to travel in comfort and it will take days to get there in safety."

In total agreement, Aunt Ermintrude gave a final dinner party for her dear girl, including not only Peter and Mary Blandford, Chloe Moore and Denzil Warwick, but a number of other interesting people Amelia had met while in London. Lord Dancy was not present.

The trip was most pleasant, although the dust from the roads was dreadful.

When they arrived at the front gates to her uncle's home, Amelia was impressed. The iron gates swung open and her post chaise brought her to the front door of the house. A man she presumed to be the butler hurried across the terrace and down the steps to open the door and escort her into the house. Behind her Chen Mei gave orders as to the disposal of Amelia's belongings.

In the long central hall Amelia was turned over to a housekeeper who took her up to a lovely bedroom decorated in shades of lavender. Once alone, Amelia hurried to the window to see that she overlooked a wandering stream where three swans leisurely paddled along.

"Oh," she exclaimed to Chen Mei when her companion tottered into the room, carrying a collection of parcels, "this is a splendid house and has a marvelous view. How odd that my uncle did not come to greet me. Perhaps I had best search him out."

With her companion's blessing, Amelia set off to find her elusive relative.

The butler directed her to the gardens off to the west of the house. "His lordship is overseeing the trimming of the topiary, miss. You can't miss him."

Intrigued by the idea of a topiary garden, Amelia wrapped her shawl about her, then left the house in search of the special garden.

It didn't take long to discover that the entire grounds

were planted with magnificent specimens of various shrubs
that lent themselves especially to topiary. She encountered
a hornbeam hedge with rectangular holes cut at intervals to
form an arcade of green. Yet trees clipped in amazing
shapes were everywhere she looked. Topiary garden? Why,
the entire estate was a topiary garden. How was she to locate her uncle?

The swans, followed by an assortment of ducks, gracefully paddled up to greet her near the edge of the stream.
The grass had been trimmed right up to the water's edge for
a neatly elegant walk.

Amelia marveled at the exquisite topiary animals that
loomed before her as she rounded the corner of the hornbeam hedge.

"Here now, this is to be a giraffe, not a tree," scolded a
deep bass voice.

Peering around a pyramid, Amelia encountered a tall
gentleman with a mop of unruly white hair. He wore a
shaggy corduroy frock coat that certainly had seen its best
days long ago. But there was an air about him that led her
to suspect that he was indeed her uncle. When he turned,
she found celestial blue eyes trained on her with disconcerting directness.

"Uncle!" Amelia cried with pleasure. He was much as
she remembered her mother—the blue eyes and the sameness of expression. She stepped forward to offer her hand.

"Ah, you are like your mother. Welcome," he said. He
shook her hand with an absentminded bow of sorts, then returned to scolding his gardener.

Taken aback at his abruptness, Amelia decided to study
what she could see of this part of the garden. To her left
grew a magnificent peacock, or what ultimately would be a
peacock, for the tail had not quite reached its ultimate
length. There was a frame over which it was to spread.

What appeared to be an extremely fat pig marched with a
dog of noble proportions. Some distance away she observed a series of boxwood cones and pyramids and cubes
in the more basic shapes seen in a topiary garden. She gave
the plant on which her uncle and the gardener worked a
critical inspection. A giraffe—yes, she could see the potential, but it had some ways to grow first.

Turning around she found a chair formed of greenery, with a fountain and a sundial not far away. "Oh my," she declared with amusement.

"You like my garden?" her uncle inquired.

"Indeed," Amelia replied, a little stunned with the magnitude of the place.

"Come along and tell me why you decided to visit in the country when London society is at the peak of its glory. Some man, I'll be bound." He motioned her in the direction of a pretty little summer house built to look like a tiny cottage ornée with a thatched roof and elaborate decoration.

"Not in the least," she declared stoutly and too quickly, confirming his views, she feared.

A footman materialized with a large tray holding tea, sandwiches, pastries, and bowls of fresh berries with a pitcher of thick cream. Amelia realized with a start that she was utterly starved.

"Gardening is hungry work, I find. But it keeps a man fit. How's your Aunt Spencer? Haven't seen her in an age. And your father, child? How did you leave him?"

"Aunt Spencer is fine. When I last saw him, my father looked tired, but he has been doing quite well, I believe. There is some problem with the opium trade he fears will lead to serious trouble."

"And so he sends you to England to find a suitable husband. Quite right, too." Lord Quainton stared at her a moment from beneath his white beetle-brows, then smiled.

For a time they both concentrated on the exquisite repast, Amelia appreciating the scents and sights when she raised her eyes from her plate to look out from the little cottage.

"Your trip to England . . . uneventful?" he inquired when he had reached his bowl of berries.

"Not in the least," Amelia replied with animation. She proceeded to tell him the tale of landing in Portugal, then the fire in Portsmouth.

"Speak Portuguese, I suppose, after living in Macao all this time. French?"

"And Cantonese a little as well," she added with a nod.

"Your aunt said you had a Chinese woman with you. A companion?"

Amelia agreed, then explained how she had been raised by Chen Mei following her mother's untimely demise.

"Well," he said as he concluded his small meal, "I must return to my giraffe. Heaven knows what that villain of a gardener will make of it if I am gone too long. Make yourself comfortable. I trust you are here for the peace and quiet, for there won't be any parties or balls or the like. I live simply. I like it that way."

He bowed, then strode off in the direction of the topiary giraffe in the making, bellowing for his hapless gardener whose name it seemed was Puddy. Her uncle's tailless coat flapped in the breeze, and his hair looked even wilder after he had run his fingers through it another time.

Amused, Amelia returned her teacup to the saucer, then leaned back on her chair. She had done it. Knowing how she might feel compelled to interfere in Lord Dancy's life, she had made the necessary break, left London, and now had to work out a future of sorts in the depths of Wiltshire.

Leaving the pleasant shade of the little summer house, she ambled in the direction of the stream. Here she reclined against a stately elm to watch the ducks and swans feast on whatever it was they ate.

After the hustle and excitement of London, could she cope with the dullness of a country life? Of course, she declared firmly. None of these die-away airs for her. She would explore the gardens, make the most of seeing what she could of the surrounding countryside, and enjoy herself.

When she reported to Chen Mei, it was with a cheerful visage and good account of her moderately eccentric uncle.

"One generation plants trees, another sits in their shade," Chen Mei said in Cantonese in an effort to find a maxim to fit the situation.

"Well, I scarce believe one sits in the shade of that giraffe, but it is charming nonetheless." Amelia submitted to having her gown changed for dinner and wondered all the while what her erstwhile lord was doing in London.

Geoffrey stared out of the window of his home at nothing in particular. He was free. He had not seen Amelia Longworth since that evening in the theater when he had attended with the elegant Mrs. Hawtaine.

"Chattel, indeed," he muttered.

"You wished for something, milord?" Evenson inquired from the doorway. "Something to eat, perhaps?"

"I am expecting Mr. Blandford. Show him up directly when he comes." Evenson had been nattering after Geoff to eat for days, but nothing had appealed in the least.

"Of course, milord." The butler left the room on silent feet, allowing Geoffrey to return to his musings at the window. At last he spoke aloud.

"She's an elegant armful, but I'll wager she's dashed expensive," he said to a passing chaffinch.

"Who is? The Hawtaine?" Peter entered the room, crossed to stand by Geoffrey, and looked out at the scene below. "Something in particular you wanted, or was it merely my company you seek?" he said when he'd decided that there was nothing of interest to view.

"Spot on," Geoffrey replied, shaking himself from his lethargy. He ought to be celebrating, and by Jove that was what he'd do. "Have dinner with me at White's. A bit of cards and then the opera?"

"Well, I am to take Chloe and her mother to the theater this evening. Tell you what, make it tomorrow. I'd like to go out to Lord's and watch that game. I have placed a few bets on it."

"Just the thing," Geoffrey replied. He settled his friend in a chair, joining him in a glass of canary while they chatted about casual concerns.

It seemed to Geoffrey that Peter was seeing more than a little of Chloe Moore. She was a pretty girl, but her eyes lacked a certain defiant sparkle, and she seemed far too docile for Geoff's tastes.

"You knew Amelia had gone," Peter inserted into the conversation. "She is visiting a relative in the country."

"I hadn't seen her for a time and wondered if she had returned to Macao or whatever."

"And you have Mrs. Hawtaine," Peter observed.

"You don't have to make her sound as though she were a serious disease," Geoffrey objected. Lila Hawtaine might appear a trifle haughty with her superior attitude, but underneath Geoffrey suspected she was warm and inviting. Certainly her eyes met his with a clear invitation in them. He had not decided whether to accept that invitation as yet.

The men set a time to meet on the morrow, then Peter strolled off to prepare for the evening while Geoffrey decided he would attend that rout for which he'd received an invitation. He'd accepted, then later repented. Now, he would go after all.

He knew it was a mistake the moment he crossed into the drawing room of the Haversly household. The rout was less well attended than in the past, no doubt because of the exodus to Paris. The young women who remained fluttered lashes until Geoffrey wondered that the candles stayed lit. They giggled and flirted, behaving in general precisely like what they were—husband-seeking girls. *Insipid, the lot of them.*

He'd have none of it. At least Amelia hadn't indicated she had wanted to marry him. All she had ever said was that it was her duty to care for him. There was a difference, was there not? He rather thought so.

He left early, drove to White's where he gambled until far too late, but winning an enormous sum.

"Lucky in cards, unlucky in love, old boy," said one of the men, thinking himself a great wit.

For some reason the remark hit Geoffrey as unpleasant, and he abruptly bid the gentlemen good night, hoping he'd feel more the thing tomorrow. He left the room, recalling the night that Amelia and Chen Mei had dared to enter the club. She had been helping him, exposing that cheat Taunton. But what a chance she'd taken. None of those simpering misses he had met at the rout this evening would dare such action, not even to help the man they loved.

Loved? Where had that word come from? Amelia didn't love him, although she should, given the number of times she had rescued him from one thing or another. Perhaps that was why she left? She became tired of rescuing him. Her face had turned pale when he suggested they become as strangers. Had he really meant it? He supposed he had at the time.

The next day he met Peter and they drove to Lord's cricket ground. They left the carriage beside one of the buildings in the care of Hemit, then sauntered over to join several acquaintances. The betting was heavy on the team Peter favored. Geoffrey had great hopes for his team, the underdog.

The day was hot, ideal for the batter. The wicket looked to have a bit of the devil in it, and the bowling was outstanding. It was the second day of this game; the innings had been running around 200 runs each with the teams very close in their scores. Luncheon was served at two, and they dawdled afterward, chatting and walking about to confer on one thing or another. The play resumed shortly after that and continued until the stumps were drawn at six-thirty with his team declared the winner.

Geoffrey found himself the recipient of a sizable amount of cash. His team had won. Amelia had not appeared to spirit him away from the grounds, nor had Chen Mei turned up with her dagger to ensure that his bowlers did well.

Peter clapped Geoff on the back, then good-naturedly walked with him to the carriage. They drove home in good spirits, but Geoffrey found himself wishing he could see Amelia's face when he told her the sum he'd won without her interference.

They drew up before Blandford's house. Before Peter left the curricle, Geoffrey said as casually as he might, "You told me that Amelia has gone to visit her cousin, I believe. When is she due back?"

"I don't recall saying it was her cousin, old man. And I have no idea when or even *if* she will return to London. She said something about finding a good husband in the country." Peter grinned, then walked smartly up to his door.

"Oh," Geoffrey said, reflecting that his good friend was less than forthcoming with any information.

Two days later Geoffrey engaged with another friend to do a curricle race from London to Brighton. The hour arrived and the race began with no celestial blue-eyed blonde to prevent it, nor a check for hugger-mugger of any sort.

He won the race. He tooled around Brighton acknowledging the acclaim of friends for the brilliant bit of driving. All the while he drove he found himself searching for that unlikely pair of women, the dainty blonde with her outlandish Chinese companion. They were not to be seen.

He endured a round of parties, more simpering misses—

Lord, would they ever cease that drooping eyelash trick to display demure demeanor?—and at last decided he had best return to London. Brighton might be gay to some; to him it appeared sadly wanting.

It proved to be no better in Town. Dinner seemed uninteresting; he had no appetite at all. Without Amelia around to liven up his life, it scarcely seemed worthwhile to get out of bed. Life had become as dull as a dead dog.

But . . . what could he do about it?

Chapter Sixteen

"What do you mean, you will *not* tell me where she is?" Geoffrey demanded of his good friend Blandford.

"Well," Peter said, shifting uneasily in his chair. "Dashed if I can think of why she insisted we keep mum about where she went, but she did." He looked across the morning room at White's as though wishing he were somewhere else—anywhere.

"You mean she really did not wish me to know where she went?" Geoffrey was stunned. He had young women flirting with him wherever he went, billet-doux by the score landing in his pile of mail. Never had he been told a woman not only did not care to see him, but refused to let him know where she had gone. And this wasn't any woman—it was Amelia!

"But she is mine, and you bloody well know it!" he raged at his friend.

Peter merely shrugged, concealing a smile beneath a hastily raised hand. "You should have told her that." He thought a moment, then added, "No need to ask Mary, because she ain't going to tell you either."

Geoffrey's mouth firmed, and he rose from the comfort of his leather armchair to pace back and forth across the fortunately empty room.

"I take it you went to see her aunt?" Peter studied a pattern in the rug with great intensity, looking quite as though he was trying not to laugh.

"She gave me some cock-and-bull story about Amelia wishing to visit a few of her relatives. Mrs. Spencer claimed she could not remember which one Amelia went to see first. A likely story!" Geoffrey kicked at a chair that happened to be in his path. He shoved his hands into his pockets, contemplating the view beyond the bow window with unseeing eyes.

"Guess you had better forget the girl. She always caused you a devilish amount of trouble anyway. Can't imagine why you wish to find her," Peter said with a perfectly straight face.

"Because . . . " And here Geoffrey paused in his striding about the room to stare at Peter for several moments. "Because life without her is deadly dull. Can't think why, but I miss her infernal interference in my life. And she did save my hide a few times, you know," Geoff reminded his friend.

"That she did, at risk to her own, I might add. Lord, do you remember her scheme to unmask Clarissa Filbert? Never laughed so hard in my life as when we saw their faces. Well and truly flummoxed. And I thought that Sands would have compromised Amelia. However, that companion of hers had him to rights quick enough with her little dagger. And then there was the matter of your curricle. Have to admit she sensed trouble there."

"Yes," Geoffrey said, "I'll allow as how she does seem to have a premonition of trouble. Perhaps it's because she brings it on?" He grimaced at the memory of the damage to his curricle and how he might have been seriously injured but for Amelia and her blessed interference.

"Well, she sensed it sure enough at Astley's. You'd have been put to bed with a shovel long ago had she not interfered then. And that balloon ride sure enough saved your hide." Peter steepled his fingers beneath his chin while he contemplated his friend.

"What about Taunton? He was no threat to my life." Geoffrey plopped down on a chair facing Peter to challenge him.

"Aye, but what if you had issued a challenge to the man without knowing for certain those cards were marked? They were devilishly hard to spot. Taunton is known to be a deadly shot. And that Frenchman, well, you proved about even there, rescuing her from that room up in Marylebone," Peter concluded.

"When I think of the disgrace she could have brought on

us all if she had been recognized at White's, I have a case of the shudders."

"So I repeat, why bother to find her?" Peter rose from his chair and sauntered to the door. "It appears you are stymied at any rate, for no one will tell you a thing."

Once alone in the room, Geoffrey sank into deep thought. Peter was right. For some peculiar reason no one thought he had a right to find Amelia. Why, he'd need a sleuth-dog to locate her at this rate.

At which thought he sat up straight. His mind working at a feverish pace, he charged from his chair, dashed past the startled porter and out of the door to hail a hackney.

"Bow Street," he snapped to the driver before they set off.

At the famous Bow Street office Geoffrey encountered Nathaniel Conaut, who proved sympathetic but scarcely as helpful as Geoffrey might have wished.

"Sorry, old chap. Ben Tobin is on a case at the moment. Missing heiress. Family thinks she has eloped with a ne'er-do-well half-pay officer. Younger son of a baronet. Without prospects, but handsome as the devil. Has a way with the ladies. Also has a record of eloping, then being paid off to forget the entire thing. Family wants him bought off and shipped out of the country."

"How soon will Tobin be available? He has some knowledge that ought to prove helpful in my search for this missing person."

"An heiress? There seems to be a rash of them at the moment." Sir Nathaniel squinted in speculation, listening politely to the man opposite him.

"I suppose she's an heiress. Never gave it much thought. I need her for other reasons," Geoffrey admitted.

Sir Nathaniel nodded, rubbing his chin while he contemplated this problem. "Well, best wait. I will send Tobin over to see you when he returns."

Geoffrey left the Bow Street office feeling frustrated. To one side sat Covent Garden Theater, looking odd in the harsh light of day when he was accustomed to seeing it at night. Around the corner stood the Drury Lane Theater, resplendent in its rebuilt glory following the fire that had destroyed it a few years back.

All Geoffrey could think about was Amelia, and that he

couldn't find her. Only when the realization that he was in an unsavory part of town hit him after he was jostled by a rough-looking fellow, did Geoffrey come to his senses and hail a hackney.

"I've been a fool," he admitted to the interior of the hackney. "But I shall find her. I believe I love that interfering minx." With that momentous admission he sat back, somewhat dazed, to contemplate life with Amelia.

Ben Tobin did not present himself at Geoffrey's door until another week and a half had passed—a frustrating time during which Geoff tried every means he could think of to uncover Amelia's whereabouts. Nothing he could dream up sufficed to convince Mary or Peter to part with what they knew. He quickly gave up on the vague Mrs. Spencer. She would merely smile and wave her hand in the air as though to swat him away.

Baffled, confounded, perplexed, Geoffrey was prepared to do violence when Ben Tobin entered the library at Dancy House.

"Tobin! The very man I wish to see." Geoffrey suspected he pumped the man's hand a bit too enthusiastically, but dash it all, he was a sight for sore eyes.

It didn't take long to explain what was needed. Ben Tobin sat on the chair facing Geoffrey, his face a mask, his eyes alive with curiosity. For a Runner, he was a strange one, his soft-spoken and polite manner at odds with what Geoff knew about the force of detectives.

"Well, I am more at home tracking down a wanted criminal or a runaway, sir," he said when the assignment had been outlined. "I confess I don't mind a change, however. Since I've met the young lady, I'll need but a few particulars before I begin pursuit."

He proceeded to ask a great number of questions, causing Geoff to believe Tobin was far too conservative in his use of the word "few." Geoffrey handed him a small leather pouch containing a sum of money to aid in loosening the tongues of reluctant witnesses. He'd found that in most cases money proved helpful—except for people like Mary and Peter who were above such things.

Once the Runner left the house, Geoff felt at loose ends.

He had run into so many stone walls in his hunt it was a relief to turn over the search to another. Yet he felt lost—useless.

He stood staring at the empty hearth while recalling the conclusion of that infamous balloon ride. She had been so sweet in his arms, and her lips had responded so deliciously to his touch. Why had he let her go . . . only to tell her that if she did something like that again, he would beat her? Guaranteed to charm the lady for sure, he berated himself. He vowed to make it up to her . . . his Celestial Delight.

Someday he would take her on a balloon trip. She had wanted so badly to go up in one that fateful day. And she had tears of worry in her lovely blue eyes when she faced him in the middle of that field.

Oh, he had been the veriest clunch, a dolt not to see where his heart was leading him. And he had the stupidity to tell her he believed they ought to be as strangers! Small wonder she had issued orders to one and all to keep her direction a secret.

The following days were the most difficult Geoffrey had ever endured. Even the forays into enemy territory to gather information for Wellington had been a snap compared to this. He contemplated the scar on his leg, relieved it had healed so well, yet knowing that if he didn't succeed in his search for Amelia, there would be a scar on his heart that would never heal. He fingered the precious silver amulet that always hung about his neck, wishing he could speak to the one who had given it to him.

When Ben Tobin again presented himself at Dancy House, Geoffrey was more than glad to see him. Friends had complained to Geoff that he had become a sorry fellow, downright blue-deviled. Most likely they were being generous in their remarks.

"So, what did you find," Geoffrey demanded before the Runner could even be seated.

"She is out in Wiltshire not too far from Salisbury. I found out her direction from the post boy who went with her on the first stage of the trip. After that it was relatively simple to go from stage to stage. The post boys were willing to talk for a sum."

"Clever. I ought to have considered that. She did not

travel in her aunt's carriage, nor did her uncle send one for her?" His frown might have daunted a lesser man. The Runner ignored it, well accustomed to reactions from worried family.

"As you say, milord," Tobin replied. "His lordship has a right fancy place, although he's a bit of a recluse. Don't entertain none. Don't go about in local society, either."

"His lordship?" Geoff had latched onto one word that struck him as interesting.

"Viscount Quainton be his title. One of the Kenyon family, I gather."

"You say he is a recluse? Is he mad?" Alarm for Amelia's safety in the house of a demented man clutched his heart.

"Not unless you think making all sorts of topiary figures mad. Place is a forest of crazy shapes. Animals, birds, cones, you name it. I could see some of it from the gates, the rest I learned from a Quainton groom while at the Star and Garter down the road a piece. Seems Quainton is a nice enough chap if you ignore his mania for trimming hedges and clipping trees."

"And Amelia is there. Tell you what, I suspect you had best come with me when I travel to Salisbury. I have a hunch you may come in as very useful."

A gleam lit Geoffrey's eyes that promised a prime bit of mischief, to Tobin's way of thinking. Having a liking for the young gentleman, he nodded his agreement, then found himself faced with a determined man.

"We shall eat first, then take off. You can leave immediately?"

Accustomed to hasty trips, the Runner agreed. Since Geoffrey had been packed for days, it needed but to inform his coachman to have the traveling coach made ready and notify Hemit they must depart.

Within an hour the men were on the road out of London. They left by way of the Bath Road, then at Marlborough turned to head southwest toward Salisbury. The closer they came to his objective, the more anxious and nervous Geoffrey became.

To Tobin the man looked nothing so much like a bridegroom waiting to say his vows and as nervous as a cat too close to a rocking chair.

Once they achieved Salisbury, Geoffrey selected a neat inn on New Canal off Catherine Street in the heart of town. Across from the Market Square, he figured that he might even spot Amelia strolling along the street. He had not failed to note the presence of a circulating library close by on Catherine Street. Amelia liked to read.

The following day, having had no sight of Amelia, Geoffrey decided he would travel out to see Lord Quainton. Tobin would go with him, in hopes the sleuth could pick up some useful information while Geoffrey went inside. That is, if the man would see him, and Geoff had doubts on that score from what Tobin had said.

After a pause before the impressive iron gates to give his identity and desire to see his lordship, Geoffrey was allowed to enter.

"I see what you mean about the topiary—Looks like some sort of green menagerie," Geoff commented as they passed a boxwood turtle.

At the front door Geoffrey found himself escorted inside with a pleasant greeting, then down a long hall that resembled something one might see in a cloister, with elegant windows along one side. Statuary, treasures, and paintings were placed along the other wall and between windows. Definitely a man with taste and the means to indulge it.

"His lordship will be with you shortly. Since it looks to rain, he elected to work at his records this afternoon," the butler said by way of explanation. Given what Tobin had said about the viscount, it seemed a day indoors was rare enough to cause comment.

Geoffrey chose to stand by the window rather than sit. He stared out at the lovely scythed lawns and the various fantastic shapes in view. A gentle stream flowed past with a few swans and a great number of ducks paddling about. Did Amelia stroll along that grassy bank to watch their antics? Was she even now a floor away from him in her room? He drew an impatient breath, turning when the door opened.

The man who entered didn't surprise Geoffrey very much, given the background from Tobin. White hair in wild disorder and a corduroy frock coat with bulging pockets fit the image Tobin had given Geoffrey. A no-nonsense country man of the soil, hardly the notion of a viscount that most people possessed.

"Sir"—Geoffrey plunged immediately to his concern without the finesse he'd have used on a mission—"I have come about Amelia Longworth."

"Fancied you'd show up sooner or later from what she's said. Sit down, my boy. What may I do for you?"

"I would like to see Amelia, if I may," Geoffrey said politely, calming down now that he was so close to his objective.

"Indeed? Pity, that, for she'll not see you." Lord Quainton massaged his jaw while studying Geoffrey as though to assess the effect of his words.

"What?" Geoffrey exclaimed, nearly starting from his chair. To be so close and denied a chance to redeem himself was more than he could tolerate. "But she must see me! I mean, I refuse to accept that. I believe the young lady cares for me, sir. And I care for her as well," Geoffrey said, deciding he might as well lay his cards on the table.

"Oh, I have no doubt as to the truth of that. You have the same love-sick look that she wears when she thinks I'm not watching her. But she is a determined young woman, and I respect her wishes. She said she will not see you if you come to the house. Mind you, if you were to casually bump into her when she goes into Salisbury tomorrow to exchange her books at Fellow's Circulating Library, it would be different, don't y'know."

Hope rose within Geoffrey at the encouraging words from Lord Quainton. It seemed the elderly lord had sized up Geoffrey and not found him wanting, and for that Geoff could only be grateful.

"She goes into town every Tuesday to shop and exchange her books. Good gel, likes my topiary and the swans. They even seem to like her, and they are rude birds as a rule."

"I am most grateful for the information, sir. Now if I can just persuade Amelia to listen to me, my battle may be won."

"She'll have that Chinese dragon with her," his lordship warned. "Don't envy you taking her on. I vow she has a

maxim for every occasion. Some of them are downright uncomfortable." He gave Geoffrey a companionable smile.

"Ah, yes. The indomitable Chen Mei. She's rather handy
in a fight. Her ability with that dagger she carries up her
sleeve is quite amazing."

"Indeed? I hadn't known about the dagger. I see I shall
have to use care not to offend her." The beetle brows drew
together in an amused frown. "I gather you have had occasion to observe its employment?"

"She uses it to defend and protect Amelia." Then, beguiled by a new listener who appeared sympathetic to his
cause, Geoffrey told Lord Quainton the entire tale, how he
had met and dealt with the determined and loyal Miss
Longworth.

"Chattel, did you say? Good grief," his lordship muttered
at the conclusion of the story. The telling had involved
some time and several glasses of excellent port.

"She is as honest and direct as a May day is long. Inven-
tive and protective, too," Geoffrey reflected.

"I suggest you slip out of here before she sees you. Don't
want to warn her in advance, y'know. As I said, she's a
good gel and deserves a good husband."

"I am pleased you allow me the chance to present my
case to her."

"The least I can do for you, my boy." The viscount rose
and offered his hand.

Geoffrey, who had been the head of his house and not
called "my boy" for many years repressed a grin at this. He
welcomed the chance to shake hands, then said, "Thanks to
you again. Wish me luck on the morrow."

"No doubt you'll need more than luck. Better devise
something that will further the match." He walked with
Geoffrey to the door, clapped him on the back, then
watched as Geoff strode along the hall to the front door like
a man with a mission.

Oh, to be young and in love again, thought the viscount
as he gently shut the door, walking to the window to stare
out at the stream. A misty rain fell, but his thoughts were
with a certain lady, now long gone, who had denied him
many years ago. This young fellow deserved a chance, one
that Quainton had not been given.

In the carriage, Geoffrey consulted with Tobin, sharing with him the viscount's advice.

"Sounds as though his lordship knows what he's about. But, what to do?"

The two men discussed the matter all the way back to the inn. At the Rose and Crown, Geoffrey and Tobin settled in a private parlor with a bottle of the best port.

"What will be the best approach?" Geoffrey muttered, staring out at the falling rain through the mullioned window.

"You say she comes to your rescue?" Tobin said, savoring the excellent wine the likes of which he rarely got to taste.

"True." Geoffrey pivoted about, frowning while he considered something at length. Then he grinned and eagerly crossed to seat himself at the table where Tobin watched him with a speculative gleam in his eyes.

"This is what we shall do, my good friend."

"What a blessing the rain has ceased," Amelia said to Chen Mei while she gazed out of the window with satisfaction. "I have looked forward to our weekly trip to Salisbury too much to be put off by it, but it does make it a deal pleasanter to have sunshine."

"Do not anxiously hope for what is not yet come; do not vainly regret what is already past," the companion quoted in her usual Cantonese from her reservoir of sayings.

"Who says that I am regretting what is past?" Amelia cried, whipping about to challenge Chen Mei. She wished to deny what was all too obvious to her, that she did regret turning her back on Lord Dancy. For one who was always truthful, it was rather difficult to pretend otherwise.

"Long face tell all," Chen Mei smugly replied.

"Well, I shall have to take care that I smile when I go to town." Amelia slipped on her peach pelisse, trimmed down the front with dainty bows of a deeper shade of peach. Her plumed bonnet was the latest thing, and when she peeked in the looking glass on the stair landing, Amelia felt pleased with her appearance. Not that she would see anyone she knew in town. Because of her uncle's disinterest in company, no one had come to call these many weeks, nor had she met any one who appealed to her.

It wasn't like London, she admitted. There, Mary and Peter and Chloe had filled her spare hours with laughter and fun. And Lord Dancy had . . . Amelia resolutely rejected the very mental image of the man, an image that had haunted her dreams every night, lurked in her mind in the day. It had become so trying that she sometimes imagined she saw him while in town. A gentleman dressed to the nines with a jaunty walk would catch her eye, then disappoint when it turned out to be someone else.

The ride to town was as uneventful as always. She thought back to the dashing times she had known in London when Lord Dancy had needed her protection and care. Oh, she missed that, she conceded. But that man . . . to tell her they would be best to be as strangers after all they had shared.

The coachman left Amelia and Chen Mei off at the corner of Catherine Street. On such a lovely day Amelia wished to saunter along to admire the objects for sale in the shop windows.

She was astounded when a gentleman spoke to her while she studied the contents of a millinery shop window. It sounded so much like the voice she had heard in her dreams that she was afraid to face him, preferring the shadowed reflection seen in the window. How much this man looked like Geoffrey. Then he spoke again.

"Amelia, I know you are upset with me, and rightly so. Will you not give me a chance to redeem myself?" he pleaded.

This time his voice seemed too real to ignore. Hoping she was not being foolish, Amelia decided to hazard facing him.

"Geoffrey!" She met that familiar green gaze with a fluttery heart. Her hand went to calm the beat within while her eyes searched the figure before her. He appeared well, although he seemed to have lost a bit of weight.

"I finally found you. And I do not intend to let you go," he declared in a low voice that thrilled her. Only Amelia had dreamed this too often. This was not a dream, but reality. In real life Geoffrey had scorned her and her love, even though she had never told him that she loved him.

"My uncle might not agree with you," she answered, feeling quite perverse now that she was close to Geoffrey again.

"Perhaps not. But I am not so bad a fellow as you may think. I own a rather nice place north of London I long to show you. And my family is acceptable. I've told you all about them. If I hadn't become so involved with a certain Miss Longworth, I'd have been to see them before this."

"Had I a family, I would wish to see them after being gone so long," Amelia couldn't resist chiding. She had no intention of allowing him to talk her around to his point of view. But she wouldn't be rude to the man, for he had obviously come some distance to see her.

"I have had a great deal on my mind, as you may know. How could I go haring after them when I needed to find you!" He glanced about with a hint of desperation, quite as though he looked for someone.

"What is it?" Amelia asked at once, her protective tendencies where he was concerned springing to life.

"Do you see a chap behind me? Wears a dun-colored coat, dark hat tipped over his eyes. Not very tall, sort of inconspicuous, you might say." He lowered his voice to a conspiratorial whisper.

Amelia grew alarmed, for the very person he mentioned lurked near a tree across the street. He looked decidedly suspicious.

"I do see him. What a frightful-looking man. Are you in trouble again?" she demanded, subtly positioning herself so she stood between the two. One never knew when a gun might be drawn from concealment—or a knife, for that matter.

"The thing of it is, I don't know. The chap looks to be a Bow Street Runner. Do you suppose that Taunton's been found dead and I am blamed?"

With a gasp Amelia placed her hand on Geoffrey's arm, leading him along with her toward the circulating library. "I thought that dreadful man had fled the country."

"But we don't know that for certain."

"Come with me. There is a back way out of the library

that we may use. From there I shall take you to my uncle's home where you will be safe from harm."

Chen Mei tagged along behind, darting looks at the Runner, then at his lordship. No smile crossed her lips, but her eyes appeared to dance with amusement had Amelia chanced to look at her.

"Here." Amelia thrust Geoffrey ahead of her into the circulating library, peering around the door to assure herself that the man still lurked in the shadows across the street. "You stay here, Chen Mei. If he dares to come inside, use your dagger. Lord Dancy and I shall escape out of the back door." She tugged his sleeve, then drew him along with her past the rows of books until they reached a hall. From here she marched along to the door.

A clerk bowed respectfully to the young woman known to be the niece of Lord Quainton. Even though a recluse, he still garnered deference. He held the door open for the pair, watching as they hurried down the alleyway.

"Now, you ought to be safe. Where do you stay? Is Hemit with you? Will you be able to come to my uncle's with me and not cause comment where you now stay?" She led him along the alley until they reached Brown Street. Swiftly drawing him along with her, it was but moments and they were at the side of Lord Quainton's crested carriage.

'Hurry. Who knows when that dreadful man may decide to explore a bit."

Once inside the carriage, they set off toward the west and Lord Quainton's estate.

Geoffrey turned to study the determined little face at his side. "You do care for me. I am certain of it."

"Well, and I would not wish anything to happen to you, sir," she primly replied, folding her hands neatly in her lap.

All of a sudden Amelia found herself picked up and deposited on his lap. His arms wrapped around her in a most beguiling manner, and before she could protest—although she actually had no desire to do so—she was most thoroughly kissed.

She melted at the onslaught. It was beyond her to fend off the kiss when she had ached for this very thing for so long. Her arms crept up to cling to those broad shoulders, and she returned his kiss with all her being.

At last, content for the moment, she was permitted to lean against his chest. She sighed with delight.

"We are going to be married. I'll not take no as an answer, my little love," he stated firmly, holding her tightly against him as though he feared to lose her. "Once married, I hope you will agree to some time at my country home, for things there have been sadly neglected while I chased after you."

She made no answer, for indeed it was quite beyond her at the moment.

"What? No contrary reply? No words of denial?"

"Think twice, say nothing," Amelia said.

"She comes along, too," Geoffrey murmured as he gathered Amelia even closer and proceeded to convince her that he never again intended to be parted from his Celestial Delight—even if she led him into one escapade after another. With Amelia life would never be dull again.

Emily Hendrickson

The Madcap Heiress

Adam Herbert yearns
for adventure. What he finds is
heiress Emily Lawrence. Together
they discover a love worth more
than any fortune.

0-451-21289-4

Now available from
REGENCY ROMANCE

The Captain's Castaway
by Christine Scheel
When a British Navy captain pulls a beautiful woman from a death at sea, he vows to help her at any cost, to earn her trust—and her love.
0-451-21559-1

The Whispering Rocks
by Sandra Heath
Fate has granted once-poor Sarah Jane a fortune. But scandal has sent her to a far-off land where evil seems to lurk in every corner—and a handsome local man is filling her with desire.
0-451-21560-5

Available wherever books are sold or at
www.penguin.com